Richard Montanari was born in Cleveland, Ohio, to a traditional Italian-American family. After university, he travelled Europe extensively and lived in London, selling clothing in Chelsea and foreign language encyclopedias door-to-door in Hampstead.

Returning to the US, he started working as a freelance writer for the *Chicago Tribune*, the *Detroit Free Press*, the *Seattle Times*, and many others. His novels have now been published in more than twenty-five languages.

Also by Richard Montanari

The Violet Hour

Kiss of Evil

Don't Look Now
(*previously published as* Deviant Ways)

The Rosary Girls

The Skin Gods

Broken Angels

Play Dead

The Devil's Garden

The Echo Man

The Killing Room

The Stolen Ones

The Doll Maker

RICHARD MONTANARI

SHUTTER MAN

sphere

SPHERE

First published in Great Britain in 2015 by Sphere
This paperback edition published by Sphere in 2016

1 3 5 7 9 10 8 6 4 2

A CIP catalogue record for this book
is available from the British Library.

ISBN 978-0-7515-4936-2

Typeset in Janson Text by M Rules
Printed and bound in Great Britain by
Clays Ltd, St Ives plc

Papers used by Sphere are from well-managed forests
and other responsible sources.

MIX
Paper from
responsible sources
FSC® C104740
www.fsc.org

Sphere
An imprint of
Little, Brown Book Group
Carmelite House
50 Victoria Embankment
London EC4Y 0DZ

An Hachette UK Company
www.hachette.co.uk

www.littlebrown.co.uk

For Dominic and Mary

For he comes, the human child,
To the waters and the wild
With a faery, hand in hand,
For the world's more full of weeping
Than he can understand.

Who are you?
I am Billy the Wolf.
Why did God make it so you can't see people's faces?
So I can see their souls.

Philadelphia, 2015

At the moment the black SUV made its second pass in front of the Rousseau house, a tidy stone colonial in the Melrose Park section of the city, Laura Rousseau was putting the finishing touches to a leg of lamb.

It was her husband's fortieth birthday.

Although Angelo Rousseau said every year that he did not want anyone to make a fuss, he had been talking about his mother's roast lamb recipe for the past three weeks. Angelo Rousseau had many fine qualities. Subtlety was not among them.

Laura had just finished chopping the fresh rosemary when she heard the front door open and close, heard footsteps in the hall leading to the kitchen. It was her son, Mark.

A tall, muscular boy with an almost balletic grace, seventeen-year-old Mark Rousseau was the vice president of his class's student council, and captain of his track team. He had his eye on the 1,000- and 5,000-meter events at the 2016 summer Olympics in Rio de Janeiro.

As Mark entered the kitchen, Laura slipped the lamb into the oven and set the timer.

'How was practice?' she asked.

'Good,' Mark said. He took a carton of orange juice out of the refrigerator and was just about to drink from it when he fielded a withering glance from his mother. He smiled, pulled a glass from the cupboard and poured it full. 'Shaved a quarter-second off my hundred.'

'My speedy boy,' Laura said. 'How come it takes you a month to clean your room?'

'No cheerleaders.'

Laura laughed.

'See if you can find an egg in the fridge,' she said. 'I looked twice and didn't see any. All I need is one for the apple turnovers. Please tell me we have an egg.'

Mark poked around in the refrigerator, moving plastic containers, cartons of milk, juice, yogurt. 'Nope,' he said. 'Not a one.'

'No egg wash, no turnovers,' Laura said. 'They're your father's favorite.'

'I'll go.'

Laura glanced at the clock. 'It's okay. I've been in the house all day. I need the exercise.'

'No you don't,' Mark said.

'What do you mean?'

'All my friends say I've got the hottest mom.'

'They do not.'

'Carl Fiore thinks you look like Téa Leoni,' Mark said.

'Carl Fiore needs glasses.'

'That's true. But he's not wrong about this.'

'You sure you don't mind going to the store?' Laura asked.

Mark smiled, tapped the digital clock on the oven. 'Time me.'

Forty-five minutes later, Laura stepped out of the shower and looked at herself in the steamed mirror. The image was blurred, smoothing over all the imperfections.

Maybe Carl Fiore is right, she thought. Maybe I *am* the hottest mom.

By the time she toweled off and dried her hair, the mirror was clear, and soon-to-be-forty-herself Laura Rousseau was back.

As she put the hair dryer in the hall closet, the house seemed strangely quiet. Usually at this time of the early evening Laura could hear Mark playing music or video games in his room, or Angelo watching SportsCenter in the den.

'Honey?'

Silence. A flat, unsettling silence.

When Laura turned the corner, heading toward the stairs, she saw shadows spill across the floor. She glanced up to see two men standing in the hallway. They were too old to be Mark's friends, too rough-looking to be Angelo's acquaintances or customers. She'd never seen them in the neighborhood. Both in their thirties, one had close-cropped hair, the other had hair to his shoulders.

Something was not right.

'Laura Rousseau,' the one with short hair said. It was not a question. It was a statement. The man knew her name.

Before Laura could stop herself, she said, 'Yes.'

The man with long hair flipped on the hall light, and Laura saw that he had a handgun tucked into the waistband of his jeans. The other man held a straight razor.

'Your family needs you in the living room,' the long-haired man said.

When they stepped to the side, Laura ran past them, into the living room, into hell.

Her husband and son were seated on dining room chairs in the center of the room, slumped forward, their feet and hands bound with duct tape. There was also duct tape over their mouths and eyes.

The floor beneath them was soaked with blood.

As the world began to violently spin from her grasp, Laura felt herself being forced onto a chair by strong hands.

'What ... have ... you ... *done*?' Laura managed. Her words sounded small and distant to her ears, as if someone else was whispering to her.

The man with long hair knelt in front of her. 'Do you know my face?' he asked.

The horror uncoiled within Laura, threatening to burst from her body.

This is real, she thought. This is really happening.

The man took a photograph from his pocket, held it next to her face. In that moment Laura thought she saw something in his cold blue eyes. A reluctance, perhaps. A moment of hesitation.

'Put this on,' the other man said.

Laura turned to see that he had one of her blouses in his hand.

After she put on the cowl-neck top, the long-haired man again looked at the photograph. He nodded, stood and slowly walked behind her. He bound her to the chair with duct tape, put his hands on her shoulders.

'*I saw a stranger today,*' he said. '*I put food for him in the eating place. And drink in the drinking place. And music in the listening place.*'

Laura dared to glance at her dead son. Mark Rousseau was suddenly a toddler again, stumbling his way around this very room, steadying himself on the wall with one tiny hand.

'*In the Holy name of the Trinity He blessed myself and my family . . .*'

She looked at her dead husband. Angelo David Rousseau, the love of her life, her pillar. He'd proposed to her on his birthday – nineteen years ago to the day – telling her she'd be the only present he would ever want.

'*And the lark said in her warble: Often, often, often goes Christ in the stranger's guise.*'

The man took his hands from Laura's shoulders, circled back in front of her.

'*O, oft and oft and oft, goes Christ in the stranger's guise.*'

He racked the slide on his weapon. The click of metal on metal echoed like the murmur of wasps, and soon fell to silence. He placed the tip of the barrel against Laura's heart.

Do you know my face?

In her last moments Laura Rousseau remembered where she had seen the man's face before.

It was in her nightmares.

I

The Pocket

1

Philadelphia, July 2, 1976

The man in the wrinkled white suit stuttered across the square like a wounded finch, the soles of his shoes strapped to the uppers with black electrician's tape, his zipper frozen at quarter-mast. He wore dark wire-rimmed glasses.

His name was Desmond Farren.

Although the man was not yet forty, his hair was a muddied gray, long but mathematically combed, the part arrowed down the middle. On the right side, just above his ear, was a small, perfect circle of white.

Desmond Farren sat down on the bench in front of the shoe store, his stick-man silhouette all but lost in the bright posters behind him – *50% Off Selected Merchandise! Beach Sandals, Buy One Pair, Get One Pair Free!*

The four boys sitting on the opposite bench – none having yet reached the age of fourteen, nor anywhere near the height they one day would – paid the man scant mind. Not at first.

Someone on the square had a radio playing Elton John's 'Philadelphia Freedom', already an anthem in the City of Brotherly Love.

The boys were one month into their summer vacation, and the girls in their tube tops and short shorts, having a year earlier endured the brunt of nervous, poorly told jokes, had suddenly reached a state of grace that eclipsed every Act of Contrition ever said.

In a city of neighborhoods, of which Philadelphia boasted more than one hundred, boundaries only moved in the minds of those not tasked to keep watch.

Follow the Schuylkill River north, from its confluence with the Delaware – past Bartram's Garden and Grays Ferry – and you will find, in the shadow of the South Street bridge, a small neighborhood of seventy or so families pleated into the eastern bank of the river, a crimp of peeling clapboard row houses, asphalt playgrounds, small corner stores and brown brick buildings as old as the city of Philadelphia itself.

It is called Devil's Pocket.

On listless July days, when the sun radiated off the colorless wooden houses and glinted off the windshields of the rusting cars that lined Christian Street, women in the Pocket wore sleeveless cotton sundresses, often with lace handkerchiefs tucked into their bra straps at the shoulder. The men wore Dickies work pants, white T-shirts, packs of Kools or Camels crafting square bulges in the front, their Red Wing boots and trouser cuffs sifted with dust from the brickyards.

The bars, of which there were a half-dozen in as many blocks, served well whiskeys and national brands on tap. On Fridays all year, not just during Lent, there were fish fries. On Sundays there were potluck dinners.

The prevailing theory on how the neighborhood got its name was that sometime in the 1930s, a parish priest said the kids there were so bad they would 'steal the chain out of the devil's pocket'.

To the four boys sitting on the bench across from the man in the white suit – Jimmy Doyle, Ronan Kittredge, Dave Carmody and Kevin Byrne – the Pocket was their domain.

Years later, if asked, the boys would recall this moment, this unspoiled tableau of summer, as the moment the darkness began to fall.

The boys watched as Desmond Farren took out a phlegm-crusted handkerchief, blew his nose into it, wiped the back of his neck, then replaced it in his pocket.

'Philadelphia Freedom' began again, this time from a second-story apartment over the square.

Jimmy put a hand on Ronan's shoulder, chucked a thumb at Des Farren. 'I see your boyfriend's not working today,' he said.

'Funny shit,' Ronan said. 'Wait, is that your sister's hand-kerchief?'

'Fuck you.'

'Not my type.'

Kevin got their attention, put a finger to his lips, nodded in the direction of the corner.

They all turned to look at the same time, all thinking it was a nun from St Anthony's, or someone's mother, and they would catch a backhand for using the F word. It was none of the above.

There, standing just a few feet away, was Catriona Daugherty.

The only child of a single mother who worked at the Naval Home as a nurse's assistant, eleven-year-old Catriona had light-blond hair, sapphire-blue eyes. She was rarely seen without a flower in her hand, even if it was only a dandelion. She always wore a ribbon in her hair.

There were some who said she was a bit slow, but none of

those people were from the Pocket, and you said such things at your peril, especially in the presence of Jimmy Doyle.

The truth was, Catriona Daugherty was just fine. Perhaps she processed things a little more thoughtfully than most people, gave things more painstaking consideration, but she wasn't slow.

'Hey, Catie,' Jimmy said.

Catriona looked away, back at Jimmy, blushed. None of them had ever met anyone who reddened more deeply, or quickly, than Catriona Daugherty. Everyone knew that she had a crush on Jimmy, but she was in sixth grade, and that made Jimmy her protector, not her boyfriend. Maybe one day, but not now. Catriona was, by any measure of a teenage boy in the Pocket, or Philly as a whole, still a little girl. They all felt protective of her, but Jimmy was her chosen knight.

'Hey,' Catriona said softly.

Jimmy slid off the bench. Catriona instinctively backed up a little, which left her tottering on the curb. Jimmy took her by the elbow, gently moved her back onto the sidewalk.

'Watcha doin'?' he asked.

Catriona took a deep breath, said: 'Going to get a water ice?'

Catriona's grandmother was from Ireland, and Catriona spent much of her summers with the woman. As a result, she had that curious Irish lilt that made all statements sound like a question.

'What's your flavor?' Jimmy asked.

Another blush. She paused, waiting for a SEPTA bus to pass. When it did, she said: 'I like the strawberry?'

'My favorite!' Jimmy exclaimed. He reached into the right front pocket of his jeans, took out his roll, which was really three or four singles with a ten on the outside. 'Got enough money?'

Catriona looked away, toward her house, back. She held up a small white handkerchief, rubber-banded around a few coins. 'Mom gave me enough, she did.'

12

Two summers ago they had watched Catriona stop on the way to the corner store to jump rope with some of the neighborhood girls.

They had all seen her drop her hankie purse while she was jumping, and saw, as it opened, coins spilling onto the sidewalk. With one hard look from the then eleven-year-old Jimmy Doyle, no one dared move. When Catriona was done with the Double Dutch, she collected the coins – fully unaware that she had dropped her own money – and ran up to Jimmy bursting with excitement and pride.

'They threw money at me, Jimmy Doyle! Money!'

'Yes they did,' Jimmy said. 'You were *great*.'

Had the two of them been older, they might have hugged at that moment. Instead, they both backed away.

On this day, as Jimmy put away his roll, Kevin sensed someone exiting the grocery store, crossing the sidewalk. It was Catriona Daugherty's mother.

'Hello, men,' she said.

They all greeted her. Catriona's mother was younger than most of the mothers of school-age children in the Pocket, her fashion sense a little closer to the teenage girls with whom the boys were obsessed, a little more in tune with the times. She was always good for a laugh.

'You boys staying out of trouble?' she asked.

'Now where's the fun in that?' Jimmy replied.

'Don't make me call your ma, Mr Doyle. You know I'll do it.'

Jimmy held up both hands, palms out, in mock surrender. 'I'll be good. I promise.'

'And I'll be Miss America next year.' She smiled, wagged a finger at them, then reached out a hand to her daughter. Catriona took it.

'Enjoy your water ice, Catie,' Jimmy said.

'I will, Jimmy.'

Catriona continued down the street, hand in hand with her mother, floating a few feet above the sidewalk.

Ronan tapped Jimmy on the shoulder, pointed at the shopping bag at Jimmy's feet, the one he'd been carrying around all morning.

'So you got them,' Ronan said.

'As if this were in any doubt,' Jimmy replied.

He reached into the shopping bag, took out four beautiful new walkie-talkies he had artfully boosted from a Radio Shack in Center City a few days earlier.

Yet as much as they wanted to use them, there was one small hurdle. Batteries.

Batteries cost money.

F&B Variety was an old-school store on Christian Street. It had been there longer than anyone could remember, and that included the three old men who sat on lawn chairs out front, by turns dumping on the Eagles, the Phillies and the Sixers. The Flyers, having won the Stanley Cup the two previous seasons, were currently exempt.

Inside, F&B wasn't any more modern than the day it opened. The store sold the staples – lunch meats, shelf breads, condiments, laundry and dish detergents – as well as a selection of gift and tourist items, such as plastic Liberty Bells and bobble-head dolls that bore only a passing resemblance to Mike Schmidt and Greg Luzinski.

Toward the back of the store were a few racks of paperback books and comic books, with an aisle dedicated to knockoff toys.

On the end cap, facing away from the register, and the watchful eye of the owner, the perpetually sour-faced Old Man Flagg, were the batteries. It was summer, and that meant portable radios came off the shelves, so F&B always had a good stock.

The plan, as always:

Ronan would stand in line at the counter. When he got to the register, he would ask for change for a dollar. Kevin would stand at the rack of comic books, looking as suspicious as possible, which was not all that hard. He was the biggest of the four boys, and therefore the most menacing.

While Dave observed through the front window, Kevin would knock a few comic books from the rack, drawing Old Man Flagg's attention for just a few seconds. But a few seconds was all Jimmy needed. He was a natural.

Contraband acquired, they coolly emerged from the store, met up on the corner and walked to Catharine Street. Once there, Dave sat down on the steps of a row house and began taking the battery covers off the walkie-talkies.

They would be on the air in minutes.

Before Jimmy could get the batteries out of his pockets, a shadow appeared on the sidewalk beneath their feet.

It was Old Man Flagg. He'd seen the whole thing.

Charles Flagg was in his sixties, a prude of the first order. He made everybody's business his business, even going so far as to form a neighborhood watch group so he could stick his nose even further into the lives of people in the Pocket. Rumor had it that Old Man Flagg got manicures at a Center City salon.

'Empty your pockets,' Flagg said to Jimmy.

Jimmy took a step back. For a split second it looked as if he might make a run for it. But they had all seen the PPD sector car parked a block away. No doubt Flagg had seen it too. Jimmy had no choice. He slowly reached into his pockets, front and back, and pulled out eight nine-volt batteries, still on the card. Each of the cards clearly displayed the small orange F&B price sticker. Flagg took them from him.

'I know you,' he said. 'You're a Doyle. I know your father.'

Jimmy balled his fists. Nothing got his blood up faster than this. 'He's not my father.'

Old Man Flagg looked slapped. "'Scuse you?'

'I said, he's not my father. He adopted me.'

Flagg shrugged, looked over Dave's shoulder. He pointed down the street, in the direction of the Well, a shot and beer tavern. This was all you had to say about the geography of Tommy Doyle's life these days. Work. Bar. Sleep. Repeat.

'I know where he is right now,' Flagg said. 'Stay put.'

The next three minutes were spent in silence. Each of the boys dedicated the time to trying to concoct the most plausible story for how this had happened. The only one who had a shot was Dave – being the smartest – but even he was stumped.

Jimmy was fucked.

A minute later they saw Jimmy's stepfather emerge from the shadowed doorway of the Well.

Tommy Doyle was over six feet tall, broad-shouldered, hands like Tim McCarver's mitts. As he crossed the street, they all saw him weave slightly. He had an unfiltered Lucky in his right hand, burned almost to the nub.

When he reached the corner, they could smell the booze from five feet away.

Tommy Doyle pointed at Jimmy. 'You don't fucking move,' he said. He swept the finger across them. 'None of you.'

There had been a time when Tommy Doyle – if you caught him only one or two beers into the day – could be the nicest guy you would ever meet. Once, when Kevin's mother got her Dodge Dart stuck in a snowdrift, Tommy Doyle spent the better part of an hour digging her out with nothing more than a bent license plate he'd found in the gutter.

Then there was the time he broke his own wife's jaw with a left hook, supposedly because there was some dried mustard left on a plate he had taken out of the cupboard.

Kevin, Ronan and Dave all looked anywhere but at Tommy

Doyle, or Old Man Flagg. Jimmy stared straight into his step-father's eyes.

'What do you have to say?' Tommy asked him.

Jimmy remained silent, the words solid and immovable inside.

Tommy Doyle raised a hand. Jimmy didn't flinch. 'I asked you a fuckin' question.'

Jimmy glared straight through him, said softly: 'I'm sorry.'

Tommy Doyle's hand came down hard. It caught Jimmy on the right side of his jaw. They all saw Jimmy's eyes roll back in his head for a moment as he stumbled into the brick wall. Somehow he found his footing. He did not go down.

'Get the fuckin' marbles out of your mouth,' Tommy Doyle yelled. 'You babble again and I swear to Christ on the cross I will take you apart right here and now.'

Jimmy's eyes welled with tears, but not one dropped. He looked at Old Man Flagg, took a deep breath, and on the exhale said, loud enough for everyone in the Pocket to hear:

'I'm *sorry*.'

Tommy Doyle turned to Flagg, reached into his back pocket, pulled out a wallet on a chain.

'How much are they?' he asked.

Flagg looked confused. He held up the batteries. 'What, these?'

'Yeah.'

'Don't worry about it,' he said. 'I got them back.'

'How much are they?'

Flagg shrugged, glanced at the batteries. 'Four bucks for the lot.'

Tommy Doyle extracted a five, handed it to the man. 'That cover the tax?'

'Sure.'

Tommy grabbed the batteries, tore open the packages, walked over to the curb and one by one threw the batteries into the sewer.

17

Red-faced, his chin flecked with spittle, he walked back to where the boys stood, flicked the empty cardboard cards into his stepson's chest.

'You're coming to work with me in the morning,' he said. 'All of you.'

Tommy Doyle worked for a company that demolished houses, but took extra work as a landscaper on summer evenings and weekends.

It was clear that Dave Carmody wanted to break rank, perhaps interjecting that he had voiced opposition to the plan to begin with, but one look from Jimmy fixed the words on his lips.

Tommy pointed at Kevin, Dave and Ronan. 'Seven o'clock sharp. Corner of Twenty-sixth and Christian. You don't show, I'm coming to your fucking houses.'

Ronan and Kevin got to the corner of 26th and Christian at 6.45, stuffed with breakfast, sugar-rushed. Ronan's father — who was a cousin to Byrne's father, Paddy — worked for the company that made Tastykake, and the boys had eaten as many powdered mini-donuts as they could. There was a pretty good chance that they were not going to get lunch.

When they turned the corner, Dave was already there, his jeans laundered and pressed. This was his mom's work, of course. Dave was going to labor on a landscaping site all day, probably kneeling in dirt, and his pants were ironed.

'Come here,' Dave said in a low voice, as if he were passing along state secrets. 'You gotta see this.'

They walked down 26th Street, across from the power plant to a vacant lot on the corner of 26th and Montrose. Dave stepped onto the lot, jumped up on an old rusted Dumpster which had been pushed up against one of the crumbling single-car garages, pulled out a pair of bricks, reached inside. A few seconds later he drew out a paper lunch bag and jumped down.

He slowly opened the bag, showed the other two boys the contents.

It was a nickel-plated .38 revolver.

'Jesus and his *parents*,' Ronan said.

'And all the fucking saints,' Dave replied.

'Is that yours?' Kevin asked.

Dave shook his head. 'It's Jimmy's. He showed it to me. It used to be Donny's.'

Donal Doyle, Jimmy's older stepbrother, was killed in Vietnam. Some said it was all Tommy Doyle needed to let go of the rail and fall head first into the bottle for good.

'Is it loaded?' Ronan asked.

Dave pushed the release, rolled the cylinder. Five rounds. He cautiously snapped it back in place, careful to leave the chamber opposite the firing pin empty.

'Wow,' Ronan said.

Kevin said nothing.

At that moment they heard the throaty sound of the Doyle landscaping truck's wired-together muffler coming up the street. Dave put the gun back in the bag, jumped on the Dumpster and replaced the bag in the wall.

A few seconds later, they joined a very morose-looking Jimmy Doyle in the back of his stepfather's rusting Ford F-150.

Jimmy had a bandage on his swollen left cheek.

No one asked him about it.

The day was hot, humid, dense with dark gray clouds. Mosquitoes by the millions. The landscaping job was in Lafayette Hill, at one of the big homes off Germantown Pike.

Around ten o'clock, the lady of the house, a heavyset woman with an easy laugh and Ace bandages on both knees, brought them frosty tumblers of ice-cold lemonade. None of them had ever tasted anything better.

Twice Jimmy – wielding the big mower around the side yard – came perilously close to flattening the perfectly sculpted spirea on that side of the house. Both times it looked as if his stepfather might run *him* over.

If the lemonade had been a godsend, it paled in comparison to the words they heard around 2.30 from Bobby Anselmo, who was Tommy Doyle's partner.

'Let's pack it up, guys,' he said. 'We're done for the day.'

They jumped out of the back of the truck at just after three, near the corner of Naudain and South Taney Street.

Jimmy was inconsolable. Not because he had been caught stealing and had to apologize for it, or because he had dragged his friends into the matter. That was what friends were for. It was that he had been berated and belittled by his stepfather all day, right in front of those same friends. Jimmy was getting bigger, filling out, and his friends secretly wondered when the day would come when he would brace the old man.

That day had not yet come.

But by these same measures they all knew this mood of Jimmy's, and it always preceded some challenge, some death-defying attempt at something, some larceny far greater than the one that had put him in his stepfather's sights to begin with. It was as if there was something slowly winding inside him, ready to spring at a moment's notice.

Without saying much, the four boys made their way up South Taney Street, heading to the park. Just after crossing Lombard, Ronan stopped, pointed.

'Who the fuck is *that*?'

They all turned to see what he was pointing at. There was someone standing at the edge of the park, behind a tree.

It soon registered. The wrinkled white suit. The twitchy movements. It was Desmond Farren. Every few seconds he would lean to his right, looking around the tree, then snap his head back like a crazed turtle. For some reason he seemed to be in motion even though he was just standing there.

Without a word of discussion, the four boys headed to the field. It went without saying that they were all suddenly very interested in whatever had drawn Des Farren there.

It was Dave who noticed first. 'Tell me I'm not looking at what I know I'm looking at,' he said.

'Holy *shit*,' Kevin said.

It soon became clear why Des Farren seemed to be in motion. He *was* in motion.

'He's whacking off?' Jimmy asked.

'Out here?' Ronan replied.

They all moved a few feet closer and saw what Des Farren was looking at.

There, sitting in the middle of the field, not thirty feet away, was Catriona Daugherty. She wore a lemon-yellow dress, short white socks, white shoes, the patent leather kind, probably from her First Communion. She sat cross-legged on the grass, oblivious to any impropriety, to any and all on-lookers.

'You sick *fuck*,' Ronan said.

At this, Des Farren turned around, spotted the boys. He turned and ran, in the direction of the copse of trees next to the ball diamond.

Jimmy reached the man first, on a dead run, and sent him sprawling.

All four boys jumped on Farren and dragged him into the bushes. Jimmy was the first to speak.

'Kevin, get his glasses,' he said.

Kevin reached down, removed Des Farren's dark glasses.

Without advance warning, Jimmy dropped to his knees and hit the man, twice, square on the nose. Fast, well-leveraged punches. Farren's nose burst in a gummy spray of bright blood. The sound of bone on cartilage seemed to echo across the park.

Dazed, Farren tried to roll to his side. Each of the boys grabbed a leg or an arm, pinning him down.

Jimmy searched the man, emptied his pockets onto the ground. Des Farren was carrying just over a dollar in change, mostly dimes and nickels. In his back pocket he had a SEPTA bus pass, and a handkerchief the color of army fatigues. There was also an Ace comb with a half-dozen teeth missing.

'What were you doing back there?' Jimmy asked.

Des Farren's lips trembled, but he remained silent.

'Gonna ask again, you warped piece of shit,' Jimmy said. 'One last time.' He straddled the man, bent at the waist. His fists were tightly clenched. 'What the fuck were you doing back there?'

'I wasn't doin' nothing.'

'You were watching Catriona,' Jimmy said.

'Who?'

Jimmy raised a fist, stopped short. 'Don't fuck with me. You know who I'm talking about. The little girl. You were watching her.'

'I wasn't.'

'You were watching her and you were playing with your puny little dick, you sick motherfucker.'

'I never.'

'Admit it and I might let you live today. All you have to do is admit it. Admit what I *saw* you doing. Deny it and I swear to Christ on the cross I will take you apart right here and now.'

'I didn't do *nothing*.'

'Do you know where you are?' Jimmy asked.

The man just stared.

'You're in our park,' Jimmy said. 'We want you out of here. We want you out of here, and to never come back.'

'I'm gonna tell my brothers.'

And there it was.

Jimmy cocked his fist again. He held off, then reached into his pocket, took out his small pearl-handled switchblade, flicked it open.

'Jimmy,' Kevin said. 'Come on, man.'

Des Farren began to sob. 'Tell . . . my brothers.'

Jimmy stuck the tip of the knife into the man's right thigh. Not deep, but deep enough. Des Farren screeched. Blood darkened the front of his dirty white suit pants.

'That's *enough*, Jimmy,' Kevin shouted. 'Let him up.'

Jimmy hesitated for a few moments.

'Thought so,' he said. 'If you ever come back to this park, if you ever even *look* at Catriona again, I will gut you with this knife and feed you to my dog. Then I will throw what's left into the fucking river. Hear me?'

Silence.

'Do you *hear me*?'

Nothing.

'Take his pants down,' Jimmy said to Dave Carmody.

'*I hear you I hear you I hear you*,' Des Farren screamed.

Jimmy Doyle stood up, closed the knife. The look of relief on Dave's face was quantifiable.

Before he stepped away, Jimmy said: 'If you're even *thinking* of telling your brothers what happened here, think twice, if you can think at all. You don't know me, you don't know my family. It will be your last fucking mistake. You Farrens are the lowest form of shanty Irish. You won't stand a fucking chance.' He held up the man's SEPTA pass, handed it to Kevin. 'If anything ever happens to one of my boys – *ever* – I will come to your house. I will come at night, and I will not come alone. Understand?'

Des Farren nodded, rolled onto his side, held his thigh, sobbing. The blood had trickled halfway down his leg.

Jimmy turned to Kevin. 'Give him his shit back.'

Kevin dropped the bus pass and the glasses.

'Now get the fuck out of here,' Jimmy said.

Des Farren slowly rose to his feet and faltered across the field, toward the Pocket. He did not turn around.

The four boys stood in silence for a long time. Finally, Dave broke the stillness.

'Jimmy?'

'Yeah?'

'Since when do you have a dog?'

They all laughed, but it was a mirthless sound.

As they watched Des Farren disappear into the trees, they each held private thoughts about what just happened, and what might happen next.

The word among residents of the Pocket was that Desmond Farren had been born wrong, something to do with his umbilical cord being wrapped around his neck, which had somehow deprived him of oxygen. None of the boys knew this for sure, but they knew two things about the man as gospel.

One, he was always talking to himself.

Two, more importantly, you didn't make fun of Des Farren. This was because he was the oldest of the three Farren brothers. The Farrens operated a shabby tavern on Montrose Street, a dive called The Stone.

Since Liam Farren had moved to the Pocket in the early 1940s, the real stock and craft of the family had not been the tavern and hospitality trade, but rather extortion, intimidation and a mad-dog violence that struck fear into homeowners and business owners alike.

In addition to squeezing protection money from local merchants, the Farren brothers had a city-wide reputation as burglars, rivaled only by the infamous K&A gang, a criminal conclave that ran their operation out of the Kensington and Allegheny neighborhood in North Philly.

Even the K&A gang stayed away from the Pocket.

One legend had Danny Farren, a few years earlier, throwing a man off a roof in Point Breeze, but not before cutting out one of his eyes with the broken beer bottle. Needless to say, there were no witnesses willing to put Danny Farren on that rooftop. Another ember of neighborhood fire had both Danny and Patrick following a man home from The Stone one night after he had allegedly insulted a barmaid. It was said that Danny held the man down while Patrick removed the man's little fingers and little toes with a pair of garden shears.

Both Danny and Patrick Farren had been in and out of jail ever since they were teenagers, but never for the most brutal of their crimes.

It was one of the reasons why, even though he was howl-at-the-moon fucking weird, and smelled like a compost heap, no one gave Des Farren too hard a time.

Until today.

Jimmy Doyle had not only threatened Des Farren, but he had cut him.

It was with these thoughts that the four boys walked back to the avenue in silence and, without a further word, went their separate ways.

The Fourth of July dawned wet and hot. The lines around the best Irish bars were two thick by 6 a.m. Every other bar was jammed by eight. News helicopters hovered over the city.

The whole country was talking about Philadelphia. There was chatter of Boston and New York and Washington DC, but they were fucking losers; everyone in Philly knew this and expressed it to anyone who would listen.

It was the bicentennial of inarguably the most important city in America's history. Very little of this was lost on Jimmy, Dave, Ronan and Kevin.

Even President Ford made a visit to Independence Hall.

The country was two hundred years old, and the beating heart of it all, the City of Brotherly Love, was electric with energy.

Jimmy Doyle had spent the night on his living room couch, his baseball bat in hand, his open blade next to him, drinking Cokes, waiting for Danny or Patrick Farren to come storming through the door.

Neither did.

The four friends met at the south end of Schuylkill River Park, where people from all over came to watch the fireworks.

They gathered near the home plate on the ball field.

When Jimmy showed up, a six-pack of Colt 45 in tow, the night officially commenced. The beer was warm, but it was Colt. Within fifteen minutes they all had a pleasant buzz. Then came the first of the fireworks.

More than once the boys turned around to see Old Man Flagg watching them, his goofy neighborhood watch badge pinned to his shirt. He had clearly noticed them drinking the beer, but now that it was gone, there was nothing he could do about it.

After the sixth massive volley, a canopy of red, white and blue sparks overhead, the four boys looked at each other.

'The Pocket,' they said in unanimity.

The fireworks show was the best any of them had ever seen. Maybe it was the Colt.

Earlier in the day, they had conscripted Dave's two cousins, Big George and Little George, to retrieve the batteries from the sewer. Big George had moved the iron grate with relative ease, and Little George had found the batteries in short order. It had not rained, and the batteries were just fine.

Tommy Doyle had paid for them, after all.

Most of the fireworks show was spent communicating the

whereabouts of neighborhood girls using the walkie-talkies.

As the crowd prepared for the big spectacular finale, the four boys noticed a sideshow through the trees at the western end of the park. Apparently, someone had set off one of those spinning fire wheels. Because it was illegal to set your own fireworks off at Schuylkill River Park, the boys were automatically drawn to the sideshow, if for no other reason than to see who got busted.

But as they made their way through the trees, they saw that it was not a fireworks side show.

It was a police car.

There were two officers standing in front of the vehicle, talking to a woman. Without getting closer, the four boys angled for a better position.

The woman, they could now see, was Catriona's mother. A man in a brown suit had his arm around her. He seemed to be propping her up.

What the boys would forever recall was the slight delay between the time Catriona's mother opened her mouth and the moment her scream reached their ears.

There, in the headlights of the police car, they saw what had made the woman scream, the small form lying on the grass.

It didn't look real, but it was.

Catriona Daugherty was dead. Catriona Daugherty was dead and the world would never be the same. The sun might come up in the morning, the *Inquirer* might hit the door on time, but nothing would ever be the same.

Catriona wore the same lemon-yellow dress she'd worn the day before, but her hair ribbon was gone.

'He's here,' Dave said.

'What do you mean?' Jimmy asked. '*Who's* here?'

'That psycho fuck. Des Farren. I saw him.'

They all looked around. Des Farren was nowhere in sight.

'Where?' Kevin asked. 'I don't see him.'

'By the tracks,' Dave replied. 'I saw him by the tracks.'

They walked as quickly as they could without drawing attention to themselves. They reached the tracks and saw him.

Des Farren was sitting on the ground, gazing at the moon. While fireworks were going off behind him, he was looking the other way. He had a single pink rose in his hands.

'I'm gonna go tell the cops,' Dave said.

'No,' Jimmy replied. He put a hand on Dave's arm, stopping him. 'I want you guys to keep him here.'

Dave's eyes grew wide. 'What do you mean, keep him here? How do we do that?'

Having earlier collected the walkie-talkies, Jimmy reached into his bag, took out three of them, handed one to Dave, one to Ronan, the third to Kevin. He held the last one in his left hand.

'I want you guys to keep an eye on him,' he said. 'If he moves, I want you to let me know.'

Dave looked confused. 'Aren't you gonna tell the cops?' he asked. 'Aren't you gonna tell them what we caught him doing yesterday?'

'What, so he can tell the cops what *I* did to *him*? Just what I need. His fucking brothers are probably looking for me right now.'

The reality of the huge mistake Jimmy had made bracing Des Farren settled over them all. They knew it was bad, but it seemed to be getting worse by the minute.

Jimmy put a hand on each of Dave's shoulders, squared the other boy in front of him. 'I want you guys to keep an eye on him. The three of you. Split up, but don't take your eyes off him. Wherever he goes, whatever he does, you tell me on the walkie. Don't let him out of your sight.'

'Where are you going?' Kevin asked.

'I'll be right back.'

A few moments later, as the final volley of fireworks began to light the night sky over Philadelphia, Kevin Byrne glanced to where his three friends had just been standing.

The boys were already gone.

The second week in July was the hottest on record. The Phillies slid to fourth place.

On July 9th, the body of a man was found in the Schuylkill River, just beneath the South Street bridge. According to police, he had been shot once in the back of the head. A .38 bullet was found lodged in his neck. No weapon was recovered.

The man was identified as Desmond Malcolm Farren, late of Schuylkill, no wife, no children, no place of employment.

The homicide unit of the PPD launched an investigation. Due to the nature of the Farren family's many criminal activities, it was thought that the murder was in some way connected to Desmond's brothers Danny and Patrick, or to the legacy of their late father Liam.

No arrest was made.

II

In the Shadow of the Spire

2

Philadelphia, 2015

They circled the block twice, watching for people who were watching for people like them.

They saw none.

It was just before midnight on an unseasonably warm spring evening. Despite the heat, only a handful of people had their windows open, especially at the ground and basement levels, even though most of the windows had iron bars over them.

Sometimes iron bars and heavily secured window air-conditioners were not enough to keep people out. There was a tale of a North Philly rapist who specialized in coming in through windows with portable air-conditioners. The man was eventually caught because he could not stop.

Billy wondered if *he* would ever stop.

As they pulled up to the curb, the driver cut the SUV's headlights. From the distance came the din of talk radio. It was too far away, too indistinct, to discern the topic under discussion.

Beneath this, the only sound was the hum of the vehicle's engine.

They watched the street. Lights went off, shades and blinds were drawn, doors were locked and chained. Televisions went black as street dogs circled three times and lay down to sleep.

As one city shed its day, the other city – Billy's city – slipped it on like a blistered skin.

The man driving the SUV looked over, pointed at the row house. The house was in fine repair, looking to have recently had a red-brick facade installed. Each window had a flower box in full bloom.

'He's awake,' the driver said.

Billy glanced at him. The desire to look inside his coat was all but overwhelming. He found a way not to do it.

'Now?' he asked.

The driver shook his head. 'Not yet.'

The driver was Billy's age. He had sandy hair. But unlike Billy's hair, which he wore to his shoulders, the driver's hair was cropped short like a soldier's. He had hard blue eyes, the color of a comic-book sky, as well as a scar on his right cheek, a ropy fingerling that ran from just below his eye to the top of his cheek, about an inch in length.

Billy could not recall with any precision or confidence how the man got this scar, although he had been present. He remembered the moment as he remembered everything from his first life, as if seeing it through a panel of glass block, a diffused and long-shadowed play, figures frozen in white ice.

They said Billy immediately picked up a broken teacup and cut his own face in exactly the same manner. A *folie à deux*, one doctor called it, an overweight woman named Roxanne. She had brittle red hair, and an ear-splitting laugh.

Like the man sitting next to Billy tonight, Billy did not go to the hospital to have his wound treated. His kind never did. It would have been impractical, they said, engendering too many questions. As it was sometimes uttered on TV, Billy did not require stitches.

But that was many years ago. Billy didn't think of himself as being this age, or see himself as others must see him. He was twenty-six years of *this* life. Ten before that.

The driver retrieved a small vial from his coat pocket, unscrewed the cap. He took a furious snort of methamphetamine, looked into the rear-view mirror and wiped his nose. He took a final hit on his cigarette, carefully butted it out in the ashtray. 'Ready?' he asked.

Without a word, Billy opened the SUV's passenger door and stepped into the night.

Having unscrewed the overhead bulb, they stood on the back porch. The driver looked at Billy, nodded.

'Coat,' he said softly.

Billy opened his coat. There were six photographs pinned inside, on the right, three rows of two. The man pointed to the second picture in the top row. It was a daytime portrait, taken against a backdrop of a painted concrete block wall such as one might find in a prison yard, or a department of motor vehicles.

The man in the photograph wore dark blue workman's coveralls, a lighter blue shirt beneath, buttoned to the top. Over the right breast of the coveralls was a ravel of red thread, perhaps where a name had once been embroidered.

The man in the photograph was wearing exactly what the man standing next to Billy was wearing.

He *was* the man standing next to Billy.

Billy looked at the name printed in blocky black letters at the bottom of the photograph.

'Sean,' he said.

'Yeah, Billy.'

With one hand on the grip of his Makarov, Billy rang the doorbell.

A few seconds later, they heard the sound of the security chain moving left to right, the turn of a deadbolt.

The man who opened the door was older than Billy had expected. He wore a lemon-yellow cotton robe over dark-blue pajamas. Billy saw that there was a brown stain on the right lapel of the man's robe. Perhaps he'd been drinking hot cocoa when the bell rang. Perhaps the doorbell startled him.

Yellow robe. Blue pajamas. Stain.

Billy glanced down. There was nothing in the man's hands. He knew to watch people's hands when they talked to him. *Watch a man's hands, watch the man*, his father always said. He noticed that the man had dirt beneath his fingernails. He might be a gardener, Billy thought, or a tradesman, though he was surely retired at this age. Perhaps he had a hobby workshop in the basement. Billy made a mental note to take a look, if there was time, even though he knew he wouldn't remember to do this.

'Can I help you boys?' the old man asked. He took turns looking at each of them, a guarded smile on his lips.

'We're having a bit of car trouble,' Billy said. He pointed over his shoulder, across the vacant lot, to the next street over. Like Billy, the SUV was in shadow. There was no street lamp above.

'Are you now?' the old man asked.

'Yes, sir.'

The old man leaned forward, glanced one way down the alley, then the other. There were only a handful of lights burning in the row houses, over the rear entrances to the small retail stores. Night lights and security lights.

'No cell phones?' the man asked.

Sean held up an empty hand, the one not on the grip of the weapon in his pocket.

'Ran out of minutes,' he said. 'Forgot to top it up at Radio Shack.'

The old man nodded in kinship. 'Happy to help,' he says. 'You boys stand tight. I'll just go get the cordless and bring it to ya. Call whoever ya like. I got the unlimited long-distance.'

Billy went through the door first, pushing past the old man with ease. The kitchen and eating areas were small, just like most row houses of this design. To the right was a stove and refrigerator. To the left, the sink and cupboards. The only thing on the refrigerator, held in place by a ceramic magnet in the shape of a banana, was a coupon for takeout pizza.

Ahead was a short hallway leading to the front room. Halfway down the hall, on the right, there was a small bathroom, long in need of upgrade, as well as staircases leading upstairs and down to the basement.

Billy heard the back door close and latch, footsteps approaching.

A few moments later the old man walked down the hallway into the living room.

Yellow robe. Blue pajamas. Stain.

Billy picked up a dining room chair and set it in the center of the living room. He then walked to the front windows, and the front door, making sure that the blinds were drawn and that there were no lights on in front of the house. He checked the deadbolt. The door was locked.

When he returned, Sean had the old man seated in the chair. The old man's face had gone slack. His eyes were open, but they were drooping. In short order Sean had his duffel bag unzipped, the duct tape removed. He tore off a length and wrapped it around the old man's head, covering his mouth. A few seconds later he had the old man's hands bound together behind him, his legs now secured to the legs of the chair, around the ankles.

Billy knelt down in front of the old man, waited for him to focus on his face. The old man no longer looked familiar. Billy had his picture in his book. He decided to look at it later, before they left.

'Is there anyone else in the house?' he asked.

The old man just stared. It seemed as if he might be about to go into shock. Behind him, in the corner, Billy noticed a green oxygen canister. There was a thin tube wrapped around the nozzle at the top; a nasal cannula dangled down. This close, he could hear a slight wheeze in the man's breathing.

'I need you to answer me,' Billy said. 'Shake your head no, or nod your head yes.' He leaned in, close to the man's right ear. 'I will ask you once again. Is there anyone else in the house right now?'

The old man slowly shook his head.

'Okay. Is anyone else expected here soon?'

Again the old man shook his head.

'Good,' Billy said. 'We're going to do what we need to do, then we will leave you in peace.'

With the old man silenced and secured, Billy fully took in the room. It was clearly a retiree's burrow, with sturdy, comfortable furniture, an oval braided rug in the center. The recliner had far more wear than the loveseat and sofa, which were all uphol-stered in a deep green plaid. There was an unopened package of butter mints on the end table, next to a small glen of amber pill vials. None of the cascaded magazines on the coffee table were current. They all had the address labels cut out.

Billy again considered the man before him.

Yellow robe. Blue pajamas. Stain.

'It's not him,' Billy said.

Sean looked at the man, back at Billy. 'Of course it's him.'

Billy reached into his bag, took out his tattered book of photographs. Strangers all. Yet each person had a face, a name, a connection, every one an ember glowing red and round like a cigarette lighter in a darkened car.

Billy found the photograph he was looking for. It was stuck to the page with a dot of child's kindergarten paste.

'Look,' he said. 'It's not him. He's not the man we want.'

Sean took the book from his hands. He walked over to the old man, held the photograph next to his face. 'It's him. I told you it's him.'

Billy tried to search his memory for the first time he saw the man, back to when he took this very picture. There was nothing there. It was blank canvas, white and opaque.

'We're making a mistake,' he said. 'It won't work if we make a mistake.'

The old man began to tremble. With lightning quickness Sean tore the duct tape from his mouth. The old man gulped for air.

'Which room is your bedroom?'

The old man opened his mouth. A few syllables tumbled forth.

'Fuh ... fuh ...'

'First room at the top?' Sean asked, his impatience boiling to the surface.

As Sean ran up the stairs, taking three at a time, Billy pulled up a chair and sat down in front of the old man, wondering how they could have made this error.

A few moments later, Sean returned to the front room, a bundle of clothing in his arms. He took the M&P 9 mm semi-automatic from his waistband and placed it on the dining room table.

He reached into his pocket, took out his straight razor, flicked it open and with four short cuts had the tape removed from the old man's hands and feet.

'Stand up,' he said.

The old man did not move.

Sean picked up his M&P, rocked back the hammer. He placed the barrel of the weapon against the back of the man's head.

'Stand up, or I will put your fucking brains in your fucking *lap*.'

The man tried to stand, but Billy could see that his legs would not support him. He stepped forward and offered his hand. The old man took it. The skin on the man's palm was soft. Whatever he had done in life, he had not been a tradesman, Billy thought.

Sean rummaged through one pile of clothing on the floor, extracted a blue dress shirt and a burgundy necktie. In the second pile he found a navy-blue two-button blazer.

'Take off your robe, take off your pajama top, and put this shit on.'

With arthritic slowness, the old man took off his pajama top, slipped into the dress shirt. His hands were trembling, his fingers knotty from the joint disease.

He put on the blazer but could not tie his tie. Billy did it for him.

Billy stepped back. Sean held the photograph next to the man, the photo in which the man was wearing these very items of clothing, the photograph Billy had taken of the man as he emerged from the courthouse on Filbert Street.

Blue jacket. Blue shirt. Burgundy tie.

It was the right man.

'You know what to do,' Sean said.

Billy reached into his right jeans pocket, took out the piece of paper, unfolded it, read the instructions. They were written in large type.

The other pocket held the handkerchief.

On it was a word written in blood.

*

Billy stepped from shadow to shadow on the second floor, a clockwork mouse opening each drawer, each cupboard, each closet.

Inside the closets were boxes; inside the boxes were folders, a Russian doll of a man's life, his history walking this earth. One box held a brittle old photo album, many of the pictures stuck to the black paper pages with the old-style gummed corners. Other pictures were gone, fallen to time.

In one box was a framed eight-by-ten of a young man in naval uniform, his arm around the waist of a young woman in a flower print dress with puffy shoulders.

Billy had seen this man before. He couldn't recall where.

Having found what he needed, he heard a noise behind him. He spun around, his Makarov drawn and held at arm's length, his hand, as always, steady.

The old man had lied. Someone *was* expected, and he was now standing in the hallway.

Billy leveled the Makarov at the stranger, his heart pounding in his chest. He had pulled the trigger many times, but was always a bit sickened by the sound of the metal as it shredded the flesh then, with a muffled *snick*, shattered the bone.

Still, if he must pull the trigger, he would. About this there was no recall needed, no debate. He had never hesitated.

The stranger put his hands over his head.

'Coat,' the stranger said.

The word.

'What?'

'Coat, Billy.'

Billy touched the barrel of the Makarov to the man's forehead. 'How do you know my fucking *name*?'

The man looked at the floor but said nothing.

'Don't you move,' Billy said.

He took a step back, eased opened the right side of his coat.

He saw the man in the blue coveralls with the light blue shirt beneath.

'Sean,' Billy said.

The man's name was Sean. Sean Patrick Farren. He was Billy's twin brother. Billy's name was Michael Anthony Farren. More accurately, that was his Christian name, the one on his birth records, the one used in sunlight.

In the shadows, where death songs knew who must live and who must die, he was Billy the Wolf.

It was time.

As Sean unfolded his straight razor, Billy knelt in front of the old man, looked at his face. It was featureless, empty. It would not remain so for long.

'I want you to know that it *has* all meant something, sir,' Billy said softly. 'Don't think it has not. I've been to the other side, and I know.'

He waited for a response. None was forthcoming.

'It is – all of it, every morning, evening and afternoon, since that day in 1960 – a palindrome, the same forward as it is backwards. It is faultless. It cannot be deconstructed.'

He placed a hand on the man's trembling shoulder, gave him a few moments to gather his final dignity.

'I am about to see it all,' Billy said. 'Everything. Every single moment of your life. Do you have any regrets?'

The man nodded. 'Many.'

'As do we all.' Billy took the man's hands, closed his eyes, drew in the man's essence, as the . . .

. . . door swings open and a gust of wintry wind blows in, the sound of bones shattering beneath skin, frozen iron on hot flesh, the primal roar of men in the grip of madness, blood splattered on virgin snow, the taller of the two men turning, his eyes feral, rimmed with fire, a man on his knees before him, his split skull a mass of glistening white bone,

the taller man running, running, his face forever stamped in red relief as . . .

Billy opened his eyes.

He felt weightless, emptied, freed. He let the images in his mind feather to blackness.

'Do you know my face?' he asked the old man.

'Yes.'

Billy took his Makarov in hand. *'I saw a stranger today,'* he began.

He took the suppressor from his pocket and attached it to the barrel of the Makarov. The tooling was perfect, the metal cool and smooth between his fingers. He'd made it himself in the cellar. He liked the welcoming warmth of the cellar, his windowless womb.

When he reached the final line of the blessing he slid a round into the chamber.

'O, oft and oft and oft, goes Christ . . .'

He reached out, felt the man's heartbeat. He gently touched the tip of the suppressor to the man's chest.

' . . . in the stranger's guise.'

He squeezed the trigger. The powerful Makarov bucked in his hand as the old man's body jerked forward then back, a rag doll in the grip of a giant.

Billy stood, watched the old man's soul escape his body, his final reckoning rising into a delicate blue light. He saw the old man as a boy, a young sailor, a father, all faces suddenly clear, rendered with a master's hand. He watched as the life force capered once about his lifeless body, then, seeing that the living world had finished its trade, shimmered into a pearlescent curl, and was gone.

Billy knew that within minutes he would not remember the old man.

Before they left the house he took two pictures.

Snap. Snap.

Just like the other times.

Back in the SUV, with Sean at the wheel, Billy pulled down the visor.

He knew the man in the mirror, even though no face stared back. The mirror was the only self-portrait he needed. The mirror was why he had grown his hair long. To recognize himself, to remember, to know himself as a tribe of one.

His name was Michael Anthony Farren, son of Daniel and Deena, grandson to Liam and Máire Farren.

But that was only when he stepped from the shadows.

Here, in this blackened rind of night, he was Billy.

3

Across the street from the death house, Detective Kevin Francis Byrne sat in his car, thinking, as he had so many times before, how there was a stillness that came to a place where murder had been done, a calm that gathered and kept to itself every spoken word, every scrape of a heel, every lament of a rusted hinge.

Even in the heart of a city, in the middle of the day, the death house was quiet.

Byrne knew this silence well. He had stood in more death houses than he cared to recall, but recall them he did, every one. As a detective in the homicide unit of the Philadelphia Police Department, he had taken part in the investigation of more than a thousand murders and, given time, could relate some relevant detail about each case. It wasn't an ability about which he was particularly boastful – he knew cops who recalled the street address of every job, even twenty years after their retirement; it was what it was.

The patrol officer standing sentry at the door was not much

older than Byrne had been his rookie year. The officer – P/O Skinner – was as white as a sheet.

When Byrne was in uniform, perhaps six days on the job, he caught a last-out call about a domestic disturbance. The domestic turned out to be a homicide. Byrne had opened the bedroom door to find a woman in her forties all but dismembered on her marital bed, blood everywhere, including the spackled ceiling. He recalled the detectives arriving that night, just a few days after Thanksgiving, cold coffees in hand, road salt caked on the cuffs of their off-the-rack suit pants. In that death house had been a radio, a big North Philly blaster, talking about how crack killed Apple Jack.

Byrne remembered the lead homicide detective at that time – a scuffed lifer named Nicky Rocks – nodding to him upon entry, touching a finger to his right ear, as if to say: *Good job, kid. Now turn that fucking shit off.*

Byrne looked in his side mirror. A clear night, a plum-colored sky. Occasional headlights cut the gloom on Morris Street.

With his seniority, Byrne could work any shift he wanted, of course, or not work at all. Most of the homicide detectives he had known throughout his career had already retired by the time they'd reached his age. Byrne was already looking at full pension.

The older he got, the more he realized that night was his time. Insomnia came with the job, but that wasn't it. He saw more in the dark, heard more, *felt* more.

If he retired, what would he do? Go private? Work security? Bodyguard to the rich and famous? He'd had offers, mostly from other retired cops who'd started their own firms.

Some nights he felt every moment of his age. But he knew that after a hot shower, a few hours' sleep and his first coffee of the day, he would be that young badge again.

A month earlier he had gotten a new assignment. He was still on the line squad, the unit that handled fresh homicides, but now led a team of rapid-response detectives. As the head of this unit Byrne could request any detective on any shift, even detectives from other divisions, in order to hit the ground running on any job for which he saw the need.

As a result, he found himself at crime scenes almost every day.

Byrne knew what he was going to see in this death house, but still had to prepare himself for it. He'd had a brief summary from his supervisor, who'd received the initial report from the two officers who had responded to a 911 call.

A man named Edwin Channing lived at this address. He was eighty-six years old, lived alone. Channing had subscribed to Med-Alert, a medical emergency alert service. At just after 1.20 this morning, the service received a signal from Channing's address and, getting no response from the man, called police dispatch.

According to P/O Raab, Skinner's partner, the back door had been unlocked. He'd entered the premises and found the victim in the living room. He had not immediately found the device that summoned the Med-Alert dispatcher. It was not in plain sight, and according to protocol, a patrol officer was not permitted to touch the body.

Byrne knew what he was going to encounter was bad, but the bigger picture was worse. As soon as he heard the circumstances, he knew. If you spent as much time in a homicide division as he had, you could all but draw a sketch of the scene in your mind after just hearing the summary. Most commercial-robbery homicides looked similar, as did most domestic homicides.

This was the second incident of similar if not identical MO in as many days. Both as a result of a home invasion, or what was supposed to *look* like a home invasion.

There were now four dead.

The first scene was on a quiet street in the Melrose Park

section of the city. The Rousseau family: Angelo, Laura and Mark. Angelo, the father, had been forty years old. He owned and operated a gift shop in Old City. His wife Laura, thirty-nine, was a home-maker. Their son Mark was seventeen. Mark Rousseau was a track star.

The timeline, as investigators understood it, was as follows:

This past Friday evening, Mark Rousseau was dropped off at approximately 6.20 p.m. by a school friend, Carl Fiore. The two had finished track practice earlier, and had stopped for a burger on Montgomery Avenue.

Carl Fiore said he did not recall if Angelo Rousseau's car, a 2012 Ford Focus, had been parked in the drive at the time.

At some time between 8 p.m. on Friday, and 7.30 a.m. on Saturday, a person or persons entered the Rousseau home – it appeared that they were granted entry, or had a key; there was no sign of forced entry – and proceeded to ransack the entire dwelling. There was not a drawer, cupboard, closet or storage box that had not been rummaged through. Investigators were currently interviewing extended family and co-workers, as well as the Rousseau family's insurance agents, in an attempt to determine what, if anything, had been stolen.

But even though the house had been turned upside down, even though the most personal items belonging to Angelo, Laura and Mark Rousseau were strewn around the living space, this was no burglary.

When Angelo's sister Anne-Marie came by at 7.30 on Saturday to take her sister-in-law to the Italian market, what she found was horrifying beyond words.

The Rousseau family were discovered, bound and gagged on dining room chairs in a small circle in the center of the living room. They had each been shot, once, through the heart. The crime-scene unit had collected three slugs, all presumptively 9 mm, all most likely fired from the same weapon.

But as brutal as these cold-blooded killings were, the killer was not yet done with Laura Rousseau's body.

Detective John Shepherd, the lead investigator on the case, spent the night at the scene carefully logging the documents and papers that were strewn about the house. Near the top of his summary was a curious finding.

Although a number of official documents were found, Laura Rousseau's birth certificate was not one of them. The birth certificates of both Angelo and Mark Rousseau were found on the floor of the small office on the first floor.

A call to the Rousseaus' bank confirmed that they did not rent a safe deposit box.

The crime-scene unit spent twenty-four hours at the scene collecting forensic evidence: hair, fibers, blood, fingerprints. To date, the only fingerprints found belonged to the Rousseau family. The firearms identification unit was currently investigating the slugs, in hopes of matching them to a weapon used in another crime.

The fact that no fingerprints were found on the duct tape suggested that the killer, or killers, wore gloves.

And now they had struck again.

Byrne would have to wait for FIU to submit a report on the discharged bullet from this scene, if recovered, but he was certain it was the same animal.

He could smell him.

Byrne flipped on the light in Edwin Channing's small kitchen. With gloved hands he opened a wall cabinet next to the stove. Inside he found geometrically arranged dry goods. Boxes of pasta, boxes of rice, boxes of flapjack mix. Another cupboard held neatly stacked cans of soup, cranberry sauce, sweetcorn. All store brands.

He opened one of the drawers. Inside he found cutlery for

two. Two knives, two forks, two soup spoons, two teaspoons. By all the evidence, this man lived alone. The pictures on the mantelpiece suggested he had been married, and for quite some time. The oldest photograph showed the victim in his naval whites, his arm around the waist of a petite woman with dark hair and sparkling eyes. The most recent photographs showed the older man and older woman sitting on a bench in the park. It looked to be fifteen or twenty years earlier.

Byrne closed the drawer thinking that the victim could not bring himself to dispose of, or put in storage, the second set of cutlery.

He put on fresh gloves, went upstairs, careful not to put his hands on the railing. There were two bedrooms on the second floor, along with a bathroom. One bedroom was used as storage.

Before stepping into Edwin Channing's room, he closed his eyes for a moment, took in the scant night sounds, the smells. Potpourri carpet deodorizer, liniment, the faint odor of a cigarette. He hadn't smelled it downstairs, nor were there any ashtrays on the tables.

Does the killer smoke?

Does the killer frequent a place where people smoke?

When Byrne had been a young detective, he'd always carried a pack of Marlboros and a pack of Newports. One regular. One menthol. He had never been much of a smoker, but the people he talked to – witnesses and suspects alike – invariably were. It was amazing what you could learn for the cost of a much-needed and well-timed cigarette.

He stepped into the bedroom, flipped on the light. A pair of table lamps came to life, one on either side of the double bed. The bed was made, military tight, with a beige brocade duvet.

But that was the only tidy thing in the room.

As with the Rousseau house, every drawer was open, their contents strewn about the room. A jewelry box lay upside down

50

on the floor. A metal box, perhaps used as a strongbox, was open and empty at his feet. Two suitcases, probably taken from the top shelf of the lone closet, were open and empty on the left side of the bed. The nightstand drawers were on the floor, upside down. Next to them sprawled a variety of generic ointments and cold tablets.

While CSU processed the first floor, Byrne went down to the basement, flipped on the light. Two bare bulbs in porcelain sockets hung from an unfinished ceiling. The cellar was mostly empty, well kept. There was a seventies-vintage Maytag washer and dryer on the far wall, beneath the glass block that bordered the sidewalk. To the left was an even older utility tub. A towel bar had been affixed to the face; a pair of powder-blue hand towels hung neatly. Furnace, hot-water heater, humidifier.

To the right was a small workbench. There was a utility lamp hanging from the low ceiling over it. Byrne pulled the chain. On the wall was a small pegboard with basic tools. Four or five screwdrivers, a claw hammer, a pair of crescent wrenches, a pair of needle-nose pliers.

None of the tools were out of place. If the killers had visited this cellar, it appeared that they had not disturbed anything, or had returned everything to its proper place. Byrne picked at a long-dried daub of carpenter's glue on the bench, trying to make some kind of sense of these crimes.

'Detective?'

The voice came from the top of the stairs. It sounded like P/O Skinner.

'Yeah.'

'The ME is here. They're going to start to process. Is there anything you want to do first?'

Byrne took a few moments to gather his thoughts. He retrieved his phone from his pocket, tapped the camera icon. 'I'm on my way up.'

He turned off the utility light and walked up the narrow stairs.

Although his photographs would not be entered into evidence – indeed, they would be kept as far away as possible from the official photos and video taken by both the crime-scene unit and the ME's office – he'd known he was going to take them from the moment he got the call.

He stood in the middle of the living room, carefully avoiding the small yellow markers that indicated possible blood evidence on the rug.

Somehow, when he looked at the screen on his phone, framing the victim's body, it seemed as if he had seen this before. He had, of course, witnessed the same horror at the Rousseau scene, but reduced this way, on a four-inch screen, it was all put into some kind of dark and primordial perspective.

After Edwin Channing was shot through the heart – as with Laura Rousseau, but not her husband and son – the killer had taken a very sharp instrument and carefully removed his face.

4

Byrne sat at the counter at the Oregon Diner. When he had walked into the restaurant just thirty minutes earlier, there were six patrons, mostly night owls at the tail end of a party, or insomniacs such as himself. Now it was starting to fill up with early-morning commuters.

On his cell phone, Byrne scrolled through the photos he had taken at both crime scenes. He had seen enough ransacking of living spaces in his many years on the force, and knew there to be only two kinds. One was when the perpetrator was trying to make it look like a burglary. The other kind of ransacking was when the thief was looking for something in particular. Although every drawer in the dressers at both scenes, as well as the nightstands, had been pulled open and dumped, contents strewn about the room, there were a few things that didn't make sense.

For one, next to the spilled jewelry case at the Channing scene was what looked to be a modest yet still valuable wedding and engagement ring set. Not expensive by today's upscale standards, but still gold.

Why were these items not taken?

At the Rousseau crime scene, a fairly expensive Canon DSLR camera was left on the top shelf of the closet in the master bedroom. There was also a PlayStation 4 game console found sitting next to the television in the living room.

While it was well known that experienced burglars knew what to look for, what was easy to get rid of – some going so far as to pass up expensive jewelry if they knew cash or coins were in the house – these were not burglars.

These victims had been executed. Two of them had been mutilated.

Why Laura Rousseau and not her husband and son? Why Edwin Channing?

The task force had already obtained a warrant for the Rousseau family credit-card records. The last charge on their main MasterCard account was Friday at 4.16 p.m. Angelo Rousseau had filled up the tank on his Ford Focus at a Sunoco station on South 17th Street. Two detectives from South had visited the station and watched the surveillance tape. Nothing appeared out of the ordinary, no one casing Rousseau or his car. When Rousseau pulled out of the gas station parking lot, the next car to pull out was a full ninety seconds later, going in the other direction. There was no lead there.

The other thing that was missing was any evidence of a struggle. The only mess at both scenes was from the drawers, closets and cupboards. There were no overturned tables, smashed chairs; no sign of any fight whatsoever.

A search of Edwin Channing's desk drawers did not yield a copy of the man's birth certificate.

Byrne closed his eyes, trying to envision the Rousseau homicides. If it was one perpetrator, he probably first pointed his weapon at Angelo Rousseau. It wasn't that Rousseau was a particularly big or fit man, but he was big enough, and any man whose family was put in danger was not only unpredictable, but potentially fierce.

The perpetrator then almost certainly bound and gagged Angelo Rousseau. But while he was doing that, what was Mark Rousseau doing? Mark was a big kid. Six foot one, one seventy, excellent physical shape. If the perpetrator put the gun down in order to tape up Angelo Rousseau – which would've been necessary: peeling off duct tape was a two-handed job – why didn't Mark Rousseau charge him?

Perhaps the killer made Mark Rousseau tie up both his father and mother. But if that were the case, why weren't Mark's fingerprints on the tape?

There were two killers. Byrne was sure of it.

Byrne had investigated many cases of serial murder, and knew that just as often as there was a signature, a cracked prism through which the killer saw the world, a psychological pattern as distinctive as any fingerprint, often there was not. Or, more accurately, there was a signature that lived in its own absence. A method that adhered to the notion that there was no method, only instinct.

Someone was walking the streets of Philadelphia who had entered two homes, put a gun to the chests of four people and pulled the trigger.

Without conscience.

Byrne believed that most people who committed murder, whether from passion or greed or vengeance, found it almost unbearable to carry with them the guilt of what they'd done. If they were never apprehended and bound over to justice for their crime, they lived the rest of their lives inside the prison of their minds, and often enough ended up taking their own life as penance.

Byrne was just about to call for his check when his phone rang. He glanced at the screen. It was his ex-wife, Donna.

'Hey,' Byrne said.

'Hey yourself, detective,' she said. 'You sound exhausted.'

'You could tell from one word that I'm exhausted?'

'What do *you* think?'

Byrne smiled. She'd always been able to read him. It was one of the reasons they fell in love. It was one of the reasons they parted.

Divorced for over a decade, he and Donna had begun seeing each other again, having come together over a property Donna had help Byrne purchase, a house that was no longer standing. Donna Sullivan Byrne was one of the top real-estate agents in Philadelphia.

'I'm okay,' Byrne said. 'It's just been a long night.'

Since they had rekindled their affair, Byrne had wrestled with the wisdom of putting Donna through the same fears and rigors of his job all over again. He didn't say more.

'How's the trip going?' he asked, hoping he was changing his tone.

'What can I say? It's New York.'

Donna was attending a conference of realtors. She was also interviewing with three of the bigger real-estate firms in the city. Byrne had known about this trip for months, but had chosen not to think about it.

'How did the interviews go?'

'Two out of three down. I think I aced them. You know I give good interview.'

Byrne closed his eyes for a moment and asked, 'Are you thinking of taking a job there if it's offered?'

'You know I love my hometown,' Donna said. 'But New York

is the center of the real-estate universe. If I got the opportunity to work here and turned it down, I might regret it for the rest of my life.'

It was Donna's idea of a soft sell. She had weeks earlier floated the notion of moving to New York, and it made Byrne's heart ache.

'It's only ninety minutes by train,' she added as a closer. 'Step into the Thirtieth Street station, read a newspaper, and an hour and a half later step into Penn Station.'

'I know.'

'You might even like it enough to move here.'

Byrne nearly choked on his coffee. '*Me?* Live in New York?'

He looked around, saw people glancing over at him. He'd said that much louder than he'd thought.

'Is that such a crazy idea?' Donna asked.

Second only to naked skydiving in the Arctic, Byrne thought. 'I guess it isn't.'

'I'm sure the NYPD would love to get you.'

Since he'd been a kid, Byrne had never thought about working anywhere other than the PPD, or living anywhere in the world other than Philly. He never would.

'Like you said, it's ninety minutes by train,' he replied.

Donna laughed. 'I've got to get going.'

'Okay.'

'Will you think about it?'

The dilemma was wrenching. He knew if they lived ninety minutes and worlds away from each other they would drift apart, and he would lose the last chance to be with the only woman he'd ever truly loved. Donna didn't say they would move in together if he came to New York, but she didn't say they wouldn't.

Byrne hated lying to his ex-wife.

He did it anyway.

'Sure,' he said.

*

Ten minutes later, while he was paying his check, Byrne's phone rang again. He was certain it would be Donna, telling him that moving to New York would indeed be crazy and she was on the first train back to Philly.

It wasn't Donna. It was Josh Bontrager, a fellow detective in the homicide unit.

'Hey, Josh,' Byrne said. 'You haven't been up all night, have you?'

'No,' Bontrager said. 'I got the call about an hour ago.'

'Where are you?'

'I'm across from the Channing scene,' Bontrager said. 'Detective Caruso and I have been trying to conduct the neighborhood interview before people leave for work.'

Byrne silently berated himself for not getting back to organize this. Maybe he had taken on too much with the new task force. Still, Josh Bontrager was as good as any cop he'd ever worked with. He didn't really need direction.

'Anything?'

'I think so,' Bontrager said. 'We have something we don't yet have on the Rousseau job.'

'What's that?' Byrne asked.

Byrne heard the lilt in Josh Bontrager's voice when he said:

'The man across the street from Edwin Channing's house saw something.'

The man standing across the street from the Edwin Channing crime scene was in his late twenties. He was tall and angular, seemed to have about him a nervous energy that did not permit him to stand still for too long. As Byrne approached the man he scanned his eyes. They were clear. Whatever made him fidgety was probably not drug-related.

Josh Bontrager made the introduction. The man's name was Perry Kershaw.

58

As a detective, Joshua Bontrager, still only in his thirties, brought to the job an uncanny ability to gain people's trust almost instantly. Raised Amish in rural Pennsylvania, he had the knack of starting a conversation with almost anyone and having that person believe that they were the most interesting person on the planet. But beneath that affability was a dogged investigator, with a keen eye for detail. In his time in the unit, Bontrager had steadily risen in the ranks, and the estimation, of the brass.

'This is a terrible thing,' Kershaw said. 'I can't believe it. This is ... this is a *good* block.'

Byrne knew that in his city – as in any densely populated urban environment – people tended to think of where they lived in terms of blocks, often indicated by a line of demarcation that served as the unofficial boundary of a neighborhood. SoHo in New York was south of Houston; TriBeCa was the triangle below Canal Street. Mostly this was an invention of the real-estate industry as a way of stating where the gentrification began and ended.

Josh Bontrager took out his notebook. Byrne would conduct the interview.

'Tell me what you remember from last night,' he said.

'Well, I was getting ready for bed – I didn't have to work today, so I was going to try to sleep in.'

'Where do you work?'

'I tend bar at Tria Café on Eighteenth.'

'What time was this last night?'

Kershaw thought for a moment. 'Let's see. I watched the news, then some of a movie on TCM.'

Bontrager made the note.

'During the commercials I got up, put away the dinner dishes from the dishwasher, went over to my front window.' Kershaw turned, pointed to the second story of his row house, the window overlooking the street. The window that faced Edwin Channing's home. 'It was pretty warm last night, so I opened the window, caught a little bit of a breeze. That's when I saw it.'

'What did you see?' Byrne asked.

'Not sure,' he said. 'It looked like Edwin turned his living room light on and off really quickly.'

'Are you referring to an overhead light? A lamp, perhaps?'

Byrne knew that there was no overhead light in the parlor. He wanted to know if Perry Kershaw knew this.

'I don't know,' he said. 'It didn't seem bright enough to be an overhead light. More like a lamp. I remember thinking at the time that he was going to need a new bulb for the lamp.'

'How so?' Byrne asked.

'Well, you know how when you turn on a lamp and the bulb has one last lighting in it? You turn it on and *bam*, the bulb burns out. It was like that.'

Byrne knew what the man was talking about. Edwin Channing did not burn out the bulb last night, or if he did, his killer or killers replaced it. Byrne had tried every lamp in the living room. They all worked fine. What this man was referring to was the muzzle flash of the gunshot that ended Edwin Channing's life.

'And what time was this again?' he asked.

Kershaw thought for a few seconds. 'Just after midnight, I think. Yeah. Right around there.'

'Do you remember anything about the color of the light?'

'The color of the light?'

'You know how light bulbs come in different types? Bright light, daylight, soft white, LED, things like that?'

'I guess I didn't think about it,' he said. 'My first thought was that it was odd that Edwin was up at such an hour. I kind of keep an eye on him because he doesn't really have any family anymore.'

At this, Kershaw took a second, his emotions reaching him. He had just spoken out loud about taking care of Edwin Channing, and now, perhaps, it seemed he had failed at this.

Byrne moved on. 'Would you say the light appeared to be more yellow, or more blue?'

Kershaw shrugged. 'I don't remember,' he said. 'I'm sorry.'

'That's okay,' Byrne said.

'You just don't think things are going to be important, you know?'

'It's perfectly all right. When that light went on and off, did you hear anything?'

'Not sure what you mean,' he said. 'Anything like what?'

'Anything at all. Anything coming from Mr Channing's house.'

Kershaw shook his head. 'No, sorry.'

Byrne was just asking this to corroborate what he already believed to be true. Although not yet confirmed by the firearms identification unit, or the medical examiner, Byrne presumed that whoever murdered Edwin Channing, as well as the entire Rousseau family, had used a suppressor. They were not just looking for a killer. They were looking for an assassin.

Suddenly it dawned on Perry Kershaw. 'Oh my God. You're talking about a gunshot. The flash was a *gunshot*.'

'We don't know that yet,' Byrne said. 'We're still putting things together.'

The man rubbed his hands together, waited. Byrne could see a slight tremble in his shoulders. He was about to go south. Byrne had to step up the interview, or he was going to lose Perry Kershaw.

'What did you do next?' he asked.

'I watched the street a little while longer. I was just about to close the window, then the blind, when I saw two more flashes of light.'

'From Mr Channing's house?'

He nodded. 'These were different from the first one.'

'Same window? The front room?'

'Yes.'

'How were they different?'

'They were not nearly as bright. In fact at first I thought it might have been the television. But I know that Edwin doesn't watch late night TV. Unless he has insomnia.'

'So you would characterize these lights as flashes?'

'Yeah. Like that.'

'Flashes as in camera flashes?'

'Now that you mention it, yes. Exactly like that.'

'And what time was this?'

'This had to be ten after twelve. Right around there.'

Byrne thought about this. The medical examiner's investigator put time of death at between midnight and 1 a.m. This new evidence – if evidentiary it turned out to be – indicated that the killer pulled the trigger at about five after midnight. And then took two photographs.

'Can you show me exactly where you were standing when you saw these flashes of light?'

Kershaw turned and looked at his row house, as if he'd never seen it before. It was clear that he did not expect the police to be entering his home on a day such as this. Or any day. Most people didn't.

'Um, sure, come on inside.'

Perry Kershaw's house was decorated in the style of a dorm room – rock posters, IKEA furniture, hastily arranged. Upstairs, in what was clearly a guest bedroom, Kershaw crossed over to the windows and lifted both sets of horizontal blinds.

The view down to the Channing living room was unobstructed. Unfortunately, Channing's front-room windows had honeycomb-style window blinds, not Venetian-style slats. Had they been horizontal slats, there may have existed the possibility, however slight, of seeing into the room through the gaps.

Because of the bright sunlight, it was impossible to recreate what Perry Kershaw had seen the night before. But there was no doubt that a bright flash of light – indeed, three bright flashes of light – would be visible on the canvas of Edwin Channing's window blinds at or around midnight.

Byrne pointed to the second floor of the victim's house.

'Did you see any activity up there last night?' he asked.

Again Kershaw considered his answer. 'No, nothing. As you might imagine, Edwin didn't do a lot of trundling up and down the stairs. I only see lights come on on the second floor once in a while. I didn't see anything last night.'

'When was the last time you saw Mr Channing?'

'It was early yesterday evening. Just as it was getting dark.'

'Where did you see him?'

'I can show you.'

They descended the stairs, crossed the small living room and exited the house. They walked across the street, to the southeast corner. Like many South Philadelphia streets, Morris Street was a pastiche of residential and commercial buildings. While the lot next to the Channing house was vacant, the corner held a recently rehabbed row house that was now a professional building for three attorneys. Directly diagonal from it was a Cambodian restaurant, closed for renovations.

'You saw Mr Channing here?' Byrne asked.

'Yes.'

'And what time was this?'

The man thought for a moment. 'It had to be around seven thirty. Around there anyway. I got home from work, took a shower, got ready to go out. I met some friends for a quick drink.'

'Where exactly did you see him?' Byrne asked.

He pointed to the rear of the block, the alleyway that cut between the row houses. 'He was standing right there, right behind his house.'

'What was he doing?'

He shrugged. 'Just standing there, really. His back was to me. I thought he might have been watering that small garden he has there, but he didn't seem to have the hose in hand.'

'Were you walking up the block?'

'No,' he said. 'I was getting into my car. Edwin looked to be lost in thought, so I didn't say anything or call out.'

Byrne just listened.

'But now that I think about it, it was kind of odd.'

'Odd in what way?'

'As I was getting into my car, I thought I heard someone singing.'

'Singing?'

'Yeah, it was soft, but I heard it.'

'Mr Channing was singing?'

'No, it wasn't him.'

'Might it have been a radio?' Byrne asked. 'Maybe someone had a television on with the windows open? Maybe a car stereo?'

'All of that is possible, I guess. But for some reason, I had the feeling that someone was standing in his garden, and that person was singing.'

Byrne took this in. 'So this was singing, not humming. Not like someone humming while they work.'

'No, it was definitely singing. Kind of a chant, actually. It was definitely a woman's voice, or maybe a girl's. Definitely female, though. Pretty voice.'

'It sounded like it was coming from behind his house?'

'It did,' he said. 'As I pulled away, I glanced over, and I thought I saw someone standing in front of him. I can't be sure, because he has those two white brick columns next to his garden, but it looked like maybe there was a girl standing there, or a very petite woman.'

'What can you tell me about this woman?'

The man shrugged. 'I'm not even sure I saw her. I thought I saw a figure in white, but by the time I turned around in the driveway on the next block and drove back past the alley, he was already inside the house, and there was no one in the garden.'

'And you didn't hear any more singing?'

'No,' he said.

Byrne glanced at Bontrager, who shook his head. He had nothing to ask or add.

'That's the last time I saw him alive,' Kershaw said. He looked at Bontrager, then at Byrne, a slight sheen to his eyes. 'You never know, do you?'

Byrne knew what he meant. He'd dealt with it for so many years, made so many notifications, that it had become almost rote. He'd always subscribed to the theory that there were two things for which a person was never prepared: the moment someone walked into your life, and the moment they walked out. Yes, if someone was in hospice care, you could see it coming, could try to prepare yourself. His mother had been in the hospice for her final two weeks. It softened the blow, but nothing could ever fully pull the punch. It had been more than ten years since his mother's passing, and there were still times when he would be on a crowded street in the city, hear a woman's laugh, and turn half expecting to see her walking toward him, her red coat on, her strawberry-blond hair pulled up into a French twist.

It was never her.

'No,' Byrne said. 'You never know.'

He wrapped up the interview, gave Kershaw his card, along with the standing request for him to call if he remembered anything, or saw the mysterious woman in white again.

While Bontrager headed off to the forensic lab to check the status of the blood evidence collected at the scene, Byrne stood across from the death house, leaning against his car. He looked at the cracked asphalt at his feet. Within the past twenty-four hours, someone had possibly stood in this same spot, about to commit murder.

As the energy of a spring morning flowed around him, Byrne blocked it all out, three questions circling:

Who triggered the medical alert after Channing died?

Why was the killer taking pictures?

Who was singing?

Byrne looked up to see Terry Nugent exiting the Channing house. Nugent was a seasoned officer in the crime scene unit, having once worked for the Delaware state police in the same capacity.

'We have it?' Byrne asked.

Nugent held up a small paper evidence envelope. He crossed the street to where Byrne was standing and, with the forceps in his right hand, gently removed the item from the bag. Although Byrne had little doubt, the single bullet confirmed what he already knew. He was far from a ballistics expert, but you did something a number of years, and certain aspects of the job became habit.

'Good work,' he said.

'All in a night.'

'Where was it?'

Nugent pointed to the house, toward the right front corner. 'It went into the middle drawer of that old breakfront in the dining room.'

Byrne knew the answer to his next question but asked it anyway. It was the way of the job.

'Just the one?'

'Yeah.'

66

He knew this because there had been one victim, bound and gagged and executed. This caliber – which Byrne estimated to be a 9 mm, perhaps a .380 – placed at the center of the chest, meant it would not take more than one shot.

Bound people didn't run.

As a second CSU van arrived, Byrne walked to the rear of the Channing property. There was indeed a small container garden, all of the plants still quite young.

Next to the garden was a large pot with what looked to be a withered orange tree. Something in the tree caught Byrne's eye. It was a piece of cloth, tied to a low branch.

He stepped inside the house and got the attention of one of the CSU techs, who followed him back out. The tech took a series of photographs of the piece of cloth *in situ*, as well as a brief video record showing the location. He then pulled a pair of latex gloves from his pocket and put them on. He reached up, gently untied the twine.

Walking over to the small patio table, he unrolled a large piece of glossy paper, put the cloth down on it to avoid any cross-contamination and smoothed it.

The cloth was about twelve inches square. It looked to be a linen handkerchief, cream in color, with a blue lace trim. At the center was scrawled a single word. The five letters, all capitals, spanned edge to edge.

As unnerving as the fact that the killer or killers might have marked their territory with this message, two things leapt out at Byrne.

The word was written in a dark brown fluid. There was little doubt that it was blood.

Then there was the word itself, a word of which Byrne knew the meaning but had no idea of the context.

There, in the middle of the cloth, like a cipher, was written: *TENET.*

5

County Louth, Ireland, July 1941

Máire Fay Glover hid behind the curtain in the small room next to the surgery.

She had long ago grown used to the smells, both septic and antiseptic, but on this day the redolence was particularly strong, thick with the metal of blood and the foul loam of feces. She tried to sip small breaths of air through her pursed lips.

At fourteen she was old enough to pass for one of the scullery maids, and often, just by tying back her hair with a kerchief, and hoisting a kettle full of water from the well into the kitchen, or carrying a lapful of potatoes in her apron from the garden to the pantry, she went all but unnoticed.

Indeed, some of the nurses, and a few of the doctors, thought she worked there, or at least was a volunteer.

Some days Máire would stop in the glen to pick flowers, if

they were in season. Young girls with flowers in hospitals were smiled at, fawned over at times, but generally passed like ghosts in blue moonlight.

The man in bed 102 had been at the hospital for more than a month now, and in all this time had received not a single visitor. Nor, in all that time, had he once opened his eyes. He was fed through a tube, washed with a sponge and a face cloth and did his dirty business into bedpans. Once a fortnight the man who owned the barber shop on the high street – Mr Theodore Ferley – would come and shave him with a straight razor. Afterwards he applied witch hazel, and a scented cream.

But still not a word from the man.

Not during the day, anyway.

Once, on an evening in June, Máire had been tidying up the kitchen and thought she heard something. She stopped, cocked her head to the sound, listened again. It was the man. He had clearly mumbled something. Máire stole to the hallway, looked about the ward. There were only two other men, both sleeping.

She took her corn broom, made little work of sidling up next to the man's bed. The man spoke again. Then again. Máire found that she had been holding her breath the entire time. After a short while he began to speak – eyes still closed – in full sentences, as if this were some sort of confessional, as if he were trying to rid himself of some terrible burden. Máire watched his eyes, saw the movement beneath his eyelids, moving side to side, upwards and downwards. She wondered if the things the man was describing were playing out in his mind like some kind of cinema.

That evening, and for many evenings after, he spoke of the places he'd been, the things he had witnessed, and the things he'd done, all the time his eyes looking at some hidden world, an inner world, a place that lived only in his mind.

Máire Fay Glover wondered if the doctors knew the things the man had seen and done.

It didn't matter. *She* knew.

And it made all the difference.

She'd finally found him.

On the last day of spring, just after the breakfast dishes were cleared and morning rounds made, the man opened his eyes.

It was so sudden, so *unexpected*, Máire nearly leapt from her skin.

She had never seen eyes so blue.

The man slowly turned his head to see her. It was then that Máire realized she'd not properly prepared for this moment. After all this time, she was not ready. She silently scolded herself for being so stupid, so ill-equipped. There was no color in her cheeks and her hair was unwashed.

But not to worry. She looked at the man with the glamour, an ability women of her kind had always had.

The man saw what she wanted him to see: the apple-cheeked fourteen-year-old County Louth colleen Máire Fay Glover.

'My name is Liam,' he said softly. His voice was thin and raspy, brittle from disuse. 'Liam Farren.'

She knew his name as she knew her own. 'I know.'

'Am I dead?'

She took his hand in hers, remained silent for a moment. Then: 'My name is Máire.'

He raised his right hand slowly, extending his forefinger, the only one not bandaged. About halfway to her face he stopped, exhausted. It appeared as if he wanted to touch her hair, which she, of course, would have none of, not on this day. She took his hand in her own again, leaned forward and ran her cheek along the back of it. He closed his eyes at her soft touch.

'Are you an angel?' he asked.

Máire smiled. 'Something like that.'

Later that day Máire returned. While tending to small chores in the ward, she caught the eye of the clinic's head nurse, a stern woman of forty who held naught for clutter or the breaking of rules.

The nurse pointed at Liam Farren. 'He says you are family.'

Máire glanced at her hands, said nothing.

'Is this so?'

Máire didn't know what to say. She just nodded.

The nurse, disbelieving, glanced between Máire and the man a few times, perhaps mining a resemblance.

Máire looked for permission to cross over to the bed. The nurse eventually stepped aside.

'Only a short while,' she said. 'Now that he is back among the living, the real work begins.'

Among the living, Máire thought.

'Yes, mum.'

While Liam Farren slept, Máire slipped into the surgery and washed her hair. She returned with her mother's silver comb in hand and began to brush her long tresses.

She took the small poppet from her pocket, stroked the straw at its feet. She recited the poem from heart:

> *Where dips the rocky highland*
> *Of Sleuth Wood in the lake,*
> *There lies a leafy island*
> *Where flapping herons wake . . .*

For the next two months Máire visited Liam Farren every day, bringing her gran's home-made soups, often sneaking inside in the gloaming just to watch him sleep. His road to recovery was slow but steady, as she knew it would be.

'You talked in your fevers, you did,' she said one morning.

His face darkened. 'Did I now?'

Máire nodded. She had secretly kept a journal of the things he'd said, some of it unintelligible, but much of it clear, as if he were dictating his life's story to a proper steno grapher. Máire had at one time thought of the secretarial life, but her grades were only average, nor was there money for university.

Before she left for the night, a fine summer evening in late August, she stopped at the foot of the bed of a man named Joseph MacRauch.

MacRauch was a local man, a farrier by trade, a father of five who had come down with the cancer nearly six months gone, a scourge that had claimed not only half his weight but also his right leg.

Máire had no feelings for the man other than pity. He was unknown to her. Still, his ravaged face, collapsed mouth and withering body weighed on her as she passed him each day.

A week earlier the doctors gave him two weeks more to live. They had told his wife so. But Máire knew differently. Her kind always did. She peered into the hallway that evening and saw that all was hushed and dimmed for the night. A gentle breeze billowed the curtains.

Máire removed her red cloth coat. Beneath it she wore her white gauze shift, as she was taught.

She put a hand on the man's shoulder. His skin was cool to the touch. It was almost as if he had made the crossing, but he still drew breath.

Máire began to sing.

On the melody she soared above the countryside, hovering

over the corn stooks, over the trees in the forest that ringed the town, ever higher into the silver moonlight.

The next morning, before the sun crested the trees, Joseph MacRauch was dead.

6

Philadelphia, 2015

Assistant District Attorney for the County of Philadelphia Jessica Balzano considered her witness. He was darkly hand-some, with coffee-brown hair, dark eyes, lashes to die for. He wore a navy-blue blazer, white Oxford shirt and tan slacks.

He was the kind of witness about whom attorneys dreamed – direct, polite, forthright and, most important of all, believable.

'Tell us, in your own words, what happened that day,' Jessica said. 'And please take your time.'

The witness took the moment. 'It was early,' he said.

'About what time was it?'

'I don't know.'

'Was it still dark or was it light?'

'It was light.'

'So, around seven o'clock?'

'I think so.'

'And we're talking about the Friday in question?'

The witness nodded.

'I'm afraid you have to answer out loud,' Jessica said.

'It was Friday.'

'And what happened?'

The witness shrugged. This was clearly not easy for him. 'The window got broken.'

Jessica let the statement settle for a moment. 'Do you know how the window got broken?'

'I'm not sure.'

'Now, you say the window was broken. Were both panes shattered?'

'I don't know what that is.'

'The window has an upper part and a lower part,' Jessica said. 'Those are the panes.'

'Okay.'

'Were both of them broken?'

The witness shook his head. 'Just the bottom part.'

'Would you say that the majority of the broken glass was on the inside or the outside?'

Another shrug. 'On the outside, I guess.'

'Would you agree that the window did not break itself?'

'Yes,' he said softly.

'And would you also agree that there is a very real possibility that the window was broken by a football?'

No answer.

'A football you have been told many times not to throw in the house?' Jessica added.

Still no answer. None was expected. Jessica walked around the table, leaned against it and crossed her arms.

'What do you have to say for yourself?' she asked.

'Am I guilty?'

'I think so, honey.'

Jessica's seven-year-old son Carlos, perched on a barstool in their kitchen, studied his shoes.

'What's my sentence?' he asked.

'We're considering time off for helping your mother with her cross-examination skills.'

'Okay.'

Jessica glanced at her watch. 'Let's get you to school,' she said. 'We'll consider the penalty phase when I get home from work.'

Carlos Balzano looked at his hands, as if they were in shackles. When he looked up and smiled, the City of Philadelphia, and his mother, forgave every one of his crimes.

The case was the Commonwealth of Pennsylvania versus Earl Carter. The charges were commercial robbery and misdemeanor assault.

When Judge Althea Gipson was seated, the opposing counsel put on their game faces.

Jessica had been ready for this moment for weeks.

Since leaving the police force, where she had been a homicide detective for nearly a decade, she had steadily risen through the ranks of newer ADAs, much to the consternation of some of her fellow prosecutors. Jessica had expected the palace intrigue. When she'd joined the homicide unit, she had pushed hard against those who whispered behind her back that she'd gotten the assignment due to her gender, or the fact that her father was one of the most decorated cops in the history of the PPD.

Back then she was more than ten years younger than most of her colleagues. Now she was at least ten years older. It just made her work that much harder. Since day one on this job she'd turned the lights on in the morning, and turned them off at night.

Because the defendant, a forty-six-year-old unemployed welder originally from Kentucky, was all but indigent, he had been assigned a public defender.

If ever there was a Hollywood prototype for the beleaguered public defender, Rourke Hoffman was that prototype. A PD for more than three decades, now pushing sixty, Hoffman, in his rumpled suits and soiled running shoes, was a fixture at the Criminal Justice Center at 13th and Filbert streets. Today was Jessica's first time at the bar with the man.

As Judge Gipson finalized a few items on her laptop, Jessica went over her notes one last time.

What had put Earl Carter in this courtroom was a happy accident. Not for Earl, of course, but rather for the people of Philadelphia. His contact with the police department that fateful day began with a 911 call about a woman screaming in her dilapidated south Philly row house. When patrol officers arrived, they witnessed a highly intoxicated Earl Carter repeatedly punching his estranged wife.

While securing and processing the scene, the assigned detective, Victor Cortez, saw something in the front room closet that nudged a memory. On the closet floor was a rather unique red plaid flannel shirt with black pockets piped with gold thread. Beneath the shirt was a pair of worn Levi's with a distinctive black stain on the left knee. Underneath the jeans were a pair of Timberland boots, tan in color, with red woven laces.

Cortez returned to the station house that day and rooted his hard drive for the raw footage of a strong-arm robbery from five months earlier. The footage had been uploaded to the Philadelphia Police Department's YouTube channel, and posted on the PPD's blog site. In the recording, a man was seen walking in the back door of DiBlasio's, a popular Italian deli in South Philadelphia. Once inside, he began to help himself to items that were in the open floor safe. When confronted by the owner, seventy-two-year-old Lucio DiBlasio, the robber grabbed the older man by the throat and threw him into a shelving unit, bringing a large can of tomato sauce down onto DiBlasio's head.

Then the thief ran out.

In the five months that the video had been on the PPD blog and the PPD YouTube channel, no leads had been generated.

Until the day Earl Carter lifted his hand in anger to his estranged wife and a solid detective named Victor Cortez got the case.

On direct examination, the state's first three witnesses – the neighbor who made the 911 call, the responding officer and Detective Cortez – sailed through the process as Jessica had expected them to, all without a single objection from the defense.

As Cortez stepped down, Jessica sneaked a look at her watch. It was just shy of 4.30. She had thought about saving her fourth witness for the following morning, but she was on a roll.

'The people call Reginald Kenneth Jones III.'

As Jones made his way across the courtroom, Jessica gently placed her pen on top of her legal pad, took a deep breath, looked up, smiled.

'Good afternoon, sir.'

'Afternoon, ma'am.

The man sitting in the witness chair in Courtroom 603 was African American, trim and fit, in his late forties.

'Could you state your name for the record, please?'

'Reginald Kenneth Jones III.'

'Are you currently employed, Mr Jones?'

'Yes, ma'am.'

'Where do you work?'

'I work for the Philadelphia Police Department, assigned to the crime scene unit.'

'How long have you been there?'

'Twenty-eight years as a police officer; twenty-two of those years in CSU.'

'If you had to distill what CSU officers do, what would you say the job is about?'

'It's all about trace evidence. Hair, fingerprints, blood, skin cells, footprints. Our job is to collect it, document it, protect it and get it to the various labs for analysis.'

'What about photographs?'

'Yes, ma'am. We photograph and videotape every scene.'

Jessica glanced at her notes for effect. She knew every line on the page by heart. 'Let me direct your attention to March 17 of this year. Were you working that day?'

'I was.'

'Were you called to a crime scene in the 500 block of West Porter?'

'Yes, ma'am. We were requested by Detective Victor Cortez.'

'When you arrived at the scene, what requests were made?'

'Among other things, Detective Cortez requested photographs of the parlor,' he said. 'Specifically the closet next to the front door.'

'What, if anything, did you notice about the closet itself?'

'I noticed that the homeowner had removed the closet door.'

Rourke Hoffman leapt to his feet. 'Objection. Calls for speculation.'

'Sustained,' the judge said.

'I'll rephrase,' Jessica said. 'Did you notice anything out of the ordinary about the closet?'

'*Objection*,' Hoffman repeated, still standing. '*Again* calls for speculation. How would the witness know what was ordinary or out of the ordinary in that house?'

'Sustained.'

Jessica took a beat. 'Officer Jones, when you looked at the closet, what did you see?'

'There was no door.'

'Thank you.' Jessica walked over to the easel where she had earlier deployed three photographs.

'I'd like to direct your attention to these three photographs. Specifically, this enlargement. Did you take this photograph?'

'Yes, ma'am.'

The photograph depicted a pair of Timberland boots. Folded on top of the boots was a pair of soiled Levi's, and on top of the jeans was a red plaid shirt with black pockets and gold piping.

'As regards these three items, did you receive any more requests or instructions from Detective Cortez?'

'Yes. He asked that I collect these items as evidence.'

'What happened next?'

'I brought them back to the forensic lab at Eighth and Poplar, logged them into evidence and locked them down.'

'Officer Jones, do you have any reason to doubt that these three evidentiary items were mishandled in any way, or in any way left the chain of evidence as regards this proceeding?'

'Absolutely not, ma'am,' he said.

At this, Jessica nodded to Amy Smith, a fellow ADA, who was standing by the door that led to chambers, waiting for the signal. Amy opened the door, and she and another ADA brought in what looked to be a life-size statue draped in a white sheet. As Jessica expected, this drew a reaction from the gallery, as well as the defendant. The two ADAs placed the item between the witness stand and the jury box, next to the TV monitor.

'I would like to once again play the videotape of the defendant in the back room of DiBlasio's,' Jessica said.

She picked up the remote, started the tape. When the recording reached the point where Carter assaulted Lucio DiBlasio, she stopped it. She nodded at Amy Smith, who snapped off the white sheet.

There stood a mannequin, the precise height and weight of

the defendant, wearing the same clothing the defendant was wearing in the surveillance video.

If the gallery and jury mumbled when the mannequin was brought in, they emitted a collective gasp now.

'Do you recognize these items of clothing, Officer Jones?'

'I do.'

'Can you verify that they are indeed the same items collected from the defendant's closet?'

Jones looked to the judge, who nodded. He rose from his seat, walked the few steps to the exhibit. Once there, he examined the bar-coded tags hanging from the shirt, jeans and each of the boots. He returned to the witness stand, sat down.

'To answer your question, yes, these are the same items of clothing.'

Jessica knew that the judge was going to adjourn for the day in thirty seconds or so, which meant she had thirty full seconds for the jury to absorb the rather striking visual of the man on tape wearing the clothes on the mannequin belonging to the man sitting at the defense table.

ADA Jessica Balzano took the full thirty.

'Don't get mad,' Jessica said.

'When do I ever get mad?'

Jessica had to laugh. Despite being the warmest, sweetest man she'd ever known, her husband Vincent had the most volatile temper and quickest fuse. She'd long ago figured a way to harness the power.

She gripped the phone a little tighter. 'I'm stuck in the office for a while.'

Silence. Then, 'Okay. What did the kids eat yesterday?'

As a detective in Narcotics Field Unit North, Vincent Balzano worked his share of overtime too. It seemed they had just barely figured out how to not be crazy at the same time.

'Chinese from China House,' Jessica said. 'Lemon chicken and vegetable lo mein, I think.'

She heard her husband open the kitchen drawer dedicated to takeout menus. 'Santucci's okay?'

Santucci's square pizza was always a go-to. 'Perfect. I won't be late.'

'I'll try and save you a slice.'

'Italians.'

'I love you.'

Jessica clicked off her phone. She turned to the pile of folders on her desk. She was still new enough to the office to have to carry her share of water and conduct deep background and research for the superstars of the DA's office.

She pulled the top folder, took out a legal pad and folded it over to a fresh page. She had five cases on her research plate. The first case being built was a firebombing of a small business in southwest Center City. The defendant, currently being held in Curran-Fromhold, was a career criminal named Daniel Farren.

7

Headquartered on the first floor of the Police Administration Building at Eight and Race streets – a building long ago nicknamed the Roundhouse – the PPD Homicide Unit employed more than ninety detectives, working all three tours, seven days a week.

On the day following the discovery of Edwin Channing's body, Byrne met with John Shepherd and Joshua Bontrager in the duty room. There were two other detectives present.

Maria Caruso was one of the youngest members of the squad, and one of the few female detectives.

In addition was a detective named Bình Ngô, a second-generation Vietnamese American who had a few years earlier transferred over from the gang unit when an opening opened up in Homicide.

Both Caruso and Bình had led their own investigations in the past. Both were excellent detectives.

The officers compared notes.

'I've got nothing linking the Rousseau family to Edwin Channing,' Shepherd said. 'The Rousseaus went to St James's, shopped at the Whole Foods in Jenkintown, had season tickets to the Flyers. I interviewed the principal at Mark's school, and as far as we know there is no relative of Edwin Channing who attends. They lived, shopped and socialized in different circles.' He flipped a few pages. 'Laura belonged to a knitting club with her sister-in-law Anne-Marie Beaudry, who discovered the bodies.'

'Have you been able to interview her at length?' Byrne asked.

Shepherd shook his head. 'Not yet,' he said. 'As you might imagine, she's devastated. She spent the first night in Hahnemann, under sedation.'

'Has she been discharged?'

'I just called over there,' Shepherd said. 'She went home yesterday.'

'Do you want someone else to conduct the interview?' Byrne asked.

Shepherd gave this a moment's thought. 'It might be best. Right now, I'm the face of the crime.'

'I'll get over there today,' Byrne said.

He put a large photocopy of the handkerchief on the table, the square linen cloth bearing the bloody word *TENET*.

'And we've combed every inch of the Rousseau property?' he asked.

'We did,' Shepherd said. 'We'll go over it again.'

'What about the word?' Byrne asked. 'Any ideas?'

Bontrager flipped through his notes. '*Tenet*, according to Merriam-Webster, is "a principle, belief, or doctrine generally held to be true; especially one held in common by members of an organization, movement, or profession".'

'A movement,' Shepherd echoed. 'I can see the execution-style MO as being political, but I don't see Channing or the

Rousseau family as being politically active or radical. They certainly showed no signs of being mobbed up.'

'What about a religious angle?'

'A few of the documents we found at Edwin Channing's house were tax statements regarding donations to his church,' Maria said.

'The Rousseaus were Catholic,' Shepherd said. 'I'm not seeing any fringe or radical elements to either of them.'

Byrne nodded in agreement. 'Then, of course, the word *tenet* is a palindrome,' he said, 'the same forward as backward. Let's run that idea, see if there is a signature that has been used in the recent past.'

Maria Caruso made the note.

'Have we run Tenet as a last name?' Byrne asked.

Bình nodded. 'Ran it through white pages in three counties, only a handful of results. Crossed those names with NCIC and PCIC and got nothing. Following up on the few who live in Philly. I found no commercial enterprise or public agency with that name.'

'What about the Channing autopsy?'

The autopsy had taken place at 9.30 that morning. Bình had met with the medical examiner at the morgue on University Avenue.

Death for all four victims had come as a result of massive blood loss due to ballistic trauma. All four victims were shot at near point-blank range in the center of the chest. Because the projectiles were of a large caliber, the bullets had exited the victims and were recovered at the scene.

The only other marks on the bodies were ligature marks where the victims had been bound to a chair.

'The preliminary on Edwin Channing was that he was relatively healthy for a man his age,' Bình said. 'He had mild emphysema, took Digoxin and Atenolol, and had a slightly enlarged prostate. Other than that, he was in pretty good shape.'

'What about that Med-Alert button?'

'The ME believes that as Edwin Channing's muscles began to collapse, his weight against the chair activated the button. The only prints on the device were Channing's.'

Byrne thought about this. If the button had not been activated, it might have been days or weeks before his body was discovered.

'What about the Rousseaus?'

'Not much. High blood pressure on the father. Laura Rousseau had bronchitis. The son was in perfect shape.'

Byrne made a note to try and red-line the toxicology reports pending on all four victims. Toxicology, like DNA matches, took time.

'And we have no police or SafeCam footage from either scene?' Byrne asked.

SafeCam was a fairly new citizen outreach program whereby the location of private surveillance cameras – those owned by homeowners and business owners – were mapped by the PPD and Homeland Security.

If and when a crime occurred near the location of a particular SafeCam camera, the department would contact the homeowner or business owner to see if there was any footage. Not all SafeCam participants had systems that recorded audio and video to a hard drive or Secure Digital card, and they were in no way legally bound by law to share the footage, if it existed.

Despite this, the program had, to date, been a resounding success, at least as far as the department was concerned. With more than three thousand SafeCams in existence, in a little over two years there had been nearly four hundred cases solved.

'We have two police cameras on that street, which unfortunately have been down for almost a month,' Maria said. 'There are two people on the SafeCam program who might have been in range on the Channing case.' She flipped a few pages in her notebook. 'One is a resident, a Marcus Boulware. He checked his DVR for the time frame and there was nothing.' A few more pages. 'The other is a commercial establishment called Nail Island. They were closed for the weekend, and I haven't been able to reach the owner.'

'Is the store camera visible from the street?' Byrne asked.

Maria nodded. 'It's attached to the small balcony on the second floor over the main entrance. If it was on, and recording, and the footage hasn't been dumped, we might have something.'

'Good,' Byrne said. 'Let's stay on it.'

Maria made the note.

'Edwin Channing was discovered wearing a blazer, dress shirt and tie,' Byrne said. 'He was also wearing pajama bottoms and slippers. A yellow cotton robe was found on top of a small pile of clothing in the corner of the living room.'

'Maybe he was getting ready to go out,' Maria said.

'The man across the street, Perry Kershaw, said that Channing was pretty much a home body. I don't see him getting dressed up like that to head out at night,' Byrne said.

'Maybe he'd just got home,' Maria said.

'It's possible.'

'I don't know about you guys,' Bontrager said, indicating Byrne and Shepherd, 'but if I'm changing from pajamas, getting ready to go out, I put my pants on first, then shirt, then tie. If I'm out, and I'm wearing a coat and tie, the first thing I take off when I get home is my tie. Not my pants, shoes and socks.'

'Same here,' Shepherd said.

Byrne agreed. 'What was Laura Rousseau wearing?'

Shepherd flipped through his notes. 'She was barefoot, wearing a pair of dark brown ... Monte Carlo pants? Maria?'

Maria nodded. 'It's a casual style. Mostly pull-on, elastic waist,' she said. 'Not quite like sweats or workout clothing, but casual.'

'She was also wearing a white cowl-neck sleeveless top,' Shepherd said. 'Calvin Klein.'

The three men looked to Maria.

'I suppose it's not that strange, but the top is a lot dressier than the slacks. When I went through the scene, especially Laura Rousseau's closet, she looked pretty well put together. It doesn't seem like an outfit she would leave the house in.'

'It looks like she was cooking dinner, or had just finished, when the home was invaded,' Byrne said. 'If she was in for the evening, you'd think she would have fully changed into loungewear.'

Maria nodded. 'When I get home from work, I'm out of my work clothes in about ten seconds. Pet the dog, pour the Chardonnay, then it's right into my sweats and a T-shirt. Some days it's straight to the wine. I have a very forgiving dog.'

'So you think the victims are being made to put these items of clothing on?' Bình asked.

'Just about anything is possible at this point,' Byrne said. He tapped the photos of Laura Rousseau and Edwin Channing. 'A big part of this is why was Laura Rousseau singled out to be mutilated? Why not her husband and son?'

No one had an answer to this.

Josh Bontrager's cell phone chirped. He stepped away, answered the call. A few seconds later he returned.

'We've got something on the ballistics,' he said.

'Channing matches the other three?' Byrne asked.

'Let's go find out.'

The Forensic Science Center was a state-of-the-art, heavily fortified building at Eighth and Poplar streets. In the basement was the firearms identification unit. On the first floor was the crime scene unit, document examination unit, the chem lab – mostly used for the identification of drugs – as well as Criminalistics, which handled the processing of blood, hair and fiber. The first floor of the FSC was also home to the DNA lab.

Firearms, Documents and CSU personnel were all sworn law-enforcement officers. Everyone else was a civilian.

In his early fifties, Sergeant Jacob Conroy was the commander of FIU. After having spent years on patrol in southwest Philly, he'd transferred to evidence intake, the unit by which all evidence was stored, collated, handed out for court.

Based out of Fort Hood, Texas, Jake had risen through the ranks of the army's 2nd Armored Division. This served him well when he applied to become a ballistics examiner in FIU. In the past few years he had consulted and worked with the FBI, the Bureau of Alcohol, Tobacco, Firearms and Explosives, Homeland Security and any number of joint task forces.

Today he was giving a brief tour to a small group of visitors, law enforcement officers from mainland China.

'The purview of the unit is to examine everything from firearms to firearm-related evidence: cartridges, cartridge cases, specimens,' Jake said. 'A lot of the time we attend autopsies, working with the ME as to ammo used, and what to look for.'

While Jake Conroy wrapped up the tour with a brief stop at the unit's small but exotic museum of weaponry, Byrne made a phone call to Anne-Marie Beaudry, Angelo Rousseau's sister. Once again, he got a voicemail recording.

He hung up just as Conroy returned.

'Speak of the man,' Conroy said.

'And up he pops,' Byrne said. 'Good to see you, Jake.'

They shook hands.

'Do you know Detective Bontrager?' Byrne asked.

'Only by reputation,' Jake said. 'Nice to meet you, detective.'

'You as well,' Bontrager said. 'And please call me Josh.'

Jake gestured to the walls around them. There were no windows in FIU, of course. He looked at Byrne.

'Haven't seen you in daylight for a while.'

Byrne smiled. 'It's the garlic.'

Conroy nodded to the items on his examining table.

'This one's got me thinking,' he said.

'Channing?'

'Yeah.'

Four bodies on one shooter got the attention of everyone, all the way to the federal level. The PPD wanted nothing more than to shut this psychopath down before there was any kind of intervention by the Feds.

'I got together with Mark DeBellis on this.' Sergeant DeBellis was the examiner working the Rousseau case. 'I think we have something.'

Jake Conroy picked up a pair of envelopes on his desk, opened each of them, then unwrapped the contents from their tissue bindings. He walked over to the microscope against the far wall.

It was a state-of-the-art universal comparison microscope, which permitted comparative investigations of traces on fired ammunition, tool marks, documents and much more. With it, the examiner could inspect and correct images directly on a high-definition monitor and immediately print them.

Jake put one of the projectiles on the right-hand side of the stage, on a piece of wax; the other on the left. He then physically turned one bullet to match the markings on the other.

Byrne looked at the image on the screen. To his eye, they looked almost identical.

'What are your thoughts?' Jake asked.

'I'm thinking a Mauser .380,' Byrne said.

'I was thinking that too.'

'Great minds.'

'But now I have other ideas.'

'Such as?'

'I'm thinking a Makarov.'

90

Byrne looked at Bontrager and back again. 'A Makarov,' he said. 'I've heard of them, but wouldn't know one if I was firing one.'

'It's a Russian design, but it's been manufactured in a lot of places over the years. East Germany, Bulgaria, Albania. China, too.'

'Available here?'

'Oh yeah. Very fine weapon. We've run across our share.'

Jake left the room for a moment, came back with a semi-automatic weapon. In the world of handguns, there was a lot of junk, but there were also works of art. The Makarov looked to be in the latter group.

He ejected the magazines, gently pulled back the slide, telling everyone present that the firearm was not loaded. They all knew as much, but the gesture was understood and always appreciated. As odd as it might sound, the FIU was one of the safest places in Philly.

'The Makarov 9x18,' Jake said.

Byrne took the weapon from the man, hefted it, sighted it. Jake Conroy was right. It had a beautiful balance. He handed it to Josh Bontrager.

'I'm running them all through NIBIN later today,' Jake said.

Maintained by the AFTE, NIBIN – the National Integrated Ballistic Information Network – was a sophisticated database that automated ballistic evaluations, replacing the tedious and time-consuming task of side-by-side comparisons.

Byrne gestured to the printed images of the four bullets taped to the whiteboard, the bullets used to kill Angelo, Laura and Mark Rousseau, as well as Edwin Channing.

'Same manufacture?' Byrne asked.

'Yes, sir. These are all Hornady.'

'You're sure?'

It was a routine question. Byrne knew that Conroy knew. He wouldn't say so otherwise.

'Of this I am a hundred percent sure.'

'Same weapon?' Bontrager asked.

'Ninety-nine percent,' Jake said. 'Fired cartridge casings I can match in my sleep. Spent projectiles leave some room for doubt, unless you have the weapon.'

'Same shooter?' Byrne asked.

Jake smiled. 'That's your job, detective. If it's metal, I can read it. People? Not so much. Ask my two ex-wives.'

Byrne considered everything they had. It was good. 'Anything else you can tell us?' he asked.

Conroy slipped each slug into its envelope. 'Get me the gun,' he said. 'All will be revealed.'

'Hopefully we will,' Byrne said. 'With the guy still attached to it.' He held up his phone. Jake nodded. He'd call immediately if there was a NIBIN match with a previous crime or a gun owner.

On the way out, Byrne noticed a poster of Clint Eastwood pinned to the wall next to the door. At the bottom it read:

I have a very strict gun control policy: if there's a gun around, I want to be in control of it.

'So, we are moving forward with the belief that we are looking for the same person or persons who committed all four of these homicides,' Bontrager said.

Josh Bontrager, when he was in the zone, got very formal. They were standing by their car in the large parking lot of the FSC.

'I think we are,' Byrne said. 'It looks like the same bullet evidence and same gun; no reason to believe it's not the same shooter.'

'That is one sweet semi-auto, by the way,' Bontrager said, referring to the Makarov.

'It is.'

Byrne knew that Josh Bontrager knew his way around service weapons, and qualified with high marks every year at the range. He wasn't so sure if the Amish used guns or not. He asked.

'Oh my gosh, yes. We used to hunt all the time,' Bontrager said. 'Varmints, mostly. Deer causing trouble.'

'What was your weapon of choice?'

'Had a Remington 700, bolt action,' Bontrager said. '.30.06.'

'Nice,' Byrne said. 'Were you any good with it?'

Bontrager smiled. 'We ate.'

Byrne glanced at his watch. 'I've got to do that interview with Angelo Rousseau's sister.'

'I'll go with you if you like.'

'You sure?'

Bontrager opened the passenger door. 'We had a saying in the church, I think it's from Proverbs: *Be with wise men and become wise.*'

Byrne laughed. 'If that's the case, I'll stop back at the shop and we'll pick up John Shepherd.'

8

The Beaudry house was a stone ranch in Cheltenham. When Byrne and Bontrager arrived, there was no room in the driveway or, for that matter, a half-block in both directions. The extended Beaudry family, it seemed, was here in full force.

The front door was wide open, the screen door closed. Josh Bontrager took the lead, rang the bell. A few moments later, a man in his late forties came to the door.

'Yes?'

Bontrager had his shield in his hand. He raised it, introducing himself and Byrne. The man looked over his shoulder, perhaps gauging whether or not now was the right time for this – whatever *this* was. He seemed to resign himself to the fact that the sooner it was done, the faster things would begin to come to a close. Not to mention the possibility of catching the person who did this unspeakable thing to Angelo, Laura and Mark Rousseau.

The man unlocked the screen door – a door that probably stood unlocked most of the spring and summer but now stood fortified. Byrne had seen it many, many times. The small points of security that had so casually lapsed were suddenly fastened in the wake of a tragedy. As the man held the door open, he introduced himself.

'I'm Don Beaudry, Anne-Marie's husband. Angelo was my brother-in-law.'

All three men shook hands.

Don Beaudry was just over six feet, broad-chested, with a full reddish beard, speckled with gray.

The living room was cluttered but comfortable.

In a high-backed chair next to the fireplace sat Anne-Marie Beaudry. For some reason Byrne had thought she would be older. She appeared to be in her early thirties, with short chestnut hair, deep green eyes. She looked better, more rested, than he had expected. Byrne knew the toll of grief, and Anne-Marie Beaudry seemed to be holding her own.

They all sat down, each perched uncomfortably on the edge of his chair. It was common. The families of murder victims rarely sat back in a chair or on a couch in those first few days and weeks. It was as if they felt that at any moment they might need to jump to their feet, to put out some fire, to throw themselves into the breach to protect a remaining member of their now dwindling family. Investigators often matched the posture.

Coffee was offered, declined.

The two detectives had decided on the way over that Byrne would conduct the interview and Josh Bontrager would take the notes.

'What can you tell us about your brother?' Byrne asked.

Anne-Marie took a few moments. 'He was a saint,' she said. 'Always willing to pitch in, always there when you needed advice, or a shoulder.' She grabbed a tissue from the box on the coffee table, dabbed at her eyes. Maybe she wasn't coping all that well, Byrne thought.

Anne-Marie Beaudry went on to give Byrne a brief history of Angelo Rousseau's life: high school valedictorian, a stint in the Marines, the birth of his son, Mark, the opening of his company, his work with the Boys and Girls Club. By her account, the victim was an outgoing, gregarious man. Byrne didn't hear a single thing that would lead him to potentially solve the man's brutally violent murder.

'Do you know if they had a safety deposit box?' he asked.

Anne-Marie looked at her husband, back. 'I don't think so. Laura never mentioned it.'

'What about Laura?' Byrne asked. 'Did she have any enemies?'

'Oh my goodness, *no*. Laura? Laura was quiet. The exact opposite of my brother. Maybe that's why they got along so well. What they say about opposites attracting, right?'

'When was the last time you saw her?'

Anne-Marie thought for a moment. 'We belong to a knitting circle. Our most recent meeting was this past Thursday. Over in Haverford.'

'And that's when you last saw her?'

'Yes.'

'Did anything happen there that might have seemed out of the ordinary?' Byrne asked.

'I'm not sure what you mean.'

'Were there any rivalries? Any harsh words? Any unpaid debts?'

Anne-Marie Beaudry looked at Byrne as if he had just touched down to earth from another planet. 'This is a *knitting* circle, detective. There were no harsh words. We're all very close friends.'

Byrne nodded, took this in his stride. Sometimes you had to ask the question, no matter how trivial or ridiculous or unkind it sounded. More than one case had broken because of a question like that.

To make her point further, Anne-Marie took out an iPad, launched the photo app, swiped back a few recent pictures, turned the tablet so that Byrne and Bontrager could see the screen. It was a photo of a half-dozen women sitting around a cozy-looking living room, each with a knitting project at some stage of completion in her lap, balls of brightly colored yarn emerging from straw sewing baskets.

The second photo was of the same women in the dark parking lot of an Applebee's, each holding up a sweater or a shawl or a scarf. The picture was more than a little out of focus.

Byrne pointed to the woman in front on the left. 'This is your sister-in-law?'

'Yes.'

'So you all went to Applebee's after the knitting circle?'

She nodded. 'Yes. The one on City Line.'

Byrne held out his hand. 'May I?'

She handed him the iPad. Byrne swiped back and forth between the two photos. Something was different. In addition to the seven women photographed in the knitting circle, there was someone else in the picture taken in the parking lot. It looked to be a very petite older woman with long white hair, but she was standing a good bit behind the group, and far out of focus. Only the right side of her face, which was mostly obscured by hair, and her pencil-thin right arm was visible.

Byrne went back to the photograph in the living room. He counted seven women, none over the age of sixty. Certainly none with long white hair. He swiped over to the photograph taken in the Applebee's parking lot. There was no question. There were eight women. The eldest stood behind a woman who appeared to be the tallest of the group. She was mostly obscured or in shadow.

Byrne turned the tablet momentarily to Bontrager, who

nodded. He knew where this might be going. He'd seen it too. Byrne handed the iPad back to Anne-Marie.

'The woman at the back, the older woman, is she part of the group?'

Anne-Marie looked closely. 'Oh my.'

'What?'

'I didn't realize she was in the photograph until just now.'

'Do you know her?'

'Yes,' she said. 'No. What I mean is, I just saw her that night outside Applebee's.'

'Under what circumstances?' Bontrager asked.

'Hang on. I took more pictures.' She swiped her finger across the screen a few more times. 'Huh.'

'What is it?'

'She's not in any of the pictures. Just that one.'

'And you're saying she's not part of your group, and that you'd never seen her before?' Bontrager asked.

'No she isn't, and no I hadn't,' she said.

'How did she come to end up in this photograph?'

'I'm not sure.' She put down the iPad, thought for a few moments. 'We were in the restaurant, getting ready to leave, and I remembered that I left my purse in the car. I excused myself from the table. I walked out of the restaurant and over to my car, which was parked at the far end. Near the high hedges that separate the lot from the lot at Costco.'

'What happened then?' Byrne asked.

'I heard singing.'

Byrne felt a cold hand close around his heart.

'Singing?' he asked.

'Yes. Someone was singing. A beautiful melody. Haunting. Definitely in another language.'

'You don't know what language?'

'No,' she said. 'Sorry.'

'And you're saying that it was this woman who was singing?'

'Yes. It was the oddest thing.'

'Was she in a car?' Byrne asked. 'On a bench?'

'Neither. She was just standing there in the shadow cast by that tall hedge.'

'Can you describe her?'

'Not really. She was pretty much hidden. But I can tell you she was old.'

'How old?'

'I'm not really good at this. Eighty, maybe. Perhaps older. Long white hair, a white dress.'

'Anything in her hands?'

'Not that I saw.'

'What can you tell us about the song?' Byrne asked.

'Nothing really. It seemed kind of . . . I don't know. You'll think I'm crazy.'

'Not at all. Just tell us what you remember. What your impressions were.'

'It sounded kind of sad. Like a requiem of some sort.'

Another glance passed between the detectives.

'A requiem,' Byrne said. It wasn't a question.

Anne-Marie Beaudry just nodded.

They stopped at a diner on Frankford Avenue. The two detectives ate in silence, their notebooks propped against their water glasses.

'Who is this mysterious singing woman?' Bontrager asked, not expecting an answer.

As they finished their coffee, Byrne's phone rang. He wanted to let it go, but those days were over. He had four homicide victims on his desk now. And he was on point for all four.

'Yeah,' he said.

'Is this Detective Byrne?'

Byrne didn't recognize the voice. 'It is. What can I do for you?'

'My name is Joe Quindlen. I'm a patrol officer in the 17th.'

'What's going on, officer?'

'I got flagged by a guy on the 2600 block of Montrose. Said he found an object of interest in this house he's working on. Looked a little pale when he waved me down.'

The address was in the heart of Devil's Pocket. 'Who is the guy who flagged you?'

'He's a painter, plasterer, like that. He's doing some rehabbing on this block,' Quindlen said. 'I was about to bring it down to the station, but this old guy stops me on the street, said I should call you.'

'What old guy is this?'

Byrne heard the sound of a notebook page being flipped. 'Name of Eddie Shaughnessy.'

The name pulled Byrne down a long hall of memory. The only time in the past twenty years that Eddie Shaughnessy had crossed his mind was when he found himself wondering if the old man was still alive.

'You're sure his name was Eddie Shaughnessy?'

'Older gentleman, built like a fireplug, unlit cigar in his mouth?'

'That would be him.'

'Yes, sir.'

'And he said you should talk to me?' Byrne asked. 'Why did he say that?'

'No idea,' Quindlen said. 'But I got the feeling that this is a neighborhood thing, and he wants to keep it in the neighbor-hood.'

'We're not talking a box full of body parts here, are we, officer?'

'No, sir. If that were the case, no matter what the old man said, I would have called dispatch first. *Then* I would have called you.'

Byrne understood. He had been there many times as a patrol officer. The network was one thing. Your job – and maybe your liberty, if something went to trial – was another. Sometimes the blue line was thick. Sometimes it was gossamer thin.

'What's the address?'

The officer told him. Byrne wrote it down. 'I'm on my way.'

Out in the parking lot, Josh Bontrager leaned against the car, tried to look uninterested in the call. Byrne appreciated the respect.

'Want to take a ride?' Byrne asked.

'Sure, boss,' Bontrager replied with a smile.

'What did I tell you about that "boss" business?'

9

It began the moment he turned onto Grays Ferry Avenue. When Byrne had been very young, and his mother had driven him all the way across the city from Pennsport, it seemed as if he were going to a foreign country. Riding down Reed Street, passing the landmarks, stopping at red lights, watching the people, it was always about the journey, not the destination.

Byrne's job had taken him to these wards many times. One case, a few years earlier, had brought him and Jessica the length of the Schuylkill, investigating bodies strewn along its banks, into a heart of darkness.

When they turned onto Montrose Street, Byrne felt the hair rise on the back of his neck. He'd forgotten how much time he'd spent in and around these blocks.

The police officer waiting for them was in his thirties, a few cheesesteaks over fighting weight.

Out of habit, as he and Bontrager approached the officer,

Byrne reached into his coat pocket for his ID. He then reminded himself that this wasn't a job.

'How you doing?' he asked.

'I am blessed,' Quindlen said. 'Thanks for asking, sir.'

'Keeping the peace?'

'Just trying not to disturb it.'

'Where is Mr Shaughnessy?' Byrne asked.

'Just around the corner on the avenue. He's out front.'

Of course he is, Byrne thought.

Still on watch.

Byrne had not seen Shaughnessy in more than twenty years. The last time he had seen him, he was probably in his mid-sixties, a short, broad man who'd worked most of his adult life for a moving company. Even at sixty-five, he could hoist a full keg on each shoulder and walk up two flights of narrow stairs without breaking a sweat. Byrne had once seen him lift the right rear end of an AMC Gremlin onto a concrete block.

For a few years, after the war, Shaughnessy had fought professionally as a middleweight, most notably on the undercard of the first fight between Bob Montgomery and Wesley Mouzon, held at Shibe Park.

'Jesus Christ,' Eddie said. 'You got old.'

'Still the charmer.'

Byrne leaned forward, hugged the man. He still felt solid.

'It's been a couple of years, Eddie,' he said.

'What's with the Eddie shit?'

'Just sayin'.'

'It's *Mr* Shaughnessy.'

'This is Detective Bontrager,' Byrne said.

The two men shook hands.

Eddie looked down the street, back. You didn't have to be a mind-reader to know what was coming. Byrne was right.

'Place is going to shit,' Eddie said.

Byrne indicated the block of row houses 'Do you know who owns these?' he asked.

Eddie pointed at a sign. It read:

Coming soon: Six New Luxury Row Homes. A Greene Towne LLC Development.

'Any idea who Greene Towne LLC is?' Byrne asked.

Eddie shrugged. 'Probably owned by some rich prick. I remember when you could buy any house on this street for ten thousand dollars. Now I hear they're a quarter-million.'

'Even this one?' Byrne asked.

Dead center in the block was a dilapidated wooden house, scarred with graffiti. Byrne had an idea about what was happening with it. The owner was refusing to sell until he got his price.

'Piece of shit,' Eddie repeated.

'How's the family?' Byrne asked, trying to move on.

Eddie shrugged. 'Half are dead, the other half – my wife's side – are in jail. The rest are nuts.'

'Two halves, and then some,' Byrne said. 'Big family.'

'Remember my grandson Richie?'

Byrne vaguely remembered Richard Huston. Half a tough guy, liked to push his women around. 'I do.'

'Jail.'

'Let me guess two things,' Byrne said. 'One, it was a domestic violence situation, yes?'

Eddie nodded.

'Two, Richie didn't do it.'

'Of course he did it. Still didn't deserve a year and a half.' Eddie looked up, squinting into the sun, which was coming over Byrne's right shoulder. Byrne stepped a few paces to his right, putting the man in shade.

'Ever meet Richie's second wife, Judy?' Eddie asked. 'The one with the fat ankles?'

'Never had the pleasure.'

Eddie laughed. 'If you'd met her, you wouldn't call it no pleasure, believe me. You'd probably have taken a poke at her yourself.'

Byrne smiled. 'Not sure about that.' He looked up the street, at a vacant lot, and realized what had once stood there. The F&B Variety Store.

'Whatever happened to Old Man Flagg?' he asked.

'That asshole? Dead for years.'

'What from?'

'Too mean to live.'

Byrne had had no argument with that.

Eddie took a few moments, made a ritual out of lighting the two-inch remaining stub of a cigar. Byrne remembered this about him. Cigar lighted, he pointed at the Loading Zone sign, and the two cars just beneath it.

'Fucking sign, right there. In English. Which is probably the problem.'

Byrne felt the Philly quid pro quo coming. Eddie continued.

'They park here anyway. I tell them to move, they give me the finger. Believe me, if I was ten years younger ...'

Byrne couldn't think of any favors he was owed by the PPA – the Philadelphia Parking Authority – but maybe someone owed someone who owed someone. It was how most things worked. 'I'll see what I can do.'

Eddie just nodded.

'So this thing,' Byrne said. 'Why did I get the call?'

Eddie fixed him in a gaze. 'You'll see. I figured if anyone knew what to do with it, you would.'

Byrne glanced at Josh Bontrager, who looked rapt at this old-school mystery.

'Who am I talking to down there?' Byrne asked.

'Guy name of Kilbane. Owen Kilbane.'

'Okay. Thanks, Eddie.' He clapped the old man on the shoulder. 'And don't smoke too many of those things.'

'What are they gonna do? Stunt my fuckin' growth?'

The staircase was narrow and steep. The basement was small, mirroring the parlor above. The man standing in the corner was seventy years old if he was a day, wore stained white overalls, a painter's hat with the Sherwin-Williams logo.

'You're Mr Kilbane?' Byrne asked.

The man nodded. 'It's Owen, but everyone calls me Owney,' he said. He held up his right hand. It was flecked with paint. 'Sorry I can't shake. No disrespect meant.'

Byrne smiled, introduced himself, stuck out his hand. 'What's a little flat latex between professional men?'

The two men shook. Gently. Owney Kilbane then picked up the driest rag at hand, handed it to Byrne.

'This is Detective Bontrager,' Byrne added, wiping his hand.

Bontrager just waved.

Byrne took a moment to take in the room. Structurally it looked as bad as any century-old row house built just a few hundred yards from the river. But it was amazing what several coats of interior white could do.

'It's looking good,' he said.

'Coming along.'

'So, you say you found something down here?' Byrne asked.

At this, Owney Kilbane pointed at a small cardboard box on his makeshift table. Once again, Byrne's instincts threatened to take over. He nearly reached into his pocket for a glove. This wasn't a job. He wasn't sure what it was, but if there wasn't a dead body, it wasn't a job.

'Where did you find this?' he asked.

Owney pointed at the opening that led to the crawlspace under the back half of the house. 'I had to replace some of the bridging. The box was shoved into the crawlspace just a few feet from the opening.'

Byrne looked back at the table. The box was about twelve inches square, perhaps ten inches deep. On it was a layer of dust disturbed only by the markings created by Owney Kilbane as he fished it out from the crawlspace.

On the side of the box was the faded logo of the grocery store to which everyone in the Pocket went back in the day.

Other than that, there was no clue as to what was inside. But it was something important. Important enough for this man to flag down a police car, and for Eddie Shaughnessy to reach out to Byrne.

Byrne opened all four flaps of the box, bent them back. On top was a long-yellowed piece of newsprint, the color comics, perhaps from the 1960s. Byrne noticed Nancy and Sluggo at the top of the page.

He pulled out the piece of newspaper, and beneath it saw an old green dish rag, soaked with dark oil. He peeled away the rag and, for the first time in almost forty years, saw the contents of the box.

A nickel-plated .38 caliber revolver.

Byrne remembered as if it were yesterday the first time he had seen it, tucked away in a box behind two bricks just over a rusted Dumpster on Montrose Street, not two blocks away from where he now stood.

Without a word, he rewrapped the gun in the rag, lifted it out of the box and placed it on the table. There were two more items in the box, both in old-style plastic sandwich bags. One looked like an ID card of sorts; the other was wrapped in newsprint.

Byrne took out one of the sandwich bags, slid it open, removed the contents. Again it was faded color comics. This time Hi and Lois. As he began to unwrap what was inside, he found that he was anticipating something, something that felt like the missing piece of a jigsaw puzzle, a piece you might find kicked under the sofa after many years, the puzzle long since donated to some charity auction or dumped in the trash.

Or hidden in the crawlspace, Byrne thought.

When he fully unwrapped it, he saw that he had been right. There, like a ghost from his past, was a pair of wire-rimmed dark glasses. Both lenses appeared to be smudged.

Beneath it, in the second bag, Byrne could now see that the ID was a SEPTA bus pass. Without taking it out of the bag, he angled it toward the light.

He didn't have to. He knew what name was on the pass.

Desmond Farren.

Byrne and Bontrager stood across the street from the row house, the box resting on the trunk of the car. They watched the traffic pass, each immersed in their own thoughts.

On the way to Devil's Pocket, Byrne thought he was doing a favor for an old man. Now he was on the job. The box could have contained just about anything, but it didn't contain just anything. It contained a gun. Every day, citizens of Philadelphia found guns – in attics, in basements, in garages, sometimes just lying on the side of the road – and had no idea what to do with them. Sometimes they tossed them into the trash, only to have them rediscovered by sanitation workers.

Although most people were unaware of it, a city ordinance called for all guns to be turned over to the police department for safety reasons.

That was the letter of the law. The police wanted them off the street, of course, but more than one case had been furthered by the sudden and unexpected appearance of a firearm.

The protocol was for Byrne to now take the box to CSU. The gun would be put in evidence. It would eventually be fired into the ballistics tank at FIU, its appearance and serial number logged, the bullet evidence stored.

On the way back to the Roundhouse, Byrne regaled Josh Bontrager with stories of his summers in and around Devil's Pocket. Neither man spoke of the three-ton elephant locked in the trunk of the car.

Byrne dropped Josh Bontrager at his car, then sat in the parking lot, the past and present colliding all around him. He needed time to think this through. Unless he was mistaken, a half-dozen lives could be impacted by the discovery of this material, material that was all but certain to be evidence in a crime.

But why should it take him any time to decide? This was his job, his oath. You find a gun, you turn it in.

He left the box in the trunk for the time being, went into the duty room of the unit. He ran a few names, made a few calls, came up empty. He was just about to head out when his phone beeped. He'd gotten a call on his cell while it had been on silent. The voicemail was from his father. Byrne tapped the icon, returning the call.

'Boyo!' his father exclaimed.

Something was wrong. Padraig Byrne was never this happy, not in the middle of the day. He never had a pint before six.

'Da,' Byrne said. 'What's wrong?'

'Wrong? What could be wrong? I'm just happy to hear your voice.'

While it was true that Padraig Byrne had the gift, it had never really worked on his son.

'*Da*.'

'Can I call you right back?'

'Why?' Byrne asked. 'You called me. What are you doing that's so important?'

'I've suddenly got my hands full,' Paddy said. 'See, I've ... got something on the stove.'

'How much are you up?' he asked.

Silence.

'How much are you up?' he repeated.

'What makes you think I'm playing cards?'

'For one, I can hear Dec Reilly coughing in the background.'

'He still smokes that shitty pipe,' Paddy said. 'I think he buys the tobacco by the metric ton.'

'I can also hear *Boil the Breakfast Early* playing in the background.' The Chieftains album was the only CD Dec Reilly owned.

More phone silence. 'You know, you could have had a career as a cop.'

'There's still time,' Byrne said.

Paddy lowered his voice. 'I'm up two hundred and change.'

'So cash out, put it in the bank.'

Paddy Byrne snorted, but out of respect to his son he said nothing.

Byrne figured he would spare his father the standard speech. Hadn't worked when he was twenty, wasn't going to work now. As Byrne's grandmother used to say, trying to change the mind of a Byrne was like whistling jigs to a stone. He moved on.

'Are you coming to Aunt Dottie's party?'

'When is it again?'

'Thursday,' Byrne said.

'Food and drink?'

'Until they call the paramedics.'

'Beautiful,' Paddy said. 'Do I have to wear a tie?'

'No,' Byrne said. 'But pants are mandatory.'

'Good. I won't lose them in the next hand.'

'Love you, Da.'

'You too, son.'

*

Byrne called the crime lab. He knew it was too soon for any-thing beyond presumption on the hair and fibers recovered at the Channing crime scene, but it never hurt to ask.

As much as he wanted to work, his mind kept returning to the box.

How many days had he spent around that row house? He thought it was possible he had even camped out behind it one night with Jimmy when Jimmy had fucked up royally and Tommy Doyle was on the warpath.

Byrne knew what he should be doing, where he should be pointing his day, but he couldn't bring himself to do it. He knew that what Josh Bontrager had seen today in the Pocket would remain between the two men. Josh was a brother cop, and Byrne didn't have to concern himself.

He tried to get back to work, but that small cardboard box, and its contents, kept calling out to him like a dark specter from his youth.

10

Anjelica Leary caught the number 40 SEPTA at the corner of 24th and South. She only had the four blocks to go, and thought about walking, but her sciatica was acting up, she'd forgotten her umbrella and it looked like rain.

If it wasn't one thing, it was everything else.

There was a time when nothing could have stopped her, a time when she took in the waists of her dresses and slacks instead of letting them out, a time when she would leave the house on a sixty-degree day without a sweater.

There was even a time, in her sixty-eight years, when she would field the advances of the corner boys, turn around and throw them back a line, cutting them off at the knees.

Now she seemed to be cold all the time. The corner boys were old men.

She mercifully found a seat at the front of the bus. There was something sticky on the floor, a small shiny pool of brown. She had to sit with her feet to the side, but it was better than treading whatever this was around with her all day, especially on her nurse's whites, about which she was fastidious. She often thought that there were two things people remembered about you: your shoes and your breath. Her work shoes were always gleaming white, even in dead of winter, and she would buy breath mints before she'd buy food.

The man next to her smelled of garlic and gasoline.

Good Lord, she thought. Was there ever a longer day?

Anjelica noticed that someone had left the two front sections of the *Inquirer* on the seat to her left. She discreetly picked them up, folded them and slipped them into her tote. She still liked to read the paper, but hadn't subscribed in years. Every penny saved.

While the bus waited to get around road construction, Anjelica glanced at her watch. She was ten minutes away from being late. If there was one thing in which she took pride – and, indeed, insisted upon in everyone she knew – it was punctuality.

As a home health-care worker she had done many jobs over the years. General care, medication management, respiratory therapy, wound management. Sadly, the days of lugging big oxygen tanks or oxygenators up the stairs were behind her. She was, though, still a licensed practical nurse in fine standing, and with that came a number of responsibilities not listed on the job description. These days, in addition to wellness checks, checking vitals and adjusting meds, she had become much more than a care-giver to the twenty or so patients on her rounds. Somehow, despite her efforts to resist, she had become a confessor, a confidante, a co-conspirator in all manners of the heart and eternal soul.

And, mostly, a friend.

When she'd left the clinical environment of the U of Penn and begun home health-care work twenty-two years earlier, she'd found herself caring too much, even more so than she

113

had in hospital work. In a large hospital, it never got quiet enough to dwell too much on your emotions. Most of the time people were discharged – mostly head first, but sometimes feet first – before you got too tangled. As hard as she tried, she could not completely wall her heart from the trespasses of her patients. Some of them had even called her at home, in the middle of the night, but only because she had given them her number.

Jack Permutter was eighty-one years old, a widower half his life, having never remarried after his wife Claudia died of colon cancer at forty-three. Anjelica herself was twice married, but had long since considered that she was the type of person who fell hard only once, and that was enough. She often thought she had been luckier than most in this.

Her first husband Johnny, the love of her life, had treated her like a queen, had never missed an anniversary or a birthday; an emerald-eyed charmer who took her down the shore every year on their wedding anniversary, treating her to a weekend in Ocean City and seaside dinners of crabs and beer.

Johnny got his cancer from asbestos and wasted away to nothing within three months, leaving this earth a husk of the young man she'd met and fallen for at the age of fifteen at a block party in Point Breeze. He was thirty-three.

She'd looked long and hard for a replacement, had even taken to the Center City hotel bars one summer, but there were none who made her shine like Johnny. None ever would. For a long spell all the men seemed to be either too old or too young.

Her second husband, Tom Leary, had been a mistake. A nearly fatal mistake: an ill-tempered drunk who more than once raised a hand to her. Anjelica had married him out of sheer loneliness. And the health insurance, truth be shouted. It was one of the reasons she still kept his name. The marriage lasted less than three years. The bitter taste lingered still.

If she saw Tom Leary on this day, she wouldn't piss on his head to put out the fire.

She got off the bus at 20th Street, walked the half-block to Rodman Street. The rain held off until she stepped inside the apartment building. Tiny blessings.

By the time she reached the second-floor landing, she had already begun to prepare herself for Jack Permutter. The truth was, he was no more special in God's eyes than any other of her patients. In fact, he could be downright irascible much of the time, but never mean. It was just that he'd found a way to steal into her heart when she wasn't looking. One of the reasons was that he did something not one of her patients over the past twenty-two years had ever done.

He always made her lunch.

The official diagnosis – one of them, anyway; he also had prostate cancer – was chronic pulmonary obstructive disease.

Anjelica knocked twice, then twice again. It was another of her affectations when it came to Jack. He had come to expect it. Once, when she forgot, he didn't come to the door, and she feared the worst. She then remembered the signal, waited ten long minutes on the steps, then retried. Two knocks. Two knocks. He answered.

They never spoke of it.

On this day Jack opened the door looking measurably worse than he had three weeks earlier.

'Hey, Annie.' His smile brightened his face, the hallway, the day.

Jack Permutter was one of the two people she let call her Annie.

'Hey yourself, sailor.'

'Where's your umbrella?'

'Left it at home.'

Anjelica stepped fully inside, unbuttoned her cardigan. Jack helped her off with it. He smoothed it, hung it on a hook behind the door, closed and latched the door.

Anjelica was a keenly observant person, and had always had the ability to take in a place in its entirety in a glance, not missing a detail. She always knew what to expect at Jack Permutter's small, cluttered place, but it always tugged at her heart. The house smelled of old age and malady. Ointments, unwashed clothes, mildew, the sweet, doughy redolence of budget microwaved meals.

The table next to the bed was crowded with pill vials, dust bunnies, half-full bottles of water. Some of the bottles were so old, so many times refilled, that Anjelica wondered if the brands were still available.

Whenever she could she would buy a few bottles of water and try to sneak them onto the end table, even going so far as opening them, dumping out a few inches, hoping Jack wouldn't notice. She had many times tried to explain to him that bottles could only be refilled so many times before they became more bacteria than water, but to no avail.

She listened to his heart and lungs, took his blood pressure and pulse.

When they finished, Jack quickly buttoned his shirt, right down to the cuffs. He was a shy man, not particularly vain, but because of his feelings for Anjelica, the indelicacy of sitting without a shirt on for even a few moments made him uncomfortable.

Anjelica made busy work of her notes, checked the oxygen supply. All was as it should be.

'I made some lunch,' Jack said. 'If you're hungry.'

It had gotten to the point where Anjelica didn't eat breakfast on the days when she knew she was going to see Jack. In the three years she had been caring for him, he had never failed to make her lunch. Most times, as today, it was a simple affair: canned soup, lunchmeat on house-brand white bread, a pair of cookies at the end, instant coffee in rinsed plastic cups.

All the time she'd known Jack, she'd never seen, or heard of, anyone else visiting this house. There was no residue of acquaintance. Jack Permutter was alone in this world.

'Starved.'

As always, he held the chair for her, then slowly stepped across the small kitchen, retrieved the pot from the stove. He ladled soup – America's Choice Chicken Rice – into their bowls, returned the pot, then reached into the refrigerator and took out two plates, already prepared with sandwiches and potato salad.

About halfway through lunch, he asked:

'Did I ever tell you about the time I met the mayor?' He dabbed his lips with a powder-blue paper napkin. 'It was Wilson Goode in those days, not like now.'

Whenever Jack began a sentence with *Did I ever tell you*, the answer was always *yes*. That was the truth, at any rate.

What Anjelica always said was:

'No. I don't believe you have.'

'Mind you, I was a young man then, I was a sailor, fit and strong. There was this time ...'

Anjelica smiled, and took a cookie from her plate.

After leaving Jack Permutter's home and company, Anjelica had just one more patient to see, a woman named Sarah Graves. A retired schoolteacher, Sarah was eighty-five, and in addition to her hypertension and anemia, she was recovering from an arterial valve replacement.

Unlike Jack Permutter, Sarah rarely spoke, rarely tried to engage Anjelica in even casual conversation. Despite Anjelica's many attempts to involve her, she could see the woman slipping slowly from this life to a place deep inside where no light could enter, a dark place of the heart.

Anjelica saw a stalled life everywhere she looked: bookmarks unmoved in her bedside reading, towels at precisely the same angle on the towel racks, the TV channel unchanged.

When taking Sarah's blood pressure, Anjelica would often look at her face, see the young woman inside, the bright and energetic woman who taught grade-school children for more than thirty years. When Anjelica had begun to care for her, two years earlier, Sarah had told her that she still dreamed of one day visiting 41 Brighton Square in Dublin, the birthplace of James Joyce.

That dream had died, along with the will to sleep in its embrace.

As Anjelica prepared to leave, she looked at the woman sitting by the window, so small and frail in the pale afternoon light.

She wondered if she would stop by for her next visit and find the place empty, the bedcovers gone, the closets and cupboards cold and hollow, the only warmth left the threadbare afghan over Sarah's thin legs, the only trace of a life the faint smell of lilac, a brittle silence.

She slipped out, softly closing the door.

Anjelica Leary knew all about death, having long ago made her bargain with it. Death was not a great horned beast. Death was a thing that stepped silently from the shadows, in the blackest wood, and stole your final breath.

11

Jessica sat at her paper-besieged desk, in her cardboard-box-besieged office. She'd made ten phone calls in ten minutes, managing to spread that morning's *Inquirer* across her lap to catch the olive oil and vinegar peppers she would surely spill from her hoagie while she tried to set a speed record for lunch.

Now all she had to do was write and rewrite her closing argument.

She had one more witness to call: the criminologist who had processed the clothing at the lab, who would testify that Earl Carter's DNA as well as Lucio DiBlasio's blood were on all three items.

Game. Set. Match.

Jessica took a big bite from her sandwich, wiped her hands, turned to her laptop. She sensed a presence at the door to her office. She turned to see it was Rodney Coyne, Judge Gipson's clerk.

She tried to say something but was thwarted by the hoagie. Rodney understood. He'd seen many an ADA eat on the run. Sometimes literally while running.

Jessica scratched a word on her legal pad: *Plea?*

Rodney shook his head. 'Better.'

He worked the moment for all it was worth.

'Hoffman is putting Carter on the stand.'

In direct examination of Earl Carter, Hoffman – who was surely allowing Carter to take the stand against his best interest – began by eliciting the boilerplate background information on the defendant. Jessica felt like stipulating it all, but that, of course, was never done.

As expected, Carter was the son of an absentee father and an alcoholic, drug-abusing mother. He was beaten repeatedly and often by her series of alcoholic, drug-abusing boyfriends, got into trouble in his early teens, did a bunch of time in juvenile facilities only to graduate to felonies in his late teens, spending eight of the ten years of his twenties in either Curran-Fromhold or the state equivalent.

In just under thirty minutes, Hoffman rested.

Before her cross-examination of the defendant, Jessica had the mannequin returned to the courtroom, specifically to a point just behind Earl Carter's left shoulder. It produced better-than-expected results. More than once Carter turned his head, as if someone was gaining on him.

Jessica stood at the table, flipped a few pages in her legal pad. Finally she introduced herself and read from the list of items taken from the back room at DiBlasio's.

'Among other items there was stolen a Dell Inspiron laptop computer, a Grundig shortwave radio, and a pair of women's rings.'

She put down her pad, retrieved two large photographs,

walked them over to the easel, displayed them. One photograph was of an older-model Grundig Satellit 700 radio sitting on a desk in the back room of DiBlasio's, right next to the safe. The other, taken *in situ* by CSU, was of the radio on the floor of the closet at Earl Carter's apartment, right next to the recovered clothing.

She pointed at the photographs. 'Do you recognize this item, Mr Carter?'

Carter cast a quick glance at the easel, back, smirked. 'Looks like *two* items to me.'

'I assure you it's the same item.' Jessica said. 'This radio was found in your apartment on the day of your arrest. Can you tell us how it came to be in your possession?'

Carter pointed at the easel. 'That radio?'

'That very one.'

'I bought it.'

'Where?'

'From some guy.'

'My question was *where*, not *from whom*, Mr Carter,' Jessica said. 'But I'll work with you on this. Where, and I mean *exactly* where, were you standing when you allegedly bought this radio?'

'On Fourth Street.'

'Fourth and what?'

Carter looked at the ceiling for a few seconds, cooking his answer. 'Diamond.'

'Which corner?'

'Which *corner*?'

'Yes, sir. There are four of them, if memory serves.'

'I don't remember.'

Someone on the jury coughed. If someone on the jury coughed, it meant they were sick or not buying it. Jessica chose the latter.

'Fair enough,' she said. 'Remember how much you allegedly paid for the radio?'

'Maybe fifty or so.'

Jessica mugged. 'Not bad for this model in such good shape,' she said. 'Now, who's the guy who allegedly sold it to you?'

Another shrug. 'Some guy, you know? There are all kinds of them people around there.'

Jessica raised an eyebrow, glanced at the jury, back at the defendant, thinking: *Please* say the word.

'*Them people*?' she asked. 'Who is *them people*?'

Carter tried to stare her down. He was a lightweight. In her time on the street, Jessica had learned how to stare down a fire hydrant. She'd learned from the best, Kevin Byrne.

'Thieves,' he said, perhaps believing he'd covered himself. 'That's who *them people* is.'

'I think we're getting somewhere, Mr Carter,' she said. 'What you're telling the court is that you admit that when you purchased this radio, from a person unknown to you, you were aware that the merchandise might have been stolen. Is that correct?'

'I didn't ask the man if it was stolen or not.'

'I can understand that,' Jessica said. 'Seeing as how *them people* can be.'

Rourke Hoffman hadn't moved this fast in years. '*Objection*.'

'Withdrawn.' Jessica took a few moments, tapped the photograph of the radio in Carter's closet.

'If we can locate this mystery thief, perhaps we can locate some of the other items that were stolen from the safe at the same time. Items, the people will freely concede, that were *not* found in Mr Carter's possession that day.'

She picked up her legal pad, referred to it once more. 'Those additional items being a Dell Inspiron laptop computer, three hundred dollars in American Express travelers checks, two women's rings, one emerald, one ruby, two Nikon DSLR cameras—'

Carter let out a snort of laughter.

Jessica stopped reading, looked up.

'I'm sorry, did I say something funny?'

Carter shook his head.

'Weren't no damn *cameras*. That's an insurance scam right there,' he said. 'Y'all ought to be looking into that, not me.'

Jessica felt a staccato heartbeat in her chest, the kind that started fast and sped up, the same one she recalled from her days as a police officer when she had a suspect on the ground, cuffs locked.

Breathe, Jess.

'I'm sorry,' she said. 'Could you repeat that?'

Carter's eyes went cold, flat-lined. Jessica saw that the judge was about to instruct the defendant to answer. She held up a finger.

'Thank goodness we live in a country where proceedings like this are preserved for posterity.' She crossed over to the court reporter.

The reporter, trying to keep her smile in check, read:

'"Weren't no damn *cameras*. That's an insurance scam right there. Y'all ought to be looking into that, not me."'

'Thank you.' Jessica returned to the state's table. She went for the nomination. Hapless, sincere, with a grace note of compassion.

Meryl Streep had nothing on south Philly girls.

'I'm so sorry,' she said, addressing her remarks to Judge Gipson. 'My apologies to Mr Carter and to the court. It seems I misread my notes. I'm afraid I have the worst handwriting possible. The note I read was not about stolen cameras, but rather about an in camera meeting with Judge Drotos earlier today.' She paused, held up her legal pad, glanced at Carter. 'You're right, Mr Carter. There weren't any cameras in that safe.'

Carter looked at his feet.

'But how could you *possibly* know that?'

It took the jury less than an hour to return a verdict of guilty on all four counts.

By the time Jessica stepped through the back door at DiBlasio's, they were all there.

Her husband Vincent, her daughter Sophie, her son Carlos, her father Peter.

Jessica had grown up a few blocks away. Lucio DiBlasio had catered her wedding, had always treated her as a daughter, or at least a favorite niece. Whenever she stopped in for bread after Mass at St Paul's – DiBlasio's stayed open until 1.30 on Sundays to accommodate noon Mass – she always left with a treat. She loved Lucio and Connie DiBlasio like family.

It was one of the reasons she had lobbied long and hard to get the case. Once she got it, she knew it would be a challenge to keep her emotions in check, especially after watching the surveillance video of Earl Carter assaulting Lucio DiBlasio.

Distancing was something she'd learned from her years on the street as a police officer. If you let every abused kid, every elderly person who was pushed to the ground and robbed get to you, you could not do your job in the cold, rational manner it called for. You would last two weeks.

When she got to the more deliberate and seemingly less volatile world of the DA's office, she thought it would be different. It wasn't. The victims were the same, the bad guys were the same; it was only the process that changed.

Now she was surrounded by the aromas of her childhood. Prosciutto and soppressata, pecorino and sharp provolone, sheet pizza with oil and garlic, the simmering sauce for the *frutti di mare*, the *baccalà*.

She hugged her daughter, kissed her husband, hoisted her son into the air.

'You won, Mom,' Carlos said.

Jessica wanted to be humble, to say it was the Commonwealth of Pennsylvania that had won, and that she'd had a lot of help, not only from the police officers involved and the team of DA's investigators, but from twelve jurors whose hearts were true and purpose noble.

Who was she kidding? Her son was *seven*.

'Yes, I did, honey. I won.'

'And I helped.'

'You sure did.'

They high-fived.

One by one, the entire DiBlasio clan came over, each giving Jessica a grateful hug. When Connie DiBlasio hugged her, both women broke into tears. Not very professional of Jessica, but she didn't care.

After everyone raised a glass, and emptied their cups, Lucio began to make the refill rounds with his gallon of *vino di tavola*.

Then, without warning or probable cause, something came over Jessica. Something that had been building a long time, ever since she first set foot in the district attorney's office. She grabbed Vincent and planted a big, wet, sloppy, long kiss on his lips. It all came out of her. The anticipation of this trial, the stress of hoping she could and would do right by one of her father's oldest friends, the release of hearing those words: *guilty on all counts*.

She looked over at her children. Sophie was staring at her phone, rolling her eyes. Carlos was covering his.

The kiss got a standing ovation.

'Wow,' Vincent said.

'Believe it,' Jessica said. She looked over her husband's shoulder, out the window, at their new SUV parked in a dark corner of the parking lot. 'I need you to help me with something in the car.'

Vincent, being the great detective he was, caught on quickly. Before he could say another word, Jessica kissed him again. This time it was shorter, but fraught with urgency.

When he pulled away, he said: 'I think I should get some body armor.'

Jessica smiled, took his hand. 'There won't be time, Detective Balzano.'

There wasn't.

12

The park was quiet. Byrne sat on the bench next to the small community garden.

He had found himself coming here more and more often lately, although he could not quite pinpoint why. There were times when the traffic was heavy on the side streets, which made it hard to think, but even then he found a way to step inside himself and visit the places he needed to visit.

Then there were times, like now, when the city was asleep, and the only sound was the wind rustling the leaves.

Woodman Park, he thought. He thought about the long road it had been for this green space to become what it was today.

He thought about the house that had once stood here. It had been a time of turmoil, a time of apprehension and fear. Perhaps he'd believed that he could save the place. Not the structure, but the very essence of this spot on earth.

Having been raised Roman Catholic, he knew he was supposed to believe in redemption. Little by little, through his time on the police force, witnessing the worst of human behavior, that belief had eroded. Recidivism for violent crime was at an all-time high. There seemed to be no redemption in the harsh solitude of prison life.

Were they going about it all wrong? Byrne knew it was not for him to say.

But now, sitting here in this beautiful space for which he had lobbied long and hard, a space that had arisen from the ashes of the chamber of horrors that once stood here, he felt, once again, that redemption was possible.

But redemption for whom?

He looked at the box next to him on the bench. The items inside brought him back to that day, the day Catriona Daugherty had been killed.

Over the nearly four decades, he had thought of her many times, thought of seeing her in the square that week, thought of her small form lying beneath the trees in Schuylkill River Park.

Byrne opened the box, looked at the .38 in the bright moonlight. He thought about the first time he had seen it, the day Dave Carmody had jumped on the Dumpster and taken it out of the wall behind the bricks. Byrne had known next to nothing about firearms at the time, but he knew it was a fearsome thing, a thing to be respected.

At this thought, a shadow came up on his left. He turned, looked.

'Hey,' he said. 'I had a feeling I was going to see you.'

He had first met the cat under rather bizarre circumstances. They had both been standing next to the old house, unaware of the other's presence. At that moment, the chimney began to crumble – having years earlier lost its tuck pointing – and a few bricks tumbled off the roof onto the cat's head, knocking him cold.

Byrne had taken the cat – whom he immediately named Tuck – to a vet, and over the course of the next few weeks nursed him back to health. He supposed he knew early on that he didn't own Tuck, nor was it the other way around. Tuck belonged to this place, even though the structure was long gone. Over the past six months, as Byrne visited this green space, the cat had shown up a few times.

Oddly enough, he seemed to know when Byrne most needed a friend.

Tuck jumped onto the bench, nuzzled Byrne's leg.

'Good to see you, buddy,' Byrne said. 'I've got something for you. I think you're going to like it.'

When he knew he was going to come here to think, Byrne stopped at Ippolito's Seafood on Dickinson Street and picked up a quarter-pound of sushi-grade tuna.

As he unwrapped the treat, Tuck jumped onto his right shoulder in anticipation. When Byrne put the paper on the bench, the cat was on it in a flash. He grabbed it, sprinted over to the hedges near the back of the lot and made short business of the fresh fish.

'None for me, thanks,' Byrne said. 'I've already eaten.'

A few minutes later, the cat trotted to the edge of the lot, turned at the hedgerow, licked his lips one more time and disappeared into the darkness.

The night once again fell quiet.

Byrne thought of the last hours and minutes of Des Farren's life, of his part in that day, the events that were set in place; of how the lifting of one's hand in anger could echo across decades, and how, in those moments of madness, lives were forever changed.

13

Billy looked at the rows and rows of photographs, each one a patchwork of features: eyes, noses, mouths, ears, chins. On many of them – most, in fact – there was a name or a word, something that would help identify the subject of the picture, or clarify Billy's relationship to the person.

On the wall dedicated to his first life there were three pictures of a man named Joseph Mula. Joseph Mula, in all three pictures, wore a white rayon smock and creased gray trousers. In each photograph there was a black Ace comb sticking out of the smock's chest pocket. Joseph Mula had a crew cut, narrow shoulders and small hands.

But no face. Try as he might, Billy could not see the man's face. Even though Joseph Mula had cut Billy's hair every six weeks or so between the ages of five and ten, Billy could not remember anything about his face. Instead, he remembered the smells. Barbicide disinfectant, Aqua Velva, Brylcreem.

Above Billy's headboard were three rows of photographs of

family he'd never met, the extended clan Farren. For many years he scanned the old photographs, looking for himself in their faces. He once thought he recognized one of them as his aunt Bridget, only to learn that the woman in the picture had died ten years before he was born.

In this room, the only picture of his father, Daniel, was a clipping from an old newspaper article. Billy had cut out the eyes one night. He did not remember why.

His was a ghost world.

He'd once waved to himself in a mirror.

Over the years, Billy had met only a handful like him, those who had crossed over and returned, people who came back with an ability and a deficit, those who found a blank spot where something used to be.

When his second life began, he spent more than two years trying to regain his strength, a painful, exhausting regimen. During those years, often long into the night, he read everything he could get his hands on, spending many hours in the library selecting books.

As he came to understand the shadows, his face blindness, he read books on his condition, and was surprised to learn how many people had some degree of the affliction, including Dr Oliver Sacks and artist Chuck Close.

In the end, Billy found it far easier to be alone. He slept in the same room he had slept in as a boy, a cluttered warren beneath the tavern his parents had once operated. The echoes of all the people who had been patrons of The Stone, in its almost seventy years, were still present. Billy heard them in the night: the din of arguments, the clink of glasses raised in tribute, the tinkling of the bell over the front door signaling an arriving or departing customer.

Sean had moved out years ago, and now slept at the long-shuttered body shop on Wharton, a business once owned by their late uncle Patrick. Heavenly Body was no longer open to the public, but Sean sometimes did chop work for friends, and maintained a small, ever-changing fleet of stolen vehicles, all at some stage of repair and repainting.

Both Billy and Sean knew that there was a chance the black Acadia SUV had been identified, or soon would be. In the next few weeks they would chop it for parts. There was a recently repainted white Econoline van ready to go.

As Billy prepared to leave for the day, he stood before the large poster next to the door, as he always did. The reproduction was of a painting called *Deux hommes en pied* by the French painter Edgar Degas. Depicted in the painting, the title of which translated as 'Two Men Walk', were two men standing side by side. The man on the left was fully rendered. Perched on his left hand was a green parrot. The man on the right – despite the fact that his vest and coat were both painted in the impressionist style – had no face.

Some said that Degas never finished the painting, having just begun to sketch the man's face. Others said he deliberately obliterated the man's features.

Billy had never seen anything in his life to which he related more. It was how he saw the world, a blank and featureless place, obscured by bright light.

The painting was in a museum in Troyes, France. When all five lines were drawn, and the fever lifted, Billy intended to make the trip and stand in front of the painting. He wondered if, after all this time, just by virtue of the miracle that awaited him, the man on the right would have a face.

Maybe the face would be *his* face.

The Queen Memorial Library was a small branch of the Free Library located in the Landreth Apartments for senior citizens on Federal Street between 22nd and 23rd.

Billy sat, as he always did, at the table nearest the door, watching her.

Her name was Emily.

Emily was a graceful, pretty woman in her mid-twenties, with soft hair to her shoulders, the color of warm butterscotch. She had long, elegant fingers, a ready and genuine laugh.

For a long time Billy did not know she was legally blind.

One of her jobs at the library was checking books out for patrons, and that consisted mostly of swiping the item beneath the bar-code scanner, bagging the books and sending the customer off happy. Because the Queen Memorial was located in a senior center, a certain proportion of visitors had some visual problems, and therefore there was a section devoted to Braille, large-print and audiobook editions.

Initially Billy had begun visiting the library to spend time with a reference book on the collected works of Edgar Degas, specifically the page that held a color plate of *Deux hommes en pied*.

One day, on a whim, he stopped at a florist on Federal and bought Emily a single white rose. He walked back and forth in front of the library for an hour, only to throw the rose in the trash and go home.

This happened three days in a row.

On the fourth day he hiked his courage, again bought a rose, entered the library, walked up to the counter and gave it to Emily.

'This is for me?' she'd asked.

'Yes.'

'How lovely.' She sniffed the rose, smiled. 'I adore white roses.'

This confused Billy. Before he could choke the words, he said, 'How did . . .'

Emily laughed. Billy saw all of it. The small smile lines next

133

to her mouth, the way her face lit up. Somehow her face was crystal clear to him.

'How did I know it was a white rose?' she asked.

'Yes.'

Emily leaned in across the counter and whispered conspiratorially, 'I'm not really blind, you see. It's just a ruse to get sympathy and government benefits.'

Billy considered himself lucky that she couldn't see the confusion that dashed across his face for a moment. She was kidding, of course.

'I know by the fragrance,' she added.

'Different roses smell differently?'

'Oh my, yes.'

Over the next few months, on Billy's weekly visits, he would sit with her as she ate her lunch. She explained how, in general, roses with the best scents were darker colors, that they tended to have more petals, and those petals tended to have a downy texture. She explained how, to most people, a 'rose' fragrance was to be found on pink and red roses. One day he brought her a yellow rose, and she explained that there were notes of violets and lemon in the fragrance. Orange roses, she said, often smelled of fruit, and sometimes clove.

For more than three months, Billy did not miss a week.

It was here that he filled the hours between the money collections he and Sean made. Here was where he rediscovered Jack London and Dashiell Hammett and Jim Thompson. Here was where he learned the true nature of his condition. There were no cures here. There were just stories.

One day, at lunch, Emily surprised him. They were sitting on the stone bench near the library entrance.

'I'm sure you have your pick of women,' she'd said. 'Why do you want to spend your time with a book mouse like me?'

'What do you mean?'

'Handsome men get to pick and choose.'

Billy felt himself begin to redden. His face felt hot. 'Why do you think I'm handsome?'

She touched his face, running her fingers on either side, from his forehead, lightly over his eyes, his cheekbones, to his lips and chin.

She sat back. 'I can see you.'

They fell silent for a few moments. Billy watched her. He found himself not looking at her name tag, her ivory cardigan sweater and white blouse, or the way she would put her hair behind one ear. He actually saw her. He had no trouble recognizing her face. The sensation was odd and disorienting, the way he imagined it felt when a person with a hearing disability put in a hearing aid for the first time and heard Beethoven's Ninth Symphony.

Many times he'd waited for her across the street, and followed her as she made her way home with her white-tipped cane. She lived only two blocks away, on Oakford Street, but Billy never ceased to be amazed at how she did it. As often as he watched her walk home, he would park across the street from her row house and watch her windows, the soft shadows cast on the blinds. She had two cats, Oryx and Crake, and often left lights on for them.

On this day, Billy just watched her at the counter. They had a date for lunch the next day, and somehow he would find the courage to ask her.

14

Nail Island was a small nail salon and spa located across the street two doors west of Edwin Channing's house. The white brick facade had two windows with hot-pink canvas awnings. The front windows boasted the salon's services: manicures, pedicures, waxing, tinting.

When Byrne and Maria Caruso pulled up out front, Byrne noticed the surveillance camera above the front door, which was the reason for their visit. He looked across the street and tried to gauge the angle, wondering if the camera's field of vision would include the area in front of Edwin Channing's house.

When Maria had spoken to the owner of Nail Island, the woman told her that the camera was indeed hooked up to a DVR, and that the recordings were kept for a week.

With a little bit of luck, if the camera was operational, and the field of vision included the Channing house – or the area to the right or left – they might have something. Byrne felt his pulse quicken as he held open the door for Maria Caruso and stepped inside.

The shop was long and narrow, with five nail stations on the right. There were two customers; one getting a manicure, one a pedicure. Both customers were women were in their thirties. A six-year-old girl sat at a vacant station, fully engrossed in an iPad.

'Welcome to Nail Island.'

The woman was coming out of the back room, carrying a plastic tray of various polishes. She was African American, in her late thirties, very slender. She wore a hot-pink smock with the store's logo, white jeans, white sandals. All of her nails, top to bottom, were painted a soft yellow.

'My name is Alvita Francis,' she said. 'How may I be of assistance?' She had a slight Caribbean accent.

Maria produced her ID. 'My name is Detective Caruso. This is Detective Byrne. I believe we spoke on the phone the other day?'

'Yes, of course. About the SafeCam.'

'Yes.'

Alvita reached out a hand to Maria, palm up. 'May I?'

Maria extended her right hand. Her nails were short. She wore no polish.

'You have very pretty nails,' Alvita said.

'Thank you.'

'You must be getting your B12.'

'Greek yogurt is my life.'

'I can make them look better,' Alvita said.

'You can?'

'Lord, yes. Beautiful nails are *my* life.'

Long nails were not just an inconvenience for a female police officer, they were a potential hazard. Although there was no departmental policy regarding long nails, it was frowned upon,

137

and almost always ruled out before the fact. Anything that might hinder or prevent you from drawing your service weapon was a bad idea.

Alvita glanced at Byrne. 'I'm not liking *those* nails at all.'

Byrne looked at his hands. 'What's wrong with them?'

'You ever get a manicure?' she asked.

'It's on my bucket list.'

She reached over to the counter, pulled out two cards, handed them to Byrne and Maria. 'Ten percent discount to PPD.' She pointed to the woman at the third of three stations. 'Mika could take you now if you like.'

'Maybe some other time,' Byrne said. 'But thanks.' He pocketed the card, pointed to the area above the front door, where the exterior camera was located.

'May I ask why you have a camera?' he said.

Both sculpted eyebrows went up. 'You from Philly?'

'Born and bred,' Byrne said.

'And you still ask people that question?'

'Fair enough,' Byrne said.

'On the phone you said that you record to a DVR,' Maria said. 'Did I get that right?'

'You did.'

'Is that activated by a motion sensor, or is it on all the time?'

'It's on all the time,' Alvita said. 'When we're closed, that is. Sometimes I just turn it off to save the hard disk space during business hours.' She pointed to the camera on the wall opposite the register. 'That one's on twenty-four-seven. I keep the cash drawer empty and open and lighted when we're closed, but you never know. They're not criminals because they're smart.'

'And you're saying you had the camera on and were recording on the night I asked you about?' Maria asked.

'Yes, ma'am. I closed up around eight o'clock that night, set the alarm and put the cameras on. Went to Cape May for the weekend.'

'May we take a look at the footage?'

'By all means.'

Alvita led them to the rear of the shop. On the way, the little girl looked up from her iPad, waved at Byrne.

The back room was piled high with boxes, hair dryers, stools and carts, manicure tables, plastic chairs, shampoo bowls. Somewhere in all this was a cluttered desk with a 21-inch iMac.

'Please excuse all this,' Alvita said. 'I've been meaning to sort this from the time Whappy killed Phillup.'

Byrne and Maria exchanged a glance. Byrne figured that she meant a very long time. He didn't ask who Whappy and Phillup were.

'I took the liberty of cueing up the recording to about an hour before the time you said you were interested in,' Alvita said.

'We appreciate it,' Maria said. She pointed at the chair. 'May I?'

'Please do,' Alvita said.

Maria Caruso was part of the younger generation of detectives who had a deep understanding and interest in all things digital and high-tech. Byrne had come to it all on the slope of a nearly vertical learning curve.

'I will leave you to your business,' Alvita said. 'Call me if you need anything.'

She pushed through the beads, and stepped back into the salon.

Maria sat at the desk, took the mouse in hand. She navigated to the period just preceding the medical examiner's estimate of Edwin Channing's time of death. She hit play. The screen revealed the area beneath the Nail Island entrance, along with the cars and sidewalks on the other side of the street. The Channing house was out of frame to the left.

On the upper right-hand side of the screen was visible the

vacant lot to the right of the Channing house and, in the distance, a small portion of the next street over.

Cars passed. A few pedestrians crossed the frame. A man walking his dogs. No one seemed to be paying much attention to Edwin Channing's residence.

At 11.25, a vehicle crossed the frame, right to left, on the far side of the street. It was a large late-model SUV, dark blue or black. As it moved out of frame, the vehicle came to a halt, the field illuminated by the brake lights. It appeared to have stopped just in front of the Channing house. Only a portion of the rear bumper was visible.

For the next two minutes it did not move. No one crossed the camera's field of vision on foot.

At 11.28, the brake lights flared again, and then disappeared in darkness. The only lights now were the street lights.

At 11.30, a dark SUV rolled to a stop at the very top of the frame on the right, parking on the next street over, just on the other side of the vacant lot.

'It looks like the same vehicle,' Maria said.

'Yes, it does,' Byrne replied.

A minute later, the driver door opened and two ghostlike shadows moved from the SUV, across the vacant lot, in the direction of the Channing house. The time code said 11.32. The two detectives watched the recording wordlessly, as the occasional car passed in the foreground. Maria put the recording on double speed.

At 12.16, the two shadows returned. The SUV started, and the headlights cut through the gloom with an ethereal yellow glow.

'Can we run that back?' Byrne asked.

Maria grabbed the scrubber bar, moved it slightly left. A few seconds later, the two shadows again crossed the vacant lot, approached the car.

'Stop it there for a second.'

Maria hit pause. Byrne knew she was thinking the same thing he was thinking.

Were these the men they were looking for?

Were these two cold-blooded killers?

'Could you ask Alvita if there is any way we can get a hard copy of this?' Byrne asked.

'Sure.'

While Maria walked into the salon, Byrne sat at the desk. He took out his phone, snapped a picture of the screen, looked at the photo. It was grainy, but not significantly worse than what was on the recording.

He rewound the recording. He paused it at the moment the SUV passed by the store. There was a good deal of motion blur, and the darkened windows prevented him seeing into the vehicle, but one thing was discernible. The left-rear fender was dented.

Maria stepped into the back room.

'Alvita said there might be a way to do it, but her only printer is up front.'

'That's okay,' Byrne said. 'With her permission, let's get someone from the AV unit out here to make a copy of this footage, bracketing it by thirty minutes either side.'

'You got it.'

While Maria Caruso headed back to the Roundhouse, Byrne spent the next hour canvassing the neighborhood with the blurry photograph of the old woman he'd gotten via email from Anne-Marie Beaudry. No one recognized her.

The night before, he had sent the photo by email to Perry Kershaw, who said not only did he not recognize the woman, but he now wasn't sure he'd actually seen her. Byrne put the so-called lead in a mental compartment he used for coincidence, and moved on.

He spent the next few hours walking around the blocks that surrounded the Channing scene. Using Edwin Channing's house as ground zero, he made ever-widening concentric circles, looking for exterior surveillance cameras.

Just because a homeowner or commercial establishment had surveillance cameras didn't mean they were available or willing to sign up for the SafeCam project. Far from it. It was only common sense to realize that people had at least as much to hide as they were willing to share. Probably far more.

In all, Byrne counted nine cameras within a four-block radius, cameras that were not signed up to SafeCam. He stopped at all the locations. Four were residences, with no answer at the door. One turned out to be a dummy camera. Three of the business cameras did not have any recording devices hooked up.

At two o'clock, he found one that did.

Four blocks east of Nail Island was a small convenience grocery called Sadik Food King. It was run by a Turkish couple named Joe and Fatma Sadik.

When Byrne walked in, he was greeted by a symphony of aromas, not the least of which was from a brass samovar of strong black coffee. He was also greeted by Joe Sadik. Sadik was in his late forties, a wiry, neat man with a firm handshake and a ready smile. He wore a cream-colored dress shirt and a cocoa bow tie.

Byrne explained what he was looking for, without giving any details on the circumstances. He also gave Joe Sadik the time frame.

Unlike the setup at Nail Island, the Sadiks – having been robbed many times – had invested in high-quality cameras, and subscribed to a cloud service that stored their surveillance recordings off site.

They met in an office in the back of the store.

'Why did you decide on this service?' Byrne asked.

Sadik became animated. He spoke with expressive eyes and hands. 'Twice we get robbed, and they took not only the tape machine, but the cameras themselves.' He pointed at the ceiling above the heavily fortified back door. There was a smoked glass dome there. 'Now it's a little harder to spot, and definitely harder to steal. And if they do steal the camera, they won't get the video.'

At this, Joe's wife Fatma, a petite woman dressed in a burgundy pantsuit, came into the room with an orange tray. On it was a pair of small cups of steaming black coffee.

'Thank you,' Byrne said. He sipped the coffee. It was strong and flavorful.

On the screen, the surveillance video lurched forward. Cars passed, people passed, the sun cast long shadows, then set altogether. As the image glowed beneath the street lamps, a familiar vehicle crossed the frame.

'Wait,' Byrne said. 'Can we go back?'

Joe Sadik hit pause. He backed up the recording.

As the recording inched forward, cars passed in starts and fits. At the 9.55 mark, a black SUV entered from the left side of the frame, stopped at the corner. A black SUV with a dented left-rear fender. The license plate was not visible in the frame, but the badge was. It was a GMC Acadia. Byrne called it in.

When he'd completed the call, he turned back to Joe Sadik.

'Okay,' he said. 'Let's let it play.'

Sadik hit play. On screen, the vehicle pulled up across the street, parked in front of the U-Cash-It store. A few seconds later, the driver and passenger got out. Without prompting, Joe Sadik hit pause.

Although the light level was low, and the vantage was a high angle and across four lanes, Byrne could see that the occupants of the SUV were white males, late twenties to mid-thirties.

They both wore black leather jackets. The passenger had long hair, nearly to his shoulders. The driver, who sported wrap-around sunglasses, had close-cropped hair. Both wore what looked to be fingerless black gloves.

'Okay?' Sadik asked.

'Okay,' Byrne said.

Sadik hit play.

Onscreen, the one with the longer hair held open the door of the U-Cash-It, and the driver walked in. The second man followed.

'Is there any way to print this out?'

Sadik was on his feet in a flash. 'We have this technology.'

The U-Cash-It store was a renovated and fortified brick row house, next to a phone and pager store. Renovated was probably the wrong word. The first floor was gutted, dry-walled and painted. That was it. There was a counter that spanned the width of the space, a U-Cash-It sign on the far wall – a garish red and yellow, with a fist holding bright green cash, and a lightning bolt forming the center of the U – but nothing else except for a small two-way mirror, and a pair of cameras in the far corners.

Byrne had never been in a more stark and uninviting commercial establishment.

Then again, if you found yourself needing to cash checks at these rates, you weren't here to socialize.

If the interior was uninviting, the man standing behind the counter was even more so. In his late twenties, he stood maybe six-two, two-forty. Shaved head, a pair of iron loops in his right ear, two of the most intricate sleeve tattoos Byrne had ever seen. Not to mention a gaudy neck tattoo. Apparently his arms and neck were where his sense of color and composition lay, such as it was.

'How you doing?' the man asked, with little interest in the answer.

'Never better.'

'You a cop?'

Byrne took a moment. 'Is it that obvious?'

'What do you think?'

Byrne needed a little bit of help from this man, so he decided to let the attitude roll, for now. He moved on, pulled his ID.

'Homicide?'

'That's right,' Byrne said.

'I haven't killed anybody.'

'Didn't say you had.'

The man continued to try and stare him down. From the look of the tattoos, the posturing, the permanent scowl, it was clear that this was not the man's first encounter with a law enforcement officer. That also told Byrne that this was a family business. If this guy was a convicted felon, no one was going to hire him to handle their cash, except Mom and Dad.

Eventually the man glanced away, over Byrne's shoulder, at some imaginary customer who hadn't just walked in.

'I didn't get your name,' Byrne said.

The man took a deep breath, flaring his nostrils.

'Dennis.'

Byrne made an elaborate gesture of taking out his notepad, flipping a few pages, clicking his pen.

'Just Dennis? Like Cher, or Madonna?'

Another flare. 'LoConti.'

'Great to meet you,' Byrne said. He put down his notebook and pen. He leaned back a bit. Just two guys talking.

'I see you've got two surveillance cameras at the back of the store.'

Dennis turned around and looked, as if he didn't know they were there. He turned back.

145

'What about them?'

'Have they ever come in handy?'

'Not sure what you mean.'

'I mean, have you ever had a problem where you had to identify someone who had come into your establishment via these surveillance devices?'

Byrne knew that Dennis knew that if there had ever been a burglary or robbery reported at this address, the PPD would have all the details. He could lie, but there would be no point if he wanted to get this cop out of his store and his life.

'A couple of times,' he said.

'Awesome,' Byrne said. 'Money well spent.' He pointed to the entry door. 'I notice that you don't have a camera outside.'

'No.'

'May I ask why?'

A slight smile came across Dennis's face, quickly receded. 'Because it never gets that far.'

As he said this, Byrne saw the man's right hand move, almost imperceptibly, back towards his body, stopping just a few inches from the edge of the worn countertop. He wondered what kind of persuader the man had under the counter. Not his business at the moment. Maybe soon, but not right now.

'Understood,' he said. 'This might explain why you're not part of the city's SafeCam project.'

'The *what*?'

Byrne gave him a brief rundown. About ten words in, he saw the man glaze. 'I can have some literature sent out if you like.'

'Yeah. Okay. Sure.'

'I'll make a note. But let me get down to business. I don't want to take up too much of your time.'

The man's face said: *Finally*.

'I need to ask you about two of your customers.'

'Which customers would they be?'

'I don't know their names,' Byrne said. 'That's kind of why I'm here.'

Nothing. Byrne moved on. He picked up his notebook, flipped a page.

'These two gentlemen paid you a visit the day before yesterday. At about 9.55 p.m.'

'*About* 9.55?' Dennis asked. 'Sounds exact to me.'

'Actually it was 9:55:31. Didn't want to burden you with the extra details. Were you working that night?'

'I was here.'

'Then you might remember them.'

Dennis rubbed a hand over his chin. 'We get a lot of people in here.'

Byrne slowly looked around the room. They were the only two people, and had been since he had walked in. U–Cash–It was not booming. When he looked back, he saw he'd made his point.

'So, these two guys were white, thirties, kind of street-looking. One had longer hair, black leather jacket, fingerless gloves. They drive a black Acadia.'

Dennis pretended to think. 'Not ringing a bell.'

Byrne nodded, held the look for a few moments. He again pointed to the front door. 'I was just talking with the folks who run that small grocery on the corner.'

'The Iraqis?'

'I believe they are Turkish, but yes. That store right there.'

'We don't run in the same circles.'

'Gotcha,' Byrne said. 'It turns out they *do* have a camera on the outside of their business, and because of how many times they've been robbed, they subscribe to a rather pricey cloud service that records and stores their surveillance video off site. It turns out also that their exterior cam has a clear view of your front door.'

Byrne reached into his suit coat pocket, took out the photocopy of the freeze-frame he'd gotten from Joe Sadik. He smoothed it on the counter. It clearly showed the man with longer hair holding the door to U-Cash-It open as the other man entered. In the corner was the date and the exact time.

While Dennis LoConti looked at the photocopy, Byrne looked at Dennis LoConti. He saw the tic. Slight, but it was there. He could all but hear the air begin to leak out of this man's game. LoConti knew these men.

'You know, people who come in here are entitled to their privacy.'

'I couldn't agree more,' Byrne said. 'But as you earlier noted, I'm with the homicide unit. These two gentlemen are not necessarily wanted for any specific crime. They've just come up as a part of a broader investigation.'

It was Byrne's oldest and best tap dance. He continued.

'And as you're no doubt aware, we have a pretty good DA's office in this town. They're aces at compelling people to discuss their clientele. Now, I'm not saying we should go that route. I'm saying that we're just a couple of guys talking.' He nodded at the photocopy. 'Do you recognize these men, Mr LoConti?'

LoConti looked at the paper, tapped his fingers. 'I might have seen them.'

'But you don't know their names.'

'Like I said, we get a lot of people.'

'If these people conducted a transaction here at this exact time, would you have a record of it?'

'Usually I would, but my computer is in for repair.'

By way of illustration, he reached under the counter, picked up a power cord and a USB mouse, neither connected to a computer. It was hardly proof.

Byrne thought about what he had, and whether or not a warrant could be cultivated. It didn't seem like enough.

He decided to hold the chit for a while, shake Dennis LoConti's tree a little more. He handed him a card.

'Give me a call the minute you get your computer back,' he said. 'Will you do that for me, Dennis?'

LoConti took the card. 'Sure thing.'

Byrne held the man's gaze until LoConti glanced away. There was a connection here, but Byrne couldn't quite put his finger on it. He suspected these two men on the video were not merely check-cashing customers, so he doubted there would be any record of their visit on Dennis LoConti's conveniently missing computer.

Before stepping out of the store, Byrne turned back and said:

'By the way, it's Mr and Mrs Sadik.'

'Who?'

'The people from the grocery across the street. The people who are keeping an eye on your business when you're sleeping.'

It was after four o'clock by the time Byrne arrived at the Rousseau house. He let himself in through the padlocked back door. The only previous time he had been in the house it had been teeming with crime-scene techs and investigators. He needed it to be silent.

He sat in the kitchen with the lights off for a while, listening for house sounds, sounds that might have preceded the ruin of the Rousseau family.

Had the killers come around to the back door? Had they knocked on the door, and had a member of the family, thinking it was a neighbor, simply opened it to them?

According to her statement, Anne-Marie Beaudry said that when she entered the kitchen at 7.30 on the morning when the victims were discovered, the oven was set on low, and inside was an all-but-dried-out leg of lamb, wrapped in foil.

Byrne flipped on the light. On the counter was a cookbook. A red ribbon place marker jutted from the top. He gently opened the book, and saw that the page was a recipe for apple turnovers. He glanced at the fruit bowl on the small table. It was full of Granny Smith apples.

He envisioned the few moments before Laura Rousseau met her killer, standing right where he was standing, her thoughts consumed by this simple, everyday task. It would be her last.

Mark's room was a typical teenager's room. Instead of rock star or hip hop posters, however, Mark's posters were of athletes. Cole Hamels, LeSean McCoy, Usain Bolt.

His daily journal was in a black lacquer box sitting on top of his dresser. Byrne opened the box. The journal itself was brown leatherette. Byrne could see traces of the black fingerprint powder.

He took out the journal, opened it to the center and began reading.

June 16. I started work today at the store. It was kind of slow in the morning, but by noon a few busloads of tourists showed up. I think they might have been Korean. Wherever they were from, they had a lot of money to spend. It was so funny to watch Dad try to figure out what they were saying. He always talks with his hands anyway, but watching him try to describe the Liberty Bell was a stitch.

Somehow it got to be three o'clock, and neither of us had taken a break for lunch.

I went down to the diner on Third Street, and guess who was there. I'm not sure there is a future for me and Jen. She might be a bit too serious for me.

I think Mom might be the bravest person I know. It was amazing when she stood up to those people when she didn't have to. When I asked her why she did it, she said it was about everyone else, and that sometimes you have to make a stand, even though it isn't the easy thing to do.

I was a little too young to understand that then, but I do now. If I can be half as brave as Mom, I will be happy.

Byrne closed the journal. No matter how many times he did this simple but necessary task – more than one case had turned on a seemingly innocuous sentence in a diary or journal – he felt as if he were invading the victim's privacy.

Still, he took out a paper evidence bag, slipped in the journal. He made a note to remind himself to log the removal in the murder book's chain of evidence. He'd read more later.

Before leaving the house, he stopped in the kitchen. On the counter was a digital answering machine. He touched the button to play the outgoing message.

They all answered together.

'*We are the Rousseau family!*'

Byrne knew the machine had been processed, and that it contained no messages. He played it again, unsure as to why. Perhaps it was because he wanted to meet these people, to experience something of them that was animate, something sentient and alive.

He played the outgoing message one last time, and as he did, he found his gaze turning to the living room, and the large brown stains on the carpeting.

'*We are the Rousseau family!*'

He felt the old anger begin to rise. He did his best to bully it back. It had never helped.

On the corkboard in the kitchen were photographs of Mark Rousseau at ten, twelve, and fourteen, the chronicle of him growing from a gangly pre-teen into a tall young athlete, on the way to becoming a man he would never live to be.

As Byrne closed and sealed the door, he felt the weight of the journal in his pocket, haunted by those two lines Mark Rousseau had written:

I think Mom might be the bravest person I know.

It was amazing when she stood up to those people when she didn't have to.

15

'I don't want one,' the old woman said. 'I will say no more on the matter.'

She crossed her thin arms over the front of her pilled blue cardigan and tried to make herself even smaller.

Anjelica tested the water coming out of the faucet with the back of her right wrist. Tepid at best. She turned up the hot water, tried it again. Too hot.

Perfect.

Just hot enough to cook the old bird.

She turned it down, swirled the water with her hand.

'It doesn't matter if you want one or not. You are going to have one,' Anjelica replied. 'And *I'll* say no more on the matter.'

'It isn't my bath day.'

'Yes it is, old woman.'

'I didn't take a bath last time.'

'Last time my sciatica was acting up and I couldn't lift you. Today it's worse. You think you're the only one with troubles?

I've already let you slip a week and it is a day neither of us will get back.'

'I know what day it is. You don't have to tell me. I *know* what day it is because you're wearing that perfume.'

Anjelica almost laughed. She always wore perfume when she visited Tess Daly. The reason was simple. The old woman talked more than anyone Anjelica had ever met. More than even her own mother, who had been a non-stop chatterbox about everything and nothing.

A year or so earlier, Anjelica got the idea to schedule the old woman to be her last stop of the day. She'd put on a little makeup, her best sweater, and perfume, telling the old woman that, as much as she would like to sit and chat, she could not do so because she had a date. At first it was clear that the old woman did not believe her, assuming – rightly so – that no one in his right mind would give a second look to someone like Anjelica Leary.

But Anjelica stuck to her story, and eventually got the old woman to believe it was true. It was the only way to get out of her apartment at a decent hour.

Truth be told, Tess Daly was a civilized enough sort at eighty-eight years. Anjelica more than once thought about what life might be like if she could hook her up with Jack Permutter.

Two old birds, one stone.

Twenty minutes later, the woman bathed and fed and planted in front of the television, Anjelica looked at herself in the mirror, straightened her blouse and skirt, both older than time.

Like clockwork, she heard the TV in the parlor veer from an ad to: '*This . . . is . . .* Jeopardy.'

She poured Tess Daly an inch of Jameson, returned the bottle to the small desk in the bedroom, locked the drawer, pocketed the key. If she didn't, Tess would drink the whole thing.

*

On this night, as with every other night she visited Tess Daly, Anjelica stopped for a hoagie at a small restaurant on Lombard, then headed back to her house, got into her robe, poured herself her own few inches of Irish and hoped for a good movie on TCM.

She had little interest in films made these days, what with the superheroes and explosions and so-called romantic comedies. Hers was the era of her parents and her own young adulthood, the movies of George Cukor and Billy Wilder and Alfred Hitchcock and Frank Capra.

As if by serendipity, tonight's movie was *Kitty Foyle*. The 1940 film starred Ginger Rogers, in an Oscar-winning performance, as a hard-charging blue-collar Philadelphia woman from the wrong side of the tracks who found herself the object of affection of two different men: the wealthy cad, played by Dennis Morgan, and the idealistic young doctor, played by James Craig. A real tearjerker.

Anjelica loved the old tearjerkers.

As she settled into her chair and watched the opening credits, it occurred to her that she had not had a good cry – a real ten-Kleenex affair – in a long time.

Almost forty years, if one were to count.

Anjelica Leary counted.

At just after eleven o'clock, she dressed in her nurse's whites, ran a brush through her hair. Before leaving the house, she looked at herself in the mirror next to the door, wondering where the years had gone.

Wasn't it just yesterday she'd stood, slender and energetic and full of youthful promise, at her graduation from Temple University?

She glanced at the small pill vial in her hand, thinking about the journey these pills had taken, and where they would go this night.

Like Kitty Foyle, who had made the most important decision in her life while having a conversation with herself in the mirror, Anjelica made up her mind.

'It is God's work, it is,' she said to the gray-haired woman in the mirror, knowing that the next time she saw this woman, the world would be different.

The world would be *better*.

She found Constantia sitting at the last booth in the small coffee shop at which they'd agreed to meet.

Small talk made, they got to the reason for the meeting.

'I can't tell you how much this means, Mrs Leary.'

Constantia Colfax was a scant twenty-five, friendly and outgoing in a way that Anjelica had never been. Even though the young woman had had as much life thrown at her as anyone, including Anjelica, she did not run for an amber vial, or a bottle, or any of the other things that made things worse. She stiffened her spine and moved on.

'You must start calling me Anjelica. Mrs Leary is my mother-in-law, and she's been in the ground for twenty years.'

And good riddance, Anjelica thought, but kept to herself.

'Anjelica, then,' Constantia said. 'It's a beautiful name.'

'Thank you,' she said. 'As is yours.'

Constantia lowered her voice, even though there was no need. 'And you have no problem with signing in as me?'

Anjelica matched the woman's subdued volume. 'None at all, love. I know you'd do it for me.'

'I truly would,' she said. 'I hope it would be under happier circumstances, but you can count on me.'

'Of course I can.'

They'd met a month earlier at a NVA conference and, despite their difference in age, became fast friends. Constantia had never worked at this clinic. No one would be the wiser.

There was no physician on duty at the clinic, but rather a rotating roster of doctors on call from nearby hospitals.

'You don't think we'll get in trouble, do you?'

'Not to worry,' Anjelica said. 'I've been doing this a long time.'

At this, Constantia smiled. She was of an age and a temperament where the smallest assurance from someone Anjelica's age would be enough to assuage her doubts about just about anything.

'Do you have any new photos?' Anjelica asked.

Constantia lit up. 'I do!'

She rummaged in her purse, took out her iPhone, clicked it on. She turned the screen to face them both, tapped the photo app. A second later there was a photo of a smiling, round-faced girl wearing a bright green jumper.

'Oh, the dear,' Anjelica said.

Another photo, this one of the girl in the tub, a crown of bubbles on her head.

'And her doctor said it's just a chest cold?'

'Yes.'

'The poor thing,' Anjelica said. Constantia's daughter, Lucia, was asthmatic, and chest colds for her were potentially serious.

'Well, if she takes a turn, you call me. I may be old, but I still have sway with the doctors at U of Penn.'

'Thanks, Mrs Leary,' Constantia said. '*Anjelica*.'

Twenty minutes later, Anjelica stood in front of the dilapidated building generously called the 24th Street Clinic and Rehabilitation Center. Even out here, she could smell the frailty, the coarse odors of sickness. The smells did not bother her – you couldn't do your job as an LPN for long if they did – but they still managed to get on her skin in a way that required showers that lasted until the water was cold. The showers had gotten longer and longer over the years.

It all begins with a step, Anjelica thought. Step to the right, your life goes this way. Step to the left, it goes another.

Step into the light, or into the darkness.

To the Lord or to the Devil.

Anjelica Leary made her choice, pulled open the door and stepped inside.

16

By the time Byrne reached the Penrose Diner, he realized he had not eaten all day.

When he entered the restaurant, he looked in both directions. He had not seen the man in a year or so, and almost walked right by him.

Graham Grande was a latent fingerprint examiner when Byrne first became a detective, a man already nearing retirement, which was not mandatory at the time. Grande had come up before the FBI created the first databases, when the science of being a latent examiner was all about the long, tedious task of comparing fingerprints side by side on paper.

Now in his eighties, he still showed up occasionally at the Survivors' Benefits and other PPD charity functions. He looked frail to Byrne, but his eyes were clear.

The two men shook hands. Byrne slid into the booth, ordered coffee, perused the menu. As hungry as he was, his nerves got the better of him. He put the menu away.

He knew that Graham's wife had been ill for a long time. He was almost afraid to ask. He wanted to enquire after her by name, but couldn't remember it. He blamed himself for letting the time pass, for forgetting.

'How is your wife?' he asked, hoping it didn't sound uncaring.

Graham shrugged. 'She has her good days and her bad days. We have her over to the Camilla House now.'

Byrne knew that Camilla House was a long-term-care nursing home in West Philly, near Cobbs Creek.

'Some days she's sharp as a tack,' Graham continued. 'Remembers what I wore to so-and-so's wedding in 1956. Other days ... '

The waitress brought Byrne's coffee, topped up Graham's cup.

The two men talked about the job as it was in the day, the job as it was now. They talked about people they knew in common – fellow cops, lawyers, police support personnel – many of whom, Byrne was sad to notice, were gone.

It was Graham who brought it around to the business at hand. He tapped the box sitting next to him in the booth. 'You want this in here or outside?'

Still the cop, Byrne thought. 'I'll get it before I leave.'

Graham took off his glasses, wiped them with a napkin. It was a gesture Byrne remembered from back in the day.

He put the glasses back on, lowered his voice.

'Well, it was a job and a half to try to process this material without my kit,' he said. Byrne had asked if it was possible to read prints off the items without using powder or tape. He knew there were other, less reliable methods. Graham Grande had never been one to turn down a challenge.

'How did we do?' Byrne asked, not really wanting to know.

Graham leaned forward as if he were on a witness stand, a

160

place that had become a second home to him over a forty-year career in law enforcement. 'Not good. I can tell you that there are prints on both items, though.'

Byrne felt his heart sink. He had hoped Graham could pull any latent or patent prints off the items without disturbing anything. 'You couldn't process them?'

Graham shook his head. 'Not without my kit.'

'So if another examiner were to process these items, he would have no way of knowing they'd been looked at before?'

'Not unless he was a mind-reader.'

'No problem, Graham,' Byrne said. He let the information settle. 'So tell me, how are things going? You making the bills?'

'Retirement sucks,' Graham said. 'Don't do it.'

Byrne pushed an envelope across the table.

'What's this?' Graham asked.

'For your trouble.'

Graham lifted the flap, dropped it. 'It's too much.'

'Well, if you can't use it . . . '

Byrne made a slow-motion, half-hearted attempt to grab the envelope. Graham snatched it in a flash. He was still pretty quick.

'I never said that.'

When Byrne reached his car, he put the box on the trunk, looked at the items inside. The dark glasses and the SEPTA pass. He had not given the .38 to Graham to examine. Processing an old pair of sunglasses and a forty-year-old bus pass was one thing. Processing something that might have been used in the commission of a crime was another.

Byrne knew that his prints were on Des Farren's glasses and bus pass. He remembered Jimmy handing him the glasses and the pass that day in the park. He couldn't remember if anyone else touched them.

But why were they in this box? Why weren't they, along with the .38, at the bottom of the Schuylkill River?

Byrne decided to drive to the Platt Bridge. He'd make up his mind when he got there whether or not to throw the box over the rail.

By the time he turned on to Market Street it came to him.

Hazel, he thought.

Graham Grande's wife's name was Hazel.

17

Every night, Billy walked the city.

For every face he could not recognize, he was doubly blessed by his clear memory of place. If he had once been anywhere in the city, he could remember the route.

He knew every dip and rise on the avenue, every turn of a side street. He knew the curbs, the cracks, the steel grates that ventilated the SEPTA cars rumbling beneath his feet. He knew every slash of graffiti, every car sitting up on blocks, every shuttered store.

Billy always walked quickly, hands in pockets, his worn boot heels soft on the hard pavement, his pace in steady syncopation with the night rhythms of traffic and traffic lights.

On some nights he began where this life began, at Carpenter Street, and headed east. Some nights he strolled up to Market Street, and walked river to river, then back.

His drive was boundless, often lifted by the thought of the

people who had walked these streets over the years, the decades, the centuries, their energies still in the very cobblestones beneath the pavement.

Whenever he passed people on the street, he looked at their faces, cataloguing their features, filing them away, adding and subtracting them, putting them in columns. He knew it was possible, even likely, that he saw many of the same people every night. People often went to the same places at the same time, for work, for entertainment, for obligations, for the need.

Sometimes people looked at his face and nodded. Billy never knew if they were doing so because they knew him, or if it was some kind of courtesy. He did not see much courtesy or respect these days, so he suspected the former.

As he walked across the city, and entered the dens where the monsters lived, he made hard eye contact. With some of the men – men who walked their own routes – he entered a silent contract, a pact that said: *If you do not lift your hand to me, I will do you no harm.*

On Sunday nights, when he reached St Patrick's, he would stop. There he would kneel at the side of the church, take off his coat and place it on the ground. As he had done once a week for as long as he could remember, he would remove a few threads from the lining, take a lighter from his pocket and burn them on the steps, releasing the essence of all he had fought and defeated.

On this night he told God of his transgressions, of his mortal sins, of the old man, of the family. He could not see their faces, but he could feel his heart heavy with their burdens, which were now his own. So many over the years, and yet his heart was not yet full.

As he strode back to Devil's Pocket, the place of his birth, the feelings got stronger.

Something was happening.

It felt as if it was all coming to a close, a time of transfiguration. He felt as if his third birth was coming, and it would be as different from his second life as his second life had been to his first, those idyllic ten years when he had been safe in his father's house, fettered by love, a time before these past twenty-six years of darkness.

Something was happening.

There were two more lines to draw and the square would be complete – unbreakable, unshakeable, the same from every direction, a perfectly contained palindromic world where there would be no questions, only answers, a place where every face he saw would be different and remembered.

Just before midnight, he found himself across the street from Emily's apartment, watching her shadows grow and recede on the sheer curtains. He'd only seen her in and around the library, and often wondered what would happen if ever he crossed the street, walked up the steps and knocked on her door.

Maybe one day, he thought.

One day soon.

'Where've you been, boy?'

'I've been walking, Mórai.'

'Where did you go?'

'I walked river to river.'

'Our Desmond used to walk.'

Billy knows this, of course. 'Did he now?'

'Oh yes. Once he walked from City Hall all the way to the museum.'

Straight down the center, Billy thinks. Billy has done it himself.

'Straight down the center of the Parkway.'

Just before dawn, Billy sat on the roof of The Stone, looking out over the Pocket. He sipped from a bottle of Tullamore Dew. It was his favorite time of day, a time when everyone saw the world as he saw it.

As the first dawn light began to paint the sky, he heard the groan of the rusted iron access ladder leading to the roof. He drew his Makarov, held it at his side.

Before the intruder was visible, Billy heard:

'It's Sean.'

He eased the Makarov back into his pocket. 'Okay.'

'We cool?'

'We are.'

Sean climbed onto the roof, sat down on a crate, looked out over the streets. Before long, he reached into his pocket, retrieved his vial, hit the meth. He then lit a cigarette.

'Remember the time we found Uncle Pat up here?' Billy asked.

Sean laughed. 'Oh yeah. We caught that beating afterwards,' he said. 'How old were we then?'

Billy thought about it. To him, time was a piecemeal cloth marked only by the seasons, by the scars on his hands and face. 'I think we were eight or nine. Something like that.'

Sean held out a hand. Billy passed him the bottle of Tullamore Dew. Sean drank from it, passed it back. 'We hit those houses that night, didn't we?'

'Yeah.'

'Where were they?'

'Cinnaminson,' Billy said. He could not remember the faces of the people he had seen this very night, but he could get in a car and drive to the house they had visited all those years ago.

It was a time in their lives when their father, Danny, and their uncle Patrick were teaching them the finer points of residential burglary, often driving to middle-class neighborhoods in New Jersey, staking out houses. When the adults were certain the dwellings were unoccupied, they would boost the boys into first-floor windows.

'That's *right*, Cinnaminson,' Sean said. 'We got those Atari 5200s.'

'Yeah.'

'Man, I loved those things. Bet you they're worth a bundle now.'

That night, after getting back to The Stone, Billy and Sean had gone to the cellar to hook up the game consoles. As usual, after a score, Patrick had been pumped full of adrenalin. He picked up a woman at the bar and brought her to the roof.

Sean hit his vial again, shook it off. 'What was her name?'

'The girl with Uncle Pat?'

'Yeah,' Sean said. 'Was it Cindy? Sandy? Wendy?'

'Mindy,' Billy said. 'Mindy Meeks.'

Sean shook his head. 'How the fuck do you remember this shit?'

Billy shrugged. His ability to read faces was the exact opposite of his ability to remember names and locations. 'Do you remember what we called her after that night?'

Sean thought for a moment. 'No.'

'Squeaky Meeks.'

Sean howled. 'That's *right*.'

'We called her that because she made those mouse noises when she was doing the dirty up here with Uncle Pat.'

'Squeaky Meeks,' Sean said. He stubbed out his cigarette, looked at his watch. The streets below were starting to come alive. Lights blinked on in the condos at Naval Square.

'I'm going to head back to the shop, get some sleep,' Sean said. 'You good?'

'Yeah.'

'We've got work to do later.'

'I know.'

As Sean made his way down the iron ladder, Billy looked out at the neighborhood, at the massive South Street bridge, the dark, churning river. He'd been born here, had lived here most of his life and knew in a way that transcended all rational thought that, like his uncles Patrick and Desmond before him, it would be in the shadow of the spire that he would die.

The Pocket buried its own.

18

Philadelphia, 1943

They had arrived in New York City the day before, spending the night in a rundown hostel in a part of town known as the Bronx.

They spent what they had on train tickets to Philadelphia, and a pair of sandwiches that were mostly fat and gristle.

They had become man and wife on the ship, married by a man who said he was a proper Lutheran minister, a man who required no papers or proof of age, just a pint of bitters. The certificate looked real enough.

As they walked from the train station, they asked after the Irish neighborhoods, if one were to be found.

There was only one place, Máire learned. Not an official neighborhood, but more of an enclave.

It was called Devil's Pocket.

After months of cold-water flats, shared bathrooms, and food on the dole, they found a modest row house on Montrose Street,

169

complete with rattling windows, leaky roof and thin walls. Liam scrounged scant work on the coal piers on the river, while Máire worked as a domestic and housekeeper in some of the mansions surrounding Rittenhouse Square.

It was on a Fourth of July in the park that they slipped into the trees and made scandalous love, all while the fireworks painted the sky above them.

Clothes returned to modesty, Liam held her.

'There's more here for a man like me,' he said. 'More than the black lung and fatty beef and patched trousers.'

At that moment, Máire wondered what he saw when he looked at her, if the glamour could any longer grip a man as powerful as Liam Farren.

She doubted, but she hoped.

For weeks they rummaged the landfills and trash bins, and with a jar of glue lifted from the hardware store and nails pulled and straightened from the abandoned lumber at construction sites, they had some wobbly but workable furniture.

They decided to open a shebeen, a small tavern in the front room of the row house. If they kept the light low – which was no great hardship, seeing the cost of electricity – the shabbiness of the furnishings might be overlooked.

Three weeks later, with only the bottles collected from friends, and a pair of old doors on saw horses, The Stone was open for business.

Máire styled the tavern as she knew them to be in Ireland, where the shebeen was, in many ways, the social center of the neighborhood. It was much the same in Philadelphia, even down to the laws that mandated closing of the doors on Sundays.

Soon after opening, to gather the Sunday trade, they established a Sunday drinking club, which was private and therefore not subject to law.

At first, the only people to come to The Stone lived on the block. Many nights there were only three or four of the local boys. No matter how clean Máire kept the place, there was always something to do.

After the first year, however, it became known throughout Schuylkill and Grays Ferry as a meeting place for mutual-aid societies, immigrant networks and ward politics.

While Liam Farren was tolerant of the bluster, it was to the darker side of things he was drawn, darker even than backroom political dealings.

As the war in Europe drew to a close, Liam's two best friends were the Malone brothers, Matthew and Kyle. The Malones were known for their ability to stay a stride ahead of the law, as foul as they might run of it. Matthew, the bigger of the two, was known to keep a small hatchet in a sheath on his belt. His brother, having learned a trade in the fisheries of County Down, preferred his *Jowika*, the two-bladed knife he seemed to carry in his hand at all times.

Each evening Liam and the Malones would meet at The Stone and go forth into the night, returning before dawn. Most mornings Liam would awaken Máire with strong tea and toast, often with a sack full of jewelry and coins.

As Liam slept through the day, Máire tried to wrest the blood from his shirts with bleach. Almost every noontime – save for Sundays – would find her in the cellar, her knees astride a utility basin.

While Liam served three months for breaking and entering a house in Fitler Square, Máire missed her curse. She was finally with child. At just the same age as her mother and her mother's mother, and all the women before them.

Eight months later brought Desmond. Desmond was born with a spell. On that night Liam went on a terror. A terrible

171

beating came to any man who dared cross him. The morning found him with damaged hands, and a scar across his stomach he would carry until the day he died.

When Máire regained her strength, she searched far and wide for her real son, certain that the boy in her house was a change-ling, a burden given to her for her lethargy in blessing the child. She became adept in sneaking into houses all over Devil's Pocket.

She did not find her son.

In the boy's sixth week she took a piece from her grand-mother's cloth coat and burned it on the front steps of the row house, held the boy above it. He did not respond.

Within two years she had two perfect boys, Daniel and Patrick. Fine and strong and pink, born one year apart to the day, the *samhain*, November Eve.

After the war, there was money to be made and money to be had. The front room of the row house was no longer fit or big enough to handle the trade, so Máire found some local trades-men who, for the cost of their pints every night until the job was complete, remodeled the space, knocking out walls and building a suitable bar with a rail. She found a man to make a neon sign at cost, and it went over the front door, facing the avenue.

Late in August 1952, a few days before Labor Day, Liam and the Malones were out. There were just three locals at the bar. Cal Murphy, who at eighty had taken up residence on the first stool most nights, and had become the de facto mayor of The Stone, was on his third pint.

Margaret, the woman who tended bar three nights a week, wiped down the counter while Máire sat at a table trying to find money for their suppliers.

At just after ten o'clock the door opened, drawing Máire's eye. Two young men walked in. Each in their late teens, one was short and portly, the other taller and hungry-looking. They did not have to announce their intentions for Máire to know their mission.

The chubby one drew a small silver pistol from his pocket and threw a lunch sack on the counter. 'Put the money in there,' he said to Margaret.

No one moved.

Máire glanced at the door to the back room. She both hoped and feared that Liam would step through. Hoped because he would know what to do. Feared because this boy might get spooked and pull the trigger.

Liam did not appear.

'Do you know who this is you're stealing from?' Cal Murphy asked.

The young man put the pistol to Cal's head, pulled back the hammer.

'Did I ask you a *question*, old man?'

Murphy remained silent, but didn't take his hard gaze from the boy with the gun. The chubby one withdrew the gun, walked to the bar. He motioned for the taller boy to stand behind Murphy.

With the barrel of the gun the chubby one nudged the empty sack closer to Margaret. Margaret looked at Máire. Máire nodded.

Keeping her eyes on the boys, Margaret opened the register and put the money in the sack.

'The coins, too,' the chubby one said.

Margaret complied.

'And we'll have that box you keep below the bar.'

'Don't know what you're talking about,' Margaret said.

The tall one drew a knife from a sheath on his belt, lifted it high in the air and brought it down through the back of Cal

Murphy's hand. The old man shrieked in agony. The tall one withdrew the knife, wiped it on Cal Murphy's shirt.

'The next one is going in his throat,' he said.

Margaret again made eye contact with Máire. Máire again nodded.

As Máire tended to Cal Murphy's hand, Margaret reached under the bar, took out the strongbox, opened it. Máire knew the exact contents. Three hundred six dollars and fifty-five cents. The barmaid put it all in the sack.

As quickly as they had come, the boys were through the door and gone.

Three days later Máire returned from the market to find a crudely made sign on the front door of The Stone:

Closed for Repairs.

Odd, that, she thought, wondering where the money was going to come from for these repairs, and how they could afford to forgo three days' earnings, especially now that they had lost three hundred dollars to thieves.

She walked around to the back, came in through the kitchen. Because they were closed, the only thing on the stove was a pot of soup for their tea. She put down her bags, pushed through the door into the bar.

There were five of them in the room. The Malone brothers, Liam, and young Danny and Patrick.

Behind the bar were a pair of tall wooden crosses, fashioned from two-by-six lumber scrapped from the demolished houses on Stillman.

The two boys who had robbed the tavern were bound to the crosses, stark naked as the day, their mouths gagged with oily rags. Máire saw the long red welts down their arms and legs. The chubby one had a gaping wound on the right side of his waist, more than a pound of flesh missing. It had been crudely stitched using Máire's leather punch and twine. She could smell the infection.

In the center of each of the boys' chests was drawn a dartboard in black paint.

Every so often Kyle Malone would down a shot of whiskey, walk around the bar, pick up four darts. One by one he fired them at the boys' chests. Each bull's-eye brought a cheer from the others. They all took turns, even the boys.

The games went on long after Máire turned in for the evening.

On the third day, the sign came down from the door, the crosses disappeared and The Stone reopened for trade. No one enquired after the boys.

When the two detectives assigned to the robbery case stopped in, they drank for free and lamented the state of a world where hard-working men like Liam Farren fell prey to the criminal element.

A week later, while washing the bar towels in the cellar, Máire saw the four pieces of lumber, dismantled, stacked in the corner. The wood smelled of bleach.

It would not be the last time they were used.

As Danny and Patrick grew toward adolescence, they watched out for Desmond, but Desmond did not make the rounds with them.

Patrick became quite the ladies' man, staying out till all hours, a woman in every ward, many of them married. He was once caught in the act, and the husband who'd found them raised a knife to him. The man walked with a cane for a full year, and never lifted his eyes as he crossed Montrose Street.

Danny married Deena Finneran and the celebration raged for four days, drawing guests from as far away as Ohio. Deena was radiant.

The Devil's Pocket Boys grew in reputation and lore. In Dundalk, Máire had never locked the door to her house, and she saw no reason to start here. While much of the neighborhood and the city proper fell victim to crimes both grand and small, no one dared steal anything from clan Farren.

1974

The black news came as a telegram. After serving just two months of a ten-year sentence for manslaughter, Liam Farren crossed paths with a Romani gang in Graterford prison. The tale was told that, on the final day, he gave as good as he got but was overpowered in the prison yard and felled by a *chivomengro*.

Liam Michael Farren was dead.

That night Máire took his clothes down to the river underneath the South Street bridge and washed them until every stain was gone and his shirts were gleaming white. She stayed until dawn, her tears falling into the Schuylkill.

She thought about her grandmother, a small but fierce woman walking the countryside in County Louth. Her grandmother had once said that she had been cursed as a girl by a *púca*:

Go n-ithe an cat thú is go n-ithe an diabhal an cat.

May the cat eat you, and may the devil eat the cat.

Máire believed that when her firstborn son was spirited away, leaving her with a changeling, the curse had come back.

Indeed, Máire Farren came to know, it had never left.

19

Philadelphia, 2015

Jessica looked at her watch. She had twenty minutes to get to court. She'd make it, but she wouldn't be ready. She had twenty-seven cases on her desk. It was always a toss-up between punctuality and preparedness.

She'd got all of her file folders jammed into her enormous canvas tote when she glanced up to see a man standing in her doorway.

'Have you got a minute?' he asked.

'For you, sir, always,' Jessica said.

The man smiled. 'How many times are we going to have to go over the sir business?'

It was true. In all the time Jessica had been with the DA's office, she had not gotten this part of the decorum correct. When she was a police officer, she'd had to deal with superiors who were sometimes younger than her. She dealt with superiors with whom she often socialized. In a two-badge household there

177

was a lot of crossover. Vincent had his bosses and underlings; Jessica had hers. The way around it in the police department was to refer to the other person by their rank. If you weren't comfortable calling your superior Joey, you called him Sarge. It was the right amount of familiarity and respect.

Add to that the fact that the automatic response of police officers when talking to the public was sir, or ma'am, no matter what mood you were in, or whether or not they deserved the respect.

It was totally different here. It seemed as if she would have to call her superiors exactly what they wanted her to call them. Saying 'I think I agree with you, unit chief' sounded slightly odd.

'You're right,' she said. 'I'll remember in the future.'

The man sat on the edge of her desk, straightened the crease of his pant leg. He was tall and broad-shouldered, had close-cropped light-brown hair, blue eyes, a great smile.

'I got the summary on the Carter case,' he said. 'It was masterful.'

'Thanks,' Jessica said. She almost said *sir*, but stopped himself. 'I have a good team.'

'Your science was a bit thin.'

It was true. Rourke Hoffman had blown cannonball-sized holes in her witness's testimony regarding the blood and fibers found on Carter's clothing, mostly due to the almost non-existent sample size. Still, she'd had to present it.

As rushed as she was, Jessica had no intention of cutting this love fest short. Standing in her office was the unit chief of the homicide division. There were those who believed – and Jessica counted herself among them – that he would not be there for long. Everyone knew he was going to run for district attorney this fall, and everyone believed he would win.

Later this day there was a thinly veiled fund-raiser for him at the Ashburner Inn.

'Are you coming tonight?' he asked.

Attendance at the fund-raiser wasn't mandatory, but it was mandatory.

'Wouldn't miss it.'

'See you there,' he said, and walked out of her office.

As Jessica was gathering her things, she thought that she could do much worse than to align herself with the next district attorney for the Philadelphia County, Mr James P. Doyle, Esq.

She wondered if she'd ever call him Jimmy.

The Ashburner Inn was a brick-oven gourmet pizza restaurant and bar on Torresdale Avenue and Ashburner Street in the Holmesburg section of the city.

The restaurant nearly earned its name in December 2012 when an electrical problem caused a fire. In the ensuing year the place was remodeled and refitted, and, since the closing of Finnigan's Wake in Northern Liberties, had become a popular place for police, firefighters and other city personnel.

Jessica had gotten home, cooked dinner, showered and dressed in record time. She'd left her two children and husband in front of the TV with their trays.

When she arrived at just after 6.30, the place was already packed. She recognized fewer than half the people. Cops, lawyers but also union reps, business people and everyone else with an interest in the way justice was meted out in the city of Philadelphia.

It was all but a coronation for ADA James Doyle.

If everything went as planned, he would be the next District Attorney of Philadelphia.

By the time Jimmy Doyle stepped to the front of the crowd, Jessica was on her second Bacardi and Coke and already feeling it. She was getting to be a real lightweight in her old age. Time was when she could knock off five or six drinks, go to bed, get up at 5.30, strap on her Reeboks and do three miles before going to the office.

Those days were gone. She looked at her watch. It was 8.36, five minutes later than the last time she had looked. Despite all the food, and all the people she had not seen outside of a professional basis in a few years, her mind kept returning to the backlog of cases she had piled up on her desk.

Somebody tapped a glass, and the crowd fell silent. Jimmy Doyle looked elegant in a navy-blue suit and burgundy tie.

He began, as expected, by thanking everyone for being there, especially the owners of the restaurant. He acknowledged the bigwigs and movers and shakers.

'I was born and raised in Philadelphia, specifically in a small neighborhood called Devil's Pocket. Now, as many of you know, this means two things. If you're from the Pocket, you don't last long if you back down from a fight. And the fact that I'm standing here today means that I won at least one more than I lost.'

Polite laughter. Polite applause.

'But just because I'm a fighter doesn't mean that I got here on my own. I've had a lot of people in my corner. From law enforcement officers to community organizers and activists, to people who work in the fields of health care, social work and yes, even the defense counsel, who have made me be at my best when we squared off at the bar.

'I'm running for district attorney to make Philadelphia a safer place to live, to work, to raise a family, at a lower cost. The county spends a high percent of its budget on the criminal justice system yet we don't feel safe in our homes and on our streets. There's something wrong when the jails have a higher occupancy rate than our hotels, and we still don't feel safe. People are disillusioned.

'I will be the first to say that there is a lot of work to be done. My Irish grandmother used to have a saying: *A family of Irish birth will argue and fight. But let a shout come from without and see them all unite.*

'This is how I see the honest, decent, hard-working people of Philadelphia, as a family. Sure, like all families we may have our disagreements on how to get things done, but let us be threatened by a criminal element and you will see a united Philadelphia, a strong Philadelphia, a determined Philadelphia.'

The crowd applauded. When the noise died down, Jimmy took a step forward, one hand in pocket.

'Today I've learned of some tragic news. You all probably know the name of Jacinta Collins. Mrs Collins was the Point Breeze woman, a mother of two, who was gravely injured in an explosion two months ago, her injuries a direct result of a deliberately set explosive. A man was arrested for that crime, a man named Daniel Farren. He is currently awaiting trial on those charges.'

Jimmy Doyle took a moment, continued.

'I am sorry and saddened to say that Jacinta Collins died today at 4.53 a.m.

'I've learned that the ME will rule that the woman died of sepsis – blood poisoning – but will rule the cause of death as homicide. Her case has been turned over to the homicide division of the PPD.'

Doyle let the news make its rounds among the crowd.

'The office of the district attorney has been preparing a case against Mr Farren, a case that included the charge of aggravated assault and attempted murder. I am here to say that the charge will now be upgraded to murder in the first degree, and that I will personally try the case.'

Now the murmurs became louder. This was a new one for Jessica and, she suspected, most people in the crowd. Things

181

like this were almost always discussed and announced behind doors.

'A vigorous prosecution needs a vigorous team, and I'd like to take this opportunity to announce my selection for second chair on this most important case.'

The crowd drew in and held its breath.

'Second chair will be ADA Jessica Balzano.'

At first, to Jessica, it felt as if all the air had suddenly been sucked out of the room. She felt a tightness in her chest.

Jimmy Doyle raised his glass in her direction. Everyone in the room followed suit. A few moments later there was polite applause.

Jessica felt faint.

'Are you sure about this?'

Jessica stood at the end of the bar with Jimmy Doyle. She had wisely switched to Diet Cokes.

For years she had trained as a boxer, having even fought a handful of professional fights. There was an old saying in the ring that someone was trying to punch above their weight. Jessica suddenly felt like a featherweight getting in the ring with Joe Frazier.

'Never been more certain,' Jimmy said. 'You've been doing good work, and you are ready.'

'I appreciate your confidence in me.'

'Add to this your experience on the street as a homicide detective, and you will be our MVP.'

Jessica knew a little about the case. She knew that the defendant, Danny Farren, was a small-time hood from southwest Philly, in and out of jail most of his adult life. The current charge was that he had firebombed a building, ostensibly as retribution upon a man from whom he and his crew had been extorting money, for failure to make a payment. She knew that Farren, as expected, was pleading not guilty, and had not said a word about the case to anyone other than his attorney.

'The Farren family has been a cancer in this city a long time,' Jimmy said. 'It's time to shut them down for good. I'm going to make a call in about ten minutes, see if we can get a grand jury together in short order. The more we present on Danny Farren, the more will stick.'

It was all moving a bit fast, but Jessica found her resolve returning. She could do this.

'Tomorrow morning, nine sharp, my office. We'll bring the walls down around Danny Farren.'

Jessica stood next to her car for a long time, taking this all in. She had just been handed something she'd wanted for a long time. Ever since she was a little girl, actually.

She had many memories of visiting a courtroom with her father, watching the wheels of justice turn. She remembered watching the prosecutors present their cases in a slow, methodical manner, leading a jury by the hand through the events of a crime.

Granted, very few of these prosecutors were women, but it never occurred to Jessica that a prosecutor *couldn't* be a woman, or that her gender would in any way be an obstacle to getting what she wanted.

She'd been on a direct course to law school until that horrible day in 1991 when her brother was killed in Kuwait. Michael Giovanni was going to be the cop, and Jessica Giovanni was going to be the lawyer.

Everything changed on the day Peter Giovanni buried his only son. Within a few years, after getting her undergraduate degree in criminal justice from Temple University, Jessica entered the Philadelphia Police Academy.

She never looked back. Even those times when she testified in court for one of her cases in the homicide unit, feeling a pull in the direction of the state's table, and the smartly dressed ADAs who worked in the homicide division of the DA's office.

Now she was there. Granted, she was second chair, but she was second chair to the unit chief, a man who had carved out such a stellar record as a prosecutor that he was the odds-on favorite to be the next District Attorney for the County of Philadelphia.

After that? Mayor Doyle? Governor Doyle?

Senator Doyle?

Jessica got in the car, started it, pulled out onto Torresdale Avenue. It was two blocks later that she realized she hadn't put her headlights on.

20

Anjelica Leary didn't often get her hair done, preferring most days to just pull it back, securing it in a rubber band. She'd lost most of her vanity – all except a nearly pathological belief in cleanliness – many years ago. The world did not look at sixty-eight-year-old women, and understandably so: not everyone had the genes or bone structure, not to mention the pocketbook, of a Hollywood star, now did they?

Still, when she'd woken this morning, a rare day off, she'd found a spring in her step. All was surely not right with the world, but Anjelica Leary could have a good day now and then. She'd earned it.

'What do you think today, Miss Leary?'

Whenever she pampered herself, she came to Nino Altieri's spa and salon on Locust Street. Nino was in his late fifties, unabashedly flamboyant, and as gossipy as a Dublin fishwife.

No matter how many times Anjelica had corrected him, he still called her Miss. Regardless of a woman's age or marital status, every female was a Miss. To that end, and in the name of equality, every man was a Master.

'Can you make me look like Helen Mirren?' Anjelica asked.

Nino laughed. 'You are already more beautiful. I can only enhance what is there, although I fear I may be gilding the lily.'

As Nino wielded his magic, he regaled her with stories about his most recent European adventures, which included stops in Palermo, Malta and Prague.

Anjelica had never been struck with wanderlust – the furthest from Philadelphia she had ever strayed was a week in Myrtle Beach – but as she listened to Nino's tales, she could find no reason not to one day soon take a proper vacation, going someplace she'd always wanted to visit. As much as she loved her job, and her patients, neither was really enough to deny her some happiness and adventure.

In the end, she treated herself to a protein treatment and a partial highlight, along with a deep clean and a soft mask.

She window-shopped on Walnut Street for a while, indulged herself with lunch at a small café on Sansom. She didn't get to Rittenhouse Square that often, and when she did, she was always reminded what a truly venerable and majestic place the city of her birth was.

It was easy to forget when you spent your days with your head down, caught up in the worries and trials of the day.

When she arrived home, she got out her cleaning supplies, for that was what she did on her days off. Before she changed into her old slacks and smock, she went through her closet, looked at the sorry state of her wardrobe. She had two nice dresses, both of them cosseted in dry-cleaning bags for the longest time. She took out her best dress, put it on and was pleasantly surprised to see that it still fit. With her freshly made-over hair and skin, and her deep-magenta frock, she thought she looked good. Still not Helen Mirren, but not bad for an old gal from South Philly.

She tried to imagine herself wearing the dress on the streets of Paris, London, Edinburgh. The thought set her pulse to quicken.

Before long she scolded herself for her schoolgirl folly, made herself a pot of Earl Grey, changed into her dowdy clothes.

As she drank her tea, she flipped on the television. The news said that a neighborhood man, Danny Farren, who was awaiting trial for the firebombing of a store, was now being charged with murder.

Tea finished, she set about her chores. This would have to be a proper cleaning; not a dust and vacuum and shut-the-shower-curtain job, but one that smelled of lemon oil.

Unless she was mistaken about such things – and she rarely was – she would soon be receiving company.

21

The DA's office had its own homicide division, which did much of the legwork that took place after an arrest had been made by the PPD and charges filed.

At nine o'clock, in Jimmy Doyle's office, in addition to Jessica and a detective from the DA's homicide unit, were three first-year ADAs.

Jessica knew she had overdressed for this meeting – not in the sense that she was wearing a ballgown and teardrop diamond earrings, as if she owned either – but her dark suit was pressed, her white blouse was starched and blindingly white, her only jewelry an inexpensive Timex watch and her wedding ring. A minimum of makeup; no perfume.

Jimmy slowly and methodically laid out the strategy they would undertake to build not only a case of first-degree murder against Danny Farren, but also a host of other charges, including racketeering and criminal conspiracy.

'I've spoken to the inspector, and the captains involved,'

Jimmy said. 'Choose anyone you like from our homicide investigation team. Jessica, you will also be on point with the homicide unit of the PPD. Your old stomping grounds.'

At this, a button on the desk phone flashed. Jimmy Doyle picked up the phone, punched the button. 'ADA Doyle.' He listened for a few seconds. 'That's fine. Thanks.'

A few moments later, Jessica sensed a presence behind her.

'I've simply got to talk to security around here,' Jimmy said with a smile, looking over Jessica's shoulder. She turned to see who was standing in the doorway.

It was Kevin Byrne.

Jessica had been so busy of late that she hadn't spoken to her old partner in a few months. They truly moved in different circles now. While she'd had dozens of police officers and detectives on the witness stand for direct examination, none had been from the homicide division.

Now, seeing her old partner filling the doorway in this place, her heart swelled. She wanted to throw her arms around him, but that would have been wrong in just about every possible way at this moment.

Byrne broke the rule for her. He gave her a quick, gentle hug. As always, despite the fact that she still carried a side arm, could handle herself with her fists and feet and had the power of subpoena, Jessica felt safe.

She'd always felt safe with her partner.

Byrne turned to Jimmy Doyle. 'Hey, brother.'

'You look good, Kev.'

The two men shook hands, did the half-hug, one-arm clap-on-the-back thing.

Tough Irish guys and their emotions, Jessica thought with an inner smile.

'Kevin will be point man and liaison with PPD Homicide on this.' Jimmy looked at Jessica. 'Will that work for you?'

'Absolutely,' Jessica said.

'Great. Danny Farren is going to be charged with murder later today. We all know that there is much more to his criminal enterprises than that. I want everything we can find on him. I want to bring the Farren chapter in Philadelphia to a close.'

Jimmy stepped around his desk, stood in front of Jessica and Byrne.

'If we do our jobs well, Danny Farren will never get out of prison,' he said. 'If we do our jobs *really* well, and catch a tailwind, he'll get a one-way ticket to Rockview.'

Jessica knew what he meant. The state correctional institution at Rockview was the only prison in the Commonwealth of Pennsylvania that carried out the death penalty.

'Any thoughts, questions, concerns?' Jimmy asked.

Jessica had a million of each. She decided to wait.

'Besides new evidence on the firebombing, what are we looking for?' Byrne asked.

'Anything and everything. Wherever the investigation takes you. I talked to your captain. You can put as many detectives as you want on this.'

'Much of this is going to be work for divisional detectives, though, Jimmy.'

Jimmy shook his head. 'Not this time. I want the best homicide detectives we have. Everything has been cleared.'

'Wherever it leads?' Byrne asked.

'Wherever it leads,' Jimmy said. 'Let's not be swayed by who the victim of this homicide was. As unsavory as the woman's lifestyle might have been, she was a citizen of this county, and if anyone counts, everyone counts.'

Jessica knew what he was saying, and that it needed to be said. Maybe not for Byrne or herself, but for the younger ADAs in the room.

The truth was, public agencies didn't always break a sweat

collecting evidence and prosecuting people who were responsible for the deaths of gang members or anyone on either side of the drug trade.

On the way out of the building, Jessica and Byrne ran into Graham Grande, who was on his way in. Byrne made the introduction.

'Graham was with the ID unit a little before your time,' Byrne said to Jessica.

'I was,' Graham said. 'My first job was dusting the Liberty Bell when it got cracked.'

'And as I recall, we closed the case,' Byrne said with a smile.

Graham turned to Jessica. He handed her a card. 'I've been doing a lot of work for the DA's office. Expert witness testimony, consulting,' he said. 'Keep me in mind if you ever need an old dab hand.'

'I sure will,' Jessica said.

After they said their goodbyes, Graham crossed the lobby, signed in and took the elevator to the eighteenth floor.

Jessica and Byrne walked to Reading Terminal Market for coffee. They sat at a table, caught up, as much as they could in the time they had.

'You guys go way back, don't you?' Jessica asked. 'You and Jimmy.'

Byrne sipped his coffee, nodded. He gave her a brief history of his summers in Devil's Pocket. He had never before mentioned any of this. Jessica wondered why, but didn't ask. There were many episodes in her childhood that she had not shared with Byrne.

She caught him up on Sophie and Carlos.

'Sophie misses you,' she said.

'I miss her. I can't believe all this time has passed. I won't let it happen again.'

'She has braces,' Jessica said. 'And a boyfriend.'

'Uh oh.'

'Tell me about it.'

'How's Vince taking it?'

'Like you'd expect,' Jessica said. 'Every time the kid comes to the door, Vincent answers it with a .45 ACP on his hip.'

Byrne laughed. 'I remember it well from when Colleen started dating. I'm not sure I'm over it yet.'

They caught up on their fathers, their extended families. Neither wanted to leave. But there was work to be done. A few minutes later they stood in front of the massive 3 South Penn Square, directly across from City Hall.

Jessica stopped, put a hand on Byrne's arm.

Byrne stopped walking. 'What?'

'I love the smell of City Hall in the morning,' Jessica said, doing her best Robert Duvall in *Apocalypse Now*. 'Smells like . . . justice.'

Byrne laughed. 'God, I've missed you, partner.'

Jessica sat in the passenger seat, Byrne at the wheel.

'Where to first?' she asked.

'I think we should take a look at the crime scene,' Byrne said. 'I've already talked to the bomb squad and a federal agent.'

Whenever a deliberately placed explosion occurred anywhere in Philadelphia County, an agent from the Bureau of Alcohol, Tobacco, Firearms and Explosives led the investigation. The PPD bomb squad took part as support personnel. Their main purview was the detection and de-arming of explosive ordnance.

As Byrne headed west on Market Street, Jessica thought about this case. She had investigated many homicides, but not from her current desk. This was different. When you were a cop, all you could think about was the arrest. When you were a DA, it was about presenting the evidence and winning the case.

As a cop, when you came across exculpatory evidence, you could go blind and deaf. As a DA, not so much.

Jessica hoped she could justify Jimmy Doyle's confidence in her. At this moment, she felt a little shaky about that.

As Byrne turned onto 21st Street, she spoke.

'The Farrens?'

'What about them?' Byrne asked.

'It seems you have a history with them, too.'

'God, are there any secrets in this town?'

Jessica just stared. Rhetorical question.

Byrne told her about Christmas Eve 1988, about the death of Patrick Farren and his role in it as a young detective working out of South, and about how, while being questioned about the savage beating of a woman named Miranda Sanchez, Patrick Farren had unwisely threatened a veteran cop named Frankie Sheehan with a gun.

Jessica had never met Frankie Sheehan, but she knew his name, his reputation, and that he had died in the line of duty.

'Frankie was never the same after that night,' Byrne said.

'How so?'

Byrne headed west on Lombard Street.

'Well, some people who are given to such things believed he was cursed.'

'Cursed?' Jessica asked. 'Like how?'

'Two weeks later his wife got into a bad wreck on the expressway. Frankie's cancer metastasized. Within two months he was first through the door at a drug house, which he had no business doing at his age. He was killed in the firefight.'

'I'm not sure any of that qualifies as a curse.'

Byrne took a moment. 'The Farrens are a menace, Jess. They harm everything they touch. Frankie's not the first person, certainly not the first cop, to cross swords with them and come out bad.'

There was something Byrne wasn't telling her, but that was okay. She could see that Frank Sheehan meant something to him, and she didn't want to press.

Still, as they turned onto 24th Street, Jessica considered what Byrne had told her, and felt a dark force, something obscure and inexorable, pulling her ever closer to Devil's Pocket.

III

Sídhe

22

Philadelphia, 1976

The city was alive with celebration over the bicentennial.

At just after 6 p.m., with The Stone packed to the rafters, Máire was in the kitchen, turning the whiskey sausages from Tully's. She sensed someone behind her.

It was Desmond. Desmond in his precious white suit.

'Where are you off to?' Máire asked.

'Going to the fireworks.'

'Are you now?'

'I like them,' Desmond said. 'I wish they were here all year.'

'Then no one would get anything done. Everyone would just stand about looking at the sky.'

Desmond laughed.

'Have you eaten?'

'I have, Ma.'

'Let me look at you,' Máire said.

Desmond buttoned his jacket, stood at attention. His suit was dirty. He had somehow cut his leg a day earlier, and there was dark brown blood on his right pant leg.

'Why don't you let me wash these trousers for you?' Máire asked. 'It won't take long.'

Desmond looked down, as if seeing the stain for the first time. He looked up. 'It's fine. I like them like this.'

'What am I going to do with you?'

Desmond again glanced down at his pant leg, thought for a moment. 'You know what they say.'

'What do they say?'

'Better good manners than good looks.'

Máire smiled. 'Character.'

'I love you, Ma.'

'You be careful crossing the street, Des.'

'I will.'

Before leaving, Desmond paused, as he always did, caught his reflection in the toaster, smoothed his hair and walked out the back door. When he got to the sidewalk, heading to the park, he turned and waved.

Máire never saw him alive again.

Later that day, at the Fourth of July festival in the park, the devil put his hands in both pockets.

At just after ten o'clock, fair little Catriona Daugherty was found strangled in the park that bordered South Taney Street.

The rumors flew fast and hot. Máire heard, and not from just one source, that people in the Pocket suspected her Desmond of the terrible sin. They said that he had put his eyes on Catriona years ago and that he had taken a length of rope that night and choked the life out of her.

The police came to The Stone, talked to Máire and Danny and Patrick. Desmond did not come home. Except for a short time in hospital, it was the first time he had not slept in his own bed.

For the next four days, Máire and her boys combed the streets from Washington to Lombard, from the avenue to the river, knocking on doors, looking in garages and alleys and basements, hoping for the best, knowing the worst.

On the morning of July 9, there was a knock at the back door. Máire opened the door to a young policeman, who told her that a man had been found, shot to death, beneath the South Street bridge. He asked that Máire come down to the morgue to see if the dead man was her Desmond.

It was.

For the second time in two years, Máire found herself at the river's edge, a bar of soap in one hand, a basket of clothes next to her. She stayed till dawn, and finally got the blood from Desmond's white suit.

1978

On the night Deena gave birth to two beautiful boys, the moon shone brightly over South Philadelphia. She named them Sean and Michael. They were light, but they were healthy.

When Máire held them both for the first time, she felt the feelings surge within her. Although Sean was beautiful, she knew the first time she saw Michael that he had the gift.

That night she stole back into the nursery, sat between them. It was Michael's small hand she held as she recited the poem.

> Where dips the rocky highland
> Of Sleuth Wood in the lake,
> There lies a leafy island
> Where flapping herons wake . . .

Christmas Eve 1988

By the time Patrick Farren was murdered – gunned down in his prime by the police – the Pocket had changed. Gone were the drinking clubs and potluck dinners. Now it was about a drug called crack cocaine. The Stone had been robbed twice in the past two years. Only once did Danny and Patrick find the men who did it and put them under the sod.

At 8 p.m., the bar was only half full, with many of the regulars drinking at home with their families. Danny and his sons were off to the mall for last-minute shopping. Patrick was cozied up with one of his girls in the corner, a pretty girl Máire had seen in the bar a number of times.

A few minutes later, the two of them left.

The call came at just after midnight. Máire knew before her hand touched the receiver.

Patrick was dead, murdered at the hands of the police.

Two of her boys gone now. Poor Desmond in 1976, and now Patrick.

But the devil was not done with the Farrens on this night. In an attempt to save his Uncle Patrick, young Michael was struck by a car. The boy hit his head on the frozen pavement.

As Christmas Day dawned, Michael Farren lay in a coma, just like his grandfather so many years ago in County Louth.

He would not wake for nearly two years.

Each night Máire would read to the boy and play music. Like his grandfather in Dundalk, Michael did not respond. Many a night found Máire watching the boy's eyes, his face, his hands, hoping for a reaction.

All the doctors and books said it was likely that Michael was aware of his surroundings, that he could hear what people said, and that it was a good thing to play music for him. While

Máire's taste in music was traditional, she felt that her grandson would not respond to ballads and laments and reels.

Patrick had been the lover boy, and had all the tools of the gigolo's craft. Dozens and dozens of LPs. Night after night Máire would put them on, hoping for a reaction from Michael. All the British and Irish bands from Patrick's era as a young man – Cream, the Groundhogs, Thin Lizzy, Chicken Shack, Taste, Roxy Music.

One evening, while flipping through them, she saw something that made her heart flutter. A strange-looking album that had depicted on its cover a mouth-puller, a carved stone icon used in medieval Ireland to ward off intruders and evil spirits. Máire's own grandmother had had one on the front door of the house when she was growing up in Dundalk.

When Máire turned it over, she saw that the band was called The Stark.

She put the album on, and just a few seconds in, she could see that Michael was responding to it. It was the first time in nearly eighteen months. As the song played, she saw his eyes move beneath his eyelids, his fingers lift and fall to the rhythm, a color returning to his face.

The song was called 'Billy the Wolf'.

1996

By the time Michael and Sean had bested eighteen, they were known throughout the Pocket, and much of south Philadelphia, as the founding members of the River Boys. Their father Daniel – Máire's last remaining son – presented a patriarchal face and presence, and no decision was made without him.

It was a long road back physically for Michael, who was weak and atrophied from his coma, but Máire had never seen anyone

201

work harder. Many a dawn found him behind The Stone, a makeshift set of barbells at his feet. He set up a small boxing ring in the cellar and took on any and all comers, regardless of their weight. Many times he was overmatched and took a beating, but he never quit.

He spent his days getting physically stronger, and his nights reading. Máire had never seen so many books as she saw in his room in the basement.

But while he overcame his physical problems, the face blindness that Michael had begun to exhibit not long after coming out of his long fever dream, the inability to recognize even members of his own family, stayed with him.

Máire did what she could to help. Placing notes on everything, making a schedule for Michael to keep, pinning pictures of everyone in his room. Still, as often as he knew who she was, he did not know her from Eve. As the boys' criminal enterprise grew, it became more and more of a problem.

In those years, Michael stuck close to Sean. Whenever someone crossed or cursed the Farren name, Sean and Michael brought the man to the cellar beneath The Stone, and there he learned his manners.

One man, a butcher by trade, had failed to make a payment for two months. He was carved with his own stag-handle knife.

As the millennium approached, Máire Farren had one son left, and two grandsons, one of them damaged. The Stone had fallen on hard times, and the Pocket was well on its way to gentrification, with talk of the Naval Home being turned into condominiums.

Máire knew that all of it was down to the curse.

Go n-ithe an cat thú is go n-ithe an diabhal an cat.

If Máire had inherited anything from her grandmother, it was patience. She would wait to find the right moment, and when that moment came, the curse would be lifted.

As she sat at the end of the bar, folding the last of five linen handkerchiefs, the ones with blue lace around the edges, she knew it would be Michael who would lift the curse.

No, she amended, it would be Billy the Wolf.

23

Philadelphia, 2015

When Byrne picked Jessica up at home, it felt like no time at all had passed.

The best part, for Jessica, was that she was able to dress down for a change.

ADAs frequently visited crime scenes, but rarely when the scenes were fresh. The possibility of witnessing evidence being collected left too much room for defense counsel to claim that it had been tainted by prosecutorial zeal and was thereby inadmissible.

This was different. This crime scene was now two months old. The forensics had long been collected, collated, analyzed and recorded. The crime-scene tape was down.

Still, even though the scene was cold, the charge was hot.

The bomb unit of the Philadelphia Police Department was headquartered in a new facility on State Road. Also in the complex was the police academy, as well as the K-9 unit.

Jessica and Byrne had visited the exterior of the crime scene building once, taking a few photos of the space, which was still boarded up. Today they would get inside.

On the way to the location, Jessica reviewed the reports generated by the South Detective Division, the unit that had investigated the original case. She knew that no detective ever wanted a case taken away from them – when you had your boots on the ground first, you wanted to cross the finish line, including testifying in court and seeing the suspect convicted, all based on your due diligence.

Still, the moment Jacinta Collins died, and the ME ruled it was a homicide, the two South Division detectives who were running the case knew there would soon be a knock on the door. Jessica felt for them – she'd worked on a number of cases with Byrne where the FBI stepped in when federal laws were found to have been violated.

Today they would meet with an officer from the PPD bomb squad and get a walk-through.

Byrne parked the car on Webster Street. Before he could get out, Jessica reached into her bag, took out an envelope. She handed it to Byrne.

'What is this?' he asked.

'Open it.'

Byrne gave it a moment. If Jessica knew anything about her partner, she knew he didn't like surprises. He slowly lifted the flap of the envelope, took out the contents.

'Oh my God,' he said. It was a 4x6 print of a photograph of Sophie Balzano.

'She took a selfie,' Jessica said. 'She wants you to have it.'

'She's so beautiful,' Byrne said. 'I can't believe how much she's grown. I just saw her two months ago. How does this happen?'

'Tell me about it.'

Sophie had changed her outfit ten times before deciding on her best navy-blue cashmere sweater and her silver crucifix pendant. Because of her braces she didn't smile, but she decided after printing off the picture that this made her look even more mature. It did.

'I love it, Jess,' Byrne said. 'Thanks. Tell Sophie thanks. I'll cherish this.'

'Ahem.'

Byrne looked over. 'What?'

'She wants a picture of you.'

He reddened a little. 'Oh. Okay. Sure. Remind me in the next day or two. I'll take one.'

Jessica held up her iPhone. 'No time like the present,' she said. 'A famous detective friend of mine used to say that to me all the time.'

'What?' Byrne asked. 'Now?'

'Fix your hair.'

The commander of the PPD bomb squad was Zachary Brooks. After twelve years as a patrolman on the street, where he worked the 14th District, a slot opened up in SWAT, the Special Weapons and Tactical Unit. At thirty-six, much older than anyone else in the highly physical unit, Zach Brooks took the job and became one of its top officers. Four years later, he moved over to the bomb squad.

The bomb squad often worked with the homicide unit on fire-related deaths.

They met outside the crime-scene location. Zach was about thirty minutes late.

'Zach, this is Jessica Balzano. She's with the DA's office now, but she was my partner in Homicide for ten years.'

'I've heard the name,' Zach said with a smile. 'A pleasure.'

'Here too,' Jessica said.

'Sorry I'm late,' he said. 'Had a job.'

'Was that the call to the Federal Building?' Jessica asked. She'd seen something about it on the early-morning news.

Zach nodded. 'A package was left on top of one of the cars in the underground parking level. We went in to assist the BATFE. Did an RSP.'

An RSP was a remove safe procedure. Depending on the device, the threat level, it could be as simple as an X-ray to determine whether the package was benign, or one that required the use of a blast containment receptacle.

'What was it?' Byrne asked.

'Believe it or not, it was a spice rack. Someone in the US Attorney's office brought it in to give to a co-worker at a bridal shower, and left it on top of her car.'

'Are you sure that was garlic powder in there?' Byrne asked.

Zach laughed. 'Situation volatile but contained, detective.'

'Glad you could make it down,' Byrne added. 'Much appreciated.'

'Any time.'

Most of the questions they were about to ask had already been asked by the detectives from South. Now that the charge was going to be murder, they needed to be asked again.

Zach held up a set of keys. 'Ready?'

'Ready.'

He took a laptop out of his shoulder bag, opened it, put it on the roof of Byrne's car. He pointed to the boarded-up window facing Stillman Street.

'According to the surveillance video shot by the pole cam on the corner, the suspect walked east on Webster Street at approximately 9.21 p.m.'

Zach played the surveillance video. On the screen, made a

207

glowing green by the low light level, they could see a man walking toward the crime scene building. It would not stand alone as evidence in court, but it was a man they knew to be Danny Farren. When he was arrested two days later, the clothing he wore on the video – a gray leather jacket and dark flannel slacks – was taken as evidence.

On the recording, Danny Farren disappeared from view at the left side of the frame.

For the next five minutes the only movement on the video was the occasional car moving up or down the street.

At the 9.26 mark, Farren re-entered the frame, walking away from the building.

At 9.28, the camera shook violently, just as a blinding flash filled the frame. Glass was blown into the street, and what appeared to be a cloud of gypsum rained down. Smoke billowed.

When the smoke began to clear, the street and sidewalk could be seen to be covered in small shards of glass. A few minutes later, a handful of residents began to gather on the opposite side of the street. Nearly all had their cell phone cameras out.

At the 9.46 mark, a PFD ladder truck arrived on scene.

'Can we see that again?' Jessica asked.

'Sure.'

Zach tapped a few keys. The video restarted.

Jessica looked closely as Danny Farren entered the frame. The image was grainy, but he seemed to be holding something in his left hand. It appeared to be a rolled-up newspaper. Perhaps a magazine.

'Can we stop it right there?' Jessica asked.

Zach did.

Jessica tapped the screen. Specifically, Danny Farren's left hand.

'Is that consistent with the size and shape of the device used here?' she asked. It looked as if Farren had his hand wrapped around the object, as opposed to carrying it like a bag.

'I've watched this a few times during the investigation by South detectives, and afterwards, in anticipation of testifying at trial,' Zach said. 'Obviously it's not the clearest picture, but I would have to say it is consistent.'

'Can we move forward to where he walks back in frame?'

'Sure.' Zach moved the scrubber bar a bit to the right. When Farren entered the frame on the left, seconds before the explosion, he tapped a key to make the recording enter slow motion. With this type of surveillance footage, there was no smooth slow motion. Instead it was a series of still shots. With Farren dead center in the frame, Zach hit pause.

Jessica looked closely. It was impossible to tell if Farren still had the object in his left hand, as it was shielded by his body. It did not appear that he swung his arms much, so his left hand did not enter the frame.

'Can anyone see if he still has something in his hand?'

Both Byrne and Zach admitted that it was impossible to tell.

Jessica knew that as an investigating police officer, it would have been enough to bring Farren in, and probably charge him. In a court of law, it would be a tough sell. It was a dilemma she was facing more and more as an ADA.

Zach let the video play. Once again, the force of the blast made Jessica wince. She'd been around firearms her whole life, had gone to a range with her father since she was ten, and had a healthy respect for weapons, but no fear.

Explosive ordnance was another matter.

When the smoke cleared, she realized that it was not only glass that was glistening on the sidewalk. According to the report, and the weather report for that night, there had been a slight drizzle on and off.

'Let's say that *is* a rolled-up newspaper or magazine in his hand,' she said. 'Was the device used the kind that needed to be kept dry?'

'With the type of fuse that was used, the drier the better.'

'And would a newspaper or magazine be enough to keep it shielded from the rain?'

'Definitely.'

Jessica took the information in. She was beginning to formulate a case. She made a mental note to talk to the detectives who'd arrested Farren, and see if there was an inventory of items found in his car.

If there was a magazine or newspaper in there, dated the day of the bombing or before, they would process it for trace evidence to connect it to the bomb.

'Can you walk us through the scene?' Byrne asked.

'Let's do it.'

Zach closed the laptop, returned it to his shoulder bag. He took out a ring of keys, found the one he was looking for, slipped it into the padlock of the temporary door on the front of the store.

He unlocked the door, propped it open.

The first thing Jessica noticed was the smell of burned wood and plastic. Beneath it all was the smell of sulfur.

Zach crossed the room to a battery-powered halogen lamp, flicked it on. The room was instantly aglow with a bright white light.

Jessica got her first look at the crime scene. She'd seen photographs on the way in, but there was no substitute for standing in the place where the crime had been committed.

To the left was what remained of three long glass display cases. The frames still stood, but the glass was in piles on the floor.

Zach pointed to an area about five feet in from the side window.

'This is the blast seat.'

'This is where the device detonated?' Jessica asked.

'Yes. The suspect broke this window, tossed the device in. I'm presuming he wanted to have it detonate in the center of the room, but it looks like this hanging conduit may have stopped the forward progress.'

Jessica saw that there was a depression in the vinyl flooring, and a black oval.

'What can you tell us about the device itself?'

'It was a pipe bomb,' Zach said. 'The container was two-inch-diameter galvanized forged steel, approximately ten inches long. Available at any Home Depot.'

Jessica knew that a running joke among BATFE agents and bomb techs was to refer to Home Depot as Terrorists R Us.

Zach broke down the type of explosive, the blasting cap and the fuse. He walked to the back wall, shone his Maglite on it. He then ran his hand over an area of about three or four square feet. 'Do you see these small fragments?'

Jessica slipped on her glasses. There, embedded in the dry-wall, were dozens of small metal shards.

'This is from the container itself. The galvanized pipe. Had the explosive been black powder or flash powder, the pipe might have broken into only three or four pieces. With this material, it exploded into a thousand.' He ran his light along the ceiling and the far walls. The fragments were everywhere.

'Did you find any ball bearings, nails?' Byrne asked.

'No.'

Jessica looked at Byrne. A silent understanding passed between them.

'It was a low-tech device, not that hard to make or de-arm,' Zach continued. 'If we'd known about it, we could have taken it out.'

'What about the projectile?' Jessica asked.

'That was one of the end caps. The subject put the explosive in, along with the cap. He then drilled a small hole in the other end cap, put it on the pipe and ran his fuse through it. He taped the fuse to the side, lit it, tossed it through the window.'

'And he could be sure that the tape wouldn't put it out?' Byrne asked.

'Absolutely. They burn hot.'

Byrne walked over to the wall opposite the window where the bomb had been thrown. The force of the blast had all but fused the sheetrock to the studs, bowing the drywall between the uprights. In the center of the wall, behind where the glass display cabinets had stood, was a hole no more than three inches in diameter, the sheetrock pushed in all around it.

Jessica had seen the crime-scene photographs, and understood what this was, but seeing it in person brought with it a wave of sadness.

'This is where the end cap went through?' Byrne asked.

Zach crossed the room. 'Yes. With something this highly explosive, a fragment – in this instance a five-ounce piece of galvanized forged steel – will travel at around thirteen hundred feet per second.'

Jessica knew enough about firearms to know that 1,300 feet per second was roughly the equivalent of a high-velocity .22 LR bullet.

On the evening Danny Farren tossed the pipe bomb into the store window, the row house just west of the scene had long ago been abandoned and boarded up.

Jacinta Collins had pushed in through the back door, apparently looking for a place to cook heroin. Detectives had found her dealer, who, on condition of immunity for this one sale, confirmed that he had sold Jacinta black tar about thirty minutes before the blast. The very definition of wrong place, wrong time. The heroin, spoon and works were found next to her body.

She was sitting on the floor in the back room, no more than fifteen feet from where the pipe bomb landed.

The projectile blasted through the old wooden lath and dry plaster, striking her on the right side of her face, between the right eye and her temple.

Firefighters responding to the call saw the hole in the wall, and subsequently found the victim. The woman had lain in an induced coma for the past two months. When the investigating detectives arrested Danny Farren, he was charged, among other things, with aggravated assault.

Now it was murder.

They stood on the sidewalk next to the window through which Danny Farren had thrown the pipe bomb. Zach Brooks had locked the building and made a DVD copy of the footage.

Byrne held up the DVD. 'Thanks for this.'

'Anything you need.'

As Zach climbed into his truck, Jessica and Byrne stood across from the store, each with their own thoughts. Even outside, two months after the bombing, the whole block smelled faintly of charred wood and plastic.

'We're not going to get Murder One out of this,' Jessica said.

'Why not?'

'Mainly because Danny Farren didn't load the bomb with ball bearings or small nails, which, as you know, is the preferred design when the criminal intent is to do bodily harm, the preferred design of homicide bombers,' Jessica said. 'The case for the defense will be that Farren's intent was to do damage to the structure, not cause injury or death.'

The fact that he would be charged with causing the death of

213

Jacinta Collins was foregone. It would be up to the DA to decide on the degree.

Still, if a case was going to be presented to a grand jury, anything was possible. Jessica knew her orders. Find anything and everything.

Byrne gave voice to the second thing they were both thinking.

'If you're extorting money from someone for protection, why would you destroy something that would generate income?'

The answer was in the mad-dog nature of men like Danny Farren. The message was in the force of his response. The man who owned the building, Kenneth Zelman, had refused to comment on the incident. He was clearly in the grip of Danny Farren's extortion scheme, and telling the police would have incurred further wrath. Jessica figured that after the firebombing, the man somehow found the money to pay.

Before she could reply, Byrne's phone rang. He took a few steps away, answered the call. A minute later he returned. He looked grim.

'What is it?'

'That was Captain Ross,' he said.

'What's up?'

'Even though the victim's grandmother has already begun funeral preparations, I have to notify her officially. No one from the department has done it.'

'Let's go and make the visit,' Jessica said.

Byrne looked up, a bit surprised. 'You don't have to go, Jess.'

Jessica opened the car door. 'Says who?'

24

Muriel Davis lived in a block of houses in North Philly that had always broken Jessica's heart.

Jessica reckoned she had gone through most of her life just this side of the glass being half full, an optimism she carried through her time in school, through the academy and then onto the street. When she got to Homicide, she noticed that the outlook had begun to erode, that she was suddenly trying to sweep the sand off the beach with a whisk broom. Working homicides, along with Special Victims, brought you into contact on a daily basis with the worst kind of human behavior.

Still, for many years she wanted to believe that people could rise above their circumstances, that being born into the kind of poverty and despair that was evident in this part of her city – a section she had not visited since her time in Homicide – was not necessarily a death sentence, or a ticket to prison.

Muriel Davis's row house was struggling. Small touches such as lace curtains on the second-floor windows were grace notes. The old trinity was badly in need of repair.

The woman who answered the door was in much better shape. Muriel Davis was thin, no more than five-four. Her silver-white hair was pulled back in a bun. She wore a bright aqua cardigan and black slacks.

Before Jessica could introduce herself and Byrne, the woman ushered them in. She'd been expecting a visit.

The parlor was clean and dust free, with doilies on the old waterfall tables, as well as the back and arms of the camelback sofa. The mantelpiece was four deep in family photos. Above was a painting of the Sacred Heart of Jesus in a gilt frame.

Without formally offering, Muriel Davis had gone to the kitchen and returned with an array of butter cookies on a plate. Even the plate had a doily.

'First of all, Mrs Davis, on behalf of the City of Philadelphia, let me say how sorry we are for your loss.'

The woman just nodded. Being so long after the moment Jacinta went into a coma, it looked as if Muriel Davis had done her grieving. Or maybe she'd gotten it done years ago in anticipation. There was pain in her eyes, but no tears.

'Jacie's mama Pearl was all part of that, you know,' she said.

'Part of what, ma'am?' Byrne asked.

'Doing the drugs, acting out. She was barely out of grade school when I lost my hold on her. Pearl had Jacie at sixteen, went in and out of jail, court-ordered rehab.'

'Where is she now?'

Muriel picked up a photograph from the end table, a faded picture of a tall, lanky girl, clearly in the grip of the Pointer Sisters fashion craze, posing in front of a vintage Delta 88. 'Oh, she passed. Long time now. Wasn't no drugs killed her, though.'

'How did she die, if I may ask?'

Muriel ran a finger over the photograph. 'She stay with this violent boy. Called him Ray Ray on account he had this stutter. He come home one night, found Pearl had spent the last of his

216

drug money on food and medicine for Jacie. Took a steak knife to her. Had to bury her closed. Couldn't fix her face.'

'I'm so sorry, ma'am,' Byrne said.

'Thank you.'

'What about Jacie's father?'

Muriel put the photograph down. 'Jacie's daddy was never part of her life. I don't think she ever met him but twice. And that was when he came around to get his benefits. When that ran out he was long gone, off to his next baby mama.'

She sat back, crossed her hands on her lap.

'You raise them up the best you can with what the good Lord give you to work with. Only got but two hands, and one of them don't work with the arthritis.'

'Before the incident when she was injured, when was the last time you saw Jacinta?' Byrne asked.

Muriel thought for a few moments. 'It was two days before. She dropped off her babies, told me she was going on a job interview.'

'Two children?'

Muriel nodded. She pointed to the Olan Mills-type photograph on the wall. It was one of those settings where the older sibling was sitting behind the infant. An adorable girl and boy.

'Tia is five now,' Muriel said. 'Little Andre is three.'

Jessica saw Byrne take a moment, gather his thoughts. 'I want you to know that before, when the case against Danny Farren was aggravated assault, it was one thing. There were some very good detectives on that investigation, and they did a great job. With the work they did, Danny Farren was going to go away for a long time.'

He paused for a moment, continued.

'Now it's different. Now it's a charge of murder, as it should be. I want you to know that Danny Farren will never take one breath as a free man.'

217

'Every breath he takes is one that my granddaughter has been denied. If I could have her alive and in jail, I'd choose that.'

Jessica and Byrne said nothing.

Muriel pointed to a spot in the center of the worn living room rug. 'Jacie used to sit there, under the Lord's watchful eye, and open her Christmas presents. Every year she'd take the longest time opening her gifts.' She looked up at Jessica. 'You know how some children just tear off the paper, like they think the gift might be gone by the time they get inside the box?'

Jessica did. She had two of them at home. 'Oh yes.'

'Not Jacie. She'd peel back the tape and gently slide out the box. Then she'd fold the paper, make a neat pile of it. See, she knew we didn't have much, and she saw no reason to waste. Every year, for years – birthdays, Christmas, Easter – we'd reuse that paper. Still have some.'

Muriel pointed to a bookshelf. On the bottom was an oversized atlas. Sticking out were a dozen sheets of brightly colored paper.

Jessica stood, wanting to leave before her emotions crept up on her.

They made their goodbyes.

At the door, Byrne handed Muriel a card. 'If there's anything the city can do to make your arrangements easier, please don't hesitate to call.'

Muriel took the card, nodded a thanks. She opened the door for them, paused.

'I know what Jacie did, Mr Byrne, who she was, who she ran with,' she said. 'I could not find a way to love her any less. Didn't want to, didn't even try. Got my own reckoning coming soon.'

'Not for years,' Byrne said.

Muriel smiled. 'Oh Lord. Listen to you.'

*

They sat at the curb, in silence, for a long time. Each of them received phone calls. They both looked at their phones, hit ignore.

Finally Byrne spoke. 'You okay?'

Jessica wasn't okay. 'I haven't made a notification in a while. This was tough. I don't ever want to forget this feeling.'

Byrne nodded. 'It's amazing how they never get easier. I mean, you know the words to say, but each time is just as difficult.'

'This poor woman,' Jessica said. 'She lost her daughter to violence, lost her granddaughter to violence.'

She glanced down the street, at the hundreds of row houses, as far as she could see. She knew there was a personal drama playing out in all of them. She knew that in many of them there were stories not dissimilar to Muriel Davis's, stories of heartbreak and sorrow and anger.

She wondered if she and Byrne and all the people who spoke on behalf of these people would ever make a difference. She glanced at Muriel Davis's house and knew that she had to focus on *this* case, *this* story, *this* life.

Grief, she had come to believe, had a half-life. It might lessen by degree over the years, but it never fully left your heart. What had once been a case, a case she'd gotten less than twenty-four hours earlier, now had a face.

She would find justice, wherever it was hiding, for Jacinta Collins.

25

Billy paced in front of the library. He had taken two showers, washed and conditioned his hair, combed and re-combed it many times. He wore new jeans and a white dress shirt he had not taken from the closet in two years.

As he walked back and forth, he saw a man in the library watching him. He had noticed the man watching him and Emily in the past.

Gray jacket. Patched elbows. Black frame glasses.

When Emily came out the front doors, Billy found that he was holding his breath. She wore a peach-colored dress.

As they walked, she took his arm.

They stopped in front of Circuit World, an old-school electronics and ham-radio emporium that had been at this location for more than fifty years. The store could not compete with the big box stores and chain outlets like Radio Shack and Best Buy, but it did carry exotic and hard-to-find items for the radio and home hobby enthusiast

'Would you like to come in with me?' Billy asked.

Emily raised her face to the sun. 'I think I'll stay out here. It's such a nice day.'

Billy assisted her to a nearby bus stop bench. She sat down. 'I won't be long,' he said.

Emily smiled. She touched her watch. 'I'll count the minutes.'

Billy entered the store, soon found what he needed, paid cash, as always, and was out of the building in short order. He sat down next to Emily on the bench. When he saw the SEPTA bus coming, he took her hand. They walked in silence toward Federal.

As they crossed the street, Emily asked: 'Did you find what you were looking for?'

'I did,' Billy said. 'They have everything in there.'

When Emily didn't respond, Billy glanced at her. She was smiling.

'What?' Billy asked.

'Aren't you going to tell me?'

'Tell you what?'

'What you bought?'

Billy looked at the package. 'It's nothing really.'

'Is it something naughty?' she asked. 'Will I be scandalized and led to a life of debauchery and hedonistic pursuits?'

Billy reddened. 'Nothing like that. It's a motion detector,' he said. 'Battery-operated. The kind with an alarm.'

'A motion detector?'

'Yes,' Billy said. 'What you do is, you put it in the corner of a room and turn it on. Then, if anyone walks across its field, it goes off with a really loud alarm.'

Emily stopped walking and waved a hand. 'Well you don't need it,' she said. 'You can just take it back.'

'What do you mean?'

'Take it back to the store and hire me.'

'Hire you?'

'Don't be fooled by my girlish looks and retiring nature. I am an expert motion detector.'

Billy laughed. 'Are you now?'

'I am,' she said. She offered a hand. 'Walk me over to this building.'

Billy took her hand. They crossed the sidewalk. They stood in front of a storefront church.

A few moments passed. When the traffic slowed, two people crossed the street, walking west on Federal.

'Two people just went by,' Emily said. 'An adult and a child.'

She was right. 'Yes. That's pretty good.'

'I'm not done.'

'Okay.'

'The adult was a woman. I'd say in her mid-to-late twenties. The child was a girl, not much older than two. And I'd say they were both dressed up.'

She was right about this, as well. 'How do you know?'

'I've had a lot of practice being blind,' she said. 'But since you ask, I knew it was a woman because I smelled her perfume. It was a modern fragrance, nothing an older woman would buy. As to the child, I heard the sound of short footsteps. I knew they were dressed up because the woman was wearing heels, and the child was wearing hard-soled shoes.'

Billy was stunned. 'You're hired. I'm taking this back.'

Emily laughed.

After their walk, they sat in silence on the stone bench outside the main entrance to the library. At one o'clock, Emily touched her watch. 'I have to get back.'

Billy took a deep breath. 'I need to tell you something.'

'Of course,' she said.

'I think I'm going away for a while.'

'Okay.'

'I just wanted to let you know.'

Emily reached out, touched his shoulder. 'I hope it's nothing bad.'

Billy had no idea what it was going to be. He said, simply: 'No. I'm just going to France.'

'Oh my goodness! How exciting!'

He wanted to explain it all to her – she was the only person in the world for whom he cared enough to tell – but he had no idea where to begin.

He glanced away for a second. When he looked back, a tear was running down Emily's cheek.

'What's wrong?'

'I'm going to miss my flowers.'

Billy hadn't expected this. 'Well, I can—'

'I always know when you come into the library. Did you know that?'

'No,' he said. 'How?'

'I can smell the roses when you walk past the front desk.'

Billy suddenly felt embarrassed. He felt like a stalker. He had often walked right in front of her and waited hours to find the courage to talk to her. Now he knew that *she* knew that.

Before he could respond, he sensed someone approaching. He instinctively brought his hand near his pocket, his weapon.

'Is everything okay, Em?' the stranger asked.

Billy turned to see a short, thick-waisted man in his thirties. *Gray jacket. Patched elbows. Black frame glasses.* It was the man who worked at the library. The man who had watched him.

'She's fine,' Billy said.

The man took a step closer.

'Emily? Are you okay?' he repeated.

'I said—'

The man put a hand on Billy's chest. 'I'd like to hear it from her.'

Billy bladed his body to the man, opened his coat. The man looked down, saw the Makarov.

'I'm fine, Alex,' Emily said. 'Really.'

Billy stared at the man's featureless face, mouthed the words: *Walk away now*.

The man backed slowly away. A few seconds later, he disappeared around the corner.

'I have to go,' Billy said. There was more he wanted to say, much more. He had even thought he might have the courage to ask Emily if she wanted to go to France with him. He thought that, somehow, if she stood in front of the painting with him . . .

It no longer mattered.

'I understand,' she said.

'You'll get back okay?'

Emily laughed, wiped the last tear. 'I've been doing it for six years. I'll make it, Michael.'

Michael.

He had never told her his other name, but she had found out because he needed a library card to access the reference books. He'd had the same library card since he was sixteen.

As he walked down Federal Street, his anger began to grow. It soon became a furious, writhing thing inside him.

Ten minutes later, he returned to the library. There, parked in front of the main entrance, was a police car. Through the window Billy could see Emily and the man she called Alex – *gray jacket, patched elbows. black frame glasses* – standing next to the magazine area, talking to two policemen.

As the white squall built inside, Billy knew two things.

One: he could never go back to the library. He would never see Emily again.

Two: the police would know his name and address.

*

Billy spent the rest of the afternoon in a dive bar on Wharton called The Jade Kettle. It was dark, with only a handful of patrons, hardcore midday drinkers.

Billy needed it dark. He needed the quiet.

As he nursed his sixth bourbon, a woman walked over.

'Hi,' she said. Billy turned to face her.

White T-shirt. Auburn hair. Silver bracelets.

'Hi.'

'Okay if I sit down?' she asked.

'I'm afraid I'm not going to be very good company.'

'Having a bad day?'

'When bad days have a bad day, it's better than this.'

She laughed. 'Sounds like a challenge.'

She slipped onto the stool.

'What's your name?' she asked.

Billy leaned back, tried to take better measure of this girl in the dim light. She was in her early twenties, too pretty for The Jade Kettle by a prison yard. The bars in Center City and Northern Liberties drew them, certainly Old City and the Sugar House, maybe Fishtown, the hotel bars. No girl this pretty who wasn't a working girl wandered into The Jade Kettle unescorted. Certainly not in the middle of the day.

Her accent said south Jersey.

'Billy,' he said. 'My name is Billy.'

'I'm Megan.'

They shook hands.

Megan leaned back, assessed him once again. 'You don't look like a Billy.'

'Really now?'

'Really.'

Billy drained his glass, called for another. It would be his seventh. He ordered one for the girl.

When they were served, he glanced at the door. He was hot.

Cops any minute now. The Makarov was heavy in his waistband. His feet were on the floor.

He looked at the girl.

White T-shirt. Auburn hair. Silver bracelets.

'What do I look like?' he asked.

'I think you look like a Malcolm.'

'I once had an uncle named Malcolm.'

She sipped her drink. 'See? I'm prescient.'

She didn't expect him to know the word. He did, of course. He'd learned it at the library. The thought of Emily's co-worker Alex brought a fresh shard of anger.

'Actually, my uncle's name was Desmond.'

'Now you're trying to confuse me.'

'I am,' he said. 'It's all part of my master plan.'

'So where is Uncle Desmond these days?'

'Long below the sod. A victim of low morals and evil intent.'

She didn't know what he meant. As the bourbon took hold, he found he didn't care.

'His middle name was Malcolm,' he added.

'I get it,' she said. 'So. Billy. Billy what?'

Billy drained his drink, rattled the cubes, got the bartender's attention. He had a pair of hundreds on the bar. They would not cut him off here.

He leaned in, whispered: 'Billy the Wolf.'

She snorted a laugh into her hand. Billy handed her a napkin. She took it.

As she finished her drink she asked: 'Tell me, Billy the Wolf.'

'What?'

'You have a place nearby?'

He took her to Sean's old room in the basement of The Stone, now just a single bed and a nightstand, a few years of dust and mildew on the floor and drapes.

He found that he had been right. She was a working girl.

He settled with her before they made love.

It was the dream of the dream.

In it he is cold and afraid. His father's hand is on his shoulder. As always, there are two men – big men in long winter coats – standing nearby. One man is on the sidewalk, one man is just on the street, at the curb, standing between two parked cars.

Uncle Pat is standing in the middle of the road.

Snow is falling.

From somewhere in the distance comes the sound of a reggae version of 'The Little Drummer Boy'.

There is an explosion of gunfire. Four blinding white lights come out of the darkness. He is flying, falling. He finds himself in the pitch dark, his face against cold stone. When he sits up, it feels as if the ceiling is very high, almost as high as the sky. But there are no stars. It is a hall of black mirrors, but every time he looks into one, there is no one there.

He hears voices. Familiar voices. He hears people praying in both English and Irish. He hears music. It seems to be coming down a long metal pipe, has a carnival sound. He hears a hissing noise, like vapor from a teakettle. It seems to surround him.

And he walks. Mile after mile. Sometimes the walls are closer, and feel like metal: cold and smooth and unblemished. Sometime he feels the presence of other people, perhaps animals, but they dart from shadow to shadow, and he never gets a good look. In the darkest places, the long distances between the mirrors, he hears them keening and crying, mournful sounds that reach the endless night sky, and fall like rain.

And he walks. River to river. He can hear the gulls, the slap of the water against the piers.

Beneath it all, beneath the sounds of keening animals and

escaping vapor, beneath the sobbing and reciting of prayers, there is always music.

He hears songs about a white room. He hears songs about blood running cherry red. He hears songs about a woman named Virginia Plain, a song about how the boys are back in town.

One night he hears a song that speaks to him in a way that no song ever has.

> *Take heed, Billy, the wolves come out at night.*
> *Run with the pack, don't turn back,*
> *Hide from the morning light.*

That's who he is. He is Billy the Wolf.

One day, as he is walking, he sees a faint light ahead. At first it is burning red; it shimmers to orange and then to gold.

As the light grows in intensity, drawing him ever nearer, he hears the scream. It is far away, but it begins to grow in volume and urgency—

Billy opened his eyes.

A woman was screaming. Billy sat up, disoriented, drenched in sweat.

White T-shirt. Auburn hair. Silver bracelets.

He tore off the covers, naked, groping in the darkness. Where was the girl?

He heard the sound of breaking glass, a struggle. He reached for the Makarov, found it, chambered a round. The sounds were coming from the next room.

His room.

He opened the door, saw her standing by his bed. She had turned on the lights and they hurt his eyes.

'What . . . what is all this?' she asked.

Billy tried to focus. The walls were covered with his photographs. On one wall, the wall devoted to the death songs, there were pictures of people, people with no faces, people with their faces drawn in. Beneath some of them were newspaper clippings.

Drug dealer found murdered.

Torresdale lawyer dead at 50.

Gang leader shot to death.

'These ... these people are all *dead*. You have pictures of them. *Real* pictures.'

'I can explain.'

The girl began to back her way out of the door. 'What did you do to their *faces*?'

'Wait,' Billy said.

The girl turned and ran. Before Billy could take a step, he heard the explosion. The gunshot shook the house.

He turned off the lights, made his way slowly across his room. He peered around the door jamb.

A man stood in the dimly lit hallway, his hand stretched out. In it was a picture. Billy flipped on the hallway light. He saw that the man had a semi-automatic pistol in his other hand. At his feet was a woman. The right side of her skull was missing. The walls were streaked with blood and bone fragments.

Billy aimed the Makarov at the man, stepped forward, his head pounding.

'It's Sean,' the man said.

Billy looked at the man's eyes. They were his own. It was his brother. It was Sean. He lowered his weapon.

Billy only remembered brief moments of the afternoon.

White T-shirt. Auburn hair. Silver bracelets.

'Who the fuck is this?' Sean asked. He was flying on the meth, pacing like a caged tiger.

'I don't remember her name. I met her at the Kettle.'

'And you fucking brought her *here*?'

Billy told Sean how his day had begun, the story of the man and the library. He had never before told his brother about Emily.

Sean hit the vial again, screeched like a bird of prey. 'God-*damn* it.'

'They were here,' Billy said.

Sean stopped. 'Who was here?'

'The police.'

'*What?*'

'I watched from the attic. They knocked front and back, tried to look in the windows, then left.'

'Have they been back?'

'No,' Billy said. 'After that I locked up and went to the Kettle.'

Sean began to pace once again.

'We have to leave, man,' he said. 'You know that, right? We can never come back. We have to get all the money that's out there. Tonight. We make our pickups tonight. Settle all accounts.'

Billy said nothing for a moment. 'But what about the last two lines? We have to draw them.'

Sean ran a hand across his chin. 'We get our money first, then we draw them. Then we leave town.'

Billy returned to the bedroom, put on his clothes. The woman's clothes were strewn about the room. Sean followed.

'Get the certificates,' Sean said.

Billy pulled out the strongbox with the documents they needed. He decided to take the whole box. It also held the cash, nearly three thousand dollars.

Sean found a bath towel, wiped the girl's blood from his face and hands. He dragged the girl's body onto an old rug and rolled it up. He bound it with strong twine.

'Let's get her to the back door. I'm going to take her to the river.'

They labored to get her to the back door. Sean left, and returned a few minutes later with the white van they had jacked in Fishtown. When they took it, the van had been green. They loaded the girl's body into the back.

Sean took another hit from his inhaler, slipped behind the wheel, rolled down the window.

'I'll be back, and we'll take care of business,' he said. 'Wait for me here, okay?'

'Okay.'

As Sean drove off, Billy walked back into the house, a lifetime of echoes thunderous in his head.

Every memory he had, every moment of his past, was gone. There was only time present, and everyone was a stranger.

There never was a Michael Anthony Farren.

There was only Billy.

26

When Jessica stepped into the duty room at the homicide unit, the feelings all but took her breath away. She'd expected a wave of nostalgia, but had not been prepared for the depth of feeling.

The first person to run up to her with a big hug was Josh. She'd really missed him.

'Josh,' she said. 'You look great.'

'Not as great as you.'

Jessica recalled the day she'd met Josh Bontrager, fresh-faced and clad in mismatched clothes. He'd hit the ground running on an investigation of serial murder that took them to the source of the Schuylkill River.

She made the rounds, talking to the secretaries up front, spent a few minutes with Captain Ross. When she got back to the duty room, she saw John Shepherd. They hugged. John was a rock, and further reminded Jessica how much time she had spent in this room, and how much she missed everyone.

'You were right about the handkerchief,' Shepherd said to Byrne.

'Where was it?'

'At the far end of the property, tied to an apple tree. There's that small fence back there, so I originally thought maybe that was where the Rousseau property stopped. I looked at a plot plan, and it continues to the other side of the trees.' He took out his phone, swiped a few photos, turned the screen to face Jessica, Byrne and Josh Bontrager.

It looked to be an identical handkerchief to the one found behind Edwin Channing's house.

The word this time was:

OPERA.

'Has this been processed?' Byrne asked.

Shepherd nodded. 'It's at the lab. They've had it since yesterday afternoon.'

'Do we have any prelim?'

'We do,' he said. 'Presumptively, they are the same handkerchiefs, part of a sct. Chandi said they're linen. Handmade.'

'New?'

Shepherd shook his head. 'She didn't think so, but she hadn't yet run any tests.'

'Can you print that?'

'Sure thing,' Shepherd said.

A few moments later, they were all staring at an 8x10 print of the handkerchief, sitting next to a photograph of the first specimen, the one bearing the word *TENET*.

Byrne glanced at his watch. 'I need to stop at the lab,' he said. He turned to Jessica. 'If you want, I can—'

'I miss the lab,' Jessica said.

Byrne smiled. 'Still Miss Subtle. You can come.'

*

On the way to the lab, Byrne filled Jessica in on the details of the cases. She knew he was not telling her everything, and she understood. While they were ostensibly on the same side, the side of justice for the citizens of their county who had been wronged, writ large or small, they had different sets of rules now.

When they parked the car in the lot at FSC, Jessica reached into her bag, retrieved an envelope, handed it to Byrne. He opened it.

'Oh God,' he said.

It was a 4x6 print of the photo Jessica had taken of him for Sophie.

'Cool, huh? Sophie printed it off for you.'

'Do I really look like this?' Byrne asked.

'Do you want the opening statement or the closing argument?'

'Which one is the bigger lie?'

Jessica didn't have to think too long about this one. 'Opening statement. Evidence gets in the way of total fabrication in the closing argument.'

'Okay,' Byrne said. 'Opening statement.'

'You look good, partner. And that's the truth.' She tapped the photo. 'Exhibit A.'

'I don't know,' Byrne said. 'I should have worn my jacket.'

In the picture, which was a close-up, Byrne wore a crisp white shirt, a navy tie.

'It's a good picture of you, and I'm not just saying so because I took it,' Jessica said. 'Your hair is a little messy, which is adorable. You have fashionable stubble.'

'So, a kind of Gerard Butler meets Brad Pitt thing?'

'Yeah,' Jessica said, keeping the laugh inside. 'Like that.'

'Tell Sophie thanks,' Byrne said. He put the picture in his inside suit coat pocket.

'I will,' Jessica said. 'But I should tell you something else about this picture.'

'What about it?'

'It's now the official screen saver on Sophie's smartphone.'

'You're kidding.'

'Nope,' Jessica said. 'You replaced Nick Jonas.'

Of all the divisions of the Forensic Science Center, criminalistics was the most varied. Its purview was the analysis of hair, fiber and blood evidence, as well as DNA.

The chief examiner was Chandi Dhawan.

Born into extreme poverty in the Basanti slum of Calcutta, Chandi, now in her early forties, had fought her way to England, where she got her degree in biochemistry at Oxford, married a man who worked in international finance, then took a position with the US Department of Agriculture before moving over to the field of forensics in law enforcement.

And she'd accomplished it all from the confines of a wheelchair. Jessica didn't know the reason she was in a chair, and never felt comfortable asking about it.

As they caught up with their recent lives, Jessica was once again struck by the woman's flawless beauty and effortless grace.

'How are things at the DA's office?' Chandi asked.

'Better hours, but the coffee is much worse, believe it or not.'

'I can remedy this,' Chandi said, with her delightful melange of urban Indian and posh English accents. She gestured to a Chemex beaker on the work table, set up with a conical filter. Next to it was the most elaborate coffee grinder Jessica had ever seen, something called a Gaggia MDF. At the other side of the room a kettle had just begun to steam.

'Can I interest you in a cup of Ojo De Aqua Geisha?' Chandi asked.

'That *is* coffee, right?' Byrne asked.

'One of the best.'

'We're in,' Jessica said, answering for both of them.

They made more shop talk and small talk until the coffee was ready. Chandi even used a timer. She poured coffee into a trio of beautiful blue porcelain cups, then, like all serious practitioners of the culinary arts, quietly observed as her guests sampled her offering.

'Oh my God,' Jessica said. It was about the best she'd ever had.

'Coffee is not cooking,' Chandi said. 'Coffee is science.'

She took her last sip, closed her eyes to the taste and aroma. When she opened her eyes, she was back in the lab.

'And now to work.'

She rolled over to the examining table. She clicked on the overhead light, swung out the magnifying lamp. On the table was the evidence collected at Edwin Channing's house and the Rousseau house, the two handkerchiefs, on which were written *OPERA* and *TENET*.

'What can you tell us about these?' Byrne asked.

'I believe I can tell you more than a few things.'

As Jessica looked at the exemplars, she was reminded of her days as a detective, and how, at this moment when the pieces started to snap together, it was such a rush. She found she got the same feeling when a witness began to get caught in their web of lies on the stand.

Not better, not worse, just different.

'These handkerchiefs are Irish linen,' Chandi said. 'Very high-quality. They measure eleven and one half inches square, including the lace edging.'

'Irish linen as in *Made in Ireland* Irish linen?' Byrne asked.

'I am not yet certain of this,' Chandi said. 'But I believe so. And they are most definitely vintage.'

'How vintage?'

Chandi shrugged. 'Presumptively 1940s. Perhaps older. If it

236

was paper, I'd have that for you. Actually, I would rely on Hell Rohmer for that. But I'm working on this.'

Helmut Rohmer was the garrulous head of the PPD's document examination unit. Jessica and Byrne had worked with him many times.

'And it's definitely a handkerchief?' Byrne asked.

Chandi glared.

'Okay,' Byrne said. 'Just a question.'

Chandi continued. 'It is hand-made, very beautiful.' She angled the magnifying lamp over the cloth. 'As you can see, there are slight flaws – as with all hand-woven items – and signs of use commensurate with its age.'

'So it's been used?' Jessica asked.

'Perhaps not,' Chandi said. 'But handlcd.' She took a small laser pointer out of a drawer, turned it on. She ran the narrow beam along the edge of the handkerchief bearing the word *OPERA*.

'Do you see how, on this sample, the color of the lace on the lower right quadrant is a lighter shade of blue than the lace on the other handkerchief? Indeed, lighter than the other three quadrants on the same handkerchief?'

Jessica hadn't noticed it at first, but Chandi was right.

'Why is that?' Byrne asked.

'Again, this is merely a presumption, but I would say that while these handkerchiefs were stored – and I believe that they were, for a very long time – they were folded into quarters, and this quadrant was uppermost in the box. As such, it was exposed to sunlight. Therefore it is lighter in color.'

Jessica couldn't wait to take the testimony of Chandi Dhawan one day. She was a DA's dream.

'So there's probably no chance of picking up a latent print off this surface,' Byrne said.

'I doubt it. While we have been able to pull latents off woven material, not many come from one so porous. Still, when I am finished, I will send this to the ID unit. I hear they are quite good.'

Chandi reached into a folder, pulled out a pair of documents, handed one to Byrne.

'We tested the fluid on both samples. In both cases it is blood – human blood – and both the same blood type.'

'From the same person?' Byrne asked.

'That will take a little time,' Chandi said. 'But I can tell you that the blood samples on these handkerchiefs did not come from any of the victims.'

'You're saying that the blood might belong to the perpetrator?'

'That is one of eight billion or so possibilities.'

'What about hair or fiber?'

Chandi pulled out a pair of photographs. Jessica recognized them as microscopic photographs of hair.

'These two samples were found on the handkerchiefs. There were a total of six hairs, but I believe only two different donors.'

To Jessica, the two samples looked identical.

'I can tell you that both samples are human hair from the scalp. I can tell you that the subjects are Caucasian.'

'Man or woman?'

'That I cannot tell you. There are no characteristics or markers that can isolate a sample as to gender. But I say, presumptively, that they are from male subjects.'

'Why is that?'

'You will think me terribly anachronistic, not to mention vile and sexist.'

'Never.'

Chandi pointed to a few spots on the hair shaft. 'I say this because this hair has never been permed, nor is there evidence of a lot of chemicals such as those found in hairspray.'

'That is so sexist.'

'I told you.'

As they prepared to leave, Byrne stopped at the door.

'I've never asked you this,' he said. 'But I've always wondered.'

Chandi looked up, said nothing. Byrne cleared his throat, continued.

'Chandi Dhawan is a very pretty name. Does it have a meaning?'

Chandi took off her glasses, batted her luxurious eyelashes. 'Detective Byrne, are you *flirting* with me?'

Byrne looked at Jessica, back. He reddened a little. 'I suppose I am.'

'How flattering,' Chandi said. 'I am, of course, a married woman. But I am also quite sure that when I discuss this at lunch, I will be the envy of every woman in the FSC. Some of the men, too.'

'I don't know about that.'

'To your point. My name, as with many Indian names, has meaning. Roughly translated, my surname – Dhawan – means "messenger on the field of battle".'

'Wow,' Byrne said. 'No kidding?'

'No kidding.'

Chandi reached up, turned off the swing-arm magnifying light, continued.

'And my first name – Chandi – means "moonlight".'

'So your name means "moonlight messenger on the field of battle"?'

'Yes,' Chandi said with a disarming smile. 'Let this be a warning to all enemies. I move at night.'

She moved her chair to the door, shook hands with her two guests.

'There is an old Hindu saying. "Many dogs will kill a hare, no matter how many turns it takes." We are many dogs, Detective Byrne. We will catch these men.'

*

They stood at the elevator, waiting for a car. Before the doors opened, they heard someone coming up the steps. Fast. They turned to see an out-of-breath Jake Conroy.

'I'm glad I caught you,' Jake said. He was amped up, big-time.

'What's up?' Byrne asked.

'I knew it,' he said. 'I *knew* it.'

FIU guys had energy, Jessica thought. They always had. Maybe it had something to do with gunpowder, steel and velocity. This sounded like a break in the case.

'Got the hit for the Makarov on NIBIN. From two years ago. An armed robbery at a coin shop in Quakertown.'

'It's a match?'

'It's a match.'

'And we have a suspect?'

'Under glass. We've got eyes on the address as we speak. He's there now.'

27

The target building was a three-story converted row house on Tasker, between Fifth and Sixth streets, in a section of the city known as Dickinson Narrows.

The perimeter team went in first and cut the bolts from the back fence. The backup team deployed in two vans, parked half a block away on either side of the target house.

Even though the detail had to wait for the go command, having a search warrant signed, there was no need for the actual paper to be delivered to the scene.

Jessica waited on the phone in the tech van. At just after two o'clock she took a call from her office.

'We've got it,' she said into her two-way.

The plan was to have a single officer approach the house in the guise of a public works employee. If the officer could get the drop on the man, and there was no further threat from inside the building, the operation could stand down.

In addition to the Makarov, there were also a half-dozen other weapons registered to the man who lived in the house. And those were the ones the PPD knew about.

Depending on how badly this suspect wanted to stand his ground, the potential for a violent encounter was great. Because this was a homicide warrant, they could take no chances. Most police-involved shootings took place in three to five seconds. There was no margin for error.

Jessica looked out the mirrored windows of the van.

She saw that there was no shortage of teenagers and even younger kids on the corners with cell phones. The possibility of the subject being tipped off and escaping was highly probable.

As she watched the scene unfold, she felt adrenalin kick in. Part of her wanted to be on the entry team, like she had been in the old days; part of her was glad she was not.

A few seconds later she heard the detail commander give the go order. On screen, she saw the officer walk up the street. In his left hand he held a clipboard. He wore a public works windbreaker and ball cap. Jessica knew he had a Kevlar vest on beneath the windbreaker.

He stood in front of the house, got a read on the windows and door. He scribbled a few things on the clipboard, in case he was being observed.

He rang the bell, waited. He rang it a second time. A few seconds later the door opened. Through the pole cam directly in front of the house, Jessica could see that the subject was in his mid-thirties, had close-cropped hair.

In a blur the officer had his weapon drawn, leveled. The subject got on the ground in front of the row house and seconds later was in custody.

A pair of SWAT officers breached the door, followed by Kevin Byrne and Josh Bontrager, all deployed in Kevlar vests.

Jessica found that she was holding her breath.

Eventually Byrne emerged, holstering his weapon as he walked down the steps. He threw a glance at the pole cam.

'Premises clear,' one of the SWAT officers said over the radio. Jessica exhaled.

The first floor of the space was currently being remodeled from what was once a residence to a retail space. Along the left side was a long display counter. Behind it were shelving units. The walls had been patched and repaired, but not yet painted.

The subject sat on a folding chair at the back end of the space, his hands still cuffed behind him. Although he had no criminal record, information gleaned from both the Department of Motor Vehicles and the Department of Licenses and Inspections identified him as Timothy Gallagher, aged thirty-eight.

Four detectives from South Division had conducted a search of the premises, as well as Gallagher's car – a 2014 Audi 4 that was parked a half-block away in a city lot – and come up empty. No weapons were recovered.

Depending on how this initial interview went, time would tell if the car would be impounded and towed to the police garage, where it would be processed for blood, hair and fiber.

While Byrne pulled up a chair opposite Gallagher, Jessica held back, sat in a chair on the other side of the counter. Josh Bontrager and John Shepherd stood near the door.

A video camera, trained on Gallagher, was on top of the display case. He had called his lawyer, who had not yet arrived. He had every right to not say a word.

'Mr Gallagher, my name is Detective Kevin Byrne. I'm with the homicide unit of the Philadelphia Police Department.'

Gallagher looked up at Byrne, but said nothing.

'Do you know why we're here?'

'My lawyer should be here any minute. We'll talk then. If at all.'

Byrne nodded. 'You have that right, of course. But there's nothing stopping me from telling you why we're here. It's about your Makarov.'

The man looked up. 'My Makarov?'

'Yes, sir.'

'I don't own a Makarov.'

Byrne reached into his coat, took out a folded document, pushed it across the desk. An official form from BATFE, the 4473 was mandatory in Pennsylvania for the legal, over-the-counter purchase of a firearm from a dealer. The man barely scanned it, perhaps only looking for his name and signature.

'Did you read the date on this?' Gallagher asked.

'I did, sir.'

'I don't have this gun anymore.'

'Who has it?'

'I have no idea. It was stolen.'

'When was it stolen?'

'Two years ago. Right before Christmas. It was about a month after I had a robbery.'

'Did you report this burglary to the police?'

He looked at Jessica, back. 'Of course I did. Who doesn't report a burglary to the police?'

You'd be surprised, Jessica thought.

'Which agency did you report it to?' Byrne asked.

'State police. This happened at my old store in Quaker-town.'

Quakertown was a town of approximately nine thousand residents in the northeast portion of Upper Bucks County, about thirty miles north of Philadelphia.

Byrne shared a quick glance with Jessica. They'd been down this road before. Communication between state and city and county and federal agencies left a lot to be desired. If they'd had the information about the stolen weapon, they could have stood down this entire operation. They still would have talked to this man, but not in handcuffs.

Josh Bontrager took out his phone, stepped out of the building. He would follow up on this. Byrne turned back to Gallagher. Until he heard that the story of the burglary was true, the man would remain in cuffs.

'Tell me how you came to acquire the Makarov,' he said.

Gallagher paused, took a deep breath. 'Not much to tell. I bought it at a gun show fifteen years ago.' He nodded at the 4473. 'It's all there.'

'Where was the show?'

'Over in Greencastle.'

'Why did you buy it?'

'I sell stamps and coins,' he said. 'I buy and sell gold. I have cash on hand. Why do you think?'

Byrne moved on. 'Did anyone ever borrow this weapon from you?'

'Never.'

'Not even for an afternoon, to go to the range or something?'

'Not once.'

'Can you tell me the general details of the burglary?'

'What's to tell? It was the middle of the night. I'd locked up, put the system on, shut the safe.'

'Where was the gun?'

'I kept it under the counter.'

'Why not in the safe?' Byrne asked.

'What the hell good would it do me there? I just tell the bad guys to hold on a minute while I get my weapon? If I hadn't had it to hand a month earlier, I'd be dead.'

Byrne took a moment. He'd meant, why not in the safe at night. He didn't care for the man's attitude, but cut him some slack. He didn't think he would be too happy if this had happened to him.

'What else was stolen during the burglary?' he asked.

'Some rare coins, some silver jewelry. A few books of stamps. Nothing precious. Maybe four to five thousand all told.'

'Was it customary to leave these items out?'

'You can't put everything in the safe, every night,' he said. 'I wouldn't leave an Inverted Jenny out. That's the—'

'First US airmail stamp,' Byrne said. 'Curtiss JN-4 printed upside down.'

Gallagher looked surprised. 'You know your stamps.'

Byrne said nothing.

'Besides, don't the police always tell you to leave a little something out?' Gallagher said.

It was true. The conventional wisdom was that if a burglar got absolutely nothing, they were more likely to trash the place in anger.

Josh Bontrager re-entered the store, caught Byrne's eye, nodded. It meant that the man's story checked out. He had been burglarized, and he had claimed the Makarov was taken. It was all in the police report.

Byrne stood, crossed the room, unlocked the man's handcuffs. 'First off, let me say I'm sorry about this.'

The man rubbed his wrists, said nothing.

'Tell us about the robbery at the Quakertown store.'

Gallagher's account of the incident matched the official police report. Two men with ski masks on had come into the store just before closing. They'd pointed a weapon at Gallagher, who managed to get the Makarov out from under the counter. Both men fired. The robbers left. It was the slug from the Makarov, dug out of the drywall, that had provided the match to the bullet evidence in the Channing and Rousseau cases.

A month later came the burglary.

'Do you have any ideas about who might have committed the burglary?' Byrne asked.

Gallagher looked at each of the detectives in turn, said: 'I have my ideas. But it was a long time ago. Doesn't really matter anymore.'

Byrne waited for more. More didn't come.

'As you might have guessed, this is an extremely important matter. It would be very helpful if you would share these ideas with us.'

Gallagher ran a hand over his chin.

'This was a long time ago, mind you. Long before the burglary.'

Byrne listened in silence.

'My father had just opened a shop over on Grays Ferry Avenue. Do you know it?'

Byrne nodded.

'We were doing all right. This was back when people collected. Now it's all bullion metals, sports memorabilia. Back then it was collectors.' Gallagher thought for a few moments, clearly unused to talking about whatever it was that he was going to say. He continued.

'So we're open a few months, and one day, just before closing – a Saturday, of course – this guy comes in. Big guy, older – fifties or sixties maybe – tough-looking, prison tats. I knew right away it was a shakedown. Wasn't my first rodeo.'

'What did he say?'

'You know the routine. He said it was all about the Irish sticking together, how the police weren't always going to help. I told him that half the police force in Philly were Irish. He didn't find the humor or the logic.'

'So you paid him protection money.'

Gallagher looked at the floor, back up. 'What was I supposed to do? I asked around, talked to the other merchants and shopkeepers. These guys were fucking animals. This one guy, Ralph Brady, used to own a little sporting goods store on South. He said he missed a payment and came home to find his family dog hanging from a tree in the back yard. Pinned to the dog's collar was a photograph of his seven-year-old daughter.'

'How long did this go on?'

Gallagher shrugged. 'Two years, maybe? We opened two more stores, and I had to pay for them, too.'

Byrne made the notes. Gallagher continued.

'Like I said, the burglary wasn't here. I had five stores back then. The Makarov was up in Quakertown.'

'And you think it was these men? The men who extorted money from you?'

'I *know* it was them. I couldn't exactly tell the police this. All things considered.'

'And you're certain that the Makarov was stolen in this burglary?'

'I'm one hundred percent sure.'

Jessica considered this. If the gun was stolen this long ago, it could have been sold and resold a hundred times. No paperwork involved.

'I take it you are no longer paying these people for protection,' Byrne said.

The man hesitated.

'After the burglary, I hired private security. They drove me to and from the bank, to and from my house. I spent about six grand on my house – alarms, motion-sensing lights, fencing; five times that much on my stores. I have three pit bulls at home that would eat you for an appetizer. After the fire, they stopped coming around. Went for easier pickings, I guess.'

On the word *fire*, Byrne glanced over at Jessica.

'There was a fire?' Byrne asked.

'Oh yeah. After they stole everything they could carry, they burned the place to the ground. I was insured, of course, but I lost a lot of irreplaceable things. Stamps, mostly.'

'Might it have been a bomb?' Byrne asked.

248

'Could have been. To me, a fire is a fire.'

'Who were these guys, Mr Gallagher?'

'I never knew the names of the guys who actually collected.'

'Do you think you'd recognize them if you saw them again?'

'I think so. It's been a while, but I'd remember.'

'We'd really like it if you could come down to the Round-house and look through some mug shots,' Byrne said.

'What, *now*?'

'It's very important, Mr Gallagher.'

Gallagher hung his head for a few moments, glanced at his watch. 'Yeah,' he said. 'It's not like I'm going to get anything done today. Let's do it.'

Back at the Roundhouse, Byrne made phone calls to not only the state police in Dublin, Pennsylvania, but also the captain of the fire department regarding the burning down of Tim Gallagher's store.

He learned that the arson investigator for that crime had ruled that no accelerant was used. He also said that no arrests were ever made, and that he had not run into this MO in all the years since.

Byrne asked if the crime-scene photos, as well as the reports, could be emailed. The chief said it would be no problem. Byrne thanked him, hung up. About ten minutes later, the files arrived. Byrne didn't bother looking at them, because he didn't have a clue as to what to look for.

He called Zach Brooks at the bomb squad, who said he had some time to look at the pictures and the files. Byrne forwarded them.

Ten minutes later, Brooks called back. Byrne put him on speaker.

'What do we have, Zach?'

'Well, obviously I can't make any concrete findings without walking the scene and collecting my own samples, but based on what you've sent me, and the findings of the arson unit up there, I'd say we have the same device.'

'You're saying it might be the same bomber?' Byrne asked.

'I can't tell you that, but the device used looks to have been identical. The blast seat is a mirror image, and the blast pattern seems to be indistinguishable. I can take a ride up there if you want. If the place hasn't been remodeled or demolished, I'll be able to tell you more.'

Byrne gave it a moment. 'I don't think we'll need that right now,' he said. 'But thanks, Zach.'

'You got it, brother.'

Byrne crossed the room to the terminal at which Tim Gallagher was sitting. Gallagher looked up. 'I'm sorry,' he said. 'I haven't seen the guy. They're all starting to look alike.'

'No problem,' Byrne said. He leaned over, tapped a few keys. A second later, a mug shot came up, front view and side view.

'Holy shit,' Gallagher said. 'That's the guy.'

Jessica felt a surge of adrenalin. She walked around to the front of the LCD monitor.

There, on the screen, was a familiar face.

The man who had been extorting money from Tim Gallagher was Danny Farren.

'Are you certain this is the man?' Byrne asked.

'One hundred percent.'

'And you say that the men who actually picked up the protection money were younger?'

'Yes.'

Byrne crossed the duty room, came back with a folder. He opened it, put a photograph on the table. It was a still taken from the surveillance cameras in front of the Sadik Food King.

'Are these the men, Mr Gallagher?'

'That's them,' he said. 'They're older here, but that's them.'

*

Six detectives met at the back of the duty room. On a white-board was a picture of Danny Farren and his two sons, Michael and Sean. Both sons had been in and out of jail over the last twenty years, ever since they were juveniles, but neither had done hard time.

Each detective took a few moments to read the Farrens' sheets – their known associates, their last-known addresses, their life histories in and around the criminal justice system. Nothing leapt out that would tie them to the Rousseaus or Edwin Channing.

As Josh Bontrager and Maria Caruso hit the phones, coordinating the various units, Jessica and Byrne met near the captain's office.

'Let's get that warrant,' Byrne said.

'If you're talking about an arrest warrant, it's not going to happen.'

'Of course it will.'

'How am I supposed to walk an arrest warrant through with what we have?' Jessica asked. 'Or, more accurately, what we don't have?'

Byrne gave it a moment. 'We've got the Farrens on the CCTV footage outside the Channing scene. We've just put the murder weapon in their hands.'

'Number one, that footage near the Channing scene is so far away and so dark that it could be anybody. Plus, the SUV looks like ten thousand other banged-up dark SUVs in Philly. The fact that the Farrens were a few blocks away two hours earlier in a remotely similar vehicle isn't going to fly. We arrest them, we have six hours to charge them. If we could find that Acadia, we might have something to work with.'

Byrne just listened. They both knew that the Acadia was probably chopped for parts by now.

'Two, that gun was stolen a long time ago, in another county,'

Jessica continued. 'We don't exactly have it in their hands. Plus, Gallagher's testimony, if it comes to that, about knowing who broke into his store would get ripped to shreds. You know how guns are bought and sold on the street. On top of everything, I'm not sure we could even compel Gallagher to take the stand on this matter.'

Jessica knew that Byrne knew all this. The two of them had tried to work the system for years together.

Figuring she was in for the pound as well as the penny, she went on. 'We've got no forensics, no DNA, no solid eyewitnesses. We arrest them, and don't charge them, they walk. Everything after that becomes harassment.'

The two of them let the fury of the moment ebb.

'So what are you saying?' Byrne asked.

'I'm saying that I'm going to make the call right now.'

Twenty minutes later, Jimmy Doyle walked into the duty room. Byrne briefed him on what they had.

The two prosecutors and three detectives huddled in a corner.

'What do you think, Jess?' Jimmy asked.

Jessica thought of everything they had, and did not have. 'I think we can get a search warrant for The Stone. It's Michael Farren's last known address. I'd say we have probable cause. We search the place, we find a shell casing, the weapon itself, or any property belonging to Edwin Channing or the Rousseaus, the arrest warrant will fly.'

'I agree.'

'Who's available?' Jessica asked.

Jimmy glanced at his watch. 'I think Judge Salcer is in chambers now.' He looked at Jessica. 'If you type it up, I'll get it over.'

'You got it.'

*

252

Within a half-hour, Jessica's phone rang. It was Jimmy.

'This is Jessica,' she said. 'You're on speaker.'

'Who am I speaking to, Jess?'

'Detectives Byrne and Shepherd.'

'We have the search warrant,' he said. 'I've been in touch with Captain Ross and Inspector Mostow. They're gearing up the fugitive squad to serve an arrest warrant if we need it.'

Jessica and Byrne said nothing.

'I've also talked to the district attorney,' Jimmy continued. 'This is all one investigation now. Four counts of conspiracy to commit murder. Danny Farren and his two sons. We are going to bury these fucking animals.'

'Yes, sir,' Jessica said. The word 'sir' slipped out before she could stop herself. Jimmy Doyle didn't seem to notice.

'I'll meet the PPD there,' he said. 'Jess, I'll need you back here on point.'

'On my way,' Jessica said.

As the entire duty room got ready for the detail, the sense of forward motion was palpable.

'Good work, counselor,' Byrne said to Jessica.

'Wait until you get my bill.'

Byrne smiled as he put on a Kevlar vest. Jessica helped strap him in.

'Be safe, detective,' she said.

'Always.'

She held up her phone. It meant, call me ASAP.

'Copy that,' Byrne said.

As Jessica watched the officers leave the duty room, she thought about what had just happened, and what they believed to be true.

The killers they sought now had names.

Sean and Michael Farren.

28

The building was a derelict clapboard row house on Montrose Street, at one time a tavern called The Stone.

In the past decade or so, the neighborhood had become gentrified, especially after the old Naval Home had been remodeled into Naval Square, a condominium and retail complex.

But that was a few streets over. Here, in this section of of the neighborhood, between 26th Street and Grays Ferry Avenue, it looked much the same as it had fifty or sixty years ago.

As detectives fanned out along the block, Byrne met Jimmy Doyle about a hundred feet from the front of the building.

'Christ, does this take me back,' Jimmy said.

Byrne pointed at the tavern. 'Did you ever go inside?'

Jimmy nodded. 'My mother made me go there a few times to drag my stepfather out. Place always gave me the creeps.'

Byrne remembered The Stone well. It had had a long-standing reputation for being a hard place for hard men. When you were ten years old, that status grew into something of a myth.

'I saw Patrick Farren literally pick up a guy and throw him out the door,' Jimmy said. 'A two-hundred-pound man and he lifted him off a stool. Dead weight.'

Byrne glanced down the block. There he saw an idling CSU van, holding back in case they were needed to process the scene. He turned back and asked the question that had begun to fester inside.

'Jimmy,' he said. 'Do you know Graham Grande?'

Jimmy looked over. For an instant Byrne thought he saw the wheels turning. The *legal* wheels. Just as quickly, the old Jimmy Doyle was back.

'Sure I know him,' he said. 'Good man. Old-school pro. Precious few left these days.'

Before Byrne could respond, he got the go command on his two-way. The team was in place.

Jimmy handed him the search warrant. 'Let's do this.'

While Jimmy got on the phone to give his boss a status report, Byrne checked the action on his service weapon.

As he approached the tavern, he noticed that the front door was double-padlocked, and the sign above, at one time spelling out *The Stone* in green neon, had broken tubes. The front window still boasted a pair of beer signs from the sixties or seventies.

The door, which was just a few feet from the street, looked even worse close up. Decades of carved names and sprayed graffiti marked it.

With Josh Bontrager, John Shepherd, and Bình Ngô behind him, flanked by four tactical officers, Byrne knocked and said, loud enough to be heard through the door: 'Philadelphia Police! Search warrant!'

He waited a few moments, and repeated the process.

No response.

The four tactical officers cautiously moved to the rear of the structure, their AR-15 rifles high.

As Byrne and Shepherd walked along the right side of the building, Byrne noticed that the boarded-up windows on the first and second stories had rusted iron bars over them. At ground level there were two windows of glass block.

At the rear of the property was a small patio. As Byrne recalled, it was at one time surrounded by a white picket privacy fence. The boards had long ago been ripped from the cross rails. The back door to the bar, as with the front door, was padlocked. There did not appear to be any other entrances to the structure; no coal chute, no delivery doors. Byrne walked up to the two windows and tugged on the iron bars. They were secure.

He got on his two-way and suggested Josh Bontrager do the same thing on the other side. In short order, Bontrager got back to him with the news he expected. The bars on the windows on that side were secure.

When the entry team was ready, Byrne knocked on the rear door, listened for any sound coming from inside the building. There was none. No television, no radio, no conversation. Best of all, no dogs.

He keyed his handset, raised Josh Bontrager. A minute later, Bình Ngô and Bontrager rounded the building.

Bontrager had a large crowbar. He made eye contact with everyone and, seeing that the team was ready, inserted the crowbar into the door jamb, right near the padlock, and pushed. It took two or three attempts, but on the final attempt the door splintered open.

'Philadelphia Police!' Byrne yelled. 'Search warrant!'

The four detectives all drew their weapons, held them at their sides. The four tactical officers entered the building. Because they did not know if the suspects were present, the detail would be a methodical search of the premises, not a dynamic entry.

The tactical officers would search the first and second floors;

Byrne and Shepherd would take the basement. Josh Bontrager and Bình Ngô would cover the exterior.

According to the plot plan they had acquired from the Department of Licenses and Inspections, the kitchen had been at the rear of the structure. Byrne and Shepherd quickly found the stairs leading to the cellar, keeping their flashlights out and away from center.

While there was some light on the first floor, sifting through the boarded windows, the cellar was pitch black. Byrne felt along the wall, found no light switch.

As they descended the steps, the old and dried-out treads announced their arrival, as did the bright white beam from their flashlights. It made the two detectives perfect targets in this confined space.

When they reached the bottom of the stairs, Byrne took in the area.

A narrow hallway. Two doors. One on the right, one on the left. Both were closed. No light spilled into the corridor from beneath them. Ahead, at the end of the hall, was an old oil furnace.

Byrne shone his flashlight at the ceiling, made eye contact with Shepherd, who nodded. There were three bare bulbs in the unfinished ceiling. Byrne reached up and touched one of them. It was cold.

He could hear the other officers moving up to the second floor.

The two men flanked the door on the right. John Shepherd reached out, soft-checked the doorknob. He shook his head. It was not locked.

With a nod, he swung the door inward. As it opened fully, Byrne rolled the jamb, his weapon in close-contact firing position. With his other hand he shone his flashlight floor to ceiling in rapid arcs, taking it all in.

Against the far wall was an army cot, a small table, a lamp. Another corner held a pile of dirty clothes. At the foot of the bed was a table, which held a hotplate. The device had a cord that ran up to the light socket in the ceiling. There was a closet with no door. The room was unoccupied.

The two detectives moved to the second door. They would reverse roles. Byrne checked the doorknob. This door too was unlocked. When Shepherd was ready, Byrne opened the door, flanked Shepherd on the right.

'Holy shit,' Shepherd said.

A few moments later, the area cleared, Shepherd holstered his weapon. Byrne stepped into the room and saw what the man meant.

As a K-9 officer and his dog made a pass through the structure, searching for possible booby traps and explosives, Byrne met John Shepherd at the back door. They exchanged a look known to veteran law enforcement officers the world over, members of the military and first responders of every discipline. It was one of relief and purpose. They'd gone into the abyss and emerged unscathed. There was always this moment of deceleration.

'The fatal funnel,' Shepherd said. 'You never get used to it.'

Byrne just nodded. The fatal funnel was a search term used when breaching a door into a room where the threat was unknown. He put a hand on his old friend's shoulder. They'd survived another one.

With the building cleared and secured, Byrne went back to the main floor, while the other detectives and officers stood down.

The layout of the tavern proper was a U-shaped bar with what had at one time been benches around the walls that faced the street. The windows had long ago been boarded up.

Only a few barstools remained. The area behind the bar was

a deadfall of broken furniture, rotting drywall, severed electrical conduits. A pile of framed posters lay on the floor near what was once the hallway that led to the restrooms, Irish tourist attractions.

Everywhere was the smell of age, of blight, of decay.

The first room to which Byrne and Shepherd had gained entry in the basement had been used as a bedroom, but clearly not for years. Discarded clothing, both men's and women's, along with fast-food trash, beer cans, magazines, none newer than five years old. A fairly typical crash pad.

It was the other room that spoke of a deep and disturbing pathology.

While it did contain a single bed and table, it was something other than just a place to sleep. Every square inch of the wall space, doors and ceiling was covered in photographs, news clippings, drawings, each with some kind of hand-written note attached. Some of the areas were ten or fifteen pictures deep, attached to the wall with ten-penny nails. Many of the people in the pictures had had their faces removed. Others had faces drawn in. Everywhere were arrows pointing from faces to buildings, identifying store owners, waitresses, mail carriers, people on the street.

There had to be thousands.

And the printers. There were more than two dozen photo printers of varying vintage strewn around the room. One corner held a half-dozen, stacked halfway up the wall, covered in dust. Byrne had stood in his share of rooms occupied by people with every imaginable obsession, but he had never seen anything like this.

'Kevin.'

He turned to see Josh Bontrager standing in the doorway. 'Yeah, Josh.'

'Found something.'

Byrne followed him into the hallway, over to the base of the steps. Bontrager shone his flashlight on the wall. There Byrne saw what was obviously blood. Above it, a hole in the plaster that looked to have been made by a large-caliber bullet. The blood was not wet, but it glistened. It was fresh.

Byrne got Jimmy Doyle on the two-way.

'Jimmy,' he said.

'Yeah, Kevin.'

'You better get down here.'

With the portable halogen lamps in place, they saw much more. In addition to the first blood pattern they'd found, there was what looked to be human tissue streaked on the walls, as well as auburn hair attached to a patch of scalp. A small pool of blood was still damp beneath the steps.

Jimmy and Byrne stood away from the area at the end of the hall as CSU officers began to process what was clearly the scene of a homicide.

After a few moments Jimmy took out his phone. He pointed at the fresh blood.

'I'll have the arrest warrant before it dries.'

29

By the time Byrne made it home, his mind was working overtime with all the new developments. The presumption – it had not become fact, not yet – that Danny Farren's sons, most likely working at the elder Farren's behest, had committed these home invasions and savage murders had widened the investigation in a way he'd never anticipated.

The Stone was secured, and detectives from South, along with officers from CSU, were combing the place for anything that would lead them to Sean and Michael Farren. Considering the vast quantity of junk, and the thousands of photographs, it would be a slow process.

Byrne was on call for the next twenty-four hours, but that was only on paper. He would probably be back at the Roundhouse in a few hours. He had to be at the center of all this.

As they suspected, it was indeed human blood on the floor and walls. A 9 mm slug had been pulled from the wooden lath near the bottom of the stairs. No body had been found, but a pattern in the dust on the floor leading to the back door suggested a body might have been rolled into a blanket or rug and dragged outside. Crime-scene techs found what they believed to be trace blood evidence on the threshold of the back door.

Try as he might, Byrne could not fully get a grasp on all the photographs and notes affixed to the walls in the basement room. They had to go back many, many years. He was certain they would find evidence of myriad crimes in that room, but that did not help the problem at hand, and that was the fact that there were psychotic killers on the loose.

Jimmy Doyle had put in a call to Danny Farren's attorney in the hope that Farren might talk to the police and shed some much-needed light. As expected, he refused.

An arrest warrant had been issued for both Sean and Michael Farren.

It was with these puzzles and questions in mind that Byrne rounded the corner onto his street and parked his car. He was so occupied with the cases that he almost didn't see the shadow.

There, in the doorway to his building, was a petite woman.

She was dressed in white.

'Sorry, Dad.'

Colleen Siobhan Byrne sat at the dining room table, spinning a teacup. Deaf since birth, she had recently graduated with honors from Gallaudet University, the nation's pre-eminent college for the deaf and hard of hearing. It had slipped Byrne's mind that she was heading up to attend her great-aunt Dottie's birthday party.

'Sorry for what?' Byrne signed.

Colleen smiled. 'For scaring you back there.'

'Scared? *Me?* Do you know how many deaf girls I've arrested and thrown in jail?'

'How many?'

'Not a one,' Byrne said. 'But I wasn't scared. I was just happy and surprised to see you.'

'Okay,' she signed, letting him off the hook.

Byrne glanced at his daughter's hand. Specifically at the ring on her third finger, left hand. She was engaged to be married. He had met the young man, had also fallen under his spell. He was a good man. Still, Byrne couldn't believe it. Colleen was just a toddler only a few months ago.

His daughter knocked on the table, got his attention. Byrne looked up.

'Something's wrong,' she signed.

Byrne shook his head, offered a weak smile. Colleen wasn't buying it, not even half a loaf. She tapped a fingernail on the table between them. Meaning: *dish*.

'I don't know,' he signed. 'The job, maybe.'

'It's always been your job. Why now?'

Another shrug. 'I define myself by what I do for a living.'

'Everybody does,' Colleen signed. 'This woman is a doctor, this man a landscaper or an architect. We are what we do.'

'If I were to stop being a cop, what would I be?'

'Lots of things.'

Byrne sipped his beer, put down the bottle. 'For instance?'

'For one, you're a great dad.'

Byrne smiled. 'Well, you've just had the one. I'm not sure you're qualified on that.'

'One is plenty,' she said. 'And on top of that, you're a great son.'

Byrne wasn't expecting that. He felt his emotions rise. 'I don't know about that one.'

'You are. Grandad couldn't be any prouder of you. You don't see it, but I do.'

'You see it?'

Colleen nodded. 'I watch him when he watches you.'

'What do you mean?'

His daughter gave it some thought. 'Whenever you're doing anything – telling a story, working around the house, pitching in to help somebody – he watches you, and he gets this look, like he wants to burst with pride and admiration.'

Byrne had had no idea. Paddy Byrne was just Paddy Byrne. Retired dockworker, union man, drinker of lager, the most diehard of Eagles fans. They'd had a few heart-to-hearts over the years – granted, more lately than before – but like a lot of Irishmen, Paddy Byrne kept most of it inside. Byrne knew his father loved him. He hoped his father knew the same.

'You were there for him when Grandma died,' Colleen signed. 'Every day.'

'It's what you're supposed to do.'

'It is, but a lot of people don't do it. He told me that he didn't know what would have happened if you weren't there.'

'He told you that?' Byrne asked. 'When?'

'In a letter.'

Byrne felt punched. 'He writes you letters?'

Colleen rolled her eyes. She tapped her father's hand. Byrne was always amazed how his daughter's smile, her touch, could change his day completely. He was blessed.

'So why today?' she asked.

Byrne just shrugged. 'Big case.'

'Bad?'

He didn't have to think too hard about this one. He nodded.

'Sorry,' Colleen signed.

'I'd love to say it's just another day at Black Rock, but I can't.'

'Want to talk about it?'

He did. 'Maybe later. Let's eat first.'

'Great. What are you making?'

Byrne laughed. His daughter could do that, even on the worst of days. 'Reservations?'

Colleen smiled, kissed him on the cheek. 'I'll find something here. It's amazing what you can throw together in a college dorm. I once made a casserole of cottage cheese and Vienna sausages.'

'Make that,' Byrne said. 'I'm going to hit the shower.'

Byrne felt a hundred percent better. He slipped into casual slacks and a pullover. When he stepped into the living room, he saw Colleen looking at two photographs that had been on top of his briefcase. He berated himself for leaving them out. He hoped they weren't too graphic.

On the other hand, Colleen was no longer a child. She knew what he did.

Before he could step across to the kitchen, she held up both photographs, a puzzled look on her face. They were of the two linen handkerchiefs.

She put down the pictures, signed:

'Are these from the case?'

Byrne nodded. Held up two fingers. 'Two cases.'

She looked at them again, wrinkled her nose.

Byrne got her attention. He knew what she was thinking. 'Yes,' he signed. 'Those words are written in blood.'

Colleen stared at the photographs a little longer. She seemed transfixed. Then: 'Are these the only two?'

'What do you mean?'

'Are these the only two handkerchiefs you have?'

'Yes,' he signed. 'They are the only two. Why would you ask that?'

She pointed at the photos. 'Because you have these two words. *Tenet* and *Opera*.'

'What about them?'

'They're part of the Square.'

Byrne was lost. He told his daughter so.

'These are two of the words in the Sator Square. Haven't you ever heard of it?'

Byrne shook his head. He had intended to plug the words into an internet search tonight. It was the main reason he'd left the photographs out.

'What is it called again?' he asked.

'The Sator Square.' She finger-spelled *Sator*.

'And what is it all about?'

Colleen thought for a moment. She held up a finger, meaning: *hang on*.

She reached into her bag, took out her phone, started texting someone with blinding speed. She put the phone down, turned back to Byrne.

'Do you remember Sister Kathleen?'

Byrne didn't. Instead of blatantly lying to his daughter, he just shrugged.

'You don't,' she signed.

'I have my own nun nightmares,' he said. 'Who was she again?'

'She was my math teacher for four years. Geometry, algebra and calculus. We're still in touch.'

'You took calculus?'

Coleen thrust both hands out, palms up. She continued.

'Anyway, she's a big fan of stuff like this. It's where I first heard about it. We did a whole class on it. It's not exactly math, but Sister Kathleen is like that. I was always in the smart-kid class, so we could afford to go off on tangents.'

Colleen's phone vibrated on the counter. She picked it up, glanced at the screen, smiled. She slipped the phone into her purse, signed:

'I just texted her about this, and she said she'd be happy to talk about it.'

Byrne felt his pulse quicken. He had no idea if what his daughter was talking about had anything to do with the cases, but it was a direction.

'That's great,' he said. 'When do you think she'll have time?'

Colleen grabbed her coat from the chair, slipped it on. 'Right now. I told her we'd be straight over.' She opened the door. 'We'll eat on the way. Even I can't make anything out of Jim Beam and stale oyster crackers.'

Gardenia Hall was a convent home and health-care center in Malvern, Pennsylvania. With light traffic, it took them less than an hour to get there.

When Sister Kathleen opened the door, Byrne was taken aback. The woman had to be in her mid-seventies but stood with a younger woman's poise. Without a word, neither spoken aloud or signed, she took Colleen in her arms. Byrne could see it was an emotional moment for both women. He stepped away.

When they broke their embrace, Colleen gestured to the nun. 'This is Sister Kathleen.'

They shook hands. Byrne was not surprised to find the woman's grip firmer than his own. He tried to remember if he'd ever actually shaken hands with a nun before. He couldn't imagine when or where it might have been. Genuflecting or running from them, yes. Shaking hands, not so much.

'Call me Kathleen if you like,' she said.

'I'd love to,' Byrne replied. 'I just don't think I can.'

She nodded in mock concern. 'Catholic education?'

'Still in progress.'

'For all of us,' she said. She stepped to the side, gestured toward the hallway at the other side of the foyer. 'Welcome to Gardenia Hall.'

'Thank you, Sister.'

*

267

Sister Kathleen's room was austere only in its size and furnishings. One wall, where there was a small desk and laptop computer, also held a poster of Albert Einstein, a whiteboard with what looked to be a complicated math problem on it, as well as a corkboard. Just about every square inch of corkboard was dedicated to pieces of paper with numbers and diagrams on.

While Sister Kathleen and Colleen caught up in sign language that was so amazingly fast he couldn't hope to keep up, Byrne looked at some of the certificates and photographs on the wall. Sister Kathleen was a graduate of Villanova University, and had received her advanced degree from Georgetown.

She saw him looking at her boards and smiled. 'You may think it's all random – that there is no order or balance to all this – and you would be absolutely right. I have no idea what, if anything, links these theories. One day, though. One day.'

She picked up a black marker pen.

'So. The Sator Square, is it?' she asked.

'Yes, Sister,' Byrne said.

She turned to the whiteboard, erased what was on it, and began to write. A minute later she stood to the side. She'd written:

$$
\begin{array}{ccccc}
S & A & T & O & R \\
A & R & E & P & O \\
T & E & N & E & T \\
O & P & E & R & A \\
R & O & T & A & S \\
\end{array}
$$

'The Sator Square,' she said.

For Byrne, two words leapt off the chalkboard. *His* words. *TENET* and *OPERA*. A moment later, he saw the puzzle.

Sister Kathleen pointed at the board. 'As you can see—'

'It reads top to bottom, bottom to top, left to right and right to left,' he said.

'Exactly.'

Byrne let his eyes again roam the square, marveling at the symmetry. But as much as he appreciated it, he was at a loss as to why two of the words would show up, written in blood, at two brutal crime scenes.

'What does it mean?' he asked.

'Well, firstly it is a four-times palindrome, and as a palindrome it has a lot of baggage, especially religious baggage.'

'How so?'

'Some people believe that because a palindrome can be read backwards and forwards, it is immune to tampering by the devil.'

Byrne looked at her, trying to gauge if the woman was about to go off-planet with this.

Sister Kathleen smiled, held up her hands. 'That's one interpretation. But only one.' She tapped the board. 'As far as I know, the first known appearance of this is about 79 AD in Pompeii, buried in the ash of Vesuvius.

'Since then it has shown up in many places. Manchester, England; Dura-Europos in Syria; the Duomo di Siena in Italy. As to its meaning, or even its translation, there are about as many theories as there are sightings.'

'For instance?' Byrne said. 'If you don't mind.'

'Not at all.'

As she spoke, she signed everything.

'The early instances were actually Rotas Squares, not Sator Squares. The words themselves, if taken to be Latin, can be loosely translated, with only the word Arepo appearing nowhere in the language. Some believe Arepo was a proper name. The sentence – again, loosely, and by no means literally – reads: "The farmer, Arepo, uses his plough for work." Or something like that. Believe it or not, I was a C student in Latin.'

Byrne waited for more. There was no more. He looked at his daughter, who smiled and shrugged.

'Granted, not an earth-shattering sentence,' Sister Kathleen said. 'It probably wasn't even proper Latin, but that's just one idea. Others consider it an amulet of sorts. The Latin words *Pater Noster*—'

'Meaning "Our Father",' Byrne said, translating.

Sister Kathleen smiled. 'Catholic.'

'I've done my share of penance.'

She pointed out the letters in the square. '*Pater Noster* is contained in the square as an anagram, along with two instances of *alpha and omega* – A and O.

'There are many who believe early Christians used it as a secret symbol to let other Christians know of their presence. There are even more who believe that the invocation of the square can lift jinxes and curses.'

'Curses?' Byrne asked, recalling his conversation with Jessica about the last weeks of Frankie Sheehan's life.

'Oh yes,' she said. 'The Prayer of the Virgin in Bartos claims that these are the names of the five nails used to crucify Christ.

'On balance, the Sator Square is seen by many, in both religious and secular quarters, as a mystical symbol, an emblem used to ward off evil.'

Byrne wasn't sure any of this had anything to do with his cases. It was only two words. Could it be coincidence? Had the Rousseaus known Edwin Channing? Had these handkerchiefs belonged to them, not the Farren brothers?

He made a note to call South Detectives to see if any sign of the Sator Square had been found at the tavern on Montrose.

'What about now?' he asked. 'Why would it show up here?'

Sister Kathleen sat down at her desk, steepled her fingers. 'I'm afraid that is a bit out of my wheelhouse,' she said. 'I don't know the context, and that's as it should be.'

She leaned forward, continued.

'I've known Colleen a long time, and I know what you do for a living, detective. It would not be a surprise if these words have come up as part of an investigation.'

'They have,' Byrne said.

Sister Kathleen thought for a moment. 'In many ways our chosen lives are similar. We try to make sense of an upside-down world, to confront and attempt to vanquish evil where we find it, to bring comfort to the grieving.'

Byrne had given this much thought over the years, still hung on to the vestiges of his Catholic upbringing. He could not find any disagreement with what this woman was saying.

'Quite often people will attach meaning to things when there is no meaning in other areas of their lives. They cling to alcohol or drugs or promiscuity.'

Sister Kathleen stood, glanced at her walls, the ongoing mathematical problems. She looked back at Byrne and Colleen.

'Einstein once said that pure mathematics is the poetry of logical ideas,' she said. 'If there is a logic to this, and I suspect there is, I know you will find it.'

As they were leaving, Byrne looked at the picture hanging on the wall next to the door.

'Where was this taken?' he asked.

She looked at the photo, ran a finger along the bottom of the frame.

'This is in Ghana.'

Byrne studied the smiling children. Twelve in number. All of them looked to be seven or eight years old.

'Four of these children are no longer with us,' Sister Kathleen said.

'I'm sorry.'

'The rest have graduated college.' She touched the smiling

271

girl in the front row. 'Abeeku is now a pediatrician, with five children of her own.'

Byrne didn't know what to say. He could now see why Colleen held this woman in such high regard. He took out a card, handed it to Sister Kathleen. 'If you think of anything else, please call.'

'I certainly will.'

'And thanks again for your time. I trust you'll keep this confidential.'

'You have my word.'

Out in the parking lot, Colleen stopped him, signed: '*I trust you'll keep this confidential?*'

Byrne didn't even bother signing. 'I know, I know. *Jesus*, am I stupid.'

Colleen hauled off and punched him in the shoulder for that one. He knew it was coming, tried to brace himself. It still hurt.

With Colleen fast asleep on the living room couch, Byrne sat at the dining room table. In front of him was his laptop, a half-bottle of Bushmills and the box. It was how he had come to think of it. *The box*. He had returned Desmond Farren's bus pass and dark glasses, and they now sat next to the .38, as they had for the past forty years.

Or had they?

Who was to say that the gun had not been removed from the box and used over and over to commit crimes? Who was to say that there was not, right at this moment, bullet evidence in an envelope at FIU that would match this weapon and bring a killer or killers to justice?

There was no question in Byrne's mind that he was being, at the very least, derelict in his duties by not turning the weapon in to FIU for examination. His failure to do so bordered on the criminal.

He went to the hall closet, took down a shoebox he used for news clippings and old photographs. He found the three items he was looking for.

One was a picture taken by the river beneath the South Street bridge. In it, Byrne stood with Dave Carmody, Ronan Kittredge and Jimmy Doyle. It had been taken sometime in June 1976. Dave, as always, wore his spotless Phillies jersey. Ronan had on his running shorts and worn Nikes. Jimmy wore a white T-shirt and Levi's.

It was the last picture they had ever taken together. After the events of the Fourth of July that year, they had drifted apart. Part of it was that they were teenagers, and, like all teenagers, had begun to leave behind those things of childhood, including friendships. Part of it was the darkness they all carried from having been in some way involved in the maelstrom of evil surrounding the deaths of Catriona Daugherty and Desmond Farren.

Byrne had never spent another summer in the Pocket. The four of them never discussed what happened that night.

The second item Byrne removed from the box was a yellowed news clipping from 1996. It was from the *Newark Star-Ledger*. The headline read: *Hunterdon County Teacher Dies in Fiery Crash*.

Byrne skimmed the short article, although he knew most of it by heart. It told how Ronan Ian Kittredge, 33, had been found at the bottom of a hill, off Route 31, burned to death in his 1995 Ford Aspire. The article said that the road had been treacherous that night due to a blinding snowstorm.

When news of Ronan's death had reached Byrne, he had called the Hunterdon County sheriff's office to find out more details. He was told that there were two sets of tracks found on the shoulder of the road that night. One set – the set that ran down the hill – belonged to Ronan's Aspire. The other set belonged to a much bigger vehicle.

The sheriff's office also said that no one had come forward with any information. They promised to call Byrne if and when there were further details. They never called.

The third item was also a newspaper clipping. Although it was newer, from August 2004, it was more worn and creased. There were rips in the paper, a few spots where liquid had been splashed. That was because Byrne had removed it from the box dozens of times, reading it over and over again with his coffee, or with his Bushmills in the middle of the night, as he was doing now.

This headline read: *Pittsburgh Man Found Shot to Death*. The article chronicled how David Paul Carmody, 41, was found dead in an alleyway in the Homewood section of the city.

When Byrne had got the call from Dave's mother, he drove to Pittsburgh and met with the homicide detectives assigned to the case. They had graciously allowed him to look at the files, the autopsy findings, the toxicology results. Nothing made sense. Dave lived all the way across town from Homewood, had no record of drug use. He did not drink, was happily married. According to the ME's office he had been killed by a single gunshot to the back of the head. No bullet or casing was found. His car was discovered a block away. No witnesses came forward.

Byrne looked at the photograph that accompanied the article. A smiling, early-middle-aged Dave Carmody looked back.

Byrne had called the homicide unit in Pittsburgh once a year since 2004. No arrest was ever made.

Of his three friends from the Pocket, Jimmy Doyle was the one Byrne had lost track of most completely. In fact, after the summer of 1976, he did not talk to him until the day five years ago when Jimmy walked into the Roundhouse, clapped him on the back and announced that he had taken a position with the Philadelphia DA's office homicide division.

They'd met at a number of functions, but had never sat down over a bottle and fully caught up.

Byrne got online, did a search for Greene Towne LLC, the company that was doing the rehabilitation on the house in Devil's Pocket where the box had been found.

He discovered that the company was based in Chestnut Hill, and had a small website by corporate standards, only a few pages deep. It appeared that the project in Devil's Pocket was their first. On one page were short bios of the four principal owners.

One of the names was familiar: Robert Anselmo. Although the man was forty years older than the last time he had seen him, Byrne had no problem recognizing him.

Robert Anselmo had once been partners in the landscaping business with Jimmy's stepfather, Tommy Doyle.

'What did you do, Jimmy?' Byrne asked of the night.

He navigated to Jimmy Doyle's campaign website. He read Jimmy's bio page.

After graduating high school, Jimmy had worked his way through Duquesne University, where he went on to obtain his law degree.

One item in Jimmy's CV jumped off the page. From January 2002 to March 2005, he had been an assistant district attorney for Allegheny County, Pennsylvania.

Byrne picked up the photograph of himself and his three boyhood friends.

As he looked at the young, smiling face of Jimmy Doyle, he felt a cold finger rake his spine.

The largest city in Allegheny County was Pittsburgh.

30

The meeting was for ADAs working the Farren case, and the unit chief of the homicide division. Unless and until arrests were made in the current string of murders, of which the DA's office was all but certain Danny Farren was the orchestrator, the focus would be on building the case in the Jacinta Collins murder, and compiling as much collateral evidence against Farren as possible.

In attendance were Jimmy Doyle, Jessica, Amy Smith and three first-year ADAs.

'We pretty much have what we had before,' Jessica began. 'We have a deposition and statement from the woman who saw Danny Farren park his car on the street that night. She saw him get out of the vehicle, walk behind the building. She said he was back there no more than a few minutes or so – which syncs with the pole-cam recording – then he returned to his car and drove off.'

'Do we have any other eyewitnesses?' Jimmy asked.

'No, that's it. But we do have that pole-cam video, and it aligns with what our witness says Farren was wearing that night.'

'And you met with a member of the bomb squad?' Jimmy asked.

Jessica nodded. 'Detective Zachary Brooks. He walked us through the scene.'

'I've had him on the stand,' Jimmy said. 'Good officer. Great witness.'

Jessica agreed. 'And then we have Farren's fingerprint on the duct tape.'

Before Zach Brooks had given her a crash course on the making, deploying and detonating of a pipe bomb, she would have bet against any kind of forensic evidence – hair, fiber, blood, DNA, fingerprints – surviving the heat and pressure of the blast. Now she knew the opposite.

A series of photographs taken in the basement of The Stone were spread out on the table.

'What do we have from this evidence?' Jimmy asked.

'It's still being tagged and collated. But I can tell you that these photographs and drawings go back many years,' Jessica said.

She tapped one photograph. It showed a picture of a heavy-set man wearing powder-blue double-knit slacks and a matching Ban-Lon shirt. It looked to be 1990s vintage.

Beneath the picture was a clipping from the *Inquirer*. The headline read: *Reputed Mobster Gunned Down in Cherry Hill*.

'We've identified this man as Carmine Sciaccia. He was a captain in the Ruolo crime family from the late seventies until his demise in 1997. The article is about his as-yet-unsolved murder in the parking lot of the Cherry Hill mall. A pipe bomb on a timer.'

'You're saying we think the Farrens carried out the hit?'

'Too early to tell,' Jessica said. 'But I can tell you that there are at least a dozen other instances where we have a covert surveillance photograph over a news clipping wherein the subject of the photograph has been killed. I've run a half-dozen of them. None so far have been closed.'

Everyone in the room remained silent for a few moments. The possibility that they were on the brink of solving a dozen more homicides was energizing to say the least.

'What about the rest of these photos? It looks like there are hundreds of them.'

'Thousands,' Jessica said.

'Good work,' Jimmy Doyle said. 'Keep me posted.'

Jessica began to build her case. Along the way she would add anything she thought might help in the criminal conspiracy counts.

She began to research the Farren family. Records went back to 1944. They were all on paper then, and she had to take her lunch over to the building where they were stored, the vast complex that used to be home to the *Philadelphia Bulletin*, at one time the largest afternoon newspaper in the United States.

Liam Farren and his wife Máire had arrived from Ireland in the early 1940s. Liam had been a fusilier in the British Army. Within a year they'd opened their tavern, The Stone.

Liam was first arrested in 1945 on a criminal complaint of assault and intimidation. The details were that he had offered protection to the owner of a small hardware store, who didn't want to pay. He was convicted and did eleven months.

Jessica made notes on the principals, dates and times.

Over the next fifteen years, Farren was arrested six times, each time on a felony charge. Due to what looked like an efficient system of witness intimidation, he was able to beat all but two of the charges, returning to prison twice for a total of three years.

One of the raps he beat was the firebombing of an insurance firm in Grays Ferry. Jessica underlined the word *firebombing*.

In 1974, Liam Farren was again arrested and indicted, this time on a charge of manslaughter for beating a cab driver to death with a claw hammer. He was sentenced to a ten-year stretch at Graterford. He never made it out. According to prison records, he was killed in a prison yard fight that year.

If Liam Farren's career in crime had been localized to Devil's Pocket and a few surrounding neighborhoods, his sons Patrick and Daniel had taken the show on the road. Between the two of them there were no fewer than three dozen indictments, ranging from assault to arson to strong-arm robbery to residential burglary in neighborhoods as far apart as Cobbs Creek in West Philadelphia, Torresdale in the northeast and the Queen Village section of South Philadelphia.

Patrick Farren was killed in a shootout with police in 1988. Byrne had already filled Jessica in on his own role, as well that of Frankie Sheehan.

After Patrick's death, Danny Farren went on to consolidate his hold on businesses in Devil's Pocket, Schuylkill, Grays Ferry and Point Breeze.

With Michael and Sean Farren, Danny's twin sons, the adage about the apples and the tree proved not to be a cliché. Each of the boys did time in juvenile detention. In 2006, Sean was arrested for menacing. He served two years of a five-year sentence.

According to current records, there was no last-known address for Sean Farren. Michael Farren's only address was The Stone.

Detectives from South were currently looking for known associates of the two men.

When Jessica got home, she took a long, hot shower. She couldn't seem to get the contents of that room full of photographs off her mind.

The photos of the mutilated faces of Edwin Channing and Laura Rousseau were beyond horrifying. Jessica knew why she had been kept out of the loop on the details of the murders. Her job had been to build a case against Danny Farren. Now that the case would include conspiracy on multiple counts, she was copied in on everything.

With Vincent taking care of the kids, she flopped into bed at just after nine o'clock.

She dreamed of The Stone, and what it must have been like in the 1940s and 1950s. Philadelphia had never had a shortage of corner taverns, ethnic neighborhood corner taverns at that. While The Stone had surely never been an elegant place, it was cozy and welcoming in her dream, certainly a contrast to the reality of the place: a den of thieves.

As light began to filter through the blinds, she opened her eyes, rolled over, reached for her husband. Vincent was already up and gone. He and his team at Narcotics Field Unit North were putting together a far-reaching sting operation, and he was working eighteen-hour days.

Jessica looked at the clock. It was nearly six, which gave her a good forty-five minutes before she got up. She needed every second of it. Thank God Sophie was old enough to take care of herself and her brother.

The job had other ideas. Jessica's cell phone rang at just after 6 a.m.

It was Byrne.

There had been another murder.

31

The murder was not in Philadelphia County, but rather Montgomery County.

When Byrne pulled to the curb at just after 7 a.m., he had two cups of Starbucks in the cup holders. Bless him.

Jessica slipped in, sipped the coffee, still clearing the sleep and her dreams from her head.

As Byrne headed toward the expressway, he filled her in on what he had learned from Sister Kathleen. He handed her a copy of the Sator Square.

'Is someone running it through ViCAP?' Jessica asked.

Started by the FBI in 1985, ViCAP – the Violent Criminal Apprehension Program – was a national registry of violent crimes: homicides, sexual assaults, missing persons, and unidentified remains.

'Josh is on it. He'll be calling.'

'How did we get this lead?'

'The detective for the Montgomery County DA's office said

the case is a week old,' Byrne said. 'He picked up our cases on the wire. He says he thinks the MO is identical.'

Jessica shuddered. If the Farren brothers had taken their madness to another county, where else would the trail of blood lead?

The seat of Montgomery County was Norristown, a city of 35,000 residents located six miles from the Philadelphia city limits.

On the way up, Jessica read the case file the lead detective had faxed Byrne.

'This is the Farrens,' she said.

'It sure looks like it.'

They met the lead investigator at the crime-scene house, a duplex on Haws Avenue, near Route 202.

Detective Ted Weaver was in his mid-forties. He had thinning blond hair, blond eyelashes, careful blue eyes. His suit coat was one size too small, and the patch pockets bulged with notebooks, receipts, bits of paper and minutiae that apparently did not fit in the bursting leatherette portfolio on which the zipper had long ago quit. He had that hunched-over posture that Jessica recognized immediately as belonging to an overworked investigator.

He smiled when they approached, and his expression lit up the otherwise depressing scene.

Jessica and Byrne introduced themselves.

'You guys up to speed?' he asked.

According to the summary Weaver had sent, the victim was a fifty-two-year-old man named Robert Kilgore. An attorney specializing in estate planning, Kilgore, according to co-workers, had left his office on the day he was murdered at 5.30. Credit-card receipts showed that he had stopped for pizza at an Italian restaurant on West Main Street at 5.50. He was not seen alive again.

When his tenant in the duplex, a thirty-two-year-old woman named Denise Joseph, knocked on his door at seven the next morning requesting that he move his car, she looked in the window and saw the horror in the living room.

Like Edwin Channing and Laura Rousseau, Robert Kilgore had no face.

'And Miss Joseph didn't see or hear anything the previous night?' Byrne asked.

'Not according to her statement. She said she got home at nine o'clock, took a shower, sat in front of her iMac with head-phones on until midnight, then went to bed.'

'What about the neighborhood interview?'

'Nothing. This is a pretty quiet place. Whoever did this was careful not to be seen or heard.'

'Did you read the summaries of our cases?' Byrne asked.

Weaver nodded. 'It looks like the same MO,' he said. 'Home invasion, single tap to the center of the chest.'

'Duct tape?'

'Yeah.'

Weaver opened the folder on the car's hood, flipped through it. Jessica saw that the crime-scene photographs were as horrific as in the other two cases.

The victim sat in a chair in the middle of the dining room, his ankles tied to the legs, his hands bound behind him. His head slumped forward. A close-up from the front showed that his chest had a single entry wound.

It looked like he was wearing an expensive cashmere sweater and paint-stained sweat pants.

'What about the forensics?' Byrne asked.

Weaver shook his head. 'Gloves on every surface. No latents on the duct tape.'

'Did you recover the projectile?' Jessica asked.

'We did.' He found two photographs of the slug. It wasn't

in good shape, but there was no reason to believe it came from anything other than the Makarov used in the other murders.

Byrne took out two photographs. They were the most recent mug shots of Sean and Michael Farren. He handed them to Weaver. Weaver studied them.

'These are our guys?' Weaver asked.

'These are our guys,' Byrne said.

The house was a large 1930s duplex on Haws Avenue, just a few blocks from the Schuylkill River. The house was set back from the road, on a rise, with a stone retaining wall. There were old-growth maples and pin oaks around the perimeter, and heavy shrubbery near the windows. Perfect cover for breaking and entering.

But the killers did not break and enter. Like the other two scenes, there was no sign of forced entry.

They stepped onto the porch. Jessica noticed that there had at one time been a porch swing. The two eyelets screwed into the ceiling had begun to rust.

Weaver cut the seal, and unlocked the door on the left.

Byrne pointed to the door on the right. 'Is Miss Joseph available for an interview?'

'Not anytime soon. She decided to go stay with her sister in Meadville. I can give you contact information, but we've got her statement, and it's pretty thorough.'

Jessica did not notice any annoyance in Weaver's tone, although no detective really wanted another investigator going over work that was done right the first time. She also knew that Byrne had to ask.

Robert Kilgore's front room was large and had too much furniture. There were two full-size couches, a loveseat, two large recliners. A bookcase ran along one wall, and Jessica noticed that many of the books were legal thrillers, with a few shelves dedicated to textbooks on estate planning law.

In the center of the almond-colored carpeting was a large dark brown stain. Jessica noticed that the dining room table had only five chairs. She assumed that the chair in which the victim had been killed had been removed and processed at the crime lab.

'Where was the bullet evidence collected?' Byrne asked.

Weaver crossed the room, pointed to a torn-out section in the drywall. 'Went in here, hit the back of the brick facade. It's not in great shape.'

'Where is it now?'

'I've got it in the trunk of my car.'

Byrne stepped back, considered the trajectory, the angle of flight. While he did this, Jessica studied the rest of the first floor. Robert Kilgore, who, according to the summary, was unmarried, was neat but not to the point of obsession. There were only two dishes in the sink, and the appliances – all about fifteen years old – were clean and grease-free. She noted the pizza box on the table. She lifted a corner, saw that there was not one piece missing. Mold had begun to grow on the cheese.

She stepped into a small room off the kitchen. In it was a large oak desk, an older-model tower desktop computer, a 20-inch LCD screen. Around the screen were a cascade of yellow Post-it notes. She read some of them.

Mom's b-day. Arc Digest sub?
Darden will!!
CD matures 8/19!

Next to the desk was a three-drawer metal file cabinet. The drawers had been rifled. The floor beneath the desk and next to the cabinet was covered in documents.

Jessica poked her head into the small room that led to the back porch. There was an old bookcase that held running shoes and hiking boots. The middle shelves were stuffed with gardening books and gardening supplies: fertilizers, natural bug sprays, seeds, ornamental bulbs. She could see a small fenced-in garden at the rear of the property.

When she rejoined Byrne and Detective Weaver, they were poring over documents spread out on the dining room table.

'I've got to ask,' Weaver said. 'And I'll understand if you have to play it close.'

'What's that?' Byrne asked.

Weaver took a moment, looked at the photos of the victim. 'The facial mutilation,' he said. 'I mean, I know Philly gets a lot more cases of homicide than we do, but I've got some time in. I've never seen anything like this.'

Byrne nodded. 'This is a new one for of all us.' He went on to explain that the ViCAP search for similar crimes had come up empty.

'When you searched the grounds and the premises, did you find anything that struck you as strange, or out of place?' he asked.

'Not sure what you mean.'

Jessica saw Byrne hesitate for a moment. She understood. While Ted Weaver was a fellow cop, and by all appearances a thorough investigator, letting him in on something known only to the PPD and the killers was not necessarily a good idea.

Byrne decided to do so.

'Did you find a large linen handkerchief?'

Weaver stared at him for a few seconds. He then picked up the thick folder, searched through it. When he reached the end he said simply: 'No.'

Byrne waited a few more seconds, then opened one of his own

folders. He took out the two photographs of the linen handkerchiefs found at the Rousseau and Channing scenes. He placed them on the table. Jessica watched Detective Weaver as he looked at them. He seemed to blanch a little, then immediately recover. He had indeed seen a few things.

'I can tell you without a doubt that we did not recover anything like this.'

'Have you ever heard of something called the Sator Square?'

The look on Weaver's face told Jessica that he knew the theories were coming in like fastballs. He took a second before answering.

'Can't say I have.'

Byrne pulled out the photocopy of the full Sator Square. Weaver took a moment to study it.

'Palindromes,' he said.

'Yes.'

Weaver tapped the photographs of the handkerchiefs. 'Where did you find these?'

Byrne explained how the first handkerchief, *TENET*, was found on a hardy orange tree behind Edwin Channing's house. The second, *OPERA*, on an apple tree at the back of the Rousseau property.

'We looked around the exterior of the house, searching for footwear impressions, checked the hedges close to the house for any fiber that might have come from snagged clothing,' Weaver said. 'There was nothing like this.'

'The tomato plants,' Jessica said.

Both men looked at her.

'What tomato plants?' Weaver asked.

Jessica pointed in the direction of the small room at the rear of the house. 'Mr Kilgore was a gardener. On one of the shelves is a bag of Burpee organic fertilizer with aragonite. My father uses it. It's not cheap, so it looks like Kilgore was serious about his tomatoes. There have to be tomato plants around here somewhere.'

Byrne caught her eye, nodded. He knew that she already knew that there were tomato plants, and where they were located. But she could not say so, could not be where new evidence was collected, if there was any to be found.

'I've got a few calls to make,' she said.

She walked out of the house, toward the car, as the two detectives slipped on latex gloves and headed for the rear of the property. Although there was no reason to think that Ted Weaver, if called to the stand at any time in the future, would betray the trust of a fellow cop, Jessica was not on the record as saying anything other than that she had seen a bag of fertilizer.

She made a few calls, one of them to Josh Bontrager, who told her that the ViCAP search for the Sator Square had come up empty. Before long, she saw Byrne and Ted Weaver walking down the driveway. She knew from her partner's gait that they had found something. She'd seen it many times before.

When they got to the car, Byrne reached into the back seat, took out a white paper bag. He slit it open, laid it across the hood. He then placed the handkerchief on the bag, gently untied the twine, unrolled it. When Jessica saw it, she felt her pulse quicken. It read:

SATOR.

Byrne took out the photocopy of the Sator Square, as well as the two photographs.

'It fits with the other two,' Weaver said.

'Yes, it does.'

'Don't know how we could have missed it.'

'We missed it too,' Byrne said.

Jessica noted that this handkerchief, having been exposed to the elements for a week, was a little more worse for wear than the others.

'Robert Kilgore was killed first, then the Rousseaus, then Edwin Channing,' Weaver said.

Byrne just nodded.

'Which means there will be two more.'

'*AREPO* and *ROTAS*.'

The fact that they'd just established that their killers had already begun their spree a week ago, and done so in another county, opened up the investigation to a whole new level of possibilities, none of them good.

'By the way,' Byrne said, 'did you make a list of important documents that were missing from Mr Kilgore's files?'

'We did,' Weaver said. 'The only major document we couldn't find was his birth certificate.'

'Can we get copies of everything you have so far?' Byrne asked. It was asking a lot, but it had to be done.

Weaver reached into his trunk, took out a shopping bag. He handed the bag to Jessica.

'All yours. I already made the call. The Montgomery County district attorney's office is here to assist. Anything you need. Bullet is in there too.'

'Thanks, detective.'

'You are more than welcome.'

Everyone shook hands.

'Next time you're in Philly, dinner is on the PPD,' Byrne said.

Weaver smiled, patted his not insubstantial belly. 'Sure you can afford it?'

They stopped at a diner on Route 202. They tried to talk about something else beside the case. It didn't last long.

'Has Robert Kilgore come up anywhere in connection with the Farrens?' Byrne asked.

Jessica shook her head. 'Not yet. But now that I have the name, we'll see.'

It was over coffee that Jessica said what was on both their minds. Neither had said it out loud because it was one more piece of this horrifying puzzle – including the Sator Square and the mutilating of faces – that added a new and opaque dimension.

'They're collecting their birth certificates.'

32

They spent the night in one of the featureless motels on the expressway, paying cash. Billy slept in his clothes, his Makarov in hand, a half-dozen photographs taped to the ceiling above him.

Sean went out at dawn and returned with Egg McMuffins and orange juice. They watched the news. There was nothing on the cases.

They parked the white van across the street from the row house. Two doors down was a pizza and hoagie shack. The aromas made Billy hungry again.

'That's her.'

Billy turned to look at the driver. It was his brother Sean. He turned back to see the woman in the lobby of her building, taking mail out of the bank of mailboxes. She was slender and pretty.

Red dress. Gold necklace. Short blond hair.

'Are you sure?' he asked.

'Positive.'

Billy looked at the photograph in his hand, the one he'd taken of the woman on the SEPTA train eight days earlier. Her face was a blank.

'Isn't she supposed to be at work?' he asked.

'Yeah. She's supposed to be.'

They were there, at the woman's apartment building, to do reconnaissance, to find a way in and a way out. They were not supposed to see the woman, not until later that night.

'Let's light her up now,' Sean said.

'No.'

It was the middle of the morning. There were too many people. They would be caught, and there would be hell to pay.

'We need to know the layout.'

Sean reached for his Phillies cap, his sunglasses. He put a hand on the door.

'Wait,' Billy said. 'I'll go.'

Billy attached the suppressor to his Makarov. He pinned the photograph inside his coat and stepped out of the van.

'Can I help you with something?'

Red dress. Gold necklace. Short blond hair.

'I'm sorry?' Billy asked. He wanted to reach into his coat, take out the photograph of the woman – Danielle Spencer was her name – but he couldn't do it, not while she was in front of him. She was standing next to the door to her apartment, keys in hand.

'I was just looking for someone who lives here.' As he said this, he pointed over his shoulder, back down the hallway.

'I know everyone in this building. Who are you looking for?'

Billy needed to come up with a name.

'Emily,' he said. 'My friend Emily.'

The woman thought for a moment. 'There's no one in the building with that name. Are you sure you have the right building?'

Billy glanced at the lobby and saw it. There was a camera pointing at him.

He looked out the front door, at the man in the van. It was Sean. Sean was right. They had to do this now.

'Maybe I do have the wrong place,' he said. 'What is the address here?'

He could see the suspicion growing in the woman; in her posture, the way she pulled the slightest bit away from him.

Before she could respond, the door to her apartment opened. Billy looked over her shoulder to see a man – a big man – standing there. The man wore a gray uniform and had a revolver on his hip, strapped into a gun belt.

'Hey, baby,' he said to the woman.

'Hi,' she replied.

Red dress. Gold necklace. Short blond hair

'Who's your friend?' the man asked.

Billy could tell by the condescending tone, the way the man all but spat the word *friend*, that he looked on him as a lowlife. He felt the fury start to build.

'I think I may have made a mistake,' he said. 'Sorry to have troubled you.'

Billy turned to walk away. He unbuttoned his coat. The man stepped fully into the hallway, put a hand on his shoulder.

'Hang on a minute, pal.'

As the man spun him around, Billy closed his hand on the grip of the Makarov. Facing the man fully, he said, 'Pal? Are we friends already?'

For a moment, the man was stopped by Billy's words. Then he dropped his hand toward his service weapon. It only took a second, but a second was long enough. Billy set his weight, reeled back and slammed a shoulder into the center of the man's chest, knocking him backward into the apartment. Before the man could recover, Billy drew the Makarov and shot him twice in the head.

An hour later, when the death song had been sung, Billy knelt in front of the woman. She was tied up in a chair in the middle of her living room. They had found her birth certificate. They had everything they needed to complete her line in the square.

AREPO.

Red dress. Gold necklace. Short blond hair.

'Do you know my face?' Billy asked.

The woman didn't move.

As Sean unfolded his razor, Billy stood, circled behind the woman. When he was done reciting the prayer, he put both hands on her shoulders, drawing in her essence, closed his eyes as . . .

. . . the afternoon sun filters through the trees, the sound of Billy Joel's 'Captain Jack' afloat on the breeze, the dark blue sedan parked on South Taney Street, doors open, the man in the black leather coat kneeling in front of the girl, her mouth a twist of fear and distress, tears streaming down her face as the man turns, a bag of M&Ms in hand . . .

Billy opened his eyes.

After he carefully placed the handkerchief, Sean paced the small living room. He hit the vial twice in rapid succession. Billy wondered if Sean had slept at all in the past two days.

Sean stopped pacing, reached into Billy's coat, unpinned his photograph. He handed it to Billy.

'I need you to hold this in your hand. You *have* to keep my picture in your hand. We're almost done. We can't have any mistakes.'

'Okay,' Billy said, but his voice sounded far away.

'We're going to get the last of the money. Then we'll draw the final line in the square.'

To Billy, it didn't seem possible. The feeling filled him with something he had never felt before, something buoyant.

He imagined it was what other people called hope.

33

The message on Byrne's voicemail was from an old friend from his academy days, Ron Cimaglio. Ron was a captain in the 17th District. He had seen the alert posted for Michael and Sean Farren, and the names triggered a recent memory.

Michael Farren had crossed Captain Cimaglio's radar just a few days earlier.

Emily Carson was a willowy, pretty woman in her late twenties. She wore a lemon-yellow dress and a delicate gold sweater pendant in the shape of a rose.

Before leaving the Roundhouse, Byrne read the summary written by the two officers who had spoken to Emily Carson on the day in question. The officers underlined the entry that Emily was legally blind.

Byrne met the woman in a small study cubicle off the main room of the Queen Memorial Library. He made notes as Emily told him how she had met Michael Farren, and how Michael had come to the library on an almost weekly basis for many months.

'He always brought me roses,' she said. 'Every time.'

As she said this, her fingers played over the gold pendant.

'Did he say where he bought them?' Byrne asked.

'It never occurred to me to ask.'

'I understand,' Byrne said. 'Do you recall your conversation with the police officers? About why they wanted to talk to you?'

'Of course,' she said. 'Alex said Michael had a gun. It was Alex who called the police.'

'Did you have any reason to doubt what Mr Kiraly was saying?'

'I had *many* reasons to doubt what he said,' she said. 'I guess I just didn't want to believe it. I mean, I don't know Alex that well, but I don't know him to be a liar or a teller of tall tales. I didn't know *what* to think.'

'And that's the last time you spoke to Michael Farren?'

'Yes. It was after we went for a walk on my lunch break.'

Byrne flipped through his notes. 'You told the officers that you and Michael went to a store a few blocks from here. Is that right?'

Emily nodded. 'Yes. It was some kind of electronics store.'

'Do you recall where it was?'

Emily gave him walking directions.

'Do you remember anything Michael said at the time that might have sounded strange, or out of the ordinary?'

'I'm not sure I know what you mean.'

'Did he seem agitated, or different from usual?'

Emily remained silent for a few moments. 'I'm sorry, detective. I just can't think straight.'

'It's okay,' Byrne said. 'Take your time. I know this must be a difficult conversation for you to have.'

Emily took a deep breath, slowly released it. 'No. I don't remember anything out of the ordinary.'

'Did Michael tell you what he bought at the store?'

'Yes. He told me he bought a motion detector.'

'A motion detector,' Byrne said. 'Did he say why he needed it?'

Emily shook her head. 'No. I made a little joke about it at the time. It seems so long ago now.'

'Did he say where he was going when you parted company that day?'

'No.'

Byrne could see that he was losing her. She was clearly on the verge of crying.

'It can't possibly be true,' she said. 'What they're saying Michael has done. All those people. It has to be a mistake.'

Byrne didn't know what to say. He had been to the crime scenes, had seen what the Farren brothers had wrought. He knew very well how people presented different faces to the world, but he was having a difficult time reconciling the horrors of what he had seen with the gentle soul being described to him by this young woman.

'We just need to talk to him,' he said. 'Do you have any idea where he might be right now?'

'I would tell you if I knew, Detective Byrne. For Michael's sake. He never told me where he lived.' She gestured to the main room of the library, to the location in general. 'This is the only world I shared with him.'

It was a long shot, but Byrne decided to go for it. He took out his cell phone.

'I need to ask you a favor.'

Emily looked surprised. 'Of course.'

'Would you be willing to help us bring Michael in?'

'Yes,' she said. 'Of course. I don't want anything bad to happen to him.'

Byrne considered what he was asking. 'I'd like us to go over to the side of the room where the magazines are. Would that be all right?'

'Okay,' Emily said. 'May I ask why?'

Byrne stood, took her hand in his and said, 'The light is better.'

Twenty minutes later, Byrne walked to the electronics store about which Emily had spoken, an old-school emporium called Circuit World. He showed Michael Farren's picture to the two clerks. Neither recognized him.

The owner went through receipts for items purchased around the day and time Byrne specified. There was a record of the purchase of a motion detector at the right time, but no credit card transaction and therefore no billing address.

As Byrne had expected, Michael Farren had paid cash.

Byrne stood in front of the huge whiteboard, the crime-scene photographs of the victims arrayed at the top. Robert Kilgore, the Rousseau family, Edwin Channing.

There was a wire, a direct line that connected all of them. Were these retribution killings? Had these people had dealings with Danny Farren or his sons?

It didn't seem likely, but if Byrne had learned anything in his time on the job, it was that there were very few coincidences, and nothing was beyond the pale.

Before he could call his contacts at South, checking on the status of Sean and Michael's known associates, his phone rang. It was Jessica.

'What's up?'

'Turns out Michael Farren was in a coma for almost two years after that accident in 1988. Did you know about this?'

'No,' Byrne said. 'I never followed up.'

'Well, when he came out of it, he had numerous physical problems, but also another problem. A neurological disorder.'

'What was it?'

'I found the doctor who treated him. He's expecting us.'

Dr Bruce Sheldon was in his late-fifties. He was now in private practice, but had worked for the county mental health system for fifteen years after graduation from Penn State.

They met at his small, comfortable office on Chestnut Street, near Fifth.

As they settled in, Jessica scanned the walls. Sheldon was board-certified in psychiatry, child psychiatry and psychosomatic medicine.

They got the small talk out of the way in short order.

Byrne produced a photograph of Michael Farren. He'd blown up the mug shot and cropped it to look more like a portrait. The effect was less than convincing, particularly to a psychiatrist who had dealt with criminals for thirty years.

'It's our understanding that you treated Michael Farren.'

'Yes,' said Sheldon. 'He was remanded to juvenile detention at the time. He spent a little over a year there.'

'What was he in for?'

'He was convicted of an assault against a county employee.'

'Did it involve a weapon?'

'No,' Sheldon said. 'But the assault was severe enough to send the victim to the hospital.'

'How did Farren come to be on your radar?' Byrne asked.

'He was considered to be uncooperative. Didn't accept authority. Of course, that's not exactly a rarity in the juvenile detention system. It's one of the reasons they enter the system in the first place.'

'Were there any violent incidents when he was inside?' Byrne asked.

Sheldon glanced at the file in front of him. 'Minor scuffles with other boys. Nothing too violent. After a while the others found out about his family and gave him a wider berth.'

'They knew his father was Danny Farren?'

'Oh yes,' he said. 'A lot of these kids – most of them, in my experience – are acting out. Not really bad kids, but acting out to get attention. Someone like Michael Farren was seen as a legacy kid, a third-generation criminal.'

'You said uncooperative. How so?'

'Well for one thing, he insisted he was not Michael Farren. He said his name was Billy.'

'He called himself Billy?'

'Yes,' Sheldon said. 'Billy the Wolf. It's from a song by—'

'The Stark,' Byrne said.

'You've heard of it?'

Byrne just nodded.

'Another of his behaviors included seeing the same corrections officers and facility personnel every day but claiming he didn't know who they were. At first it was thought that this was part of the con. You'd be amazed at some of the things these kids come up with.'

'Can you tell us what your initial findings were?'

'Because Michael had suffered a severe head trauma, and indeed was in a coma for a long time, it was somewhat difficult to diagnose his condition. I think we went through three months straight of tests. In the end, among other findings, we discovered that he suffered from a somewhat rare neurological disorder called prosopagnosia.'

'What is that?'

'It is a cognitive disorder of face perception, sometimes called face blindness, where the ability to recognize faces is impaired. Other traits of visual processing – for instance, object discrimination and intellectual functioning, such as decision-making –

often remain intact. Sometimes these functions are enhanced. People with prosopagnosia can be quite brilliant. Oliver Sacks, for one.'

'The doctor?'

'Yes,' said Sheldon. 'The term wasn't even coined until 1944 or so. Men with post-traumatic stress disorder and severe head trauma were returning from the war and not being able to recognize their own wives and families.'

'How does this manifest in the real world?' Byrne asked.

'Well, if you suffer from this syndrome, even in its mildest form, you could meet someone, spend a good deal of time with them, then a day later not know them from Adam.'

'So is it possible that you might use clothing as a recognition strategy?'

'Absolutely. The color, texture and style of clothing can be a very powerful tool. Prosopagnosics sometimes use a fractional strategy that involves clues such as clothing, body shape and hair color.'

The changing of clothes, Jessica thought. This was why Farren was making them put on other clothes. He needed the clothing as a marker.

'Might the person use a photograph as a reference point?' she asked.

'Yes,' said Sheldon. 'Would you like to see some of the tests we use as diagnostic tools?'

Jessica looked at Byrne, back. 'Sure.'

Sheldon got up, crossed the room to a table against the wall. On it was a 27-inch iMac. He hit a few keys. The screen defaulted to a screen saver depicting Robert Indiana's *LOVE* sculpture. He turned back to his guests.

'This is a pure test of facial recognition,' he said. 'Shall we begin?'

'Okay,' Jessica said.

Dr Sheldon tapped a key. On the new screen were six ovals: three across, two down. In each oval was a different face. Just a face, from cheek to cheek, hairline to the bottom of the chin. No hair, no ears, nothing below the chin. Four of the faces were white; two were black.

Sheldon then handed Jessica and Byrne each a blank piece of paper with six empty ovals.

'Without consulting each other, I want you to fill in the name of each of the people on the screen, if you recognize them. If you don't, just leave it blank.'

To Jessica – and she was certain Byrne – this didn't seem too difficult. She wrote down six names; Byrne followed suit.

Dr Sheldon tapped a key. The faces disappeared. The screen went blank.

'How did we do?' he asked.

Both Jessica and Byrne handed in their sheets. Jessica saw that they had identical responses: Carroll O'Connor, Andy Reid, James Earl Jones, Ringo Starr, Sidney Poitier, Jackie Gleason.

'You both get an A,' Sheldon said. 'Now I'm going to show you six more faces. I want you to tell me if you recognize any of them.' He handed them blank sheets. 'Ready?'

'Ready,' Jessica and Byrne said in unison.

He tapped a key.

What seemed to be another simple test was anything but, Jessica found. The faces were all upside down.

'You probably want to tilt your head to the side, but don't,' Sheldon said.

He was right. It was Jessica's first instinct. And it was maddening. She couldn't identify any of the faces.

'I don't know any of these people,' she said.

Sheldon looked at Byrne. 'Detective?'

'I think I know one,' Byrne said. He wrote on his sheet.

'Ready to see who these strangers are?'

Sheldon tapped a key. A moment later, all six pictures flipped, right side up. It was astonishing. Jessica recognized them all. B. B. King. Goldie Hawn. Richard Gere. Harry Dean Stanton. Anthony Hopkins. Donna Summer.

Byrne turned his paper over. He'd written *B. B. King*.

'Awesome,' Jessica said.

'I'm a blues fan,' Byrne said. 'What can I say?'

'Not as easy as you might think, right?' Sheldon asked.

'I would have bet against this,' Byrne said. 'I would have bet I could recognize them all.'

'Most people would. All the parts are there – eyes, nose, mouth, eyebrows, chin – but there is no whole. No connection. We've run tests where the subject's child or parent were in the mix, the right-side-up mix, and there was no recognition whatsoever.'

'And you're saying that this is what the world looks like to Michael Farren?'

Sheldon took a moment. 'You know how sometimes you see footage on TV and people will be pixelated out?'

'Sure.'

'Some people with prosopagnosia describe it that way. They'll fixate on a feature – hairstyle, perhaps – and use that as a marker.'

'What about context?' Byrne asked.

'Very important.'

'So if someone with this disorder is in a place with which they are very familiar, it might aid them in recognizing people they expect to be there.'

'Absolutely,' Sheldon said. 'Place, time of day, even smells can be used as markers.'

'This affects recognition of family members?'

'Yes. Mothers, fathers, sisters brothers,' he said. 'I've read case histories of women who left their children at playgrounds because they could not recognize them.'

'How pronounced is Michael's Farren's condition?'

'I haven't seen him in twenty years, but because there is no cure for this, no drug therapy, I'd say it's as pronounced as anyone suffering from the syndrome.'

'Is this something that can get progressively worse?'

'Yes, it can.'

Sheldon turned off the computer.

'I don't get many visits from the homicide division and the DA's office,' he said. 'I know you're bound by confidentiality, so I won't ask. But obviously this is something serious.'

'It is,' Byrne said.

Sheldon turned away for a moment, looked out the window, at the people passing by his office. He turned back. 'I've seen thousands of patients in my thirty years of practice. Some had very minor issues, some had conditions that required a lifetime of in-patient therapy. I'd like to think I remember them all. I remember Michael Farren. I hoped that he would learn to cope with his condition, but I was not optimistic.' He crossed his hands in his lap. 'If ever I get the opportunity to see him again, I will start over.'

They stood on the sidewalk, leaned against the car. The heat was rising. Byrne loosened his tie.

While they were waiting, two more patients entered Sheldon's office. Life goes on, Jessica thought.

'Face blindness,' she said.

'I have to admit, I'd never heard of it.'

'It's why the victims were dressed the way they were dressed.'

'I think you're right.'

'Farren has to have them dressed in a certain way before he knows he has the right person.'

Byrne just nodded.

'But where does he know them from?'

There was still no direct link between the Rousseau family, Edwin Channing and Robert Kilgore. The only connection seemed to be their violent deaths, and a cryptic message painted in blood on a fine linen handkerchief.

34

Josh Bontrager stood in the small lobby of an eight-suite apartment building in Germantown. He was as pale as Jessica had ever seen him. She'd never known him blanch at a crime scene.

Around him walked a flurry of crime-scene technicians.

Byrne and Jessica had gotten the call after leaving Dr Sheldon's office.

There had been a double murder.

In the center of the small living room sat the victim. She looked to be in her late twenties. Her hands and feet were bound with duct tape. There was a single entry wound to the center of her chest. The rug beneath her, as well as the white leather loveseat behind her, was splattered with blood.

The woman was barefoot. It appeared she was wearing a knee-length red skirt and a dark blue Robert Morris University sweatshirt.

There was little doubt that Michael Farren had made her put on the sweatshirt, confirming that she was the intended victim.

Her name was Danielle Spencer. Like Edwin Channing, Robert Kilgore and Laura Rousseau, the Farrens had peeled away her face.

After the investigator for the medical examiner made his pronouncement, and finished taking pictures, the crime-scene officers began processing the scene.

Jessica and Byrne stayed out of the way, standing on the other side of the dining room table, a silent understanding passing between them. They had both dealt with serial murder, with multiple murder, but they now knew that this rampage was as bad as anything they had ever experienced, and that predicting where the Farrens would strike next would become a priority for every law enforcement officer in the county.

As Josh Bontrager stepped in to begin his investigation, Jessica looked at the victim on the floor by the door. He wore the grey uniform of an armored car security service. The revolver on his hip was still strapped in, and looked to have not been drawn. The two holes in his forehead, in a very tight pattern, explained why he did not get the chance.

The crime-scene officer taking photographs moved closer to the dead man. Jessica returned to the dining room, saw the handkerchief on the table, unfurled on a large piece of glossy white paper.

AREPO.

Josh Bontrager stepped into the dining room.

'Where was it?' Jessica asked.

'She has one of those AeroGardens.'

'Not sure what that is,' Jessica said.

Bontrager led them to the kitchen. On the counter was an indoor garden, a plastic receptacle with white lights over a hydroponic base. It was thick with basil, parsley, cherry tomatoes, peppers.

Bontrager took out a pencil, lifted one of the large basil leaves. 'It was tied right there.'

'Same twine?' Byrne asked.

'Looks like it.'

Byrne gestured to the papers strewn around the living room. He pointed to a folder titled 'Legal'.

'Did you find the victim's birth certificate?'

'No birth certificate,' Bontrager said. 'Everything but.'

Bontrager's phone rang. He answered, stepped away, spoke for a few moments.

'Can you send it to me?' he asked. He then gave his email address, said: 'Thanks very much.'

He turned back to Jessica and Byrne. 'That was the security firm that handles this building. There's a camera in the lobby, as well as the parking lot and the rear delivery door. There's also one in the elevator. The cameras feed to a cloud.'

'Do they have something?' Byrne asked.

'I'm going to say they do. The guy I just spoke to made a clip of the lobby camera from earlier today. He sounded pretty shaken up.'

Bontrager's phone beeped. He looked at it.

'We have it.'

They stood in the back hallway, near the delivery entrance. Bontrager propped his phone on the table used by the delivery services. He launched the file from the security company.

The recording was a high-angle shot of the front hallway. A few seconds in, a woman walked down the hallway, stopped in front of apartment 102. It was the victim, Danielle Spencer. Jessica felt a chill run up her spine. This woman had been alive just a few hours ago.

The woman dug around in her purse, extracted her keys. After a few moments she looked up, towards the lobby. A figure approached her, a man with hair to his shoulders, wearing a leather jacket.

The man was Michael Farren. It was the same coat he'd been wearing in the other surveillance video, taken from the Sadik Food King.

Farren and Danielle appeared to talk briefly.

A few seconds later, the door to 102 opened. A man stepped out. He was the victim on the floor near the door. He kissed Danielle, then turned his attention to Michael Farren. They exchanged a few words. Farren turned away from the man and unbuttoned his coat. The man put a hand on Farren's shoulder. The scene seemed to freeze for a long moment, then Farren pivoted and drove his shoulder into the man's chest, pushing him back into the apartment.

Then, with lightning speed, Farren drew a silenced weapon and fired two shots into the apartment.

They gathered in the lobby as CSU geared up for another long day. They watched the activity in silence, as they had many times before. Finally Bontrager spoke.

'I've never taken the life of another person,' he said. 'It is something I have been trained to do, and will do, if necessary, to save my life or the life of a citizen of this city. But beyond this, I have never wished death upon anyone, no matter how evil their acts. Not once.' He paused for a moment. 'Until today. Today I wished death upon the people who did this terrible thing, and at some point I am going to stand before God and explain myself.'

Jessica and Byrne said nothing.

Bontrager pointed at the crime scene. 'I have to get back in there. I'll keep you posted. Be safe.'

'You too, Josh,' Jessica said, but he had already turned on his heels and was walking down the hallway.

Jessica and Byrne stood on the sidewalk in front of the building. Jessica could not get the video out of her mind. She looked at the steps, the door, the lobby, the hallway. Rare was the instance when she had arrived at the scene of a clearly premeditated murder so soon after.

'How do we stop them?' Jessica asked.

Byrne took a moment. 'If the Sator Square is their pathology for these killings, they are going to stop themselves, if we don't find them first. Then it becomes a matter of hunting them down.'

His phone rang. He looked at it. 'I don't recognize this number.' He hesitated a few moments as it rang again. He decided to answer. He put it on speakerphone.

'This is Byrne.'

'Detective Byrne, this is Joe Sadik.'

'Yes, Mr Sadik. What can I do for you?'

'The two men. The two men that were on the surveillance video. The one you made the print out of.'

'What about them?'

'I just got back from the bank. Those men are in the U-Cash-It right now.'

35

Dennis LoConti sat on a chair in the middle of the office. His hands were taped behind him.

Billy watched from the doorway.

Yellow shirt. Blue jeans. Sleeve and neck tattoos.

A man stood behind LoConti.

Sean.

Sean took another hit of the meth. His eyes were red glass.

'Let me see if I can make this a little clearer for you,' he said. 'You are going to open the safe. You are going to take out everything in there. You are going to give it to us.'

'I *paid* you for this month, man.'

Sean put the M&P to the man's head. 'Are you really this fucking stupid? Are you really going to argue with me?'

LoConti said nothing.

'Here's how it works. I'm going to untie you. You're going to stand up, walk over to that safe and open it. If you take too long, or make a move I don't like, I will empty this mag into your lowlife, white-trash, skank-tat fucking head. Do you under-stand?'

LoConti nodded.

Sean took out his razor, cut the man loose. LoConti stood up on shaky legs, crossed the room slowly, knelt down. He reached out to the electronic keypad.

'Wait,' Sean said. 'Billy.'

Billy crossed the room, stood just behind Dennis LoConti. He leveled his weapon, pointing it at the man's head.

'You don't have a gun in there, do you, Denny boy?' Scan asked. He hit his vial, shook it off.

'No,' LoConti said. 'There's no gun.'

'There better not be. Let's go. Open it.'

Due to his trembling hands, it took Dennis LoConti a few attempts to open the safe. On the second blown attempt, Sean began to pace. Finally the tumblers fell and LoConti gently turned the handle.

'Stop,' Sean said.

LoConti did.

'Get up – slowly – and get back over here.'

LoConti obeyed. Sean tossed Billy the duct tape. Billy again secured LoConti to the chair. Sean grabbed his duffel bag, opened the safe fully, peered inside.

'Holy *shit*,' he said. 'Look, Billy.'

Billy looked. Inside the safe was what appeared to be fifteen thousand in cash, all banded hundreds. There were also some clear plastic bags containing gold watches, bracelets, necklaces. Sean made short work of shoveling it all into the duffel bag. Before he zipped it, he saw something else in the safe.

'Oh *no*,' he said. 'Denny, Denny, *Denny*.'

Sean reached into the safe, extracted a revolver. It looked to be a .38 Police Special. He put his M&P in his waistband, got up, crossed the room. He tapped LoConti's lips.

'Wrap him,' he said.

Billy wrapped the duct tape around the man's head, gagging him.

Sean knelt in front of LoConti. 'You lied to me, Denny. That's the lowest thing a man can do. You lied to me, and it hurts my feelings.'

He stood. He pointed at the camera staring down at them.

'Is the camera on?'

Dennis LoConti nodded.

'Recording?'

Another nod.

'Good.' Sean walked up to the camera, stared into it for a few moments.

'This is what happens to liars,' he said.

He walked back to where Dennis LoConti was seated, put the gun to the man's head and pulled the trigger. The force of the point-blank explosion sent LoConti onto his side on the floor. Blood and fragments of his skull streaked the garish yellow walls.

'What about *now*, asshole? What about *now*? Got some fucking smartass response now?'

Sean emptied the revolver into LoConti's chest, then tossed the gun aside.

'Billy.'

Billy looked at the man.

Sean.

Sean reached into Billy's coat, took out his picture, put it in Billy's hand. 'I told you to keep the fucking picture *out*. Keep it in your hand.'

Billy stared at the photo. There was not much left of Sean.

'You have to say you know who I am.'

'Sean,' Billy said.

'Go around back, get the van, drive around to the front. I'm going to light this place up.'

'Okay.'

Sean ran to the front of the store, leapt over the counter, just as sirens rose in the distance. It sounded as if every police car in the city was on the way. And they were getting closer.

Billy looked at the photograph in his hand, and the man at the front of the store.

Sean.

'We have to split up, Billy.'

Billy remained silent.

'You know where to meet me, right?'

The sirens drew nearer.

'You know where to meet me, right? We have to split up.'

'I know,' Billy said. 'By the Trolley Works. I know.'

Sean looked at his watch. 'Midnight.'

'Okay.'

Billy watched the man run out the back door, down the alley, and vault the fence at the end. He looked at the photograph.

Sean.

Midnight.

Billy parked near the old warehouse at the end of Reed Street, far from the nearest street lamp, just fifty or so feet from the entrance to the Philadelphia Trolley Works. Every so often a police car drove by.

Billy watched for Sean. It was past midnight, and Sean had not shown. Something was wrong.

He stepped into the darkened doorway of the warehouse, pulled the Makarov from his holster, held it at his side. He listened for footfalls, the rapid panting of a K-9 dog coming up the street, but heard neither. He had once been attacked by a German Shepherd with silver eyes when he'd boosted a pair of candlesticks from a house in Torresdale. That had been when he was nine or so, before his dream, and he remembered every detail, every creak of a stairway tread, even the way the dog smelled.

He looked around the building. There were two policemen by the white van, lights flashing. Billy slipped the suppressor from his jeans pocket, threaded it onto the barrel. He chanced another glance as a second patrol car arrived.

He looked to his right, at the block of row houses on Earp Street. He knew that there was an alley behind them, an alley that emptied onto South 36th Street. Beyond that, a block or so away, at Wharton, he would be able to catch a SEPTA bus.

Billy closed his eyes, tried to organize his thoughts. He'd spent much time around this area when he was small, following the tracks. He once spray-painted his name on this warehouse. He wondered if it was still there. Maybe if he saw it, it would take him back.

He opened his eyes, peered down the length of the building. Somehow, Emily was standing on the corner, just beneath the street light. She wore a powder-blue dress and a thin strand of pearls. When she turned to look at him, Billy raised a hand to wave. He saw then that the right side of her head was missing.

It wasn't Emily. It was the girl from The Jade Kettle. The dead girl.

It was shadows.

Billy took a deep breath, arranged the weight of his bag on his shoulder. Before he could take a step, he saw a shadow pool on his left. The man was less than five feet away. Billy had not heard him approach. His footfalls were masked by the sound of a siren.

'Police!' the man yelled.

Billy spun, his weapon out and leveled. He squeezed off a single round.

The bullet entered the police officer's right eye and exited the back of his skull in a violent gout of scarlet blood. The policeman slumped onto his right side, rolled onto his back. Billy put the barrel of the weapon over the man's heart and once again pulled the trigger. The force of the blast caused the man's body to lift slightly from the ground.

Billy stepped back, looked at the man, saw the ravel of red thread over the pocket, now soaked in blood. He holstered his weapon as a police car turned the corner, just twenty yards away. He looked inside his coat, at the photograph.

The man on the ground wasn't a policeman.

It was Sean Farren. His brother.

Sean was not saying that he was police. He was trying to warn him.

Billy watched as Sean's spirit began to rise. He saw their mother, Deena Farren, so thin in her hospital bed, purple bruises on her arms, her skin the color of bones. He saw his brother standing in front of their father, taking the beating that put the scar over his eye. He saw the broken teacup on the floor. He saw his brother standing over him that Christmas Eve on Carpenter Street. He saw himself being born into darkness.

Billy removed Sean's picture from his coat. In it he could suddenly see everything. Every feature on Sean's face. He placed the photograph on his brother's body. Then he reached into Sean's pocket, removed the straight razor. It would be up to him to draw the final line now.

ROTAS.

Billy knew the way.

Billy ran.

36

The scene at U-Cash-It had been a bloodbath. Dennis LoConti was found in the office, bound to a chair, the walls painted with his blood. At first it appeared he had been shot once in the head and twice in the chest. A review of the surveillance recording showed that Sean Farren had emptied the .38 Police Special, which was found on the floor near the office door, into the man's chest.

Joe Sadik, who had been watching from across the street from the moment he made the call, had seen a white Econoline van speed away from the scene. He wrote down the license plate.

Within five minutes of the shooting at the end of Reed Street, a perimeter was established. A boat from the marine unit was scrambled. The ID unit had an officer on scene to fingerprint the victim.

When Byrne arrived with John Shepherd and Josh Bontrager,

there were twenty sector cars on scene, more than forty patrol officers on foot.

Byrne pulled up to the warehouse. The three detectives exited the car. Byrne spread a map on the hood of the car.

There were dozens of row houses on the three nearest blocks.

Byrne took the block on Reed Street. While two patrol officers covered the front of the houses, he slowly made his way down the alley behind them. One by one he stepped close to the back doors, the windows, listening. Only four of the houses had lights on.

He knew that the patrol officers would be knocking on the front doors, ringing the bells.

When Byrne got to the third house from the end of the block – a house with no lights on – he looked at the door jamb.

The back door was slightly ajar.

He stood on the top step, listened. The house was silent. He turned down the volume on his two-way radio, tapped lightly on the door jamb. No response. He tapped again. No lights, no response.

His weapon at his side, he bumped the door with his shoulder, rolled into the kitchen. The only illumination was from the small light on the range hood.

The kitchen was empty. Byrne took a deep breath, moved down the short hallway toward the living room. There was a door in the hallway, probably leading to a pantry or powder room. He tried the knob. Locked.

When he got to the end of the hallway, he paused. The lights from the sector cars on Reed Street washed the living room walls with red and blue light.

In the flashing light he saw the layout of the living room, saw his pathway to the stairs leading to the second floor. As he turned the corner into the dining room, he felt something against his foot. Something heavy.

The woman was face down on the dining room carpet. Byrne knelt down, put two fingers to her neck. She had a pulse. He shone his Maglite on the back of her head, saw the blood.

Before he could get his two-way radio in hand, he saw the shadow to his left.

He turned. Michael Farren stood behind him. In one arm he held a three-month-old child. A little girl in a red one-piece. In his right hand he held the Makarov. Attached to it was a suppressor.

'Put your weapon on the floor,' Farren said.

Byrne complied.

'Hands out.'

Byrne put his hands out to his sides.

'Who are you?' Farren asked.

Byrne slowly rose to his feet. 'My name is Byrne. I'm a detective with the Philadelphia Police.'

Farren pointed at Byrne's weapon. He held the baby closer to his chest. He stepped behind Byrne, out of eyeshot.

'Very slowly, take the magazine out.' Byrne did as instructed. 'Now jack the round out of the chamber.' Again Byrne followed directions.

'Empty your pockets.'

Byrne did. He imagined that the killer wanted to know whether he had a second gun, or an extra magazine. He had neither.

'Lift your pant legs. One at a time.'

Byrne complied.

Michael Farren stepped back in front of Byrne, indicated with the barrel of the Makarov for Byrne to cross the room, sit on the chair by the fireplace. When he did, Farren picked up the magazine, removed all the cartridges, put them in his pocket, along with the single cartridge removed from the firing chamber.

The two-way radio chattered. Byrne cast a glance to the passageway into the kitchen. He knew that the back door was still

320

open. He waited for one of the rookie patrol officers to stumble into the house, weapon drawn. He waited for disaster.

'I want you to get on the radio,' Farren said. 'I want you to tell them that you've cleared this house and that you're going to keep searching the other houses.'

Byrne didn't move. He was waiting for permission. Farren touched the barrel of the suppressor to the baby's head.

'I saw the address on my way in,' Farren added. 'I know where we are. Do it now.'

Byrne slowly reached for the two-way, got on channel.

'I'm in 3702,' he said. 'The third house from the corner. It's clear. Moving on.'

'Fine,' Farren said. 'Now turn the volume down, but not off. Put it on the floor.'

Byrne did. He kept his hands out to his sides.

'The block is pretty tightly cordoned off,' he said.

Farren nodded, but said nothing. He shifted the baby's weight.

As the headlights of a sector car washed across the walls, Byrne got a better look at Michael Farren. In the grainy photograph taken from the surveillance footage from Sadik Food King, as well as the most recent mug shot, he'd seen a suspect – male, white, mid-thirties, brown hair, blue eyes, medium build, scar on his right cheek.

But in this moment, in this place, he saw the ten-year-old boy running out into the middle of the street.

Byrne remembered the night as if it were yesterday. He remembered the snow. He remembered the song, 'The Little Drummer Boy', coming from the tinny speakers in the bodega. He remembered Danny Farren standing on the corner with his two ten-year-old sons. He remembered the car coming around the corner, the sickening sound of the impact, the snow falling on bright red blood.

'It's time for me to go,' Farren said. He held the baby closer. 'You better hope your fellow officers aren't too trigger-happy.'

'No one's going to do anything, Michael.'

'Michael is dead, detective. Your kind killed him on Christmas Eve 1988. There's only me now.'

'Okay,' Byrne said. 'What do I call you?'

Farren looked at him as if this might be common knowledge. 'Billy.'

Billy the Wolf, Byrne thought.

He nodded. 'Billy, then.'

A siren screamed to life a half-block away, began to fade. Farren tensed, drew himself closer to the passageway into the kitchen.

'Why all this, Billy?' Byrne asked. 'Why these people?'

Farren stared into the darkness for a few moments.

'Grandfather, Uncle Patrick, Sean. They were all cursed. As am I.'

He lowered his weapon, kept it at his side.

'And now my father. There is only one way.'

The Sator Square, Byrne thought.

Five words, five lines.

The invocation of the square can lift jinxes and curses.

'What do you mean?' he asked, trying to buy time. 'How is your father cursed?'

Every few seconds Farren would open the left side of his coat and glance inside. Byrne finally realized what he was doing. There were photos inside the coat. He was trying to mark Byrne as someone he knew, or someone he was supposed to kill. He reached in, touched the photograph on the bottom right. Byrne only saw it for a second, but he could see that the photo was older, vintage, color leached by time. The photo next to it was a close-up of Michael's father, Danny.

'It all started with my grandfather when he came to this place.'

'What place, Billy? Devil's Pocket?'

Farren nodded. 'My family has been cursed ever since.'

'You don't have to hurt the child, Billy.'

Farren looked down, as if he'd forgotten he was holding the baby. She was asleep.

'When you are face-blind, people think you're stuck up,' he said. 'People think you're stupid. If they only saw it from the inside, they would think differently.'

'Of course they would,' Byrne said. He stole a glance at the window. He could see the reflection of a sector car's lights washing the wall opposite. It was getting closer.

'Kick the police radio over to me,' Farren said.

Byrne did so.

Farren grabbed a blanket out of the crib, wrapped it around the little girl.

'We are alike, you and me,' he said.

'What do you mean?'

Farren hesitated a long moment, looking at Byrne as if he were a curiosity in a jar. 'You have been to the other side. Like I have.'

Byrne had no idea how Farren would have known this, about how more than twenty years ago he had been shot, plunged into the Delaware River and been pronounced dead. How ever since, there had been moments when something akin to a vague and unfocused second sight channeled his thought. It had been a while since he'd had the sensations, but he knew it was something that would never leave him.

'You came back with an ability, as I did,' Farren said. 'But there is also a deficit. A blind spot. Am I right?'

Byrne said nothing.

'With me it is faces,' he said. 'What is your blindness, Detective Byrne?'

For some reason Byrne was unable to speak. He'd never thought about it, but it was true.

Farren held up the two-way radio. 'I will be taking this with me and listening to the cross-talk. If I hear a word on this radio in the next two minutes about our encounter, you'll find this baby in the river. Do you understand?'

'I understand.'

'Do you care about the life of this child?'

'Very much,' Byrne said.

'As do I. I wish her no harm. Do not force my hand.'

And then he was gone.

The baby was found, unharmed, behind a Dumpster at the end of the alley.

Unless Farren was holed up in one of the hundreds of row houses in the neighborhood – and all police could do was knock on the doors – there was a good chance that he had slipped through the perimeter.

Byrne met with Josh Bontrager and John Shepherd on the corner of 36th and Wharton. Two helicopters hovered overhead. Shepherd's phone rang. He answered, listened.

'Okay,' he said. 'Thanks.'

He hung up, remained silent.

'What is it?' Byrne asked.

'The body by the warehouse.'

'What about it?'

'It's Danny Farren's son Sean.'

'Michael Farren shot him,' Bontrager said.

'Yes,' Shepherd said. 'A patrol officer saw him do it.'

'He doesn't have anyone to help him now,' Byrne said. 'He's on his own.'

The detectives looked out over the city.

Michael Farren could be anywhere.

37

The last time Byrne had stood this close to Danny Farren was more than twenty-five years earlier. It was on a street corner in Devil's Pocket the night a woman named Miranda Sanchez was savagely beaten by Danny's brother Patrick. It was Christmas Eve. It was the night Michael Farren died and Billy the Wolf was born.

At that time Danny Farren had looked as intimidating as his reputation and rap sheet indicated.

Now, even though he was in his seventies, his biceps were still big. Still the mad dog, maybe with a few less teeth.

They met in a small room off the main cell block at Curran-Fromhold Correctional Facility on State Road. CFCF was opened in 1995, and named in honor of Warden Patrick N. Curran and Deputy Warden Robert F. Fromhold, who were murdered at Holmesburg Prison on May 31, 1973.

On a monitor in a nearby room, Jessica watched Farren's penetrating blue eyes. There was a good chance that the man knew what Byrne was going to say, but it was protocol for a member of the PPD to make the notification.

Byrne entered the room. Danny Farren sat waiting. His hands were shackled to a bolt in the steel table. Jessica knew that the man's attorney was standing by, watching the proceedings from another room. He had surely advised his client not to meet with Byrne alone. It was not surprising that a man like Danny Farren would want to do things his way.

The two men sat across from each other for a full minute without speaking.

'I remember you,' Danny Farren finally said.

'Mr Farren, I'm sorry to inform you that your son Sean has been killed.'

Farren just stared at Byrne. No reaction at all. Jessica couldn't imagine living a life where the slightest tic of emotion would be read as weakness. Even when learning about the death of a child.

'Was it a cop who did it?' he asked eventually.

'The incident is still under investigation,' Byrne said.

'Was it a cop?'

Byrne took a moment. 'It was not.'

Farren looked away for a moment, back. 'And I'm supposed to believe you?'

'I have no thoughts on that,' Byrne said. 'I'm just telling you what I know.'

'You killed my brother. And now you've killed my son.'

'I didn't kill your brother, Danny. I think maybe your memory is failing you.'

'My memory is perfect.'

'I was there, yes. But I didn't kill him.'

'Then what the fuck do *you* call it?'

'I call it an unfortunate incident. Your brother pointed a firearm at a police officer. A man he *knew* was a police officer.'

'And for that he should be killed?'

Byrne leaned forward. 'Yes. Every single time.'

Nothing.

'Call your son off,' Byrne said.

Farren raised his eyes.

'I don't know what you're talking about,' he said.

'Call Michael off.'

'I know who my boy is. I've just got the one now, you see. Going to make quick work of my Christmas shopping this year.'

'Every cop in the PPD is looking for him. So is the FBI.'

'Good luck with that.'

'That's thousands of armed men and women. I think your son is the one who needs the luck.'

'And yet he's managed to elude custody.'

'Get word to him that if he surrenders, I will personally see to his safety.'

Farren lifted his iron-clad hands, looked at the walls around him.

'I'm in a fucking cage. How am I supposed to get word to anybody about anything?'

'If he turns himself in, I will see to his safety,' Byrne repeated.

'What, like my brother Desmond? Like the PPD worked on the case in '76 when Desmond was found floating in the Schuylkill with a bullet in his fucking head? That kind of safety?'

Byrne said nothing.

'My mother sent a letter to that dago piece of shit Rizzo. He didn't have the fucking decency to answer.'

Frank Rizzo was the controversial mayor of Philadelphia from 1972 to 1980. Before that he had been the commissioner of police.

'I was in junior high school then, Danny.'

'So was your boy.'

'What are you talking about?'

327

Danny Farren rolled his shoulders, his neck. It was the kind of thug move that always preceded a left-hook sucker punch thrown in a bar, something at which Farren had a lot of experience. Unfortunately for him, that was not going to happen today.

'That Doyle punk,' he said. 'Jimmy Doyle.'

'What about him?'

Farren leaned forward. 'You think I don't know what happened in the park that day? You think I didn't know how he cut my brother?' He leaned back. 'Now he wants to put away the last of the Farrens.'

The two men fell silent.

'I'm fucking dying,' Farren said.

He turned his arms. There, amid the Celtic crosses on each forearm, were the marks left by the chemotherapy treatments.

'I've done a few things in my life,' he finally said. 'I'm no fucking choirboy. But this thing? This murder charge? It wasn't me.'

Jessica knew that when Farren was arraigned, he had pleaded not guilty to all charges. It was SOP for men like him. Still, with so little to lose or gain at this point, she wondered why he was still clinging to the claim that he had not committed the firebombing of the store.

'You're on surveillance tape, Danny. Your prints were on the bomb.'

Men like Farren, if they knew who had done it, would still take the hit, and bide their time, waiting and plotting revenge.

He said nothing.

Jessica saw Farren give a look to the corrections officer standing at the door. It meant this meeting was over. Byrne had done his duty by notifying a citizen of the death of a family member. He'd also made a plea on behalf of the people of Philadelphia.

Byrne stood up.

'This isn't going to end well for your son, Danny. If you really gave a shit about him, like you pretend to do with all this talk of family and legacy, you'd call him off.'

'You done?'

'Right now there are a lot of cops gunning for him. Think about it. You know how to get hold of me. I can get a news crew here in ten minutes and we can put it on TV in twenty.'

'I won't be calling.'

'I don't imagine you will,' Byrne said. 'But on your last day in this life you'll remember that I was here. On your last day you'll remember that I tried to save your only son, and you did nothing.'

Danny Farren remained silent.

'You did what you could,' Jessica said. As soon as the words left her lips, she realized how inadequate they sounded. She trusted that Byrne knew what was in her heart.

They were standing in the visitors' parking lot at CFCF.

'I remember, when we were kids, the Farren brothers were like the boogeymen,' Byrne said. 'I mean, we all postured like we were Irish tough guys, but the Farrens were the real thing.'

Jessica remembered her own neighborhood growing up. It was the Italians, but it was the same thing. Her father was both proud and ashamed to be Italian-American whenever a story was told about the local gangs.

'Some of us could have gone that way, but we didn't,' Byrne said. 'Do you know why?'

Jessica had a pretty good idea. She asked anyway.

Byrne pointed at the facility. 'It was because of places like this. We were scared shitless of ending up here. It stays your hand, cools your temper. Men like Danny Farren never have that fear, that governor of their actions. Inside or outside, doesn't matter. They are going to do what they want to do, they are going to take what they want.'

Jessica considered this. 'But don't you think that privately, when the lights go off and they're alone with their thoughts, they regret those choices?'

'I hope they do. For me to think otherwise would be to give up on the entire concept of rehabilitation.'

Jessica considered their options. 'I might have an idea.'

'What is it?'

'I'd have to clear it with my boss, but what if we offered Danny something?'

'What do we have to offer that he would want?'

'We can offer him his only son back.'

'I'm not sure I follow,' Byrne said. 'How do we do that?'

Jessica lined up her thoughts. 'We can promise him that if Michael is taken into custody, tried and convicted, he'll be sent to the same facility as his father.'

'The DA is not going to go for that,' Byrne said.

'We don't necessarily have to deliver; we just have to make him think we will.'

Byrne gave it a second. 'You think the DA will make the offer?'

Jessica took out her phone. 'Let's see.'

Twenty minutes later, Jessica glanced across the parking lot. A man was walking quickly toward them. It was Farren's lawyer.

'You said you can get a TV crew out here quickly?' he asked.

'Yes,' said Jessica. 'Why?'

'My client said he's willing to make a televised appeal to his son.'

All three local stations were on site within fifteen minutes. They agreed to use pool footage from the NBC affiliate.

Jessica and Byrne returned to the Roundhouse. They entered the video monitoring unit at just after ten. The large room had three tiers of curved tables, each bearing a number of terminals where video devices could be patched into the thousands of cameras deployed around the city. Any table monitor could be mirrored on the ten-foot screen at the front of the room. When Jessica and Byrne arrived, this was showing color bars. They were soon replaced by a live feed from the local news stations. After a brief introduction, they cut to the recorded plea made by Danny Farren.

As Byrne watched, he thought about his encounter with Michael Farren. He'd had Farren and he'd let him get away.

Anyone else that Michael Farren harmed would live in his soul forever. Byrne knew that the man had had the drop on him – and had a baby in harm's path – but it didn't ease his conscience, nor, he suspected, would it ever.

He was a guardian, and he had failed.

He looked at the television, at Michael Farren's mug shot superimposed in the upper-right-hand part of the screen.

The eyes looked out at him.

Feral eyes.

Billy the Wolf.

38

Billy spent the night and most of the day in Fairmount Park. By the time he made his way back to the motel room, it was just after three o'clock in the afternoon.

A pair of PPD sector cars were parked about a block away in either direction.

It mattered little. Billy had everything he needed in his knapsack. One change of clothes, a hundred rounds for his weapon, over fifteen thousand dollars.

He lifted his collar, walked back down the street, toward the river.

Billy sat at the end of the bar, his right shoulder to the wall. There were only a few patrons at this hour. The televisions above the bar showed the Phillies game.

He finished his beer, ordered another. Before it arrived, he grabbed the bills from the bar, pocketed them, entered the men's room.

He drew some paper towels from the dispenser, wetted them and washed his face, his neck, his hands. He ran his hands through his hair, dried them.

He stepped back, looked into the mirror.

It was empty.

When he returned to his seat, there were a few more patrons. He looked at the bartender as the man brought over a fresh beer.

Blue T-shirt, red hair, small ears.

Billy dropped a five on the bar. The barman took it.

The television now had a news break-in. It showed the photograph of a man.

'Police have identified the subject as Michael Anthony Farren of Schuylkill,' the newscaster said. 'He is wanted in connection to multiple counts of aggravated murder. In an unprecedented move, police have released a plea from the suspect's father, Daniel Farren, himself awaiting trial for the firebombing death of a Philadelphia woman.'

The conversations in the bar all but ceased, a few dozen eyes glued to the four TV monitors. The image switched to an older man in an orange jumpsuit. He looked right at the camera. Right at Billy.

'Mickey, you have to turn yourself in. I talked to the police. They told me if you walk into any police station, put your weapon on the floor and your hands in the air, no harm will come to you. I believe them. You have to do this.'

A few seconds later the screen image returned to the local anchor, with a still photograph of a man superimposed on the right side of the screen.

'If you see Michael Farren, do not attempt to apprehend him. He is considered armed and extremely dangerous. Call the police.'

Underneath it all they put the phone number.

As the TV returned to the game, the conversations in the bar slowly picked back up. Billy could not discern the topics, but he didn't need to. They had nothing to do with him.

He glanced to his left, saw a man in his twenties.

Black hoodie, ripped jeans, full beard.

Next to him, another man in his twenties.

Yellow T-shirt, curly blond hair, bandage on his left wrist.

Billy turned back to his beer, finished it. He collected his change and walked out the door.

Since he had been in the tavern, a thick bank of gray clouds had settled over the city. At first Billy was a bit disoriented, thinking it was early morning, or much later in the day.

It was only rain clouds.

He put on his watch cap and sunglasses, began to make his way to the tracks. He would follow them until Ellsworth Street, and make his way across the Pocket on foot.

'Hey, stud.'

Billy turned to the sound of the voice. There stood two men.

'You're a TV star.'

Black hoodie, ripped jeans, full beard.

Billy said nothing.

The other man, the shorter of the two, said, 'They say you're some kind of desperado. Killed an old man and a woman. Somebody's mother. That true?'

Yellow T-shirt, curly blond hair, bandage on his left wrist.

Billy watched the tall man's hands. They were at his sides, but his light hoodie was unzipped. He held a beer bottle in his right hand; his left hand was empty.

'I don't know you,' Billy said. 'I don't know what you're talking about.'

The shorter man took a step forward, as did his comrade. The tall one chucked a thumb over his shoulder, in the direction of the tavern. 'Just saw you on the TV, stud. Michael Farren. Or do they call you Mike?'

Billy felt the ground tremble slightly. A train was coming.

'Michael Farren is dead,' he said. 'Whoever, whatever you saw isn't me.'

'Maybe I'll just call the police right now, see what they have to say about it.'

Billy put his hand in his coat pocket – through the hole in his pocket – and eased it onto the grip of the Makarov. 'I wouldn't presume to tell you what you should or should not do.'

The taller one looked at his friend, pulled a face, as if to say that Billy was mocking them. Like many young men, they felt no fear.

They each took a few more steps forward.

'You got a smart mouth, motherfucker,' the tall one said.

Billy remained silent.

'What, nothing to say to that?' the other one asked.

Billy dropped his knapsack, squared himself in front of the two men.

At this, the taller one swung his beer bottle against a lamp post. It did not break on the first attempt. It did on the second.

The sound of the approaching train grew to a roar. The conductor gave two blasts of his horn as it approached the crossing.

The shorter man drew a knife from his waistband.

In an instant, Billy had the Makarov out and aimed. The two men froze.

'Throw the knife to the other side of the tracks,' Billy yelled.

The man did what he was told. The other man dropped his broken bottle.

Billy tried to place the two men. The rumble of the train made it difficult to think.

He remembered. They were the men from the bar.

Black hoodie, ripped jeans, full beard.

Yellow T-shirt, curly blond hair, bandage on his left wrist.

Billy approached them, his weapon out front, his finger inside the trigger guard.

'Get down on your knees.'

The two men slowly sank to their knees. Billy was now less than five feet away. The train rolled the earth beneath his feet. He glanced at the man on the right, aimed the Makarov at the one on the left.

'Beg me for his life,' he shouted.

The taller man opened his mouth, but no sound emerged.

Billy pulled the trigger. Twice. The shorter man's skull imploded.

Yellow T-shirt, curly blond hair, bandage on his left wrist.

The other man began to cry. Billy stood over him.

Black hoodie, ripped jeans, full beard.

'Just one question,' Billy yelled.

The man looked up, but fear had taken his words.

Billy asked, 'Have we met?'

The sound of the next two shots was swallowed by the thunder of the passing train.

39

The duty room at the homicide unit was on full alert. Six hundred photocopies of Michael Farren's last mug shot were being printed and readied to go out to the district headquarters and disseminated to patrol officers. Detectives from all divisions were arriving every minute.

In the background, the local news channels were showing Michael Farren's face, and his father's appeal, on an almost constant loop.

At five o'clock, a desk phone rang. Josh Bontrager punched a button, listened. He turned to Jessica and Byrne.

'We've got two bodies in Grays Ferry, down by the tracks. White males, twenties. Collecting IDs now.'

'Any witnesses?' Byrne asked.

'Dave Sipari from South said a man matching Michael Farren's description was in a bar on Dickinson Street when the news break-in happened. He said these two guys might have followed Farren out.'

Jessica glanced at Byrne. It would be his call on how many people to get down to that area.

'How long ago did Farren leave the bar?' Byrne asked.

Bontrager put the phone to his ear, asked the question. 'Less than half an hour.'

There were two undercover cars on The Stone, and it was a good bet that Farren knew it. He wouldn't be going back there.

'Josh, check with dispatch. See if anybody has reported a stolen car or a carjacking in a five-block radius of that tavern in the past half-hour.'

'You got it.'

While Bontrager got on the phone to dispatch, Byrne huddled with Captain John Ross. Detectives from the fugitive squad were gearing up to hit the streets, pulling on Kevlar, checking their weapons.

Jessica's phone rang. It was Amy Smith.

'What's up, Amy?'

'That search you wanted is done.'

Amy was talking about a cross-reference search Jessica had requested earlier in the day.

'I'm at the Roundhouse. Can you fax it over?'

'Sending it now.'

Jessica crossed the duty room, stood by the fax machine. She berated herself for not having Amy scan the documents and send them to her iPhone as a PDF. If there was a more ancient technology than the standalone fax machine still employed by law enforcement, Jessica did not know what it was.

She was just about to call Amy back when the fax machine rattled to life. It was only three pages, including the cover sheet. It seemed like a full minute until the machine rolled them out.

Jessica tore off the sheets, found an empty desk, began to read.

Within seconds she saw it.

'Oh my God.' She was on her feet before she knew it. She found Byrne across the room. He walked over. 'Look.'

Byrne looked at the fax. Suddenly everything – from the moment investigators had stepped into the Rousseau household – snapped into place.

'We cross-referenced the names of the victims with the Farrens, referenced them through court documents going back to 1943,' Jessica said.

'Liam Farren went on trial in 1960, and was convicted of first-degree battery. The prime witness was Edwin D. Channing.

'Patrick Farren went on trial in 1987 for attempting to lure an underage girl into his car on South Taney Street. Her name was Danielle Spencer.

'Sean Farren went to prison in 2006 for menacing. The primary witness was Laura Rousseau.

'Michael Farren went to juvenile detention in 1994 for assault. His accuser was a lawyer doing pro bono work for a community center in Point Breeze. His name was Robert Kilgore.'

'And now Danny Farren,' Byrne said. 'There's only one eye-witness to the pipe bombing, the fifth name. It would complete the square. *Sator. Opera. Tenet. Arepo. Rotas.* Killing the last accuser would lift the curse.'

Jessica got on the phone, called her office. In a few seconds she had the name and address of the sole witness to the pipe bombing.

She checked the action on her Beretta, holstered it.

'What are you doing?' Byrne asked.

'She's my witness, Kevin. I'm going.'

40

Billy sat in the red car at the curb. He knew that the police must certainly have a report of the vehicle he'd taken from the woman. She was at that moment bound and gagged in the trunk, but otherwise unharmed.

When he'd stopped at the florist shop, he'd taken a magic marker and tried to camouflage two of the letters on the rear license plate. He knew it would not get him far, but he had a full magazine in his Makarov, and a hundred rounds in his knapsack.

The last thing he wanted was to bring some fresh-faced, trigger-happy rookie cop into his curse, but he would not hesitate to do so.

He looked up, at the second floor, at the room over the front of The Stone. He saw his mother sitting by the window, smoking a cigarette. She always thought that no one knew she smoked because she did it by the window.

But it wasn't The Stone. It wasn't his mother.

It was Emily's apartment.

Billy saw a light come on inside. He wondered what Emily knew of all this. He wondered if she believed the stories the TV stations were telling about him.

He closed his eyes for a moment, thought about standing in the museum in France, about describing the painting to Emily.

He knew now that would never happen. He knew what would replace the dream in his last moments: Emily sleeping in the embrace of every rose in the world.

'Remember Tully's?'

Billy did. He and his brother had many times crawled Tully's sandwich shop, not for money or goods, but rather for food.

'I do, Mórai.'

'Remember the rings of black pudding and Martin Tully's whiskey sausages? Such a treat, they were.'

Billy could taste them still. 'I do.'

'The attic touches up to the house, it does.'

Billy remembered the attic at Tully's. From there, he and Sean would slip into the row houses on either side.

Who are you?

I am Billy the Wolf.

Why did God make it so you can't see people's faces?

So I can see their souls.

41

The house was next to the corner unit on Bainbridge and South Taney Street. By the time Jessica and Byrne arrived, a half-dozen sector cars were on the scene, parked a half-block from the house.

While four officers deployed behind the target house, Byrne and two others approached, tapped on the door, listened.

Her weapon in hand, Jessica stood to the right side of the door.

Byrne knocked a second time.

The woman who opened the door was in her sixties. Jessica's first impression was that she was not in danger.

'Good evening,' Byrne said.

In one hand he held his badge and ID. In his other hand he held up a note that read:

If you are in any danger, I want you to blink three times, but say nothing.

Jessica watched the woman carefully as she read the note. She did not blink three times. She did not react in any way. Jessica looked at the crack between the door and the jamb, on the hinge side. She did not see a shadow. There was no one behind the door. She looked at the floor, saw no shadows cast by footwear.

'Is there anyone else here, ma'am?' Byrne asked softly.

'No,' she said. 'I don't understand. What's happening?'

'May I come inside?'

She hesitated, looking over Byrne's shoulder. She seemed to snap out of it. 'Of course. I'm sorry. Please come in.'

Byrne keyed his two-way radio, bringing John Shepherd from around the corner.

'With your permission, we'd like to take a quick look around your house.'

The woman said nothing.

'Ma'am,' Byrne began, 'I'll explain everything in a moment, but we need to look around, and we'd like to have your permission to do so.'

'Yes,' she said, a little shakily. 'I mean, yes, you have my permission.'

Byrne opened the screen door. He introduced Jessica. 'This lady is from the DA's office. She's going to stay with you while we look around.'

The row house was red brick with white trim, and had only a partial basement. Byrne and Shepherd were able to clear it in just a few minutes.

When Byrne returned to the front room, Jessica and the woman were seated next to each other on the couch.

'I'd first like to thank you for your cooperation, ma'am,' Byrne said.

The woman just stared.

343

'You are Mrs Leary, am I correct?' he asked.

'Yes,' the woman said. 'I am Anjelica Leary.'

As the PPD set up a secure perimeter around the house, Jessica and Byrne spoke with Anjelica Leary.

'We need to protect you, Mrs Leary,' Jessica said. 'We have a safe house in the city, known only to a few people. You'll be comfortable and secure there.'

'For how long?' she asked.

Jessica had known the woman would ask this. She did not have an easy answer. 'I can't say for sure. Until the trial is over. Danny Farren's murder trial, that is. When the charges were arson and aggravated assault it was one thing. A murder trial is a bit more complicated.'

'I'm not going to leave my home.'

'Mrs Leary, it's just that—'

'I won't,' she repeated. 'Certainly not for the likes of Danny Farren.'

Jessica regrouped. 'Danny's in jail. He can't hurt you.' As soon as the words left her lips, she realized how inadequate and stupid they sounded. If Danny Farren was not the source of the threat, what was she doing here?

'Who, then?'

Jessica was getting in deeper. But this woman had the right to know.

'It's his son. Michael.'

Anjelica Leary turned to her. 'Little Michael Farren? The boy who was hit by the car?'

'Yes,' Jessica said. 'He's not little anymore. He's a very violent and dangerous man.'

Anjelica rose, walked to the window.

'I thought I was doing the right thing,' she said. 'The *decent* thing.'

'You did do the right thing. A lot of people would've said they didn't see anything. You stepped up. It's important.'

Anjelica Leary was silent for a few long moments. At last she turned to Jessica, a look of defiance on her face.

'I'm not leaving my home. I'm not abandoning my patients, or passing them off to people who don't care about them the way I do. I won't do it.'

Jessica had half expected this, but it was clear she had lost the woman.

She caught Byrne's eye. He nodded.

He would take over.

42

While Jessica drove back to her office to begin the process of coordinating a protection detail with the DA's homicide unit, Byrne stayed behind.

'This will all be over soon,' he said. He gestured to the sector cars on the street. 'You're in good hands.'

They sat over coffee in the woman's small, tidy kitchen. Every few seconds Byrne looked at the doors, the windows, waiting for hell.

The woman just stared at him.

'What is it?' Byrne asked.

'I remember you.'

As soon as she said the words, the memories began to sift back. The heat of that night, the mosquitoes, the explosions overhead.

'I'm not sure I understand,' Byrne said. 'Remember me from where?'

'You were much younger then, of course. The world was much younger.'

Byrne said nothing.

'My name was different,' she said. 'It wasn't Leary. Back then I had my first husband's name.'

'Ma'am?'

'It was Daugherty.'

The word was a roundhouse. 'You're Anjelica Daugherty?'

'Yes,' she said. 'Catriona was my little girl.'

43

She had never been what one would call beautiful – her features were a bit asymmetrical, a heavy-boned girl they would say – but she'd had a twinkle, an easy laugh, and it served her well.

Of all the adults Byrne had known from the Pocket, Anjelica Daugherty had seemed closest to his age. She knew the music and the movies and the TV shows.

The woman sitting in front of him looked long passed by.

'My God,' she said. 'Kevin Byrne.'

She ran a hand through her hair, straightened her skirt.

It was a moment captured by the reality that here were two people who'd met on one field of life and now, nearly four decades later, were meeting on another. Time was the great leveler, Byrne thought.

'She would be old enough to be a grandmother, she would.'

Byrne just listened.

'It sounds so phony to simply ask how you are,' Anjelica said. 'It's been nearly forty years. How you are today is because of those forty years. How we *all* are.'

Byrne had his own memories of that time, that night. He remembered seeing Catriona on the street the day before her murder. He remembered how her face lit up when she talked to Jimmy Doyle. He remembered how the slightest breeze would brush back her fine blond hair. He remembered her blush.

He looked up, into Anjelica's eyes. He'd never really seen it before, but now he did. Little Catriona favored her mother.

'Catie would sometimes stay with her gran in those days, those summer days. It was just a few blocks away. I had to work two jobs.' She wiped a tear. 'All those nights my ma tucked her in. It should have been me.'

'You did what you thought was right. You were providing for your family. Catie was *with* family.'

He almost said she had been safe, but that wasn't true.

'You weren't from the Pocket, were you?' Anjelica asked.

Byrne shook his head. 'We were living in Pennsport at the time. My father was a longshoreman. I used to visit my cousin a few times a year. Mostly summer.'

'That's right,' she said. 'The Kittredges.'

Byrne nodded. 'Ronan was my second cousin. I stayed with my aunt Ruth and uncle Matt.'

'I liked Ruth. She was a dear woman.'

'She was.'

'Always one to visit with a pie when troubles came.'

Byrne remembered the aroma of his aunt's mincemeat and rhubarb pies. It took him back.

'Are you still close to any of them?' Anjelica asked.

Byrne thought about the most recent funeral in his family, three years earlier; about his aunt Ruth, decimated by cancer, herself widowed ten years earlier.

'Both Uncle Matt and Aunt Ruth have passed.'

'I'm so sorry. '

'Thank you.'

Byrne recalled that he and Ronan would do odd jobs around Anjelica Daugherty's house in the weeks following Catriona's murder. Anjelica always tried to pay them, but they refused. She made up for it by feeding them to burst on home-made stews and spaghetti.

He looked over, caught her smiling. It erased so many hard years.

'What?' he asked.

'You look the same.'

'I don't think so.'

'You do,' she said. 'It's different for boys than it is for girls, you know. Boys get bigger. They might lose a little hair. But that which made them look like they did when they were ten or so remains. My father looked like a big boy until the day he died.'

Byrne couldn't see it, but who was he to argue with someone who said he still looked young?

'I remember Ronan,' she continued. 'He was always walking around with a baseball bat or a ball of some sort. Either that or he was running somewhere. I recall being envious of his energy.'

It was true. Ronan always played with the big kids. He was on the varsity squads in baseball and football at school in his freshman year.

'So many years have passed,' she said. 'I'm almost afraid to ask how he is these days.'

Byrne remembered exactly where he was and what he was doing when he heard of Ronan's death. He considered that there was no need to add this sorrow to Anjelica Daugherty's already weighted heart.

He shrugged. 'I'm afraid we lost touch.'

As Anjelica looked out the window, Byrne studied her profile. He recalled seeing her in the park that terrible night, the way she opened her mouth to scream but no sound emerged, not for

350

the longest time. Perhaps the real scream had been trapped inside her. Perhaps it still was.

'What about you?' she asked. 'Did you marry?'

Byrne nodded. 'I did.'

'Are you two still together?'

'That one's a little tougher to answer,' he said. 'We divorced years ago, but last year we started seeing each other again. It's too soon to tell, but I think we're doing okay. She's in New York now on business.'

Anjelica smiled. 'That's a good story. I like a story like that.'

Byrne took out his wallet, retrieved the photograph of Colleen, taken just a month or so ago on the campus of Gallaudet University. He showed Anjelica. 'My daughter.'

'My God,' she said. 'She's beautiful.'

'Favors her mother.'

As Byrne took back the photo and put it away, his phone rang. It was Josh Bontrager.

'Yeah, Josh.'

'Perimeter is in place,' Bontrager said. 'Two detectives from the DA's homicide unit are coordinating. They need to see you.'

'I'll be right out.'

He glanced out the window, saw Jessica pulling up.

'ADA Balzano is back. She's going to sit with you.'

Anjelica stood up. Before Byrne knew what was happening, she pulled him into an embrace.

44

'I saw it on the news,' Anjelica said. 'I can't believe that is little Mick Farren.'

Jessica said nothing.

'And the father. Danny Farren. He looked so ... old is what I guess I want to say. I imagine we all do.'

'Now that the news has broadcast this, it will only be a matter of time,' Jessica said. 'There's nowhere for Michael Farren to go. We have his place of residence covered. Every cop in five counties is looking for him.

'I'm going to stay the night,' she continued. 'In the morning, the city will send an armored car for us and we'll go down to the courthouse together.'

'It seems like a lot,' Anjelica said. 'For Michael Farren.'

'He's a very bad man, Anjelica. There really is no telling what he will do.'

Out of the corner of her eye Jessica saw the K-9 Unit arrive. She recognized the officer and the dog, had worked with them both.

'There's a very good chance that Michael Farren will be apprehended soon,' she said.

'Then we can stop all this?'

Jessica shook her head. 'We don't know the full extent of the threat. He may be working with other people.'

Because of the Farren family's history with pipe bombs, the K-9 officer was sweeping the grounds for explosives. Another pair of officers from K-9 were en route. These dogs would search for Farren, based on the scent of some clothing they had collected at The Stone.

'I thought I was done with all this,' Anjelica said. 'Back when my Catriona was taken.'

'It will all be over soon.'

Jessica's phone rang. It was Byrne.

'Perimeter is locked,' he said.

'Is it quiet?' Jessica asked.

'It's quiet,' he said. 'I'm coming in.'

A few seconds later, Jessica opened the door. Byrne entered.

Anjelica stood, walked over to the sideboard, where a pot of tea sat in a cozy. She turned to Byrne. 'Would you like a cup of tea?'

'No thanks,' Byrne said. 'I'm fine.'

Anjelica stood looking at the old, chipped tea service. 'I just remembered. I bought this set at a house sale. From Máire Farren, of all people.'

'Who is that?' Jessica asked.

'Danny's mother,' Byrne said. 'Michael's grandmother.'

'She was a rummager, that one,' Anjelica said. 'A scrounger and a thief. Once a year she would set up a yard sale behind that bar she owned, sell all kinds of things. What people didn't realize was that they were buying things stolen from each other's houses.'

Jessica and Byrne just listened.

'After Desmond died, she moved into that house at the end of the lane. Just a few blocks from here, near the avenue. The blue one with the shutters. Do you remember it, Kevin?'

'You're saying the Farrens owned that house?' Byrne asked.

'I'm sure they did. They were not a family to be beholden to anyone, especially a bank or any manner of landlord.'

Byrne got on to dispatch. If the Farrens owned that house, Michael Farren might be holed up there.

'I'm going down there,' he said. Jessica saw him adjust the Kevlar vest, tucking in the flaps.

'Who's out back?' she asked.

'Two officers from the 17th. They're both experienced men.'

Byrne moved to the front door, peered through the blinds. He turned to Jessica, held up his rover. 'I'll be on channel.'

When Byrne left, Jessica deadbolted the door, slid over the security chain, pulled on the handle. It was redundant, but redundancy saved lives.

'What is it?' Anjelica asked.

'There's no cause for alarm. We just need to take a few extra precautions.'

Anjelica pointed at the television, which was on but had the sound muted. Jessica glanced over. It was a news alert. A picture of Michael Farren was splashed across the screen.

'Michael Farren,' Anjelica said. 'Little Michael.'

45

Byrne remembered the house from when he was younger. It had been pretty beat up back then, had always been in need of a coat of paint. He didn't recall who had lived there, but he remembered well seeing it the other day.

It was the lone dilapidated row house in the middle of the block being rehabbed by Greene Towne LLC.

Four patrol officers established a perimeter at the corners of the house. Bình Ngô took the rear, while Byrne mounted the steps to the front door. He looked through the window. He saw no movement.

He drew his weapon, knocked on the door. No answer. He tried again with the same result. He raised Bình Ngô on his two-way.

'Any movement back there?'

'Nothing,' Bình said.

Byrne had to make a decision. There was no time to wait for a search warrant. They did not know for certain that this property still had anything to do with the Farrens. A call to Licenses and Inspections had not been returned.

'I'm coming back there.'

By the time Byrne reached the rear of the property he'd made the decision. He shouldered open the back door with ease.

They cleared the scene in minutes.

The house was unoccupied.

As Byrne walked through the old house, it felt as if he were stepping back in time to his own grandmother's house. Everywhere he looked was another bridge to the past. The old furniture, the ancient drapes, the threadbare area rugs, the double bed with the depression on one side, the ceramic bowl and pitcher on the dresser.

In the parlor there was no television, but rather an old console radio. Dozens of books on faeries and Irish folk legends. One of them was written by Francesca Esperanza Wilde, Oscar Wilde's mother. There were a handful of books on the *ban sidhe*.

And everywhere there were framed pictures. Pictures of Liam Farren in uniform, pictures of Danny and Patrick, pictures of Michael and Sean, pictures of more than fifty years of customers at The Stone.

On the wall over the antique sofa was a large picture of corn stooks. Seeing it gave Byrne a chill. At the bottom was written *Where the faeries live* in a childlike scrawl.

Room after room was a museum to antiquity.

Before leaving, Byrne found a door at the back of a closet. He opened it, clicked on his Maglite, descended a narrow staircase. At the bottom was a small stone room.

There, chiseled into the wall, as large as the wall itself, were five words that made Byrne's heart race.

The entire wall was a Sator Square.

In a ring around the square were thirty or so framed photographs. Michael and his grandmother when he was an infant. Michael and his grandmother when he was a toddler, a young boy, a pre-teen. One was of Michael in a hospital bed, his eyes closed. In this photograph his grandmother held a white rosary.

It was the last picture that gave Byrne pause, one that answered a question that had circled him since he interviewed Perry Kershaw outside Edwin Channing's house.

In the final picture, the adult Michael Farren stood with a wizened, white-haired woman on a street corner in Grays Ferry. In the background was a billboard advertising a movie. The movie was *American Sniper*.

My God, Byrne thought. She's still alive.

Máire Farren was the old woman.

She was the one singing the death songs.

46

Jessica moved through the living room, down the short hallway to the kitchen. She poured herself a few inches of coffee, tried the back door for the tenth time. It was an old habit, and died accordingly.

She'd gotten a call from Byrne telling her that the house in the Pocket was clear. There was no sign of Michael Farren. Byrne and Bình Ngô were on the way back.

She stepped into the small bathroom, closed the door. She splashed some cold water on her face, toweled off. Then she walked back down the short hallway leading to the front room.

At first she thought it was some kind of mannequin, a tailor's model perhaps. The figure was petite almost to the point of being childlike. Her face was deeply lined, but her skin was clear, almost translucent. She wore a white gauze dress that draped off her slight shoulders.

But the shock of seeing this stranger in this house – a house with which Jessica had become quite familiar in the past few hours, even to the point of moving furniture to create clear paths to the doors and windows – nearly paled in comparison to the sight of the woman's hair. It was long and surprisingly silken for a woman who had to be in her eighties.

Jessica knew that she had just encountered a threat. She knew this as deeply and completely as she had ever sensed a threat on the street, both in her time in uniform and as a detective.

But still she did not draw her weapon.

Just as the spell was broken and Jessica reached for her Beretta, the woman began to sing. At first it was a low, keening sound that quickly grew to a melodious song. It only stopped Jessica for a few seconds, but a few seconds was long enough.

'I'll have that,' came the low voice.

Before she could turn around, ADA Jessica Balzano felt the cold steel barrel of the Makarov touch the side of her head.

IV

Billy the Wolf

47

Standing in front of Anjelica Leary's house, Byrne checked and rechecked the action on his weapon, then chided himself for the redundancy. He walked the perimeter of the block, around the side of the row houses, through the back alley, every so often testing doors, windows.

If a car slowed down near the Leary house, he would slip his hand onto the grip of his weapon until the vehicle passed.

It was on his second perimeter check that the call came over the radio.

He clicked his handset. 'Byrne.'

'Kevin, it's Josh. K-9 has a hit. I'm in the building next to Mrs. Leary's house.'

Byrne felt his skin go damp.

'Explosives?'

'No,' Bontrager said. 'The search dogs. They hit for Farren's clothing.'

*

When Byrne rounded the corner, Josh Bontrager was standing next to a K-9 officer named Brad Summers. At his feet was a two-year-old male German Shepherd named Calhoun.

They stood at the entry to the corner unit next to the Leary house. It was a shuttered store. An old sign over the door read *Tully's*.

'Officer Summers,' Byrne said. 'What do we have?'

'Calhoun was working his way around the second floor and alerted me to the stairs leading to the attic. We went up the stairs and he sat in front of this half-door built into the adjoining wall.'

'That's how he alerts you?'

'Yes, sir.'

'And he is alerting to Michael Farren?'

'Yes, sir.'

'Show me.'

With Calhoun anxiously taking the lead, they walked to the second floor, then took the stairway to the attic. The ceiling was low and sloped, so Byrne had to bend over. The room was crowded with boxes and old furniture.

The dog sat in front of a half-door built into the adjoining wall. Byrne slipped on a glove, reached out, gently pushed on the door. It gave only an inch or so before touching something. Because of the Farren family's history with explosive ordnance, Byrne decided not to push it any further.

'Kevin,' Bontrager said in a loud whisper. Byrne looked over. Josh had his Maglite pointed at a piece of paper next to the door, a handwritten note.

The note read:

There is a motion detector alarm in the room on the other side of this door. You will not disarm it before I hear it. If I hear it, everyone will die.

Byrne recalled what Emily Carson had said to him:

He told me he bought a motion detector.

'Can you see anything?' he whispered.

Bontrager got on his knees, slowly edged his face toward the opening. It was only a half-inch or so. Byrne could make out dim light.

'I see it,' Bontrager said. 'It's one of those portable battery-operated types. I've seen this model. You can't get anywhere near it without triggering it, and they are loud as heck.'

'Are there any lights on it?'

Bontrager got in a better position. 'There is one. A red light in the center. It's armed.'

Michael Farren was inside Anjelica Leary's house.

And so was Jessica.

48

Jessica sat on a dining room chair in the middle of the living room. To her right sat Anjelica Leary.

Michael Farren stood near the front door. Being this close to him, she marveled not for the first time just how ordinary people could appear, especially those you knew to have committed monstrous acts of cruelty.

Although he appeared ragged, and in need of sleep, he was an average-looking man in his thirties – slender but muscular, with long, unkempt hair to his shoulders. He wore a black leather coat, black T-shirt, muddy jeans, black work boots. The pistol in his hand was immaculate, pristinely maintained.

Jessica's Beretta was now stuck into the waistband of Michael Farren's jeans.

On the wall next to the front door were pinned about a dozen photographs. One was clearly of the older woman, perhaps taken when she was in her fifties. Set off to the right was a picture of Anjelica Leary.

In front of the fireplace were stacked five birth certificates, with Anjelica Leary's on top.

The curtains over the front window were sheer. There were no other drapes. Even with the low light – the television was the only light in the room; it was tuned to a news channel showing a live shot from the block, alternating between street level and helicopter footage – Jessica knew that SWAT, with their sophisticated weaponry and scopes, could see anyone and anything that passed in front of the window.

When the house phone rang, Jessica looked at Michael Farren. He nodded, tapped one of his ears. She knew what he meant. She slowly got to her feet, crossed over to the phone, which was on a small table at the foot of the stairs. She pressed the speakerphone button.

'This is Jessica Balzano.'

'Jess, are you on speaker?'

It was Byrne.

'Yes.'

'Everyone okay in there?'

She again looked at Farren, who nodded. She kept her eyes on the man as she said:

'Yes. All four of us are okay.'

Farren didn't react. It was a risk, but Byrne had to know there were four people inside. She couldn't yet think of a way to tell him that the fourth person was an old woman. Plus, it was a way to let him know that there were at *least* four people. Jessica really didn't know if there was anyone else in the house.

'Billy? I just want you to know that nothing bad is going to happen,' Byrne said. 'There's no reason for anyone to get hurt.'

Farren crossed the room.

'Call back later,' he said. 'We have business.'

He hit the button, ending the call. He pointed at the empty chair.

Jessica sat down again.

Finally Anjelica Leary spoke.

'How many years has it been, Mrs Farren?'

The old woman raised a delicate hand, as if to brush away a spider web. 'It's been so many years that you needn't call me that any longer. It's Máire.' She spoke with a deep Irish accent.

'*Mrs Farren* will suit, thank you,' Anjelica said.

The old woman nodded, said: 'It was a grand time, wasn't it? Back then?'

'For some,' Anjelica said. 'Not for all.'

'I've buried my husband, two of my three boys,' Máire said. 'One of my grandsons.'

'This is the life you chose, Máire Farren.'

The old woman shrugged. 'We all serve somebody. I chose my God. You chose yours.'

Anjelica pointed at Michael. 'Yours has a gun.'

'Sometimes it is necessary to protect your own.'

'The men can take care of themselves.'

'Really?' Máire asked. 'Like my Desmond?'

'He killed my Catriona.'

'He did not.'

'He was seen with her.'

'How do you know this?' Máire asked.

'A mother knows.'

'Yes,' the old woman said. 'A mother does.'

'What do you know of it?'

'I know the pain of loss. When my Desmond was shot down like a dog in the street, and thrown into the river, my husband was already in the ground. Danny and Patrick wanted to take a match to the entire Pocket, but I said no.'

'And why is that?' Anjelica asked. 'Because you knew what Desmond had done?'

'Because we live in each other's shelter, do we not? Where do you think the police would have come if Devil's Pocket ran red with Irish blood? Your house? No. *Mine.*'

Anjelica waved a dismissive hand. 'You Farrens are a cancer. It all ends here and now. You've lived these many years, and your life ends in shame.'

'I'm not dead yet.'

'No, not yet,' Anjelica said. 'That will come in a cold jail cell. Just like your husband. An old woman in a stone coffin. Fitting.'

Jessica wanted to enter this conversation – it seemed to be escalating. She looked to the side window, next to the fireplace. Although she could not be sure, she thought she saw a thin cable rise into the lower-right corner, just below the bottom slat of the venetian blinds. If she was right, this would be an endoscope camera deployed by SWAT.

She glanced at Michael Farren. He had not seen it.

'Or maybe it will all end here, in this room,' Anjelica said. She gestured to the window. 'The police are everywhere. Do you think you will just rise from that chair and walk away? You may think yourself the *sídhe*, but you are delusional. You always were.'

The old woman smiled, but did not respond. Instead she reached into her bag on the floor, pulled out a white linen handkerchief. She spread it on the table in front of her. Then she took out a small cruet, deep amber in color, took off the top, tilted it to a finger and made a line on the handkerchief, all the while singing softly.

My God, Jessica thought. She is writing the last line in blood.

Before long, Máire Farren put the cruet away, left the handkerchief on the table to dry. She had written:

ROTAS.

The phone rang again. No one moved.

'They're going to come storming in here if I don't answer,' Jessica said.

'No they won't,' Michael said.

After ten rings it stopped.

The old woman pointed at Anjelica, then looked at Jessica. 'She is the only one left. The Farren curse will be lifted tonight. You can't harm us.'

'It doesn't matter what you do to me,' Anjelica said. 'Your place in hell has been reserved for years.'

Michael Farren crossed the room, put the barrel of the Makarov to Anjelica Leary's head. Anjelica closed her eyes.

'Not one more word from you, woman,' Farren said. 'Not one.'

49

Byrne watched the shadows move on the sheer curtains. He turned around to see the two SWAT marksmen on the roof of the building across the street.

He walked to the tech van, stepped inside.

The endoscope camera on the west side of the row house showed two walls. Jessica, Anjelica Leary and an old woman with long white hair. It was Máire Farren.

Byrne could see part of the wall that led from the front door to the kitchen. Farren had pinned the photographs to the wall next to the door. He needed to look at them to know who was whom.

While Byrne was watching, he saw Michael Farren cross the room, turn off the television.

He got on the radio to the two SWAT officers.

They did not have a shot.

*

Byrne found Maria Caruso in the crowd. He caught her eye, beckoned her over. When he told her what he wanted her to do, she only hesitated a split second. Moments later she was in a patrol car with a uniformed officer. They left the scene code two, no lights, no siren.

The three media vans were parked just beyond the police cordon at the corner of 23rd and Bainbridge. In addition to the reporters who were waiting to do their stand-ups, and the camera personnel, a crowd of more than a hundred people had gathered.

Byrne searched the crowd, found a face he recognized, a veteran field reporter for the local CBS affiliate named Howard Kelly. Although Byrne didn't often deal with the media – the brass preferred to leave those things to the media relations officer – he had been cleared to give an interview a few years earlier after the resolution of a string of gruesome murders in the Badlands. To whatever degree a law enforcement officer could have a professional relationship with a member of the media, Byrne felt he had a foundation for asking what he was going to ask.

He ducked under the tape, approached Kelly.

'Detective,' Kelly said, extending a hand.

'Good to see you, Howard.'

They shook.

'It doesn't look like you're getting ready to give a statement,' Kelly said.

'Not just yet,' Byrne said. 'But I need to ask a favor.'

Rare was the depth and breadth of the silence that followed a statement like that from a police officer to a member of the broadcast media.

'I'm all ears,' Kelly said.

'This has to be off the record for now.'

'Understood.'

'Do you have a cameraman you can trust?'

Kelly pointed at a man leaning against a van. At his feet was a hand-held HD camera with the station's logo on the side. 'I trust that man with my life,' Kelly said. 'Literally. We work North Philly.'

Byrne laid out his plan. Kelly listened, rapt.

'Is this something you can do?' Byrne asked.

'It is.'

'And to answer your next question, yes, when this is all over, I will give you an exclusive.'

Kelly smiled. 'Hadn't crossed my mind.'

The two men shook again.

'What do you want to do first?' Kelly asked.

'Your tie,' Byrne said.

'What about it?'

'Is it blue or black?'

Five minutes later, Maria Caruso returned. She had with her the item Byrne had requested. He returned to the tech van, put on a headset, called Anjelica Leary's landline again. After five rings, it was answered. No one said anything.

'This is Kevin. I'm with the police department. Who am I speaking to?'

A pause. Then: 'This is Billy.'

'Good. Billy. Is everything all right in there?'

'Everything is fine.'

Byrne had twice visited Quantico, had twice attended a seminar that addressed hostage negotiation techniques. He knew the five steps: active listening, empathy, rapport, influence and behavioral change.

Right now, he couldn't remember a thing. He knew that a highly trained agent was en route from the FBI's Philadelphia field office, but he was not there yet. And Jessica was inside.

'How do we make this better?' he asked.

'There is only one way.'

'Okay. I'm listening. What can I do?'

'You can pack up your guns and your badges and go home.'

'Well, that will be a tough sell to my boss, I'm afraid. Is there another way?'

'There is not.'

Byrne had to think. He reached into his pocket. He had no choice.

'I have something for you,' he said.

A long pause. 'What do you have?'

'It's kind of hard to describe,' Byrne said. 'I can send it to your cell phone. Do you have one?'

'No.'

'Okay,' Byrne said. 'Tell you what. Jessica has an iPhone. Have her give it to you, and I'll send it over.'

Byrne closed his eyes, waiting for it all to fall apart.

'Send it,' Farren said.

50

Billy could feel it. He was close. He had been so long a time in the shadows that he had all but forgotten there was light.

But now that he and Sean and Gran had drawn four lines of the square, it felt as if a great weight had lifted from his shoulders, his heart.

One more line and there would be sun.

He looked down.

It was Emily. Her beautiful face was gazing right at him.

'Michael. It's me.'

'You're here.'

'I'm so confused and sad. They say that you've done some very bad things, but I don't believe it to be true. It *can't* be true. They say that if you put down your gun, and put your hands in the air, nothing bad will happen to you.'

Billy just listened. Emily was right there. His heart soared.

'You might think I'm just saying these things because they're making me say them,' she said. 'But it isn't so. I believe them when they say you won't be harmed. This is what I want too.'

Billy looked at his grandmother.

'This is Emily,' he said. 'The girl I told you about.'

'It's a trick,' his gran said.

'No,' Billy said. 'You don't understand. She's going to come with me. To France.'

Movement now, just outside the windows. A slice of light, then it was gone.

Billy looked at the iPhone again. Emily was gone too.

Had she really been there?

He glanced around the shadowed room. It was a roomful of strangers. All women.

None of them were Emily.

'Billy,' the old woman said. She wore a white dress.

Billy turned to the wall behind him. First picture, bottom row. It was his grandmother.

'Take this,' she said. 'It is time.'

Billy crossed the room. His grandmother picked up the straight razor, opened it. The blade winked blue in the light streaming through the windows.

Billy put down the iPhone, picked up the telephone. The man was still on the other end.

'Can Emily come in here?' Billy asked.

'I don't think we should do that,' the man said.

'Why?'

'What if something went wrong? There are people with guns all over the place. You wouldn't want something bad to accidentally happen to Emily, would you?'

'No.'

'But she does have something for you.'

'She does?'

'Yes,' the man said. 'I could bring it inside.'

Billy looked at the door. He had to think.

'Billy?'

51

The phone was silent for a full thirty seconds.

'You can bring it in,' Farren said.

Byrne felt a cool wave of relief wash over him. It was instantly replaced by a warm wave of fear.

'Maybe when I get in there, we can talk about letting Jessica go. She's not part of this. She has a son and a daughter.'

Byrne waited.

'One lie. One trick. All their blood will be on your hands,' Farren said.

'No tricks. You have my word.'

'You'll have to come soon. We have to go to Midnight Mass.'

52

It was Christmas Eve dinner. Billy could smell the spiced beef, the colcannon, the plum pudding. They were gathered in the small parlor above The Stone. The Christmas lights flashed outside on the avenue.

His mother was there and she wasn't sick. She looked robust and healthy. There was high color in her cheeks. She wore a white pullover with a blue blouse beneath.

'Where's Sean?' Billy asked.

'Don't listen to these people,' his grandmother said.

Billy turned to the voice. Something was wrong with Gran. She looked so old. It was just today when her hair was black. Black Irish, she would say with a wink, but he and Sean had seen the coloring in the trash. The Clairol. They never let on they knew.

Now it was cloud white.

'It's a trick,' his gran said.

Billy looked at his mother. The woman was not Deena

Farren. Billy checked the pictures on the wall. The photo where his mother should be was blank.

This woman was younger. He had never seen her before.

Billy looked at the window, at the flashing lights.

They were expecting Uncle Pat and his father. Later that night they were going out for some last-minute shopping. Then it was off to Midnight Mass at St Patrick's.

The doorbell rang.

'Don't,' his gran said.

'It's okay.'

'Michael.'

Michael Anthony Farren.

Billy crossed the room and opened the door.

53

When Byrne stepped inside the front door, with his hands over his head, Jessica saw him take in the room, the layout, the entrances and exits, the players.

In his right hand he had a yellow rose. He placed it on the entry table.

'Close the door and lock it,' Michael Farren said.

Byrne did as he was told.

Farren gave Byrne a thorough pat-down, gestured for him to cross the room, where Anjelica Leary was seated, the opposite side from the front door and the wall of photographs.

Before doing so, Byrne took off his suit jacket, laid it across the arm of the couch. As he did so, he glanced at Jessica, then at his jacket. She followed his gaze and saw what he wanted her to see.

She then looked at his hands, which were shielded from Michael Farren. He had three fingers extended on each hand.

And Jessica knew.

Byrne turned, walked to the other side of the room. He stood next to the television.

Máire Farren rose slowly to her feet, crossed to the fireplace, opened the flue, struck one of the long kitchen matches there and lit the fire. As she did this, she began to make a keening sound.

Jessica looked at Michael Farren. He gave no indication that he knew he'd met Byrne at the row house on Reed Street.

'You can let my partner go,' Byrne said. 'You have me.'

Michael Farren said nothing for a moment. 'You said she has a family?'

'Yes. A son and a daughter.'

'You're trying to protect them.'

'Yes.' Byrne turned on the television. 'Just like I'm trying to protect you now.'

Michael looked over at the TV, back. 'You?'

The old woman continued to sing softly, seemingly oblivious to the conversation happening around her. One by one she put the birth certificates into the fire. With each piece of paper she changed her song.

'Let me help you,' Byrne said.

Farren looked back at him. 'Why? Why do you want to help me?'

Byrne slowly began to drop his hands to his sides. 'Don't you know me, Michael?'

The old woman stopped her wailing. She had one birth certificate left. It was Anjelica Leary's. 'Don't listen to him,' she said.

Michael Farren looked between his grandmother and Byrne. 'What do you mean?'

'I can help,' Byrne said. 'I can take you back. Back before the accident.'

'Stop it!' the old woman screamed.

'Back to The Stone?' Michael asked.

'Back to The Stone,' Byrne said. He gestured to the street. 'Back to before all this.'

'Shut up,' Máire Farren said.

'Don't you know me?' Byrne repeated. 'I'm your father.'

Michael just stared.

'I'm your father,' Byrne repeated.

Michael Farren turned around, looked at the wall. There, on the bottom row, on the right, was where his father's picture was pinned. Daniel Farren. He wore a white shirt, a blue necktie. He was wearing exactly what the man in front of him was wearing.

He *was* the man in front of him.

'Da.'

'Yes.'

'Don't listen,' Máire said. 'It's a trick. He's using the glamour.'

'Look at the picture, Michael.'

'That's not my name.'

'It *is* your name. Billy's not real.'

'Don't listen to him,' the old woman hissed.

'Your name is Michael Anthony Farren,' Byrne said. He pointed at the TV. 'You are my son.'

Jessica saw that the TV was not showing a news break-in at all. The AV unit had attached a cable to the house, running to a disc player in the tech van. Byrne had recorded the plea in the news van. The appeal was on a continuous loop. The photograph on the wall was the one Jessica had removed from Byrne's suit jacket and pinned there. It was the photo she had taken of Byrne.

'That's me,' Byrne repeated. 'You're my boy.'

Michael looked at the TV, then at the photo, then at Byrne. Jessica could see the struggle. He really couldn't recognize anyone.

'All you have to do is put the gun down and we'll get you some help,' Byrne said. '*I'll* get you some help.'

'He's *lying*.'

Jessica saw Máire Farren struggling to keep her balance. She couldn't. Her skin was starting to turn ashen; her breathing was shallow.

Michael Farren took a step toward Byrne. 'Will you take me shooting? Me and Sean?'

'Of course,' Byrne said. 'Anywhere you want to go.'

Michael Farren began to unscrew the suppressor from his weapon.

'Can we go to that place in the woods?' he asked. 'I know the way.'

'We'll go right now. All you have to do is put the gun down.'

Michael Farren dropped the suppressor. 'I'm a better shot than Sean. Always was.'

'I can't take sides on that one,' Byrne said.

'I can shoot the deer, and Sean can skin them. He's always been better with the knife.'

'That's what we'll do then.'

Farren squared himself in front of Byrne.

He held the gun at his side.

54

The dream was over. His father was home and they could start Christmas.

'What did you bring me, Da?' he asked.

His father pointed to the table by the door. It was a single yellow rose. Billy picked it up, smelled it. It reminded him of lemons. Someone had once told him this, and it was true.

'*Nollaig Shona Duit*,' he said.

'Happy Christmas to you, son.'

'Let's say a prayer, Da.'

'Sure,' his father said. 'Which one?'

'"A Familiar Stranger". We'll say it together.'

'*Stop*,' his grandmother said.

Michael turned to look at her. It was not his gran. This was an old woman.

'Michael.'

Michael turned back to his father.

'The prayer.'

He was Michael. Michael Anthony Farren.

He ejected the magazine from the weapon. One by one he took the bullets from the magazine. He no longer needed them. His father was home.

'*I saw a stranger today,*' he said. '*I put food for him in the eating place. And drink in the drinking place. And music in the listening place.*'

He dropped three bullets to the floor.

'*In the Holy name of the Trinity He blessed myself and my family. And the lark said in her warble: Often, often, often goes Christ in the stranger's guise.*'

He dropped the second last bullet.

'*O, oft and oft and oft goes Christ . . .*'

55

'... *in the stranger's guise.*'

Michael Farren dropped the last bullet on the floor.

Jessica glanced at Máire. She was breathing heavily. Anjelica Leary had not moved, had not spoken a word.

Michael began to cross the room, the gun out front.

'Just put it down, Michael,' Byrne said. 'Just put it on the floor.'

Still he continued across the room. He was going to hand the gun to Byrne.

'Stop!' Byrne yelled.

He did not stop.

'*Oft goes Christ ...*'

He stepped in front of the sheer curtains.

Jessica saw it, the red dot on Michael Farren's back.

No, she thought. *Byrne has him.*

Wait.

She looked at her phone. She'd never make it.

'*In a stranger's guise.*'

Michael Farren lifted both hands. His right hand held the Makarov.

Jessica closed her eyes, heard the glass shatter, the sound of the copper-jacketed round tearing through Michael Farren's chest, slamming into the wall, the dull thud as his body hit the floor.

'No!' Byrne screamed. In two strides he was across the living room, and had Jessica on the floor.

As the sound of the gunshot echoed in the room, all Jessica could hear was the labored breathing of Máire Farren, and the fading song of death.

56

Two days after the dark events in Anjelica Leary's row house, Jessica, Byrne and all the detectives involved in the case met at the office of the district attorney.

The charges against Sean and Michael Farren were still pending, even though they were both deceased.

The possibility of there being confederates with whom the Farrens had worked was likely, and the investigation into the circumstances surrounding the horrible crimes was ongoing.

On the surface, what investigators were all but certain about was that Michael and Sean Farren, most likely at the behest of their grandmother, Máire Glover Farren, had caused the deaths of Robert Kilgore, Angelo, Mark and Laura Rousseau, Edwin Channing, Danielle Spencer and Benjamin Porter. Porter was the man engaged to be married to Danielle Spencer. He worked for Brinks.

The blood evidence discovered in the basement of The Stone matched that of a woman whose body was found floating in the Schuylkill River. She had been shot once in the head. The recovered bullet matched Sean Farren's M&P. The woman was identified as Megan Haupt, aged twenty-six, late of the Francisville section of the city.

The two bodies discovered next to the tracks in Grays Ferry were twenty-four-year-old Raymond Darden, and Gary Uchitel, twenty-one, both of Olney. The pair were said to have exchanged words with a man who fit Michael Farren's description. Ballistics tied the recovered spent cartridges to Farren's Makarov.

Máire Glover Farren was pronounced dead that night at U of Penn. The cause of death was given as congestive heart failure. According to her immigration record, she had been eighty-eight years old.

The cruet of blood found in her pocket did not belong to any of the victims. There was presumptive evidence that the blood was more than seven decades old. There was speculation that it belonged to the woman's late husband, Liam Farren.

Before anyone involved in the case thought to make the move to seal the old woman's house, it was ransacked and burned to the ground. The newly rehabbed row houses on either side were mostly spared.

The woman whom Farren assaulted in the house on Reed Street, as well as her infant baby, fully recovered from the ordeal.

After the events leading up to the shooting of Michael Farren had been published in moment-by-moment detail in the *Inquirer*, the lead reporter on the story got a call from a woman named Carole Stanton, who said she had a new detail to add to the timeline.

Ms Stanton was the owner of City Floral. She said that on the night of the events, she received a visit from a man answering Michael Farren's description. She said the man ordered flowers – specifically roses; a different variety each time – to be delivered once a week to a woman named Emily Carson at Queen Memorial Library, until the money ran out.

She said the man left a shopping bag on the counter.

Inside was fifteen thousand dollars.

They stood across the street from the ruins that were Máire Farren's house. Every so often people would walk by, take cell phone pictures and videos.

'It was a museum,' Byrne said. 'I don't think anything in there was any newer than sixty years old.'

He'd told her of the Sator Square carved into the basement walls, the photographs of the corn stooks.

'Do you really think the old woman thought she was some kind of mythic creature?'

Byrne didn't answer right away. 'I don't know. But you know as well as I do that when people have a deep belief – any kind of belief – it can be a powerful thing.'

Jessica said nothing.

'You saved us in that house, partner,' Byrne said.

Jessica thought back to the moment Byrne had walked in, his hands held high. When he'd put his suit coat on the arm of the couch, he made sure the photograph was sticking out, the photograph she'd taken of him for Sophie. When he showed her three fingers on each hand, she knew she had to find a way to replace Danny Farren's photograph on the wall. It was the third picture in the third row. It all came down to the last second.

'I think it was a team effort,' she said. 'And we didn't save everyone.'

Byrne glanced over at The Stone, back. 'They couldn't be saved, Jess.'

At five o'clock that afternoon, the mayor and the police commissioner held a news conference.

Byrne declined to attend.

57

When Byrne pulled up across the street from Anjelica Leary's house, there were still a few rubberneckers taking photographs. A CSU van was parked a half-block away, wrapping up their processing of the general scene. Because three or four agencies were involved, a multitude of Ts had to be crossed.

The aftermath of an officer-involved shooting, especially in the past few years, warranted a higher level of scrutiny than a shooting that did not involve a law enforcement officer.

As to Anjelica Leary's house, except for the sheets of plywood that covered the front window, you would never know what had taken place here.

Byrne passed a few words with the CSU techs. They were in the process of releasing the shuttered store that was next to the Leary house. Because Farren had entered the store in order to gain access to Anjelica Leary's house, the building had to be gone over inch by inch.

The bomb-sniffing K-9 had cleared it for explosives. But that didn't mean there weren't other dangers deliberately set.

Byrne rang the bell, stepped back off the porch. A few moments later, Anjelica answered the door. Despite the stress of what had happened in her house, she looked younger, more alive than the last time he had seen her.

'Kevin,' she said. 'What a lovely surprise.'

'I'm not intruding?'

'Never. Please come in.'

'Thanks.'

'Can I get you something?' she asked. 'I haven't yet packed the coffee or tea.'

'No, I'm fine. Thanks.'

'I might have a wee dram somewhere.'

'It's tempting, but I'm on duty for a few more hours.'

Byrne stepped into the living room. It seemed as if he'd never been there. When he'd walked in the first time, all he could think about was saving the innocent lives in the room, defusing the situation. Now it just looked like the front room of a pleasant older row house. No ghouls or demons. The only remnant was a mover's tarp over the spot where Michael Farren had fallen.

Along the wall where Farren had pinned his photographs were dozens of mover's boxes, taped and ready to haul away.

'The last time I moved away from this area was after Catriona was killed. I was in such a fog. I just knew I could no longer be in a place that held her spirit.'

Byrne had decided on coffee after all. They sat at Anjelica's small dinette table.

Byrne thought about the little girl, how she'd brightened the place with her gentle manner and quiet ways. He thought about her flowers and her hair ribbons. Time had not diminished her memory for him at all. She would always be a little girl.

'Why did you move back?' he asked.

Anjelica gave it a moment. 'When my second marriage failed, I was at a loose end. I guess one yearns for the familiar.'

'We do,' Byrne said. His apartment now was less than a mile from where he was born and grew up. He'd tried buying and rehabilitating a house, but it turned out to hold too many ghosts.

'Where will you go?' he asked.

'I'm going to Ireland, believe it or not.'

'I'm envious.'

'My mother was born there. County Clare.'

'Sounds like a dream.'

'You've never been?' she asked.

Byrne shook his head. 'Only in the movies.'

Anjelica smiled. 'What's your favorite?'

Good question, Byrne thought. There was no shortage. '*Odd Man Out* is a good one,' he said. 'But I'd have to go with *The Quiet Man*.'

'You like the old ones, then.'

'I do.'

'So do I,' she said. 'That Maureen O'Hara was the one, wasn't she?'

Byrne had often thought that his late mother resembled the actress in some ways. It was one of the reasons he always watched that movie alone. 'She was.'

He drained his cup. 'I won't keep you. I know you have a lot to do. I just wanted to see how you're getting along.'

'Sure you won't stay for another?'

'No, but thanks. Philly's misbehaving, and my desk is full.'

'All right, then,' she said. 'It's nice to have a man looking in on me again.'

She stepped to the sink. The moment she put her hands into the soapy water, the doorbell rang. She glanced at Byrne.

'Do you want me to get that?' he asked.

'Would you mind?'

'Not at all.'

'You're a dear.'

Byrne left the kitchen, walked across the living room. He expected Anjelica's caller to be someone from the moving company, or perhaps a stray city official with yet another document to sign. It was neither. He opened the door to find a man in his eighties wearing a mismatched navy blue suit and a yellow necktie. His thinning white hair was carefully combed, and even through the screen door Byrne could smell the after-shave, a brand from the seventies. In the man's hands was a large white cardboard box of the type used for storing legal documents.

'Well hello,' Byrne said.

'Hello to you, sir.'

Byrne propped open the screen door. 'Can I help you?'

'I'm here to see Anjelica Leary. Is she around?'

'She is indeed,' Byrne said. 'May I tell her who's calling?'

'Name's Jack,' the man said. 'Jack Permutter.'

Byrne opened the door wide. 'Please come in, Mr Permutter. I'll tell her you're here.'

As Jack tried to negotiate the step over the threshold, Byrne saw that he was struggling a bit.

'Let me take that.'

'Much obliged.'

Byrne took the box, put it on the hall table. It was heavy. Anjelica soon came out of the kitchen, drying her hands. She smiled.

'Two gentleman callers in one day,' she said. 'A girl's head will spin.'

She crossed the room, took Jack in a deep embrace. When they parted, Byrne could see a mist in the man's eyes. It was clear they had some sort of personal relationship. Byrne suddenly felt as if he should be anywhere but this room.

Perhaps sensing his unease, Anjelica made the introduction. 'Kevin, this is my dear friend Jack.'

Byrne extended a hand. 'Pleasure.'

Jack glanced out the window, at the cab waiting at the curb. He looked back at Anjelica, and pointed at the entryway table. 'I brought over the box you asked me to keep. I didn't know when you were leaving.'

'You didn't have to do that,' Anjelica said. 'I could have come for it.'

'It was no bother,' Jack said.

Anjelica held him again. 'I'm going to miss you, you old swab.'

Jack wiped a tear, waved a hand. 'We'll see each other again.' He turned to Byrne. 'Honored to meet you, young man,' he said.

'The honor was mine.'

Byrne watched the man walk slowly toward the waiting cab. As the cab pulled away, a moving truck slid into its place.

Anjelica was silent for a few moments.

'Jack is ill,' she said.

She went on to tell Byrne about the man's prognosis, as well as that of some of her other patients. It was clear she cared about them all.

When the conversation drifted to silence, Byrne pointed at the box Jack had brought. 'Do you need this in the truck?' he asked.

'Oh, don't trouble yourself. I can do it.'

'Let me help,' Byrne said. 'It's no trouble at all.'

'No you don't have to—'

Before Anjelica could get to the box, Byrne picked it up. When the top slid off, he looked inside. There he saw the cut lengths of pipe, the galvanized-steel end caps, the duct tape, the fuse.

It all came rushing toward him. In an instant he saw it. Forty years distilled into a single moment. How could he have been blind to it?

He turned to face Anjelica. She was looking straight at him. Her eyes told the whole story.

'You?' Byrne asked.

Anjelica said nothing. She lowered herself onto the chair near the fireplace.

'You planted the bomb that night,' Byrne said. 'Danny Farren is innocent.'

'Innocent?' She laughed, but it was a grave and mirthless sound. 'Danny Farren and his terrible clan are many things, Kevin Byrne. Innocent isn't one of them.'

She looked out the window for a moment, back.

'The building next door was supposed to be empty. I watched it for weeks. Longer. It was boarded up. I didn't know the woman would be inside. She wasn't supposed to die. Nobody was supposed to die.'

'Why, Anjelica?'

She shrugged. 'Because the Farrens needed to be stopped. If Danny went away for ten years for the firebombing, I knew he would die in prison, just like his mongrel father.'

Byrne tried to add Anjelica Daugherty into the timeline of horrors. He could not. He asked. 'How?'

Anjelica worried the dish towel in her hands.

'It took years,' she said. 'I had my looks then, mind you, not like now.' She smoothed her hair. 'It was not hard to get Danny Farren into my bed. Over the years he began to talk, to brag. You know how men like that are.'

'And he talked about the bombs?'

'Oh my God, yes. And so much more. What he didn't tell me I learned from the internet. Always at the library. I was very careful.'

'How did you get him there that night?' Byrne asked. 'We have him on surveillance video.'

'I told him that I had talked some sense into the man who refused to pay him, the man who owned that building. I told him I had his money. I was across the street when Danny came, in shadow. When he drove away, I threw the bomb.'

'And his fingerprints on the duct tape?'

Anjelica glanced at the roll of tape in the box. 'Danny Farren touched many things in my house.'

Byrne's mind was reeling. He knew he hadn't seen any of this because he wasn't looking.

'What are you going to do?' he asked.

'Are you recording this?'

'No.'

'How do I know that?'

Byrne lifted his shirt, spun in place, tapped his chest.

'Then I will exercise my right to remain silent,' she said.

Byrne pointed to the materials in the box. 'They're going to tie you to all this. It won't be difficult.'

'You don't have to tell them any of it,' she said. 'And why would you? To protect a Farren?'

'They'll put it together with or without me.'

'If it's what God wants, He will have it.'

'Jacinta Collins,' he said. 'She died in the clinic.'

'That's what I hear.'

'Did you visit that clinic, Anjelica? Did you finish her off to make it a murder charge for Danny Farren?'

Anjelica took a long moment. 'I did visit the clinic that night, truth be known. I did sign in. I'm sure you have people in your department who will be able to identify my signature, even though it is a name other than my own.'

Byrne said nothing.

'I collected the pills from my patients for weeks, one at a time.

I thought Danny might escape on the charges and would be a free man. I couldn't have that. But when it came time to do it, I walked away. I couldn't.'

'Why?'

'The poor woman had not harmed my family. The Farrens destroyed it.'

'They're going to order a second autopsy on Jacinta Collins.'

'I'm no doctor, but I am a *very* good nurse, detective. I believe they will find that the woman died of blood poisoning, as it said in the papers.'

'Who killed Desmond Farren, Anjelica?'

Anjelica rose, crossed over to the window overlooking the street. In this soft light, Byrne could see the younger woman, the woman whose world imploded that night in Schuylkill River Park.

'I remember when I saw him for the first time,' she said. 'Des Farren, that is. Him and his funny white suit. Do you remember that awful suit?'

'I do.'

'Mind you, I didn't know then that he was daft,' she said. 'I thought he was kind of handsome, actually. Like all the Farrens.

'And then, one time, we were at the market. The one on South. Catriona was just a wee girl. Still had the baby teeth, you know? Desmond was out front that morning, cracking walnuts with his foot on the sidewalk, and eating them. Can you imagine?'

Byrne said nothing.

'He put his eye on her that day. My Catriona.'

'How do you know?'

Anjelica eased the creases in her skirt. 'A mother knows, she does.' She turned to face Byrne. 'I've never gotten that out of my mind. The smell of the bus exhaust, the sound of the cracking walnuts. I've not been able to experience either in the past forty years without the walls of my heart crumbling.'

She sat back down.

'I don't know who killed Des Farren, detective. I surely would have done the deed myself, and burned what was left of him, but I was still frightened then. I'm not now.'

'Was it Jimmy?'

Anjelica said nothing.

'He's going to be district attorney, Mrs Leary.'

'So we're back to *Mrs* now, are we?' she asked. 'How time works against you when you've got a few spots on your hands and a bit of gray.'

Byrne waited for a reply.

'District Attorney James Doyle, God love him,' she said. 'A boy from the Pocket. A boot-strapper.'

'Are you really ready for what's about to happen to you?'

'I've been in hell for forty years, Kevin Byrne. A few more won't break me. When the last of the Farrens is dead I'll sleep like a baby, no matter how cold and hard the bed.'

She glanced at one of the moving boxes. On top was a framed photograph. It was a close-up of a smiling Catriona Daugherty.

'I may not know much, but there is one thing I know for certain,' she said.

She turned to look at him. Gone was the grieving young mother he recalled from the park that night. In front of him now was a murderer.

'What is that?' he asked.

'The world is full of weeping.'

58

On July 4, four days after Jimmy Doyle secured his party's nomination to become the next District Attorney for the City of Philadelphia, Byrne stood at the edge of Schuylkill River Park.

After the fireworks had finished and the last of the revelers had staggered off, he walked over to the grove of trees near the ball diamond.

He'd thought he would find the man there, and he was right.

'Congratulations, counselor.'

Jimmy Doyle turned to look at him. He seemed surprised, but not shocked.

'Thanks, Kevin.'

They did not shake hands. After a few moments, Jimmy knelt down, picked some grass, smelled it.

'It's the smells that bring me back,' he said. 'You?'

Byrne nodded. 'Always.'

'Soft pretzels, water ice, caramel corn. Were we really that young?'

'We were.'

Jimmy stepped over to the area where Catriona's body had been found. Byrne had not remembered it being so close to the slope that dropped toward the railroad tracks and the river. He imagined that a lot of things seemed bigger when you were that age. Relationships seemed closer, events more dire, more intense. Time was a great thief of detail. This far from the avenue, he could hear the sound of the river. He thought for a moment of the water that had passed this very spot over the past forty years, the secrets that had been carried with it.

He had turned over the gun and the other items in that box, the bus pass and the glasses. He'd given a full statement regarding his involvement in the incident with Desmond Farren in this very park. The chips would fall where they fell.

It hadn't taken long to discover that James Patrick Doyle was a minority partner in Greene Towne LLC, the company that was rehabbing the row houses in Devil's Pocket. Byrne knew that the news of his submission of the items had crossed Jimmy's radar. There was no point insulting the man's intelligence with that detail.

'The *Inquirer* is going to dig,' he said. 'There's going to be blowback about that gun being found in a building you own. About Des Farren's bus pass, his glasses.'

Jimmy turned to look at him. 'I'll answer the question,' he said.

'What question?'

'The one you want to ask.'

Byrne said nothing.

'I didn't put the box there, Kevin. Not forty years ago, not twenty years ago, not last month. I don't know who did. The last time I saw that gun was a few weeks before the Fourth. Back in '76.'

'Did you go back to where you'd originally hidden it?'

Jimmy hesitated before responding to this. 'I did. If for no other reason than to prove to myself it was still there, that it could not have been used in Des Farren's murder.'

'And?'

'It was gone.'

'Who knew it was there?'

Jimmy laughed. 'Who *didn't* know it was there? You knew about it. Dave and Ronan. My stepfather.'

'Tommy knew about the gun?'

'Tommy Doyle knew everything. Drunk, violent bastard that he was.'

Byrne took a few steps away. 'Ronan died in that wreck in '96. Cops said there was another set of tire tracks. You weren't there, were you, Jimmy?'

The man said nothing.

'And Dave. Dave gets shot to death in Pittsburgh while you were there. Know anything about it?'

'Only what I read in the papers.'

'What happened in the park that night in 1976?' Byrne asked. 'Where did you go?'

Jimmy looked out over the river. 'I went looking for my step-father. Him and Bobby Anselmo.'

'What for?'

'I might have talked a good game, Kevin, but I was just a skinny kid. I knew my stepfather hated the Farrens. If there was even the slightest possibility that Des Farren had something to do with Catriona's death, Tommy would have killed him.'

'Why didn't he?'

'I couldn't find either of them that night. I just went home.' Jimmy turned to look at Byrne. He let a few long moments pass. 'What did *you* do, Kevin?'

Byrne had expected this. 'After you left, I lost Des Farren in the crowd. I lost *everyone* in the crowd.'

'I tried to get you on that walkie-talkie,' Jimmy said. 'You never answered.'

'That's because the battery was gone.'

'Gone? You mean dead?'

'I mean gone, as in not there,' Byrne said. 'I got to the corner of 27th and Lombard, you were nowhere in sight. I tried to get you on the walkie, and it was dead.'

'I remember a battery being in there when you gave it back to me.'

'That's because I replaced it.'

Jimmy nodded. Byrne wondered if he was processing all this in his lawyer's brain, weighing how it would sound to a judge and jury.

'Dave Carmody,' Jimmy said. 'He was always the weakest.'

'He was strong in other ways,' Byrne said. 'There was never a more loyal kid.'

'He always felt like he was part of it. He felt like we made Des Farren kill Catriona. So did Ronan. I don't think the guilt and shame ever lifted from their hearts.'

'The Des Farren case is still open,' Byrne said.

'As is Catriona Daugherty's,' Jimmy said. 'You turn up anything, you bring it to me and I'll present it to a grand jury. You have my word.'

Byrne took a moment, shaping his thoughts. 'I recall a meeting in your office where I was told to go wherever the case took me,' he said.

'It was true then. It's true now.'

'Are you sure that's what you want?'

'You've never been one to be talked out of doing the right thing, Kevin.'

'Despite my many times being complicit in all manner of larceny, both *petit* and *grand*.'

'Despite it all,' Jimmy said. 'But I stand by what I said. The district attorney stands by it. The City of Philadelphia stands by it.'

'Sounds like a campaign speech.'

Jimmy broke out the smile that had helped get him to where he was today. 'You're right,' he said. 'A little too much salt.'

Jimmy Doyle looked out over the park. In that moment Byrne once again saw the cocksure kid from Devil's Pocket.

'You go where your heart takes you, Kevin,' Jimmy added. 'You go where your oath takes you. You were always the best of us.'

The two men fell silent. There was just the sound of the river. It was Byrne who spoke first.

'You're going to win.'

'Nothing is a lock in Philly politics,' Jimmy said.

'You're going to win,' Byrne repeated.

'You should think about coming over to the homicide unit at the DA's office, Kevin. No more running and gunning; you still keep the shield and the title. You'd head the unit on your first day.'

'I'm happy where I am,' Byrne said.

Jimmy reached to his lapel, took out the carnation that was there. He crouched, put it on the spot where Catriona Daugherty's body had been found.

'You know, Catie had this way about her. She looked sometimes like she was so light, so ethereal, that the slightest breeze might carry her away.' Jimmy stood up. 'She looked up to me. I couldn't take care of her. Maybe I don't deserve this job. I couldn't even protect an eleven-year-old girl.'

'One last question.'

'Sure.'

'You asked to have Jessica put on the case the same day that box was found. How did that happen, Jim?'

'It scares me when you call me Jim.'

'Did you get Eddie Shaughnessy to reach out? Did you expect Jessica to keep an eye on me? To keep an eye on the investigation?'

Jimmy Doyle said nothing.

'My God.'

'What?' Jimmy asked.

'You don't know her at all.'

59

By the end of August, what had begun with one wall of his bedroom now encompassed all four. Dates and times and places and sketches and photographs and transcripts.

It was right there, but he couldn't nail it down.

On Labor Day he took it all down and made five neat piles. He decided to put it all back up again, but not right away.

He made the calls he'd been putting off, each call a slice opening an old wound, places he had no business going, places he'd never thought he'd go.

Over the past six weeks he'd made it a point to not let so much time pass between visits with Jessica. Each time she would talk of the coming regime in the DA's office, of how things might change when Jimmy Doyle became district attorney, of her future.

Although it pained him deeply to do so, for the time being, Byrne kept what he thought about Jimmy Doyle, what he suspected, to himself.

The day after Labor Day, Byrne flew to Cleveland, rented a car at Hopkins International Airport and called the CPD. He spoke to a detective named Jack Paris, a good cop with whom he had worked once before. Paris made contact with the Summit County sheriff's office.

Byrne then drove to a small town near Akron.

The next day he was back in his apartment with a new box to add to the growing clutter.

He went back to the day it all began.

July 4, 1976.

60

He had seen her in and around the park for a few weeks. She was a shy girl, always blushing.

On the day – the only one that had mattered for forty years, the anniversary of his own daughter's murder – he saw her standing alone.

He knew.

He knew the two sides of his mind, his heart, the explosions overhead, the shelling of Cape Esperance, the smell of the rose, the scent of orchids.

The pale yellow ribbon. All the pale ribbons.

They watched the fireworks together.

'What do they call you?' he asked.

'Me?' she replied.

'Yes. Do they call you Cyndi June?'

'No, silly,' she said. 'My name is Catriona Margaret.'

61

The text was from Byrne. Jessica was preparing an opening
statement in a robbery case. She dropped what she was doing
and drove to East Falls.

Laurel Hill was a sprawling cemetery, with 33,000 monuments
and more than 10,000 family plots. It was the second oldest rural
cemetery in the United States.

Jessica found Byrne in a section near West Indiana. He looked
as if he hadn't slept in days.

'Hey, partner.'

'Hey,' he said. 'Thanks for coming.'

'Did you think I wouldn't?'

Byrne shrugged. 'I didn't know who else to tell.'

'You look like a hundred bucks.'

Byrne smiled. 'Sweet talker.'

'My only virtue.'

'What's going on with Anjelica Leary?'

'We're starting to build the case against her. The DA has released Danny Farren. He's in the hospital now. He doesn't have long.'

Byrne gestured to a bench. On it was a white box. They sat down.

He told her the story, the whole story, of his summers in Devil's Pocket, and that terrible night of July 4, 1976. While the whole city was celebrating the bicentennial, a dark story had begun to take shape in Kevin Byrne's life, his heart.

He told her the story of how he and his friends had seen Desmond Farren watching the girl, how Jimmy Doyle had braced the man.

'Jimmy stabbed him?'

'He cut his leg, yes,' Byrne said. 'We kept waiting for the Farren brothers to react, to take Jimmy out, but they never did. Even when Des Farren turned up dead. It never happened.'

Jessica knew there was more. She waited.

Byrne pointed to a low monument nearby. Jessica looked at the headstone. It read:

Flagg
Charles Ann Cynthia

'Who is this?' she asked.

'His name was Charles Flagg. Ex-army chaplain, Second World War. Served at Guadalcanal. He owned a variety store in the Pocket called F&B. He was also part of a neighborhood block watch.'

Jessica just listened.

'Turns out that Charles Flagg shot himself that night of July 4th, just a few hours after Catriona was killed. I worked backward from there.'

'Backward to what?'

Byrne opened the box, took out a typed page, handed it to her.

Jessica immediately saw the pattern. It was a summary of five homicides.

July 4, 1936. Cynthia June Flagg, 10. Unsolved.

July 4, 1946. Anna Blossom Gresham, 10. Unsolved.

July 4, 1956. Constance Lenore Schute, 11. Unsolved.

July 4, 1966. Victoria Francis Jones, 10. Unsolved.

July 4, 1976. Catriona Margaret Daugherty, 11. Unsolved.

'Desmond Farren didn't kill the girl,' Jessica said. 'He didn't kill Catriona Daugherty.'

'No,' Byrne said. 'It was Flagg.'

He again reached into the box next to him. He took out a worn leather edition of the King James Bible and five clear plastic envelopes. Each contained a hair ribbon, each of a different pastel color.

'I made some calls,' Byrne said. 'I located Flagg's grandson, who it turns out works for the sheriff's office in Summit County, Ohio. After Flagg's death, his effects were boxed up and moved a dozen different times. His confession is in there. No one opened that bible in forty years.'

Jessica looked back at the sheet. 'All on the Fourth of July, all the victims around ten or eleven years old. And then it stops.'

Byrne nodded. 'I checked every July since. I ran June and August just to bracket the crimes. Nothing even close.'

'Why didn't anyone pick up this pattern?' Jessica asked. As soon as she said it, she wished she hadn't. At one time – still – she *was* the *anyone*. Byrne said what she was feeling.

'No one was looking.'

'So all of this, the dominoes that started falling after Catriona Daugherty's murder, didn't have to happen.'

Byrne didn't answer. He didn't need to. They'd both heard and felt the repercussions of the music of chance.

'Flagg lived in every one of those neighborhoods at the times of the murders,' Byrne said. He held up a thick file folder. 'These investigations start here and now. I've already talked to the captain.'

Jessica was going to ask him if he was sure this was what he wanted, but she knew that it was. She watched as Byrne gently put the ribbons back in the box, followed by the old bible.

She glanced at her watch. As much as she hated to leave, she had a ton of work on her desk.

'Call me if you need me,' she said. 'Day or night. Even if it's just to talk.'

'Thanks, partner,' he said. 'It means everything.'

Jessica got up, walked back to her car, slipped inside. She thought about the cases. Her daughter wasn't much older than those girls had been when they were murdered. She couldn't imagine the shackles of grief.

She knew that Byrne would now embark upon a passage to visit the surviving family members of these murdered girls, to tell them the story as he believed it.

She got out of her car, crossed the cemetery to where Byrne stood, put a hand on his shoulder.

She would not let him make the journey alone.

Acknowledgements

With thanks to:

Jane Berkey, Meg Ruley, Peggy Boulos Smith, Rebecca Scherer, and everyone at the Jane Rotrosen Agency;

Ed Wood, Catherine Burke, Thalia Proctor, Kirsteen Astor, and the great team at Little, Brown UK;

Michael Krotz, David Najfach, David Wilhite, Kevin McKenzie, Kathleen Heraghty, Mike Driscoll, Jimmy Williams, Annette Haralson, and Kathleen Franco MD;

The men and women of the Philadelphia Police Department;

The people of Devil's Pocket. Thanks for letting me borrow the neighborhood, move a few boundaries, and set my tale on your streets.

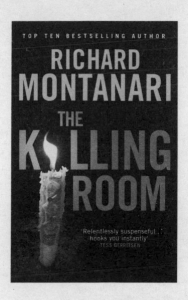

Deepest winter. Darkest Philadelphia.

A murder shocks the frozen city: an ex-cop has been lured to the basement of an abandoned chapel, wrapped in barbed wire – and kept alive for ten days.

Twenty-four hours after the discovery, Detectives Kevin Byrne and Jessica Balzano find another victim in another church, encased in a pristine block of ice.

Someone is transforming the city's cathedrals into killing rooms; someone who is determined to raise hell on earth.

*

'Scary good! You will leave the lights on long after finishing this book' Lisa Gardner

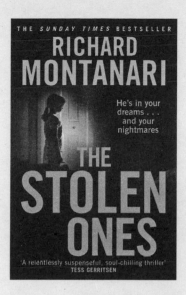

THE *SUNDAY TIMES* BESTSELLER

RICHARD MONTANARI

He's in your
dreams . . .
and your
nightmares

THE
STOLEN
ONES

'A relentlessly suspenseful, soul-chilling thriller'
TESS GERRITSEN

Destroyed by fire years ago, the infamous Philadelphia State
Hospital was known as a warehouse for the criminally insane.

But one man never left.

Detectives Kevin Byrne and Jessica Balzano are called to a bizarre
murder scene: a man has been killed by a railroad spike driven into
his head. But this is just the beginning of a trail of evil that will lead
the detectives back to the hospital, to a missing girl and to a horror
they could never have imagined . . .

*

'Byrne and Balzano make a great cop duo'
Peterborough Evening Telegraph

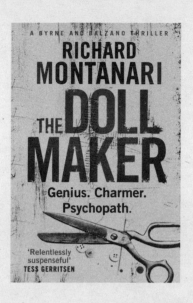

A BYRNE AND BALZANO THRILLER

RICHARD MONTANARI

THE DOLL MAKER

Genius. Charmer. Psychopath.

'Relentlessly suspenseful' TESS GERRITSEN

Mr Marseille is polite, elegant, and erudite. He would do anything for his genteel true love Anabelle. And he is a psychopath.

A quiet Philadelphia suburb. A woman cycles past a train depot with her young daughter. And there she finds a murdered girl posed on a newly painted bench. Strangled. Beside her is a formal invite to a tea dance in a week's time.

Seven days later, two more young victims are discovered in a disused house, posed on painted swings. At the scene is an identical invite. This time, though, there is something extra waiting for Detectives Kevin Byrne and Jessica Balzano.

A delicate porcelain doll. It's a message. And a threat.

With Marseille and Anabelle stalking the city, Byrne and Balzano have just seven days to find the link between the murders before another innocent child is snatched from its streets.

*

'Longtime fans of the series will not be disappointed, nor will readers who favour thrillers with a high creepiness quotient'
Booklist

RICHARD MONTANARI

A CHRISTMAS KILLING

Silent night
Deadly night

An ebook-only short story

Meet the young Detective Kevin Byrne, rising star of the
Philadelphia police force.

Christmas Eve, 1988. Partnered with streetwise veteran Frankie
Sheehan, Byrne is called out on a freezing night to investigate the
brutal assault of a young woman in a crime-ridden neighbourhood,
The Devil's Pocket.

There, with the rest of the city celebrating, relentless rookie
Byrne must step out from his partner's shadow to outwit a terrifying
predator on the same vicious city streets he will later revisit with
his future partner, Jessica Balzano.

*

'A master of the pulse-pounding novel of suspense'
Good Book Guide